Alexander Cunningham

The Stpa of Bharhut

a Buddhist monument ornamented with numerous sculptures illustrative of

Buddhist legend and history in the third century B. C

Alexander Cunningham

The Stpa of Bharhut
*a Buddhist monument ornamented with numerous sculptures illustrative of Buddhist legend
and history in the third century B. C*

ISBN/EAN: 9783337247027

Printed in Europe, USA, Canada, Australia, Japan

Cover: Foto ©Andreas Hilbeck / pixelio.de

More available books at **www.hansebooks.com**

THE

STÛPA OF BHARHUT:

A BUDDHIST MONUMENT

ORNAMENTED WITH NUMEROUS SCULPTURES

ILLUSTRATIVE OF

BUDDHIST LEGEND AND HISTORY

IN THE

THIRD CENTURY B.C.

BY

ALEXANDER CUNNINGHAM, C.S.I., C.I.E.,

MAJOR GENERAL, ROYAL ENGINEERS (BENGAL RETIRED).
DIRECTOR GENERAL ARCHÆOLOGICAL SURVEY OF INDIA.

" In the sculptures and inscriptions of Bharhut we shall have in future a real landmark in the religious and literary history of India, and many theories hitherto held by Sanskrit scholars will have to be modified accordingly."—
Dr. MAX MÜLLER.

Published by Order of the Secretary of State for India in Council.

LONDON:

WM H. ALLEN AND CO., 13, WATERLOO PLACE, S.W.;
TRÜBNER AND CO., 57 & 59, LUDGATE HILL; EDWARD STANFORD, CHARING CROSS;
W. S. WHITTINGHAM AND CO., 91, GRACECHURCH STREET;
THACKER AND CO., 87, NEWGATE STREET.
1879.

CONTENTS.

LIST OF PLATES.

PREFACE.

The remains of the Great Stûpa of Bharhut were first discovered by me in the end of November 1873; but as the whole of my camp was then on its way to Nâgpur, I was not able then to do more than to ascertain the fact that portions of two gateways, with the included quarter of the circular railing, were still *in situ*, although nearly all thrown down and buried under a mound of rubbish from 5 to 7 feet in height. On my return from the Chânda district in February 1874, I spent 10 days at Bharhut, when I succeeded in uncovering the whole quadrant of the buried railing. The curious sculptures were a source of much wonder to the people who visited the place by hundreds every day. But the inscriptions excited even greater curiosity when it was known that I was able to read them. At every fresh discovery I was importuned to say what was the subject of the writing, and great was the disappointment when I made known the simple records of gifts to the Stûpa, or of the names of the guardian Yakshas, Devatas, and Nâgas. Few natives of India have any belief in disinterested excavations for the discovery of ancient buildings, or of works of art, or of records of ancient times. Their only idea of such excavations is that they are really intended as a search for hidden treasure, and from the incredulous looks of many of the people, I have no doubt that I was regarded as an arch deceiver who was studiously concealing the revelations made by the inscriptions as to the position of the buried treasures.

In the beginning of March the work of excavation was taken up by my zealous assistant Mr. J. D. Beglar, who continued the excavation round the whole circle of the railing. To him we owe the discovery of the valuable Prasenajit Pillar, of the famous Jetavana scene, and of many of the most interesting coping stones. He made photographs of the sculptures as they were found; but as each day's discoveries only showed how much was still left to be explored, the work was closed in the beginning of April. In the middle of that month I forwarded to Government a statement of the discoveries that had been made up to that time. This statement was published in the London papers, and I was much gratified to find that my discovery was everywhere received with much interest. To it I owe the beginning of a correspondence with Professor Childers which ended only with his too premature death. The age which I then assigned to the Stûpa, between 250 and 200 B.C., has not been shaken by any subsequent discoveries, and I have reason to believe that it is now almost universally admitted.

In November 1874 I again returned to Bharhut with Mr. Beglar to make a complete exploration of the mound of ruins, and to photograph all the sculptures systematically on the fixed scale of one-sixth of the original size for all basreliefs, and of one-twelfth for all statues and larger objects. It was during these excavations that all the smaller pieces of the East Gateway were found; from which I was able to make the restoration shown in Plate VI. The exploration was carried on until the end of December, by which time the whole extent of ground covered by the railing to a breadth of 10 and 12 feet, both inside and outside, was completely excavated. At the same time all the neighbouring villages within a circuit of 10 miles were carefully explored for portions of the missing sculptures. This search was rewarded with the discovery of two pillars of a second or outer railing of which portions had already been found *in situ* at Bharhut. The basrelief of the *Indra Sâla-guha*, or "Indra's Cave Hall," was then discovered at Batanmâra, and the missing half of the famous *Chhadanta Jâtaka* at Pataora, 7 miles distant, degraded to the ignoble position of a washerman's plank.

During 1874 I had written an account of the discoveries made during the first season's excavations, but all these important additions necessitated a re-arrangement of the plates and the re-writing of the whole account of the Stûpa. This was in great part done during 1875, at the same time that I was carrying on the arrangement of Asoka's inscriptions to form Vol. I. of the projected "Corpus Inscriptionum Indicarum." The discovery of a new inscription of Asoka at Sahasarâm, in which I believed that there was a figured date, similar to some unknown symbols in another recently discovered record of Asoka at Rûpnâth, made it necessary that I should visit Sahasarâm myself, which I did during November 1875.

During all this time I was in frequent correspondence with Professor Childers in London, and with the learned Buddhist priest Subhûti of Ceylon, regarding the subjects of the Bharhut sculptures, and more especially of the *Jâtakas*, or previous Births of Buddha. In the summer of 1876 I completed the present account of Bharhut, but as I had reason to believe that some further discoveries might still be made, Mr. Beglar and myself visited the place a third time, and once more thoroughly explored the whole neighbourhood. The remains of the corner pillar of one of the missing gateways were then discovered together with several fragments. These are not included in the plates; but I may mention that the story represented on the pillar was almost certainly the celebrated *Wessantara Jâtaka*. About two thirds of each face have been cut away, but in the remaining portion of one of the scenes there is a four-horse chariot with a boy and girl being led by the hand, which leave no doubt in my mind that these are intended for the two children of Prince Wessantara.

This last visit proved of value in another way, which, though not quite unexpected, serves to show how judicious was the course which I took for the acquisition and despatch of these valuable sculptures to Calcutta. When Professor Childers heard of the intention to get these sculptures removed to a place of safety, he wrote, "It is " impossible to read General Cunningham's most interesting account of these sculptures " without a sigh of regret that they should be so far beyond the reach of our inspection. " *I hear of a proposal to remove them from Bharhut.* The scheme carries with it a certain " aroma of Vandalism (fancy carting away Stonehenge!)."[1] I am willing to accept the *aroma* since I have saved all the more important sculptures. Of those that were left behind *every stone that was removable has since been "carted away"* by the people for building purposes. So inveterate is this practice in India that Babu Rajendra Lál, when he first heard of the Bharhut discoveries, boldly addressed the Government of India, suggesting that the sculptures should be removed to a place of safety to prevent the people from carrying them off. At my request the whole of the sculptures were liberally presented to Government by the Raja of Nágod, in whose territory Bharhut stands, and I am happy to say that they have arrived safely in Calcutta, where the fine large view of the famous Jetavana monastery, given in Plate LVII., was kindly taken for me by Captain Water-house. This view will show that the sculptures have not suffered in their long travels of 600 miles. In his letter already quoted Professor Childers expressed a "hope that the " sculptures may find their way to the India Office [in London] instead of being " consigned to the peaceful oblivion of an Indian Museum." In this hope I should most cordially agree were I not afraid that they might be consigned to the still more oblivious vaults of the British Museum, where some 10 years ago I discovered no less than seven Indian inscriptions in the full enjoyment of undisturbed repose, unseen, uncared for, and unknown. At present there is no Indian Museum in London, while there is one in Calcutta where the sculptures are now deposited. And there I may hope that they will fare better than did my Srávasti statue of Buddha in the Museum of the Bengal Asiatic Society. This ancient statue of Buddha, which certainly dates as early as the beginning of the Christian era, was placed in the midst of a herd of stuffed deer and antelopes, which completely hid its inscribed pedestal from view. The result was unfortunate, as the chief value of the statue was its ancient inscription. But perhaps the Naturalists, who then monopolised the direction of the Museum, may have considered this arrangement a highly appropriate compliment to Buddha, who in several previous births had been a "King of the Deer."

---

[1] "Academy," 28th November 1874.

STÛPA OF BHARHUT.

I.—DESCRIPTION OF STÛPA.

1.—POSITION OF BHARHUT.

The village of *Bharhut* is situated six miles to the north-east of Uchahara, and nine miles nearly due south of the *Sutna* station of the Jabalpur Railway. It is exactly 120 miles to the south-west of Allahabad, and rather more than halfway towards Jabalpur: The village belongs to the small state of Nâgod, and forms the Jâgir of the present minister, by whose family it has been held for the last 60 years. In our maps it is entered either simply as *Bharaod*, or sometimes with the addition of *Chhatri*. But the Chhatri is a large stone on the top of the neighbouring hill of *Lâl-Pahâr*, and should not, therefore, be connected with the name of the village.

Bharhut is said to be the site of an old city, by some named Bhaironpur, which extended for 12 kos, embracing Uchahara on the south. The houses were scattered; and all the surrounding villages of the present day are believed to have been the several *Mahallas*, or divisions of the ancient city. In proof of this the people argue that the same huge bricks are found all over this space, which is quite true, but they were no doubt all originally taken away by the people themselves from the great brick Stûpa at Bharhut. The best proof of this origin is the fact that carved stones from the Buddhist Railing of the Bharhut Stûpa may be seen in most of the large villages for several kos around Bharhut, particularly at Uchahara, Batanmâra, Pathora, and Mâdhogarh (or Patharhat). It is certain, however, that Bharhut itself was once a considerable city, as I found the greater part of the ground around the present village, for upwards of one mile in length by half a mile in breadth, covered with broken bricks and pieces of pottery.

So little is known of the ancient geography of this part of India that it is almost useless to make any attempt to identify Bharhut with any one of the few places mentioned by early writers. But in any attempt that is made we must not forget the happy position of Bharhut at the northern end of the long narrow valley of Mahiyar near the point where the high road from Ujain and Bhilsa to Pâtaliputra turns to the north towards Kosâmbi and Srâvasti. That Kosâmbi itself was one of the usual halting places on the high road between Ujain and Pâtaliputra we have a convincing proof in the curious story of the famous physician Jivaka of Râjagriha. According to the legend Pradyota Raja of Ujain, who was suffering from jaundice, invited Jivaka to his Court, to which the physician was very unwilling to proceed, as he knew that the cure of Pradyota who strongly disliked oil could not be effected without its use. "When the great "physician had seen the king, it occurred to him that he might endeavour to give the

B

" medicine by stealth; were he to administer it openly, it might cause both his own
" destruction and that of the king. He therefore informed him that he could effect the
" cure of his disease; but there was one thing that he must mention to the monarch,
" which was that doctors are unwilling to make known to others the ingredients of which
" their medicines are composed; it would be necessary for him to collect all that he
" required with his own hand, and therefore the king must give directions that he be
" permitted to pass through any of the gates of the palace whenever he might choose.

" Chandapprajota had four celebrated modes of conveyance: 1, a chariot called
" *Oppanika*, drawn by slaves, that would go in one day 60 yojanas, and return; 2, an
" elephant called *Málágiri*, that in one day would go 100 yojanas, and return; 3, a mule
" called *Mudakési*, that in one day would go 120 yojanas, and return; 4, a horse called
" *Telekarnnika*, that would go the same distance."

" When the king heard the request of Jivaka, he gave him permission to use any
" of the royal modes of conveyance, and to pass out of the palace gates at any hour of
" the day. Of this permission he availed himself, and went hither and thither at his
" will, now in this conveyance and then in that, so that the wonder of the citizens was
" greatly excited. One day he brought home an abundance of medicine, which he boiled
" in oil and poured into a dish. He then told the king that it was exceedingly powerful,
" so that it would be requisite for him to take it at once, without tasting it or the virtue
" would be gone. The king stopped his nose with one hand, and with the other put the
" medicine into his mouth. At this moment Jivaka, after informing the attendants what
" to give the king, went to the elephant hall, and mounting the elephant Baddrawati set
" off towards Rájagriha like the wind. After going 50 yojanas he arrived at Kosámbi,
" where he remained a little to refresh himself, as he knew that the king had no army
" that could come so quickly."[1]

In the legend of Báwari, the *purohit* or family priest of Raja Prasenajita, I find the
names of some places on the route between Ujain and Kosámbi noted as follows:
" Ujjain (or Ujain), Godhi, Diwisá, Walsewet, Kosámbi."[2] Here Diwisa is most probably
only a corrupt reading for *Vedisa* or *Besnagar*, near Bhilsa. We thus have *Wal-Sewet* left
as the name of a city on the high road between Bhilsa and Kosámbi; but as no further
indication of its position is given, all that can be said is that Bharhut agrees with the
recorded position of Wal-Sewet, and as it was certainly a place of some consequence in
the time of Asoka, it was most probably in existence as early as the time of Buddha.

In Ptolemy's map of this part of India the names are very few, and of these the only
ones that can be identified with absolute certainty are *Ozene*, or Ujain, and *Madura vel
Deorum*, or the holy city of *Mathura*. We have also the rivers Ganges and Jumna, and
the capital Palibothra. Two rivers join the Ganges on the south; one is without name,
but as the town of *Tamasis* is placed on its bank it must almost certainly be the *Tamasa*,
or Tons; the other is called the *Sona*, and as it joins the Ganges just above Palibothra it
is beyond all doubt the Sona or Son River of the present day. Now taking a nearly
straight line from Ozene to Palibothra I find the following names: *Osta, Soara, Adisathra,*

---

[1] Hardy's Manual of Buddhism, pp. 244–45. There seems to be some mistake in the elephant's name;
Málágiri was the famous elephant of Ajátasatru, which he intoxicated with arrack for the purpose of killing
Buddha.

[2] Hardy's Manual of Buddhism, pp. 333–34.

Agara, Bradama, Bardaotis, and *Sigalla.* The first four I would identify with Ashta, Sihor, Vedisa (Besnagar close to Bhilsa), and Sâgar. *Bradama* may be Bilhari, and *Bardaotis,* as I have already suggested, may be Bharhut. *Sigalla,* which Ptolemy places on the left bank of the Sona near its junction with the Ganges, may be Ekachakra, or the modern Ara (Arrah of maps.) Bardaotis and Sagabaza are the only two cities of the *Bolingæ,* who might readily be identified with the *Bhagelas* if we could be certain that they occupied this part of the country at so early a date.

There is one more name which in the total absence of any more certain record, one is glad to catch at, as it is just possible that it may be the same name under a somewhat different form. In the Tibetan Dulva it is related that a certain Sâkya named Shâmpaka on being banished from Kapila, was granted by Sâkya, " in an illusory manner, some hairs " of his head, some nail-pairings, and teeth." He went to a country called *Bagud* or *Vagud,* where he was made king, and built a *Stúpa* (in Tibetan *Chhorten*) over the holy relics, which was called "the fane or chapel of Shâmpaka."[1] Perhaps Ptolemy's *Sagabaza* may have some connexion with Shâmpaka, or Sabaga, as I believe a Greek would have written the name.

In the present day the joint name for the two districts of Nâgod and Uchahara is *Bharmd,* of which no one can give any explanation. It seems probable, however, from the long inscription on the East Gateway of the Bharhut Stûpa that the Stûpa itself was situated "in the kingdom of Sugana" (*Sugana râje*). Now this name, in spite of the difference of spelling, we can hardly keep ourselves from identifying with the ancient *Srughna* or *Sughana,* which was situated on the upper course of the Jumna, and extended along both banks of the river from the foot of the hills to some unknown distance. In the time of Hwen Thsang Srughna was reputed to have a circuit of 6,000 *li* or 1,000 miles,[2] and as it was limited by the Ganges on the east, by the kingdom of Satadru on the west, and by high mountains on the north, it must have extended far to the south. But in this direction lay the equally large district of Sthâneswara, or Thânesar. Perhaps the latter may have been confined to the west of the Jumna, while Srughna included the whole of the Gangetic Doab from the foot of the hills down to Mirat, and perhaps as far as Baran or Bulandshahar. But even with this extension the frontier of Srughna proper would have been about 450 miles distant from Bharhut. But it is not likely that there were two countries of this name; and I see no more difficulty in Raja Dhanabhuti of Srughna holding possessions on the banks of the Tons, than in the Râhtors of Kanoj holding possessions on the banks of the Son. I accept, therefore, as an undoubted fact, the sovereignty of the Raja of Srughna over Bharhut, and with it must be included the intervening provinces of Mathura, Kanoj, Gwalior, and Mahoba.

At a later date we know that it must have belonged to the wide dominions of the Gupta dynasty, whose inscriptions have been found at Garhwâ, Eran, and Udayagiri. During the rule of that powerful family, the country around Bharhut would seem to have fallen into the hands of petty chiefs, as a number of copper-plate inscriptions have been found within 12 miles of the Stûpa referring to two different families who were content with the simple title of Mahârâja. These inscriptions range in date from 156 to 214 of the era of the Guptas, or from A.D. 350 to 408. Somewhat more than two centuries

1 Csoma de Körös, Analysis of Dulva, in Bengal Asiatic Researches, XX., 88.
2 Julien's Hwen Thsang II., 215.

later Bharhut was under Harsha Vardhana of Kanoj as lord paramount, but it is almost certain that the district had also a petty chief of its own. After the death of Harsha the Bâghels and Chândels rose to power, the former ruling in Bândhogarh, the latter in Khajurâho, Mahoba, and Kalinjjar.

In addition to the magnificent stone railing of the old Stûpa, there are the remains of a mediæval Buddhist Vihâra, with a colossal statue, and several smaller Buddhist figures which cannot be dated much earlier than 1000 A.D. It seems probable, therefore, that the exercise of the Buddhist religion may have been carried on for nearly 15 centuries with little or perhaps no interruption. Everywhere the advent of the Muhammadans gave the final blow to Buddhism, and their bigotry and intolerance swept away the few lingering remains which the Brahmans had spared.

2.—DESCRIPTION OF STÚPA.

When I first visited Bharhut in the end of November 1873 I saw a large flat-topped mound, with the ruins of a small Buddhist Vihâr, and three pillars of a Buddhist Railing, with three connecting rails or bars of stone, and a coping stone covering them, besides a single gateway pillar which once supported the *toran* or ornamental arch of the entrance.[1] The three pillars were more than half buried in the ground; but there were three inscriptions still visible; one on the gateway pillar, the second on the first pillar of the railing, and the third on the coping stone. To the north I found some fragments of a pillar, as well as a piece of coping, but they had evidently been disturbed. On the south side, however, I was more fortunate, as I discovered some pillars of that entrance after a few hours digging, and as one of these proved to be the corner pillar of the south-west quadrant I was able to obtain an accurate measurement of the chord of the quarter circle of railing by stretching a tape to the first pillar of the south-east quadrant. This distance was 62 feet 6 inches, which gives an interior diameter of 88 feet 4½ inches for the stone railing. I then tried to ascertain something about the Stûpa itself, but there was nothing left in the middle of the mound except a mass of rubbish formed chiefly of earth and broken bricks. I made a wide excavation in the middle of this heap, but without any result save the finding of a number of rough blocks of stone which had formed a part of the foundation of the brick Stûpa. I then made two excavations from the stone railing inwards towards the Stûpa—and in both places I found that the terraced flooring ceased abruptly at 10 feet 4 inches. This point was therefore the edge of the base of the Stûpa, which was consequently 67 feet 8½ inches in diameter. Afterwards, while excavating the railing, I found numerous specimens of the bricks of which the Stûpa had been built. Most of them were plain, and square in shape, and of large size 12 × 12 × 3½ inches; but there were others of much larger size, of which I could obtain only fragments from 5 to 6 inches in thickness.

On my second visit to Bharhut, in company with my assistant Mr. Beglar, the whole of the space inside the railing was excavated to a width of from 12 to 15 feet. This extensive digging brought to light the sole remaining portion of the Stûpa, on the S.E. face, where the rubbish had been accumulated over it. The portion remaining was a mere fragment, 6 feet in height, by about 10 feet in length at bottom. It was entirely covered with a coat of plaster on the outside. The lower half was quite plain, but the

---

[1] See Plates XI, and XII, for two views of these remains.

upper half was ornamented with a succession of triangular-shaped recesses, narrow at bottom and broad at top, formed by setting back a few of the facing bricks. I conclude that these recesses were intended for lamps. The sides of each recess were formed in two steps, so that each would hold five lights. These recesses were nearly 13½ inches broad at top and 4½ inches at bottom, and from 8½ to 9 inches apart. Consequently there would have been 120 recesses in the whole circumference of 212¾ feet. Each row would therefore have held 600 lights for an illumination. But as each row of these recesses would have given three lines of lights, and as there were several rows of recesses the illumination would have taken the form of a diamond-shaped network of lights covering the whole of the lower part of the Stúpa up to the spring of the dome.

The present village of Bharhut, which contains upwards of 200 houses, is built entirely of the bricks taken from the Stúpa. The removal of bricks continued down to a late date, and I was told that a small box (*dibiyá*) was found in the middle of the brick mound, and made over to the Rájá of Nágod. This must have been a Relic casket; but my further inquiries were met by persistent ignorance, both as to its contents and as to whether it was still in the possession of the Rájá.

According to the information which I received from the present Jágirdar, the site of the Stúpa was entirely covered with a thick jangal so late as 60 years ago, when his family first got possession of the estate. The stone railing is said to have been then nearly perfect. This perhaps is doubtful, as the castle of Batanmára, which contains several of the Bharhut stones, is said to be more than 200 years old. But when the wholesale removal of the Stúpa was once begun, part of the railing of the north-east and north-west quadrants on the side towards the village would have been first pulled down, and afterwards gradually removed. With the exception, however, of the rail bars, which weigh from 1½ to 2 cwt. each, the greater part of the railing, consisting of pillars and coping stones, was too heavy for convenient removal. Several of them were accordingly split lengthwise by regular quarrymen. Some of these split pieces yet remain on the ground, and amongst them there is one coping stone showing a row of quarrymen's holes or drifts along the top, but which is still unsplit. From this it would appear that the process of general spoliation may have been suddenly stopped, perhaps at the time when the present Jágirdar's ancestor first got possession. This is also Mr. Beglar's opinion, who thus writes, "The cause of the sudden stoppage is doubtless the granting of the " land on which these ruins stand in Jágir to the ancestor of the present holder, a poor " Brahman, who naturally would not allow the Thákur of Batanmára to carry off " building materials lying on his land without payment. And being probably too poor " to be able to split and move the heavy stones, he was obliged to content himself with " pulling down the Stúpa, and carrying off the bricks to build his own house. To this " circumstance, as I believe, we are indebted for the preservation of what still remains " of this once magnificent Stúpa."

While the Stúpa was being excavated on the side towards the village, the rubbish, consisting of a great mass of broken bricks and earth, was thrown out to the south-west and south-east, on the sides away from the village. The weight of this rubbish at last threw down these two quadrants of the railing, as I found that the pillars had fallen outwards with most of the rail bars still sticking in their socket holes. The rains of many successive years gradually spread a mass of earth over them, until they were effectually buried to a depth of from 5 to 8 feet.

Although only a fragment a few feet in length now remains of the Stûpa itself we know from the pavement that its shape was circular, and its general appearance we learn from the bas-reliefs of three or four Stûpas which are found amongst the sculptures, all of which present the same common features.[1] The dome was a hemisphere which stood on a cylindrical base ornamented with small recesses for lights arranged in patterns. A bas-relief on one of the longer rails, found at Uchahara, gives a good representation of the cylindrical base, with the addition of a regular railing in the usual position surrounding the Stûpa at a short distance. On the top of the hemisphere there was a square platform, also decorated with a Buddhist railing, which supported the crowning Umbrella, with streamers and garlands suspended from its rim. Large flowers also spring from the top as well as from the base of the square summit, and a cylindrical ornament is hung in undulating folds completely round the hemisphere.

The great stone railing which surrounded the Stûpa had four openings towards the four cardinal points. It was thus divided into four quadrants, each of which consisted of 16 pillars joined by three cross-bars and covered by a massive stone coping. From the left side of each entrance the railing was extended outwards for two pillar spaces so as to cover the direct approach to the Stûpa. With these four return railings of the entrances the whole railing forms a gigantic *Swastika* or mystic cross, which was no doubt the actual intention of the designer.[2]

The railing thus contained 20 pillars in each quadrant or 80 in the whole circle, including the returns at the four entrances. But on each side there was an ornamental arch, called *Toran*, supported on two curiously shaped pillars, which are formed of a group of four octagons joined together, and crowned by four distinct bell capitals.[3] These four capitals are covered by a single abacus on which rests a large massive capital formed of two winged lions and two winged bulls. One of these curious pillars was still standing on the south side of the east entrance, and the excavations brought to light the lower half of the second still standing in its original position, the upper half having been broken off and carried away. The mutilated capital of the second with four winged bulls was also found in clearing away the rubbish lying in the entrance; but only a few fragments were discovered of the horizontal stone beams which must have covered these pillars, and which form such a remarkable feature of the similar entrances to the Sânchi Stûpa.

But in the walls of a garden tank, one mile to the westward, I discovered the broken end of a stone beam, which from its dimensions would exactly fit the capitals of the gateway pillars. The end of the beam, which is straight and heavy in the Sânchi examples, is here sloped downwards, and a spiral is formed not unnaturally of the curled tail of a crocodile.[4] Three other crocodile ends of beams were found afterwards in excavating the ruins of the East Gateway as well as a middle portion of the lowermost beam.

Other portions of the *Toran* or upper part of the gateway were subsequently discovered. Of these the principal piece was found built into the wall of the castle at

---

[1] See Plates XIII. and XXXI. for good specimens of Stûpas.
[2] See Plate III. for the plan of the railing; and Plate V. for that of the gateways.
[3] See Plates VI., X., XI., and XII.
[4] See Plates VI. and IX. The three specimens in the latter plate are one-sixth.

Batanmâra.[1] This piece formed nearly the whole of one face of the middle beam of the Toran. The Thâkur of Batanmâra kindly permitted me to take it out of the wall. The sculptured face presents a central throne with a clump of bambu trees behind, to which two leonine animals are approaching, one each side. The animal on the right has a human head and that on the left a bird's head, but the two in the middle are true lions with huge open mouths. All have thick manes regularly arranged in two rows of stiff tufts. This face of the beam is complete with the exception of a very small piece at the left end, so that nothing is lost except the hind quarters of the bird-headed lion.

The fragment of the other Toran beam, which was found in excavating the rubbish in front of the East Gateway is unfortunately short; but as it presents both faces of the beam, the whole can be restored without any difficulty. This beam represented a procession of elephants—two on each side of the centre, where I presume there must have been a banian tree with a throne—corresponding to the bambu tree on the other beam.

From these two fragments I infer that the *Toran* consisted of three beams, as in all the gateways of the Sânchi Tope. My reasons for coming to this conclusion are as follows :—

1. The lion beam is pierced, *both above and below*, with a series of small mortice holes, 11 in number, for the reception of the tenons of other portions of the Toran. This beam must therefore have been a middle one.

2. The short portion of elephant beam shows some mortice holes *above* but none *below*. Accordingly this must have been the lowermost beam.

3. The left-hand lower fragment of the great pinnacle of the gateway shows a portion of a very *large* tenon below, which must have had a corresponding mortice hole in the upper side of the beam on which it stood.[2] It could not therefore have been placed on the lion beam, and consequently there must have been a third beam, of which unfortunately not a single fragment was discovered.

The projecting ends of the Toran beams have already been described as composed of open-mouthed crocodiles with curled tails. The square part of the beam, between the curved centre and the crocodile end, was ornamented with a Stûpa on one side and a temple or shrine on the other.[3]

Of the square block, or *dado*, which was placed between the Toran beams and immediately over the pillar, no complete example was found. But from an examination of a number of fragments I have been able to restore this member of the Toran with certainty. It presented a face of three Persepolitan half-pillars standing on a Buddhist railing, with large lotus flowers in the spaces between the pillars. A specimen will be found in the same plate with the ends of the Toran beams.

The long spaces between the central curved parts of the Toran beams would appear to have been filled with a number of small balusters and pillar statues placed alternately. Many fragments of these were dug up, some of which were found to fit one another. The pieces were accordingly glued together, and as both their tops and bottoms were sloped it was clear that they must have stood upon the curved Toran beams. On placing them along the lion beam it was found that the two kinds of balusters must have been placed alternately, as their tenons were of somewhat different sizes, and would only fit into the alternate mortice holes. Their height also was found to fit exactly

---

[1] See Plate VIII.   [2] See Plate VII.   [3] See Plate IX., figs. 1 and 2.

with the distance between the curved beams as determined by the size of the square block, or *dado*, above described. I have accordingly arranged them in this alternate order in the accompanying Plate.[1] These little balusters are of considerable interest, as their sculptured statues are much superior in artistic design and execution to those of the railing pillars. They are further remarkable in having *Arian letters* engraved on their bases or capitals, a peculiarity which points unmistakably to the employment of Western artists, and which fully accounts for the superiority of their execution. The letters found are *p*, *s*, *a*, and *b*, of which the first three occur twice.[2] Now, if the same sculptors had been employed on the railings, we might confidently expect to find the same alphabetical letters used as private marks. But the fact is just the reverse, for the whole of the 27 marks found on any portions of the railing are *Indian* letters. The only conclusion that I can come to from these facts is that the foreign artists who were employed on the sculptures of the gateways were certainly not engaged on any part of the railing. I conclude, therefore, that the Rája of Sugana, the donor of the gateways, must have sent his own party of workmen to make them, while the smaller gifts of pillars and rails were executed by the local artists.

I have ventured to restore the pinnacles which crowned the East Gateway from the existing fragments, of which enough have been found to make the restoration of the great central symbol quite certain. This is shown in Plate VIII., where all the restorations are given in outline. The wheel at the top has been taken from one of the Dharma Chakras, as the end of the hanging garland shows that the symbol was crowned by a wheel. The whole symbol is of common occurrence in Buddhist sculptures and coins.[3] The smaller symbol of the *Tri-ratna*, or "Triple Gem Symbol," has been restored from a single fragment of one of the bars. The existing fragment is doubtless a small one, but, like the point of an elephant's trunk, it is the significant portion from which the whole can be restored with certainty.

Toran is a well-known name at the present day for an ornamented archway as well as for the ornamental frames of wood which are placed over doors and archways at the celebration of weddings. Some of these have a single horizontal bar, some two, and others three, just like the stone *Torans* of the Sánchi Stúpas. In the wedding *Torans* the ornaments placed on the top are birds and flowers.[4] In the religious *Torans* the ornaments would appear to have been confined to well-known Buddhist symbols, which occur on the old Hindu coins, and which still crown the summits of the gateways of the Sánchi Stúpa. I have given a photograph of one of the entrances restored, with its three *Toran* beams, its baluster pillars, and its crowning symbols.[5] It is very much to be regretted that no portion of the upper Toran beam has been discovered, so that the restored gateway might have been made more complete. Amongst the numerous existing fragments I found none that could have belonged to the missing beam, which has accordingly been left blank in the restored elevation.

---

[1] See Plate VIII.

[2] I think it probable that these letters may be numerals, the initials of the words *pánch* = 5, *sát* = 7, *áth* = 8, and *ba* = 2.

[3] See Archæological Survey of India, Vol. III., Plate X., figs. A., C., and D.

[4] See Plate IV. for two of these marriage Torans, above which I have placed the *Anguli Toran*, or "Finger mark form," more commonly called *Tri-pundra*, which the Hindus still place on their foreheads.

[5] See Plate VI.

The Pillars of the Gateway are 1 foot 4¼ inches thick, and 9 feet 7½ inches high; the four grouped capitals with their abacus are each 1 foot 1¾ inches high, and the large single capital 1 foot 10¼ inches, making the total height of the Pillars 12 feet 7½ inches.[1] With its three Toran beams, or architraves, each gateway must have been upwards of 20 feet in height without its crowning symbols.

The coping, or continuous architrave, which crowned the circle of Pillars, is formed of massive blocks of stone, each spanning two intercolumninations. The blocks are upwards of 7 feet in length, with a height of 1 foot 10½ inches, and a thickness of 1 foot 8 inches. They are secured firmly to each other by long tenons fitting into corresponding mortises, and to the tops of the pillars by a stout tenon on each, which fits a socket on the under side of the coping stone.[2] Each block is of course slightly curved to suit the circumference of the circle, and this curvature must have added considerably to the stability of the Railing; for as each set of three tenons formed a triangle, each coping stone became an efficient tie to keep the three Pillars on which it was set in their places.

The total length of the coping, including the returns at the four entrances, was 330 feet, the whole of which was most elaborately and minutely sculptured, both inside and outside. As before mentioned only one coping stone now remains in situ, resting on the three Pillars of the south-east quadrant, which abutted on the Eastern Gateway. But no less than 15 other coping stones have been found in the excavations out of an original total of 40, so that exactly three-fifths of this most important part of the Railing is at present missing. My second season's operations failed to bring to light any of the missing stones, although several fragments were recovered. The value and importance of this coping will be at once acknowledged, when I mention that amongst the sculptures which adorn the inner face there are no less than nine *Játakas*, or legends of previous births of Buddha, *with their titles inscribed over them*. But besides these Játakas there are no less than 10 other scenes with their names labelled above them, and about double that number of uninscribed scenes, some of which are easily identified; such for instance as the *Asadrisa Játaka*, or legend of Buddha when he was the Prince Asadrisa;[3] and the *Dasaratha Játaka*, or legend of Dasaratha, including the exile of Ráma and the visit of Bharata to his hermitage.[4] There is also the story of *Raja Janaka*, and the Princess *Sivala Devi*, both of whose names are duly labelled above them. These human scenes usually alternate, with bas-reliefs of various fruits or female ornaments, all boldly designed, and generally well carved.

At the end of the coping stone which faced the visitor as he approached each of the four entrances there was a boldly carved Lion, with a curly mane and long bushy tail, sitting on his haunches. The remains of three of these Lion statues were found, but all were unfortunately broken, and the head of only one of them was discovered.[5] Next to the Lion, on both the inner and outer faces of the coping, there is a kneeling Elephant, from whose mouth issues a long undulating stem, which continues to the end of the quadrant, and divides the face of the coping by its undulations into a number of small panels, each of which is filled with sculptures. On the inner face some have flowers and fruits, some necklaces and earrings, and other personal ornaments, while the rest are

---

[1] See Plate IV.
[2] See Plate IV. for the arrangement of these tenons and mortises.
[3] See Plate XXVII., fig. 13.
[4] See Plate XXVII., fig. 14.
[5] See Plate XXXIX., figs. 1 and 2.

occupied with the *Játakas* and other scenes which have been noticed above. On the outer face all the spaces marked off by the undulations are filled with repetitions of the same elaborate representation of a full blown lotus flower.[1] This broad line of bas-reliefs is on both faces finished by two rich borders, the lower one consisting of a continuous row of bells. The carvings are bold and deep; and where not injured by actual breakage, they are still as sharp and as perfect as when first set up.

The *Pillars* of the Bharhut Railing are monoliths of the same general pattern as those of other Buddhist Railings. They are called *thabho* throughout; the invariable ending of the record of a "Pillar gift being either *thabho dánam* or *dánam thabho*. The word is the Pali form of the Sanskrit *Stambha*, a pillar. They are 7 feet 1 inch in height, with a section of 1 foot 10¼ inches face for sculpture, by 1 foot 2½ inches side for the mortises of the Rail-bars.[2] The corner pillars at the entrance are 1 foot 10¼ inches square, which is the very same section as that of the Railing Pillars of the great Sánchi Stúpa. The Bharhut Pillars are, however, 1 foot less in height. The edges of all of them, except the corner Pillars, are slightly bevelled on both faces, and they are orna-mented, after the usual manner of Buddhist Railings, by a round boss or full medallion in the middle, and by a half medallion at top and the same at bottom. All of these medallions are filled with elaborate sculpture, chiefly of lotus flowers, or of flower com-positions. But there are also several of animals, and a considerable number of scenes taken from Buddhist legend and history. A few have single figures either of Yakshas or Yakshinis, or of Devatás or Nága Rájás,[3] and in one instance of a soldier. Several of these single figures unfortunately have no inscriptions by which to identify them.

Amongst the sculptured scenes of the Pillars there are several *Játakas* with their titles inscribed above them.[4] The conception of Máyá Devi, with the approach of the White Elephant is also suitably labelled.[5] There is besides a curious view of the *Tikutika*, which seems to represent the world of Serpents and Elephants, with its name duly inscribed above it.[6] And lastly there are representations of the Bodhi trees of six different Buddhas with their respective names attached to them.[7] The whole of these scenes will be described hereafter in a detailed account of the sculptures themselves.

The scalloped or bevelled edges of the Pillars are also sculptured with various ornaments, which add greatly to the decorative enrichment of the whole Railing. These consist chiefly of flowers and fruits with human figures, both male and female, standing on the flowers, with their hands either in an attitude of devotion, or reaching upwards to the fruits. On some Pillars the flowers bear Elephants, winged Horses, Monkeys, or Peacocks, while Parrots and Squirrels hang from the branches and nibble the fruit.[8]

The ornamentation of the corner Pillars of the entrances is quite different from that of the others. The Pillars of the inner corners generally bear figures of *Yakshas* and *Yakshinis*, *Devatás*, and *Nága Rájas*, to whom was entrusted the guardianship of the four entrances. Thus at the North Gate there are figures of *Kupiro Yakho*, or Kuvera King of the *Yakshas*, and of *Chandá Yakhi*; while at the South Gate there are figures of *Chulakoka*

---

[1] See Plate XL. for specimens of both faces outside and inside.
[2] See Plate IV. for plan and elevation of the railing.
[3] See Plates XXI., XXII., and XXIII.
[4] See Plates XXV. and XXVI.
[5] See Plate XXVIII., fig. 2.

[6] See Plate XXVIII., fig. 1.
[7] See Plates XXIX. and XXX.
[8] See Plates XI. and XII. for these ornaments.

Devatá and of the *Nága Rája Chakavako.*[1] On the two outer corner Pillars there is a quite different arrangement. The faces of these Pillars are divided into three compartments or panels by horizontal bands of Buddhist Railing. Each of these panels is filled with sculpture representing some scene or legend in the history of Buddha. Several of these are extremely interesting, as the inscriptions attached to them enable us to identify the different stories with the most absolute certainty. Amongst these curious records of the past is a scene representing the procession of King Ajâtasat on his elephant to visit the shrine of Buddha's foot prints, which is appropriately labelled *Ajâta Satu Bhagavato vandate,* that is " Ajâtasatru worships (the foot prints) of Buddha."[2] Another interesting scene, which represents the Nâga Rája Erâpatra kneeling at the foot of the Bodhi tree, is labelled in a similar manner *Erapato Nága Raja Bhagavato vandate,* or " Erapatra Nâga Rája worships (the Bodhi tree) of Buddha."[3] Another scene of great interest represents the Rája Prasenajita in a four-horse chariot proceeding to pay his devotions at the Shrine of the Buddhist Wheel Symbol, which is labelled *Bhagavato Dhama Chakam,* or " Buddha's Wheel of the law."[4] Other scenes present us with views of the famous Bodhi tree of Sâkya Muni, and of the Banian tree of Kâsyapa Buddha being worshipped by wild Elephants, both sculptures being duly inscribed with their proper titles.[5] Lastly, there is a scene representing a dance of Apsarases, with the names of four of the most famous of those heavenly nymphs attached to the four dancers.[6]

Altogether 35 Pillars, more or less perfect, have been found on the site of the Stúpa, along with numerous fragments of others. Six other Pillars were discovered at the neighbouring village of Batanmâra and no less than eight more at Pathora, making a total of 49, or considerably more than one half of the original number of 80. I think it is possible that some more Pillars may yet be found about Pathora; but they will most probably be split down the middle, and their sides cut off, to fit them as beams for present buildings. Four of the eight which have already been seen at Pathora were found in this state.

The Stone Bars or Rails are of the same pattern as those of the Buddhist Railings at Buddha Gaya, Bhilsa, and Mathura. They measure 1 foot 11¾ inches in length by 1 foot 10½ inches in breadth, with a thickness of 6 inches.[7] The dimensions of the Bars of the great Sânchi Railing are 2 feet 1½ by 2 feet 1½ by 9½ inches. The Bharhut Rails are therefore very nearly of the same size, the chief difference being in their inferior thickness, which makes the curved surface very much flatter. The Rails have circular bosses or medallions on each side, which are sculptured with various subjects similar to those of the Pillar medallions. Amongst them, however, there are very few Jâtakas.[8] But they present us with several humorous scenes, and with a very great variety of flowered ornaments of singular richness and beauty.[9] There is only one specimen of a geometrical pattern, which will be found in the photograph of the Railing outside.[10]

The total number of Rail-bars in the complete Railing was 228. Of these about 80 have been found, of which six are at the neighbouring town of Uchahara. As they

---

[1] See Plates XXI., XXII., and XXIII.
[2] See Plate XVI., fig. 3.
[3] See Plate XIV., fig. 3.
[4] See Plate XIII., fig. 3.
[5] See Plate XV., fig. 3.
[6] See Plate XV., fig. 1; and Plate XVI., fig. 1.
[7] See Plate IV. for section and elevation.
[8] The *Latuwa Jâtaka* is on one of the Rail-bars.
[9] See Plates XXXIII. to XXXVIII.
[10] See Plate XI.

weigh only about two maunds each their removal was easy, as a single bullock would have been sufficient to carry off one Rail, whilst a camel might have taken three.

The Rail-bars of the entrance, owing to the wider intercolumination of the Pillars, were considerably longer than those of the main Railing, the side openings being 2½ feet and the front openings 3½ feet wide. The 19-inch round medallion which was sufficient to fill the surface of a 23-inch rail, would appear to have been considered too meagre for the decoration of the longer Rail of 30 to 40 inches. The round medallion was therefore changed to an oblong panel 25 inches in length which covered the greater part of the surface. I have seen only two of these long Rails, one of which I found in the village of Bharhut, and the other in the neighbouring town of Uchahara. The latter has been ingeniously split down the middle, and the two sculptured faces are now utilised as the ornamental capitals of the Pillars of a small Dharmsala erected by a Gosain. The sculptures of these long Rails present only religious scenes, such as the worship of the Stupa, the Bodhi Tree, and the Dharma Chakra.[1]

From several of the inscriptions we learn that these Rail-bars were appropriately called *Suchi*, or "needles," a name that must have been bestowed upon them from the duty which they had to perform of threading together the Pillars by passing through their mortises or eyelet holes. One of these inscriptions may be seen in the sketch of the *Latuwa Játaka*, which is also inscribed with the name of the donor, ending with the words *dánam suchi.*[2] Other examples give *suchi dánam,*[3] which is the more common form. It seems probable that in the former cases the inscriptions originally ended with *dánam*, and that the nature of the gift was afterwards added at the request of the donor. There are several similar instances of this kind of addition in the "Pillar gifts," which read *dánam thabho*, as well as *thabho dánam.*

Between the magnificent Railing and the Stúpa there was a clear space of 10 feet 4 inches wide for the perambulation of the pilgrims round the sacred building. The whole of this space was covered with a thick flooring of lime plaster, which has lasted well even to the present day. The outer edge of the floor was finished by a line of curved kerb stones, cut exactly to the circumference of the inner circle of the Railing; and the pillars were set against the kerb stones which just touched the diameter of the lower half medallions. The foot of each Pillar, which was quite rough, rested on a square block laid directly on the earth. The terraced floor was continued all round the outside of the Railing for a width of several feet. Here some traces of brick walls were found, as well as some Votive Stúpas of stone. These scattered foundations would appear to have been the plinths of Votive Stúpas and other small objects.

The excavation also brought to light the remains of a second stone Railing of much smaller dimensions than the Inner Railing. Only two Pillars were found, and only four pieces of the curved stone plinth in which the Pillars were fixed. But no less than 10 specimens of the curved coping stones have been exhumed, and all in positions outside the line of Inner Railing, which shows that they must have belonged to an *Outer* line of Railing. These coping stones are quite plain, but there is no mistaking their purpose.

---

[1] See Plate XXXI. for these four specimens.
[2] See Plate XXVI., fig. 1. For other examples of the same form see the inscriptions, Plate LV., Nos. 9 and 12, and Plate LVI., No. 28.
[3] See Plate LV., Nos. 16 and 17, and Plate LVI., Nos. 30, 31, 32, 41, 46, 53, 61, and 64.

At first I took them for outer kerb stones, but the mortises on their under sides showed that they must have formed part of the coping of an Outer Railing.[1] The Pillars of the Great Railing in falling outwards overwhelmed the Outer Railing wherever it was still standing, as several pieces of the outer coping were found beneath the fallen Pillars of the Inner Railing. There is, however, good reason to believe that the greater part of the Outer Railing had already been removed long before the excavation of the Stûpa in the last century, which caused the overthrow of the Great Railing. The only two Pillars yet found were discovered in two of the adjacent villages where they have been worshipped for many years on account of the figures sculptured upon them. There must have been about 240 of these small Pillars, and it is difficult to believe that so large a number could have been utterly destroyed. They were most probably split into two pieces, and then used as building stones with the sculptured faces turned inwards. The entire disappearance of the Rail-bars is also very mysterious, as there must have been about 750 of them —each being 18 inches long and 7 inches broad. Of the two Pillars that have been found one belongs to a corner position and the other to a middle place. They are both 2 feet 1 inch in height with a breadth of 7 inches. As the plinth was 7 inches in height, and the coping the same, the total height of the Railing was only 3 feet 3 inches. The corner Pillar has a single human figure on each of the two outer faces, and the middle Pillar has a similar figure on its outer face. The figures are standing fully draped with their hands joined in respectful devotion. I believe, therefore, that both of these Pillars must have belonged to one of the entrances, and that the figures were placed on the adjacent Pillars as guardians of the Gateways, while the Pillars of the Railing itself were perhaps quite plain.

Respecting this Outer Railing I have a suspicion that its erection was necessitated by the gradual accumulation of the remains of many buildings around the Great Railing; and consequently that it must be of a much later age. But however this may be, it is quite certain that the accumulation led at last to the necessity of adding a flight of steps, at least on the western side, where I found a solid stone ladder 3 feet 1 inch in width. As this ladder still possesses seven steps of 10 inches each, the height of the accumulated rubbish, from which the visitor had to descend into the area of the Stûpa Court, was certainly not less than 6 feet. Where this ladder was placed can now only be guessed, and my conjecture is that it probably occupied the actual entrance between the two lines of Railing as shown in the accompanying Plate.[2]

Amongst the fragments collected from the excavations there are pieces of two stone Pillars of different dimensions, and with a different arrangement of the medallions from those of the Great Railing of the Stûpa. Both of these pieces are inscribed, but the letters do not differ from those of the other inscriptions except in being much thicker and more coarsely executed.[3] The medallions are placed much closer together, within 6¼ inches, so that unless there were two whole medallions as well as two half medallions, these Pillars must necessarily have been much shorter than those of the Railing. But as the remains of one of the medallions shows a diameter of 19 inches these Pillars must have been of the same breadth as those of the Railing, and therefore most probably of about the same height.

---

[1] See Plate V. for the plan, elevation, and section of this Railing.
[2] See Plate V. for the conjectural positions of these ladders.
[3] See Plate LVI., fragments, figs. 19 and 20.

I do not, however, believe that they had any connection with the Great Railing itself, but that they belonged to some other distinct enclosure, which may have surrounded a Tree, or a Pillar, or a Dharma Chakra.

Their inscriptions do not throw any light upon the position which they may have occupied, unless the word *ásana*, a "throne" or "seat," may refer to the famous *Vajrásana*, or Diamond Throne of Buddha. The inscription in which this word occurs has lost the first letter of each of its two lines, but they may be readily restored as follows:

(Ba) hu hathika ásana—

(Bha)-gavato Mahadevasa—

It is possible, therefore, that this Pillar may have formed part of the Railing surrounding a *Vajrásan*. It is certain at least that the inscription does not refer to the medallion below it; firstly, because it is placed far away from it, immediately beneath the upper ornament; and secondly, because enough yet remains of the medallion to show that it was a large lotus flower. In two other instances where the words *bahuhathika* are found, they clearly refer to the "great herd of Elephants," which appears in the sculpture. Here, however, they are placed immediately beneath a row of human hands, which suggests the probability that *bahu hathika* may refer to the "many hands" of the sculpture.

Similar rows of human hands are found in another sculpture, which apparently represents a row of four altars or seats placed inside a Temple.[1] I think it very probable that these also are thrones or seats of the four Buddhas to whom "many hands" are held up in adoration. If this explanation be correct then the inscription above quoted must refer to the number of hands lifted up before the Throne (*ásan*) of *Bhagavata Mahádeva*. The *Vajrásan*, or *Bodhimanda* as it was also called, was the name of a seat on which a Buddha had obtained his Buddhahood. This Throne was an object of great reverence, and is frequently represented in the sculptures. I believe that the middle and lower bas-reliefs of the Pillar on which Ajátasatu's name is inscribed present us with actual representations of the *Vajrásan*, or Seat of Sákya Muni, with his footprints on the step below.[2] The Throne seems also to be represented in all three of the right-hand scenes of the same Pillar, under the shadow of the Bodhi tree, which was omitted in the other scenes for want of room. The *Vajrásan* of each different Buddha is also represented under the shadow of its appropriate Bodhi tree in the special scenes which are inscribed with their respective names.[3] In two of these sculptures the seat is supported on Pillars, which very forcibly illustrates my suggestion that the broken Pillar with the inscription containing the word *ásana* was most probably one of the supporters of a *Vajrásan* or Throne of Buddha.

3.—PROBABLE AGE OF THE STÚPA.

Before proceeding to describe the different subjects of the sculptures, I wish to say a few words as to the probable age of the *Stúpa*, which I have assigned to the Asoka period, or somewhere between 250 and 200 B.C. We know with absolute certainty the shapes of all the letters of the alphabet used in the time of Asoka, whose date is fixed within the very narrow limits of error of not more than two or three years. That these characters

---

[1] See Plate XXXI., fig. 4.   [2] See Plate XVI., fig. 3.   [3] See Plates XXIX. and XXX.

were in general use from Kabul to the mouth of the Ganges, and from the foot of the Himálayas to Suráshtra, we learn from the Indian legends of the coins of Pantaleon and Agathokles, as well as from the numerous inscriptions of Asoka himself and of Dasaratha, one of his successors, who reigned shortly after him, or from about B.C. 215 to 209.

That a marked change in these characters was introduced before B.C. 150 is almost equally certain. Just four years ago a small hoard of silver coins was found in a field near Jwála Mukhi, which comprised five coins of the native princes *Amoghabhuti, Dhára Ghosha*, and *Varmmika* along with some 30 specimens of the Philopator coins of Apollodotus. Now the date of Apollodotus is known within a few years, and has been fixed by myself as ranging from B.C. 165 to 150. As there were no other Greek coins in the find, and as these particular coins of Apollodotus are most probably his earliest mintage, whilst all of them were quite new and fresh, I conclude that the whole must have been buried in the early part of his own reign. The coins of the three Indian Princes must consequently be of the same age, or not later than B.C. 150. All of the letters on these coins have got *mátras*, or heads, added to them, and several of them have assumed considerable modifications in their forms, more especially the *j*, the *m*, and the *gh*, which have become angular, while their forms are invariably round, in all the Bharhut inscriptions, exactly like those of the Asoka records. According to my judgment the absolute identity of the forms of the Bharhut characters with those of the Asoka period is proof sufficient that they belong to the same age. On this evidence I do not wish to fix upon any exact date, and I am content with recording my opinion that the alphabetical characters of the Bharhut inscriptions are certainly not later than B.C. 200.

I may add also that the simple character of the pillar capitals, which are exactly the same as those of Asoka's own pillars, fully corroborates the early date which I have assigned to the Bharhut Stúpa.

I have already pointed out that Bharhut was on the high road between Ujain and Bhilsa in the south, and Kosámbi and Srávasti in the north, as well as Pátaliputra in the east. I may here add that on this line at a place called Rupnáth, only 60 miles from Bharhut, there is a rock inscription of Asoka himself. As he was governor of Ujain during his father's lifetime Asoka must often have passed along this road, on which it seems only natural to find the Stúpas of Bhilsa, the rock inscription of Rupnáth, the Stúpa of Bharhut, and the Pillar of Prayága or Allahabad; of which two are actual records of his own, while the inscriptions on the Railings of the Stúpas show that they also must belong to his age.

I have already also alluded to the inscription of Raja Dhanabhúti, the munificent donor of the East Gateway of the Stúpa—and most probably of the other three Gateways also. In his inscription he calls himself the Raja of Sugana, which is most likely intended for *Sughna* or *Srughna*, an extensive kingdom on the upper Jumna. I have identified the capital of Srughna, with the modern village of *Sugh* which is situated in a bend of the old bed of the Jumna [1] close to the large town of Búriya. Old coins are found on this site in considerable numbers. In this inscription on the East Gateway at Bharhut Raja Dhanabhúti calls himself the son of Aga Rája and the grandson of Viswa Deva, and in one of the Rail-bar inscriptions I find that Dhanabhúti's son was named Vádha Pála. Now the name of Dhanabhúti occurs in one of the early Mathura inscriptions which has

---

[1] See Archæological Survey of India, Vol. II., p. 226.

been removed to Aligarh.[1] The stone was originally a corner pillar of an enclosure with sockets for rails on two adjacent faces, and sculptures on the other two faces. The sculpture on the uninjured face represents Prince Siddhârtha leaving Kapilavastu on his horse Kanthapa, whose feet are upheld by four Yakshas to prevent the clatter of their hoofs from awakening the guards. On the adjacent side is the inscription placed above a Buddhist Railing.[2] At some subsequent period the Pillar was pierced with larger holes to receive a set of Rail-bars on the inscription face. One of these holes has been cut through the three upper lines of the inscription, but as a few letters still remain on each side of the hole it seems possible to restore some of the missing letters. I read the inscription as follows:

1. *Kapa*——(Dhana)
2. *Bhitisa* * * * *Vátsi*
3. *Putrasa* (Vâdha Pâ) *lasa*
4. *Dhanabhūtisa dânam Vediká*
5. *Torana cha Ratnagraha sa—*
6. *-va Buddha pujáye sahá máta pi-*
7. *-tá ki Sahá* * chatuha parishâhi.*

There can be little doubt that this inscription refers to the family of Dhanabhûti of Bharhut, as the name of *Vátsi putra* of the Mathura pillar is the Sanskrit form of the *Váchhi putra* of the Bharhut Pillar. This identification is further confirmed by the restoration of the name of Vâdha Pâla, which exactly fits the vacant space in the third line. From this record, therefore, we obtain another name of the same royal family in Dhanabhuti II., the son of Vâdha Pâla, and grandson of Dhanabhuti I. Now in this inscription all the letters have got the mâtras, or heads, which are found in the legends of the silver coins of Amoghabhûti, Dâra Ghosha, and Varmmika. The inscription cannot, therefore, so far as we at present know, be dated earlier than B.C. 150. Allowing 30 years to a generation, the following will be the approximate dates of the royal family of Srughna:

B.C. 300. Viswa Deva.
    270. Aga Raja.
    240. Dhanabhûti I.
    210. Vâdha Pâla.
    180. Dhanabhuti II.
    150. ————

Now we learn from Vâdha Pâla's inscription, Plate LVI., No. 54, that he was only a Prince (*Kumára*) the son of the *Raja* Dhanabhûti, when the Railing of the Bharhut Stûpa was set up. We thus arrive at the same date of 240 to 210 B.C. as that previously obtained for the erection of the magnificent Gateways and Railing of the Bharhut Stûpa.

To a later member of this family I would ascribe the well-known coins of Raja *Amogha-bhûti*, King of the Kuninḍas, which are found most plentifully along the upper Jumna, in the actual country of Srughna. His date, as I have already shown, must be about B.C. 150, and he will therefore follow immediately after *Dhana-bhûti* II. I possess

---

[1] See Archæological Survey of India, Vol. III., Plate XVI., No. 21. The gift of Dhanabhuti at Mathura included a *Vediká*, or open building for reading, a *Torana*, or ornamental gateway, and a *Ratnagriha*, or treasury.

also two coins of Raja *Bala-bhúti*, who was most probably a later member of the same dynasty. But besides these I have lately obtained two copper pieces of *Aga Raja*, the father of Dhana-bhúti I. One of these was found at Sugh, the old capital of Srughna, and the other at the famous city of Kosambi, about 100 miles to the north of Bharhut.

I may mention here that my reading of the name of the Kuniṇḍas on the coins of Amogha-bhúti was made more than ten years ago in London, where I fortunately obtained a very fine specimen of his silver mintage. This reading was published in the "Academy," 21st November 1874. I have since identified the *Kuniṇḍas*, or *Kuliṇḍas*, as the name is also written, with the people of *Kulindrine*, a district which Ptolemy places between the upper courses of the Bipasis and Ganges. They are now represented by the *Kunets*, who form nearly two-thirds of the population of the hill tracts between the Biás and Tons Rivers. The name of *Kunáwar* is derived from them; but there can be little doubt that Kunáwar must once have included the whole of Ptolemy's *Kulindrine* as the Kunets now number nearly 400,000 persons, or rather more than *sixty per cent.* of the whole population between the Bias and Tons Rivers. They form 58 per cent. in Kullu; 67 per cent. in the states round about Simla, and 62 per cent. in Kunáwar. They are very numerous in Sirmor and Bisahar, and there are still considerable numbers of them below the hills, in the districts of Ambála, Karnál, and Ludiána, with a sprinkling in Delhi and Hushiarpur.

II.—SCULPTURES.

The subjects represented in the Bharhut sculptures are both numerous and varied, and many of them are of the highest interest and importance for the study of Indian history. Thus we have more than a score of illustrations of the legendary Jâtakas, and some half dozen illustrations of historical scenes connected with the life of Buddha, which are quite invaluable for the history of Buddhism. Their value is chiefly due to the inscribed labels that are attached to many of them, and which make their identification absolutely certain. Amongst the historical scenes the most interesting are the processions of the Râjas Ajâtasatru and Prasenajita on their visits to Buddha; the former on his elephant, the latter in his chariot, exactly as they are described in the Buddhist chronicles. Another invaluable sculpture is the representation of the famous *Jetavana* monastery at Srâvasti,—with its Mango tree, and temples, and the rich banker Anâtha-pindika in the foreground emptying a cartful of gold pieces to pave the surface of the garden.

But besides these scenes, which are so intimately connected with the history of Buddhism, there are several bas-reliefs, which seem to represent portions of the history of Râma during his exile. There are also a few scene of broad humour in which monkeys are the chief actors.

Of large figures there are upwards of 30 alto-relievo statues of Yakshas and Yakshinis, Devatâs, and Nâga Râjas, one half of which are inscribed with their names. We thus see that the guardianship of the North Gate was entrusted to Kuvera King of the Yakshas, agreeably to the teaching of the Buddhist and Brahmanical cosmogonies. And similarly we find that the other Gates were confided to the Devas and the Nâgas.

The representations of animals and trees are also very numerous and some of them are particularly spirited and characteristic. Of other objects there are boats, horse-chariots, and bullock-carts, besides several kinds of musical instruments, and a great variety of flags, standards, and other symbols of royalty.

About one half of the full medallions of the Rail-bars and the whole of the half medallions of the Pillars are filled with flowered ornaments of singular beauty and delicacy of design, of which numerous examples are given in the accompanying plates.

I will now describe the sculptures in detail according to the following arrangement:

A.—SUPERHUMAN BEINGS.

1. Yakshas.
2. Devas.
3. Nâgas.
4. Apsarases.

B.—HUMAN BEINGS.

1. Royal Persons.
2. Religious Persons.
3. Royal and Lay Costume.
4. Military Costume.
5. Female Dress and Ornaments.
6. Tattooing.

C.—ANIMALS.

D.—TREES AND FRUITS.

E.—SCULPTURED SCENES.

1. Jâtakas, Previous Births of Buddha.
2. Historical Scenes.
3. Miscellaneous Scenes—inscribed.
4. Miscellaneous Scenes—not inscribed.
2. Humorous Scenes.

F.—OBJECTS OF WORSHIP.

1. Stûpas.
2. Wheels.
3. Bodhi Trees.
4. Buddha-pada, or Footprints.
5. Tri-ratna, or Triple-gem Symbol.

G.—DECORATIVE ORNAMENTS.

H.—BUDDHIST BUILDINGS.

1. Palaces.
2. *Punyasâlas,* or Religious Houses.
3. *Vajrâsan* Canopies.
4. *Bodhimanda* Thrones.
5. Pillars.
6. Ascetic Hermitages.
7. Dwelling Houses.

K.—MISCELLANEOUS OBJECTS.

1. Vehicles.
2. Furniture.
3. Utensils.
4. Musical Instruments.

A.—SUPERHUMAN BEINGS.

1. YAKSHAS.

The most striking of all the representations of the demigods are the almost life-size figures of no less than six *Yakshas* and *Yakshinis,* which stand out boldly from the faces of the corner pillars at the different entrances to the Courtyard of the Stûpa. According to the Buddhist cosmogony the palace of Dhritarâshtra and the Gandharvas occupies the East side of the Yugandhara rocks, that of Virudha and the Kumbhandas the South, that of Virupaksha and the Nâgas the West, and that of Vaisravan and his Yakshas the

North.[1] Two of these guardian demigods I have been able to identify with two of the *Yakshas* figured on the entrance pillars of the Bharhut Stûpa. The Pali name of *Waisra-wana*, in Sanskrit Vaisravana, is a patronymic of *Kuvera*, the king of all the Yakshas, whose father was Visravas. To him was assigned the guardianship of the *Northern* quarter; and accordingly I find that one of the figures sculptured on the corner pillar of the Northern Gate at Bharhut is duly inscribed *Kupiro Yakho*, or *Kuvera Yaksha*.[2] To *Virudhaka* was entrusted the guardianship of the South quarter, and accordingly the image of *Virudako Yakho* is duly sculptured on the corner pillar of the South Gate. With Kupiro on the North are associated *Ajakâlako Yakho* and *Chadâ Yakhi*, or Chandâ Yakshini;[3] and with Virudaka on the South are associated *Gangito Yakho* and *Chakavâko Nâga Râja*.[4] The West side was assigned to Virupâksha; but here I find only *Suchiloma Yakho* and *Sirima Devatâ* on one pillar, and on a second the figure of *Supâvaso Yakho*. Dhritarâshtra was the guardian of the East side; but unfortunately the two corner pillars of this Gate have disappeared. There is, however, in a field to the west of the Stûpa a corner pillar bearing the figure of the *Yakhini Sudasava*, which could only have belonged to the Eastern Gate. We have thus still left no less than six figures of *Yakshas* and two of *Yakshinis*, which are most probably only about one-half of the number which originally decorated the Bharhut Railing. I may note here that the corner pillar of the Buddhist Railing which once surrounded the Great Temple at Bauddha Gaya bears a tall figure of a Yakshini on one of the outward faces as at Bharhut.

The *Yakshas* were the subjects of *Kuvera*, the guardian of the North quarter of Mount Meru, and the God of Riches. They had superhuman power, and were universally feared, as they were generally believed to be fond of devouring human beings. This must certainly have been the belief of the early Buddhists, as the legend of the *Apannaka Jâtaka*[5] is founded on the escape of Buddha, who was then a wise merchant, from the snares of a treacherous Yaksha, while another merchant who had preceded him in the same route had been devoured with all his followers, men and oxen, by the Yakshas, who left "nothing but their bones." I suspect that this belief must have originated simply in the derivation of their name Yaksha, " to eat,"[6] for there is nothing ferocious or even severe in the aspects of the Yakshas of the Bharhut sculptures. These must, however, have been considered as friendly Yakshas, to whom was entrusted the guardianship of the Four Gates of the Stûpa. The ancient dread of their power has survived to the present day, as the people of Ceylon still try " to overcome their malignity by Chaunts and Charms."[7] I think it probable also that the *Jak Deo* of Kunâwar and Simla may derive its name from the ancient *Yaksha* or Jakh.

Of Kuvera, the king of the *Yakshas*, there is frequent mention in the Buddhist books under his patronymic of *Wessawano* or *Vaisravana*, as on attendant an Buddha along with the guardian chiefs of the other three quarters. His image also is amongst those of the

---

[1] Hardy's Manual of Buddhism, p. 24. Also Burnouf, Le Lotus de la Bonne Loi, p. 3. Also Foucaux, 195–288. They were called the Four Great Kings.
    [2] See Plate XXIII., fig. 1.   [3] See Plate XXIII., fig. 3.
    [4] See Plate XXI., figs. 1 and 2.   [5] Hardy's Manual of Buddhism, p. 108.
    [6] See Wilson's Vishnu Purâna, p. 41, where this derivation is given. Sir William Jones, however, looked upon them very differently, as he translates Manu's " Yakshas," by benevolent genii.—Institutes, L, 87.
    [7] Hardy's Manual of Buddhism, p. 45.

other gods, which bow down before Buddha as he enters their temple.[1] According to the Purânas Kuvera was the son of *Visravas* and *Irâvirâ*, and the grandson of *Pulastya*. He is therefore just as well known by his patronymics of *Vaisravana* and *Paulastya*, derived from his father and grandfather as by his own name. From the Bharhut Sculptures we see that the power of *Kupira Yakho* was as well known and fully recognised in the time of Asoka as in that of the Lalita Vistara and other Buddhist works. It seems probable, therefore, that he was one of the early demigods of the Hindus prior to the rise of Buddhism. I have failed to find any notice of him in the Rig Veda. But I believe that I have been successful in tracing him under both of his patronymics in the early Greek Mythology. As the god of Wealth he of course corresponds with the Greek Ploutos, who according to Hesiod and Diodorous was the son of *Iasion* by *Demeter*.[2] Now *Kuvera* was the son of *Visravas* by *Irâvira*, or the Earth, who is therefore the same as Demeter. He accordingly received the well-known patronymic of *Vaisravana*, or in its spoken Pali form *Wessawano*, which appears to be the very same name as *Iasion*. But as *Kuvera* was likewise the grandson of Pulastya, he was also known by the patronymic of *Paulastya* which in the spoken dialects takes the forms of *Paulast* and *Paulat*, just as *Agastya* becomes Agast and Agat, as in the well-known name of Agat Sarai. Now the latter form of *Paulat* may, I think, be taken without much hesitation as the possible original of the Greek *Ploutos*. Here, then, we see that the god of Wealth was known to the Greeks under both of his Indian patronymics as early as the time of Hesiod, or about the eigth century B.C. But if we accept this much, we must be prepared to accept much more, and must admit that the demigod *Kuvera*, the lord of Riches, was known at least as early as the period of the separation of the Eastern and Western branches of the Aryan nation.

Regarding the general appearance of the Yakshas we are told that they resembled mortal men and women. That this was the popular belief is clearly shown by the well-known story of Sâkya Sinha's first appearance at Râjagriha as an ascetic. The people wondered who he could be. Some took him for Brahmâ, some for Indra, and some for *Vaisravana*.[3] This is confirmed by the figures of the Yakshas and Yakshinis in the Bharhut Sculptures, which in no way differ from human beings either in appearance or in dress. In the Lalita Vistara also *Vaisravana* is enumerated as one of the chiefs of the Kâmâvachara Devaloka, of which all the inhabitants were subject to sensual enjoyments[4].

In the Vishnu Purâna *Vaisravana* is called king over kings ; but in other Purânas he is simply styled Kuvera, king of the Yakshas.[5] His capital was called *Alaka ;* and so the banished Yaksha of Kâlidâsa thus addresses the cloud who is to be his messenger, " you must set out for the habitations of the Yaksha chiefs, called Alaka, the palaces of " which glance white in the moonlight of the head of Siva, placed in the exterior

[1] Lalita Vistara, quoted by Burnouf, Introduction a l'histoire du Buddhisme Indien, p. 132. See also Translation of ditto by M. Foucaux from the Tibetan, p. 115. In the original passage the name of Kuvera is inserted as well as that of Vaisravana, which leads M. Foucaux to think that Vaisravana may be a different god from Kuvera. But this insertion of the two names is clearly a mistake, as only a little later I find the following passage, " N'est-ce pas Vaisravana le Maître des richesses," which thus places his identity with Kuvera beyond all doubt.

[2] Hesiod Theog, 969 ; Diodor V., 4.

[3] Lalita Vistara, translated by M. Foucaux from the Tibetan, pp. 228-229.

[4] See Hardy's Manual of Buddhism, p. 29.

[5] Wilson's Vishnu Purana, p. 153. He is also called king of kings by Kâlidâsa in his Meghduta ; Sloka, 3.

" gardens." [1] Hence mount Kailása was also called *Kuveráchala* and *Kuverádri*, or " Kuvera's hill."

The Lalita Vistara speaks of the 28 chiefs of the Yakshas, [2] apparently exclusive of Kuvera who must be included amongst the four great kings that are mentioned separately. Six names are found in the Bharhut Sculptures, and an equal number may be gathered from the legends in Hardy's Manual of Buddhism. But the only name of any note is that of Aláwaka, who contended with Buddha; and was of course overcome by him. During the conflict he attempted to frighten Buddha by calling out in a loud voice which was heard over all Jambudwipa, "I am the Yakho Aláwaka." [3] His place of abode was a Banian tree, and he possessed a peculiar weapon called *Chela* which was as irresistible as the thunderbolt of *Indra*, the club of *Vaisravana*, or the mace of Death.

With reference to the name of *Kuvera*, which means " deformed," and is said to refer to the mal-formation of three legs, I believe that this meaning of the word gave rise to the modern representations of him as three legged. But as there is no allusion to any deformity in the Buddhist books, while there is a distinct testimony to the contrary in the story of Sákya, who possessed all the 32 points of beauty being likened to him, I accept the representation of him by the Bharhut Sculpture as a true portrait of the ancient god of the Yakshas. Perhaps the derivation of the name may be found in *Ku*, the earth, and *vrinh* or *bri*, to nourish, that is, " what is nourished by the earth,"—to wit " gold " or wealth. But I am more inclined to accept *Ku*, the " earth," and *vira* a " hero," as the real original, as the *Yakshas* would appear to be the " demigods of earth," just as the Nágas are the " demigods of water."

2. DEVAS.

Of the figures of Devas I have already noticed that of Sirimá Devatá; but there is also a second of *Chulakoka Devatá* which is joined with the Yaksha *Virudhaka* and the Nága Rája *Chakaváka* in the guardianship of the South Gate. [4] There are two other female statues, but as they are not inscribed it is difficult to determine whether they are Yakshinis or Devatás. *Sirimá Devatá* may be simply *Sri Máyá Devi*, the mother of Sákya Muni, or the " auspicious mother goddess." But I have a suspicion that the figure may be intended for the celebrated beauty named *Sirimá*, the sister of the physician Jivaka. Her story as told by Bishop Bigandet from the Burmese chronicles is as follows: [5]

" A famous courtesan named Sirima, sister of the celebrated physician Jivika, " renowned all over the country for her wit and the incomparable charms of her person, " wished to show her liberality to the disciples of Buddha. Every day a certain number " of them went to her dwelling, to receive with their food, abundant alms. One of the " pious mendicants, in an unguarded moment, moved by an unholy curiosity, looked at

---

[1] The Meghaduta of Kalidasa, translated by Colonel Ouvry.

[2] M. Foucaux's translation from Tibetan, p. 72.

[3] Hardy's Manual of Buddhism, p. 261.

[4] See Plate XXIII., fig. 3, for Chulakoka, or the " Little Koka." A corner pillar at Bauddha Gaya bears a Yakshini in the very same position as Chandá and Chulakoka. There was also a Mahákoka Devata, or " Great Koka," but her statue is now at Pathora, inside the temple.

[5] Legend of the Burmese Buddha, p. 234. I have changed the spelling of the Burmese names throughout. The Burmese write Thirima and Dzewak, &c.

" her, and was instantly smitten by her charms. The moral wound was widened and
" deepened by a fortuitous occurrence. On a certain day Sirima fell sick. But she did
" not relax in her daily work of charity. Though weak and in her *neglige*, she insisted
" on the mendicants being introduced in her room, that she might pay her respects to
" them. The unfortunate lover was among the company. Her incomparable charms
" were heightened by her plain dress and drooping attitude. The poor lover went back
" with his brethren to the monastery. The arrow had penetrated to the core of the
" heart. He refused to take any food, and during some days, completely estranged
" himself from the society of his brethren. Whilst the intestine war raged in his bosom
" Sirima died. Buddha, desirous to cure the moral distemper of the poor religious,
" invited King Bimbasara to be present, when he would go with his disciples to see the
" remains of Sirima. On the fourth day after Sirima's death he went to her house with
" his disciples. There was laid before them her body, with a livid appearance, all
" swollen. Countless worms already issuing out through the apertures, rendered
" lothsome its sight, whilst a horrible stench almost forbade a standing close to it.
" Buddha coolly asked the King, What is that object which is stretched before us?
" Sirima's body, replied the King. When she was alive, retorted Buddha, people paid a
" thousand pieces of silver to enjoy her for a day. Would any one take her now for half
" that sum? No, replied the King; in all my kingdom there is not one man who would
" offer the smallest sum to have her remains; nay, nobody would be found who would be
" willing to carry her to any distance, unless compelled to do so. Buddha, addressing
" the assembly, said, Behold all that remains of Sirima, who was so famous for her
" personal attractions. What has become of that form which deceived and enslaved so
" many? All is subjected to mutability, there is nothing real in this world."

3. Nâgas.

In the history of Buddhism the *Nâgas* play even a more important part than the
Yakshas. One of their chiefs named *Virupaksha* was the guardian of the Western quarter.
Like the Yakshas the Nâgas occupied a world of their own, called *Nâgaloka*, which was
placed amidst the waters of this world, immediately beneath the three-peaked hill of
Trikuta, which supported Mount Meru.[1] The word Nâga means either a "snake" or an
" elephant," and is said to be derived from *Naga*, which means both a "mountain" and a
"tree." In the Purânas the Nâgas are made the offspring of Kâsyapa by *Kadru*. In
Manu and in the Mahâbhârata they form one of the creations of the seven great Rishis,
who are the progenitors of all the semi-divine beings such as *Yakshas, Devas, Nâgas*, and
Apsarases, as well as of the human race. The capital of the Nâgas, which was beneath
the waters, was named *Bhogâvati*, or the "city of enjoyment." Water was the element of
the Nâgas, as Earth was that of the Yakshas; and the lake-covered land of Kashmir was
their especial province.[2] Every spring, every pool, and every lake had its own Nâga,
and even now nearly every spring or river source bears the name of some Nâga, as *Vîr
Nâg, Anant Nâg*, &c., the word being used as equivalent to a "spring or fount of water."

---

[1] Hardy's Manual of Buddhism, pp. 11 and 44.

[2] Raja Tarangini I., 30. Abul Fazl also notices that in 700 places there are carved figures of snakes, which
" they worship."—Gladwin's Ain-i-Akbari—II., 126.

Even a bath was sufficient for a Nâga as we learn from the story of the birth of Durlabha the founder of the Karkotaka, or Nâga dynasty of Kashmir Rajas in A.D. 625.

In Buddhist history the Nâga chiefs who are brought into frequent contact with Buddha himself, are generally connected with *water*. Thus *Apalâla* was the Nâga of the lake at the source of the *Subhavastu*, and *Elâpatra* was the Nâga of the well-known springs at the present Hasan Abdâl, while *Muchalinda* was the Nâga of a tank on the south side of the Bodhi tree at Uruvilwa, the present Bauddha Gaya. At Ahichhatra also there was a Nâga Raja who dwelt in a tank outside the town, which is still called *Ahi-Sâgar* or the "serpent's tank," as well as Adi-Sâgar, or "king Adi's tank." The connection of the Nâgas with water is further shown by their supposed power of producing rain, which was possessed both by Elâpatra and by the Nâga of Sankisa,[1] and more especially by the great Nâga Raja of the Ocean, named *Sagara*, who had full power over the rains of heaven. In the Vedas also the foes of Indra, or watery clouds, which obscure the face of the sky, are named *Ahi* and *Vritra*, both of which names are also terms for a snake. The connection of the Nâgas with water would therefore seem to be certain, whatever may be the origin of their name.

In all the early Buddhist stories of the Nâgas they are invariably represented either as worshippers of Buddha, or as hostile at first until gradually overcome by his teaching. Nowhere is there any trace that the Nâgas were objects of worship to the Buddhists, although they were certainly held in respect by them for their supernatural powers. In later times their supposed power of being able to cause a fall of rain would seem to have led to a certain amount of reverence being shown to them, as in the case of the Nâga of Sankisa, of which Fa Hian relates as follows: "It is he who causes fertilizing and " seasonable showers of rain to fall within their country, and *preserves it* from plagues " and calamities, and so causes the priesthood to dwell in security. The priests, in " *gratitude for these favours*, have erected a dragon chapel, and within it placed a resting " place (seat) for his accommodation, and moreover they make special contributions in " the shape of religious offerings, to provide the dragon with food."[3] The later pilgrim Hwen Thsang makes no mention of the *Dragon Chapel*, although he notices the Nâga himself as the *staunch guardian* of the Buddhist buildings.[3] The Sankisa Nâga was therefore looked upon by both pilgrims as the guardian of the sacred edifices, and as such he must have been considered a true worshipper of Buddha.

The first Nâga whom Buddha encountered was the blind Muchilinda, who, during the seven days of Buddha's continued abstraction, coiled himself around the Sage's body, and formed a seven-hooded canopy over his head, which effectually screened him from the cold winds and rain, to which he had been exposed by the practices of his enemies.[4] The praises of Buddha were also sung by the great Nâga Raja Kâlika with joined hands, while the Nâgnis offered flowers, incense, and perfumes.[5] The powerful *Apalâla* also was subdued by the teaching of Buddha, and gave up his wicked practices against the people of the Subhavastu valley (Suwât).[6]

[1] See Julien's Hwen Thsang II., 152, for the former, and Beal's Fa Hian, p. 66, for the latter.
[2] Beal's Fa Hian, C. XVII., p. 67.
[3] Julien's Hwen Thsang II., 241. Il est le défenseur assidu des vestiges du Saint (Buddha).
[4] Lalita Vistara, translated by M. Foucaux from the Tibetan, and Hardy's Manual of Buddhism, p. 182.
[5] Ibid, pp. 269-271.
[6] Julien's Hwen Thsang II., 134.

These Nâga legends are all much the same, and invariably end in the submission and conversion of the serpent king. But there are some curious details in the account of the contest between the Nâga King Nandopananda and Buddha's left-hand disciple, the great Mugalâna, which are worth quoting as they throw some light not only on the relative position of the Nâgaloka but also on the nature of the superhuman powers possessed by the Buddhist priests as well as by the Nâgas.[1] "At the time that Buddha visited the " dewa-lóka Tawatinsa, the Nâga King Nandopananda said to his subjects: 'The sage " ' Gótama Buddha has passed over the world on his way to Tawatinsa; he will have to " ' return by the same way again, but I must try to prevent his journey.' For this " purpose he took his station upon Maha Meru. When one of the priests who " accompanied Buddha, Rathapâla, said that he had often passed in that direction before, " and had always seen Maha Meru, but now it was invisible, Buddha informed him that " it was the Nâga Nandopananda who had concealed the mountain. Upon hearing this, " Rathapâla said that he would go and drive him away; but the sage did not give him " permission. Then Mugalâna offered to go and subdue the Nâga, and having obtained " leave, he took the form of a snake, and approached Nandopananda. The Nâga " endeavoured to drive him to a distance by a poisonous blast, but Mugalâna sent forth " a counterblast; and there was a battle of blasts, but that of the priest was more " powerful than that of the Nâga. Then the Nâga sent forth a stream of fire, and " Mugalâna did the same, by which he greatly hurt the Nâga, whilst the other stream " did no injury whatever to himself. Nandopananda said in anger, 'Who art thou who " ' attackest me with a force sufficient to cleave Maha Meru?' And he answered, I am " Mugalâna. After this he went in at one ear of the Nâga and out of the other; then in " at one nostril, and out at the other; he also entered his mouth, and walked up and " down in his inside, from his head to his tail, and from his tail to his head. The Nâga " was still further enraged by this disturbance of his intestines, and resolved to squeeze " him to death when he emerged from his mouth, but Mugalâna escaped without his " perceiving it. Another poisonous blast was sent forth, but it did not ruffle a single " hair of the priest's body. After this Buddha imparted to Mugalâna the power to " overcome the Nâga, and taking the form of a garunda (or eagle), he began to pursue " him; but Nandopananda offered him worship, and requested his protection."

In the Bharhut sculptures there are several Nâga subjects, all very curious and interesting, of which the principal are the *Trikutaka Chakra*, and the conversion of *Elâpatra Nâga*. The first of these I take to be a representation of the Nâgaloka itself. It is carved on a circular boss on the inner face of one of the pillars of the S.W. quadrant.[2] In the upper left quarter there is a highly ornamented triangular recess, in which is seated a three-headed serpent apparently on a lotus throne. In the lower left quarter there are two lions, and the whole of the right half is filled with elephants in various attitudes of eating and drinking, and throwing the trunk backwards over the head. As the word *Nâga* means an "elephant" as well as a "serpent," I take the sculpture to be a comprehensive view of the *Nâgaloka*. The presence of the two lions is puzzling; but it seems quite impossible to doubt that the scene is intended to represent the Nâgaloka as it is labelled on the upper rim of the circle with the words *Tikotiko-chakamo*, that is the *Chakra* or division of the ancient Indian Universe called *Trikutika*. According to the

---

[1] Hardy's Manual of Buddhism, pp. 302 and 303. [2] See Plate XXVIII. fig. 1.

H 255.   E

Buddhist cosmogony, already quoted, the Nâgaloka was situated under the *Trikuta parvata* or three-peaked mountain, which supports Mount Meru.[1] Following the Vishnu Purâna the Trikuta mountain was situated on the south side of Mount Meru, and accordingly I find the figure of *Chakavâko Nâga Raja* placed as one of the guardians of the South Gate of the Bharhut Railing. But according to the Buddhist cosmogony it was the *West* quarter that was entrusted to the guardianship of Virupaksha and the Nâgas. The triangle seems to be rather an uncommon way of representing a three-peaked mountain, unless we consider that such a mountain would most probably have a triangular base, and as the serpents quarter was underneath Trikuta I take the triangle to represent the base, with the Nâgaloka exposed below.

The next subject is a figure of a Nâga King 4½ feet in height which occupies the inner face of the corner pillar of the South Gate.[2] The figure differs in no respect from that of one of the human kings, except that the head is canopied by a five-hooded snake. On the left side is the inscription *Chakavâko Nâga Râja,* or "the Nâga King *Chakravâka.*" The figure is standing in an attitude of calm repose, with the hands crossed upon the breast. Its dress is in all respects similar to that of other kings in these sculptures. Strings of pearls and bands of embroidered cloth appear to be bound round the hair, and in the ears there are the same large earrings which are worn by all the royal personages. There are also necklaces, armlets, and bracelets. A light scarf is thrown over both shoulders—with the ends hanging down nearly to the knees. The upper part of the body appears to be naked ; but from the hips downwards the Nâga Chief is clad in the Indian *dhoti,* the end of which reaches to the ground in a succession of very formal plaits. The attitude is easy, and the face has much better features than most of the other large figures.

The third subject is another Nâga Raja attended by two Nâgnis or females of the serpent race. This Raja is also in human form, and is clad in the same human dress as the other, with the same light scarf over the shoulders, and with the same five-hooded snake canopy over his head. On each side he is attended by a Nâgni, who is a woman only to the waist, or rather the loins, below which she ends in many a scaly fold of serpent tail. She is apparently quite naked, her only dress being the usual female ornaments of the time, namely huge earrings, necklaces, and a girdle of several strings. Her hand on the side towards the Râja holds a *chauri,* and the other rests on the upper serpent coil.

It is very generally believed that when the Nâgas appeared on earth among men they took the human form down to the waist only ; but in the Bharhut Sculptures the Nâga Râjas are certainly represented in complete human forms, and are only distinguishable from men by the canopy of snake-hoods over their heads. I observe, however, that the Nâgnis are invariably represented as only half human, and that they are always naked. Sometimes the lower half of the figure is not represented at all, but is concealed behind an altar or platform, from which it seems to rise. This was a very common device with the Buddhist sculptors, which is particularly noticeable in the semi-Greek bas-reliefs from the Yusafzai district, as well as in the Bharhut Sculptures.

The next subject is of even greater importance than any of the preceding, as it represents a Nâga Raja, attended by Nâgas and Nâgnis, paying his devotions before a Siris tree, or Acacia. The sculpture is a square panel on one of the corner pillars of

---

[1] Hardy's Manual of Buddhism, pp. 11 and 44.   [2] See Plate XV. fig. 3.

the South Gate.[1] On the left is the Siris tree rising from the midst of a square altar before which is kneeling a Nâja Raja in complete human form; with a five-hooded snake canopy over his head. Behind the Râja to the right are the half figures of a Nâga and two Nâgnis, also in human form, and with snake-hoods over their heads, but with their lower extremities concealed. In the midst of the piece is a five-hooded snake rising apparently from the ground, and above are two small trees, and two half-human Nâgnis. The purpose of the sculpture is told in a short label which is inscribed immediately behind the principal figure: *Erapato Naga Râja Bhagavato vandatê*, that is "*Erapâtra*, the "Nâja Raja, worships [the unseen figure of] Buddha." The great five-headed snake apparently rising from the ground I take to be the Nâga Raja on his first appearance from below in his true snake form amongst the trees and rocks. In the time of *Kasyapa* Buddha Erapâtra is said to have been condemned to lose the power of assuming his human form until the next Buddha should appear in the world. Accordingly when he heard of Sâkya Muni's attainment of Buddhahood he repaired at once to the new Buddha in his serpent form with five heads as shown in the sculpture, and on approaching the six Siris trees where Buddha was seated he instantly regained the power of appearing in human form.

The last Nâga sculpture in the Plate is taken from the coping of the Railing.[2] It represents a five-headed snake with expanded hood resting on a wide ring of coils, before an ascetic seated in front of his hermitage. The ascetic has his right hand raised and appears to be addressing the Nâga. In the absence of any inscription the precise identification of the scene is difficult; but there can be little doubt that it represents either Buddha himself or one of his chief followers expounding the Buddhist religion to some Nâga King.

It is very much to be regretted that any of these curious and interesting scenes should have been lost. There is no doubt that there was at least one more Nâga sculpture, as I found a fragment of a bas-relief belonging to a corner pillar with the title of *Nâga Raja* carved on one of the small pillars of a Buddhist railing. The name itself, which preceded the title, must have been a short one of not more than three letters, as it was inscribed on the same small pillar with the title which occupied rather more than one half of the space.

4.—APSARASES.

The Apsarases were divine nymphs who were said to have sprung from the churning of the Ocean. They were as famous for their skilful singing and dancing as for their beauty. The best and most detailed account of them is given by Goldstücker,[3] from which the following facts have been derived. "The Rig-Veda mentions the Apsaras "Urvasi, and in the Anukramini of the Rig two Apsarases are named as the authoresses "of a hymn." In the Vâjasaneyi Sanhita of the Yajur-Veda there occur five pairs of Apsarases, amongst whom there are the well-known names of Menakâ and Urvasi. "In the Adi-parvan of the Mahâbhârata, several of these divinities are enumerated under two heads." Amongst the first class I find the names *Misrakesi* and *Alambushâ*, both of whom are portrayed in the Bharhut Sculptures; to the second class belongs Urvasi.

"As regards their origin," Goldstücker continues, "the Rámáyana makes them arise
"from the Ocean, when it was churned by the gods obtaining the Amrita. Manu
"represents them as one of the creations of the seven Manus, themselves created by the
"seven Prajápatis, Marichi, Atri, &c. In the latter Mythology they are the daughters
"of Kasyapa by Muni." According to the Harivansa they were the daughters of
Kasyapa by Prádhá—and amongst their names I find Subhagá, Alambushá, and
Misrakesi.

As to their creation, Goldstücker thinks that, in the few hymns of the Rigveda in
which mention is made of them, "these divinities seem to have been personifications
"of the vapours which are attracted by the sun and form into mist or clouds." * * *
"At the subsequent period, when the Gandharva of the Rig-Veda, who personifies these,
"especially the Fire of the Sun, expanded into the Fire of lightning, the rays of the Moon
"and other attributes of the elementary life of heaven, as well as into pious acts referring
"to it, the Apsarases become divinities which represent phenomena, or objects both of
"a physical and ethical kind, closely associated with that life. Thus in the Yajur-Veda,
"Sunbeams are called the Apsarases associated with the Gandharva, who is the *Sun*;
"Plants are termed the Apsarases associated with the Gandharva *Fire*; constellations are
"the Apsarases of the Gandharva *Moon*; waters are the Apsarases of the Gandharvas
"Wind," &c.[1] "In the last Mythological epoch, when the Gandharvas have saved
"from their elementary nature merely so much as to be the Musicians in the paradise of
"Indra, the Apsarases appear, amongst other subordinate deities which share in the
"merry life of Indra's heaven, as the wives of the Gandharvas, but more especially as
"wives of a licentious sort; and they are promised too as a reward to heroes fallen in
"battle, when they are received into the paradise of Indra; and while in the Rig-Veda,
"they assist Soma to pour down his floods, they descend, in the epic literature, on earth
"merely to shake the virtue of penitent sages, and to deprive them of the power they
"would otherwise have acquired through unbroken austerities."

It is in this last character as tempters of ascetic sages that they make their first
appearance in Buddhist history. When Sákya Muni after six years asceticism was on the
eve of obtaining Buddhahood, Pápiyán despatched a troop of Apsarases to try their
powers in disturbing the sage's meditations.[2] They were of course unsuccessful, but the
description of their various wiles shows that the Apsarases had already become the
Húris of Indra's heaven. Some sang, some danced, and some extended their arms in
various positions. Some smiled to show their teeth, while some laughed, and suddenly,
as if ashamed, became grave; some half exposed their bosoms; some displayed their
figures through transparent garments; whilst others dropped their clothes and exposed
the belts of gold which girdled their loins.

Much of this description can be realized in one of the most remarkable scenes of
the Bharhut Sculptures.[3] The sculpture is broken towards the top, but fortunately very
little has been lost, and all the inscriptions that remain are perfect. On the right are
four female figures and a child dancing, all in different attitudes, and with their arms

1 Sanskrit Dictionary, pp. 222–223.
2 Lalita Vistara, translated by M. Foucaux from the Tibetan, p. 306.
3 See Plate XV., outer face of pillar. The sculpture formed one of the panels of the corner pillar of the
South Gate.

extended in various positions. In the middle and to the left are eight other female figures, all seated, one handling a pair of cymbals, and four playing the seven-stringed harp, while three more without instruments seem to be singing. In the left upper corner is a tree, but the greater part of it is missing, and any inscription which it may have borne is lost. Fortunately the labels attached to all the four dancing figures are still perfect, and from them we learn that the ladies are intended for Apsarases. The left upper figure is *Subhadá Achhará* or "the *Apsaras Subhadrá*;" that to the right is *Sudasana Achhará* or "the *Apsaras Sudarsana*;" the right lower figure is *Misakosi Achhara* or "the *Apsaras Misrakesi*;" and that to the left is *Alambusá Achhará* or "the *Apsaras Alambushá*." [1] The scene itself bears a label which is inscribed on two pillars of the Buddhist Railing beneath it. It appears to be *Sádikasam madam turam devánam*, which I am unable to translate; but it most probably refers to one of the common scenes enacted before the *Devas* (*devánam*) in Indra's heaven. But when I first saw this sculpture I had an impression that the tree in the left upper corner was the Bodhi tree, and that the scene represented the temptation of Sâkya Muni by the Apsarases.

In the Mahâbhârata Indra promises that heroes slain in battle will obtain Apsarases in the next world:—" Let no one ever lament a hero slain in battle. A hero slain is not " to be lamented, for he is exalted in heaven. * * Hear from me the worlds to which " he goes. Thousands of beautiful nymphs (Apsarases) run quickly up to the hero, who has been slain in combat, saying to him, Be my husband." [2] It is sufficiently clear from this quotation, as well as from the Bharhut Sculpture, that the Apsarases had quite lost every trace of their original conception as personified watery vapours or mists, or as sunbeams attendant on the Sun, and had been already degraded into the position of the courtezans of Indra's heaven, whose sole occupation was to sing and dance and minister to sensual enjoyment. This also was their condition at the time when the Râmâyana was composed, as Râwana tells Rambhá, that the Apsarases, of whom she was the most beautiful, were mere courtezans. [3]

B.—HUMAN BEINGS.

1. ROYAL PERSONAGES.

The only representations of human beings on a large scale in the Bharhut Sculptures are the busts of some Kings and Queens on the rail bosses, a full length figure of a Soldier on one of the pillars, one royal relic-bearer on an elephant, and two standard bearers, male and female, on horseback. But as all the Yakshas and Yakshinis, the Devas and the Nâga Rajas, are represented in human forms as well as in human costume, they may be taken as real representations of human beings. In the smaller sculptures the figures of men and women are of course numerous, and we have several representations of royal personages about whom there can be no doubt, as they are labelled with their names. Such are the figures of Râma, of Janaka Raja and Sivalá Devi, of Magha Deva (Buddha in a former birth as a Raja), of the Rajas Prasenajita and Ajâtasatru, and of the Royal

---

[1] See Plate LIV., Nos. 33, 34, 35, and 36, for these inscriptions, and Plate XV. fig. 1. The name of Misakosi is on the pillar to the right, that of Alambusha is just above the head of the child, and the other two names are at the top close beside the two figures.

[2] Muir's Sanskrit Texts, IV. 235, note 210.   [3] Muir's Sanskrit Texts, IV. 394.

Princess Mâyâ Devi. But there are others, which though not inscribed, are almost equally certain from their dress, as well as from their seated positions amongst standing attendants. Such beyond all doubt is the figure seated on a throne with numerous attendants in the *Nava Majhakiya Jâtaka*.[1] There are also several representations of *Ascetics*, but they are all of small size, so that only a few of the details can be made out distinctly, although the general appearance is striking and consistent.

2. RELIGIOUS PERSONS.

There are no priests with bare heads in these sculptures; and the only figures which appear to me to be almost certainly priests are those which are represented in the different scenes of the corner pillar of the South Gate, as seated, all of whom have the right shoulder bare.[2] But the whole of these figures have much the same tall and elaborate head-dresses as the kings and other laics, although I cannot trace any appearance of interwoven braids of hair. Supposing them to be priests, therefore, I infer that in the time of Asoka the priests shaved their heads, but kept them covered. They also wear the common *dhoti*.

Some flying figures, which I thought at first might be Arhats, wear collars, and necklaces, and girdles, and may, therefore, be intended for Devas, or Gandharvas, or other superhuman beings. In a few instances of ascetics who wear beards and head-dresses somewhat in the shape of Pârsi hats, I observe striped kilts, like the regular Buddhist *Sanghâti*, which was made of numerous strips of cloth sewn together.[3] There would also appear to have been female ascetics who wore the same head-dresses as the men.[4] All these figures are probably intended for Brahmanical ascetics (*Parivrájikas*) who are described by the Buddhists as letting their nails, hair, and beards grow, and wearing clothes of leaves and bark.[5] They are generally accompanied by vessels of fire, which show that they were also fire-worshippers.

According to all Buddhist tradition Sâkya himself set the example of wearing short locks by cutting off his own hair with his sword on his assumption of an ascetic life. In imitation of their teacher every novice on taking the religious vows appeared before the elders with his hair and beard of only seven days growth.[6]

I notice that the seated figures which have their right shoulders bare have the top knot or upper portion of the head-dress exactly over the top of the head. Now Prince Siddhârtha before he became an ascetic is described as having his hair plaited and braided, and gathered into a knot on the *right* side. This peculiarity is seen in all the Sânchi sculptures in the head-dresses of the kings and great men; and strange to say it is still preserved by the Buddhist laity in Burma. I infer, therefore, that the 'men who wear the top knot over the very top of the head may be priests and not laics. In the ladder scene of the same pillar there are also some standing figures which have the right shoulder bare; but as they all wear necklaces, and have the top knot on the right side,

---

[1] See Plate XXV. fig. 3. The figure, according to my identification of the story, is that of King Nanda.
[2] See Plate XV. in the right upper scene and the two middle scenes.
[3] See Plate XXV. fig. 6, and Plate XXVII. figs. 1 and 2.
[4] See Plate XXIV. fig. 7.
[5] Foucaux's translation of the Lalita Vistara from Tibetan, p. 200.
[6] Burnouf, Introduction à l'Histoire du Buddhisme Indien, p. 179.

they should be laymen. Perhaps they are lay brothers, or *Bhddantas*, who did not assume the priestly garb, but who might easily bare the right shoulder at religious festivals.

3. ROYAL AND LAY COSTUME.

Of the lay costume I can speak with more certainty, as there are several good examples of it, both male and female. The main portion of the male dress is the *dhoti*, or sheet passed round the waist and then gathered in front, and the gathers passed between the legs, and tucked in behind. This simple arrangement forms a very efficient protection to the loins, and according to the breadth of the sheet it covers the mid thigh, or the knees, or reaches down to the ankles. In the Bharhut Sculptures the *dhoti* uniformly reaches below the knee, and sometimes down to the mid leg. As there is no appearance of any ornamentation, either of flowers or stripes, it is most probable that then, as now, the *dhoti* was a plain sheet of cotton cloth. That it was of cotton we learn from the classical writers who drew their information from the companions of Alexander. Thus Arrian says, " The Indians wear cotton garments, the substance whereof they are made " growing upon trees. . . . They wear shirts of the same, which reach down to the " middle of their legs, and veils which cover their head, and a great part of their " shoulders."[1] Here the word rendered *shirt* by the translator is clearly intended for the well-known Indian *dhoti*, and the *veil* must be the equally well-known *Chaddar*, or sheet of cotton cloth, which the Hindus wrap round their bodies, and also round their heads when they have no separate head-dress. Similarly Q. Curtius states that " the land is prolific of cotton, of which most of their garments are made," and he afterwards adds that " they clothe their bodies down to the feet in cotton cloth (*carbaso*)."[2] To these extracts I may add the testimony of Strabo, who states that " the Indians wear white garments, white linen, and muslin."[3] But though the cotton dress was white, it was not always plain, as Strabo mentions in another place that " they wear dresses worked with gold and precious stones, and *flowered* (or variegated) robes." These flowered robes must have been the figured muslins for which India has always been famous.

Above the waist the body is usually represented as quite naked, excepting only a light scarf or sheet, which is generally thrown over the shoulders, with the ends hanging down outside the thighs. In some cases it appears to be passed round the body, and the end thrown over the left shoulder.[4]

The head-dress is by far the most remarkable part of the costume, as it is both lofty and richly ornamented. I have already quoted the description of Prince Siddhârtha's hair as braided and plaited, and gathered into a knot on the right side of the head. This description seems to apply almost exactly to the head-dresses in the Bharhut sculptures. But judging from some differences of detail in various parts, and remembering how the Burmese laymen still wear their hair interwoven with bands and rolls of muslin, I think that of the two terms *braided* and *plaited*, one must refer to the hair only, and the other to some bands of cloth intertwisted with the hair. The most complete specimen of the male head-dresses is that of the royal busts on two of the bosses of the rails.[5] The head

---

[1] Indica, XVI.; Rooke's translation.
[2] Vit. Alexand., VIII. 9.
[3] Geograph, XV. 1, 71.

[4] See the statue of the Nâga Raja in Plate XXI, right hand.
[5] See Plate XXIV. figs. 1 and 2.

is about the size of life, and the details are all well preserved. In this sculpture, and in the companion medallion of a queen, I observe the bow of a diadem or ribbon, which I take to be a sure sign of royalty. A head-dress of a similar kind is worn by all the Nâga Rajas,[1] and in the case of the larger figure of the Nâga king Chakavâka I think that I can distinguish the plaited hair from the bands of interwreathed cloth. The two bands which cross exactly above the middle of the forehead appear to be cloth, while all the rest is hair, excepting perhaps a portion of the great knot on the top. Similar cross bands or rolls of cloth may be seen in the head-dresses of the soldiers and standard bearer in Plate XXXII. figs 2, 3, 4, and 5. This interwreathing of muslin with the hair is also described by Q. Curtius, who says that "they wind rolls of muslin round their heads."[2] The *plaiting* of hair, which I have described above from the Lalita Vistara, was likewise noticed by the Greeks, as Strabo records that "all of them plait their hair and bind it with a fillet."[3] These quotations seem to describe very accurately the peculiar style of head-dresses worn by all men of rank in the Bharhut Sculptures; and as the chief classical authority for such details was Megasthenes, who resided for many years at Palibothra, their close agreement with the sculptured remains of the same age offers a strong testimony to his general veracity. The only exception that I have observed to the use of this rich head-dress is in that of *Kupiro Yakho*, or *Kuvera* the *King* of the Yakshas, who wears an embroidered scarf like that of the females as a head covering.

The ornaments worn by the men will be described along with the female ornaments, as several of them are exactly the same.

4. MILITARY COSTUME.

Amongst the Bharhut Sculptures there are no battle scenes or sieges as in the later sculptures of Sânchi. There is, however, a single figure of a soldier, nearly of life size, and in such fine preservation, that all the details of his costume can be distinguished with ease.[4] His head is bare, and the short curly hair is bound with a broad band or ribbon, which is fastened at the back of the head in a bow, with its long ends streaming in the wind. His dress consists of a tunic with long sleeves, and reaching nearly to the mid-thigh. It is tied in two places by cords; at the throat by a cord with two tassels, and across the stomach by a double-looped bow. The loins and thighs are covered with a *dhoti* which reaches below the knees, with the ends hanging down to the ground in front in a series of extremely stiff and formal folds. On the feet are boots, which reach high up the legs, and are either fastened or finished by a cord with two tassels, like those on the neck of the tunic. In his left hand the soldier carries a flower, and in his right a monstrously broad straight sword, sheathed in a scabbard, which is suspended from the left shoulder by a long flat belt. The extreme breadth of the sword may be judged by comparing it with the thickness of the man's arm, which it exceeds, while its length may be about $2\frac{1}{2}$ feet, or perhaps somewhat more. The belt of the sword is straight, and without a guard. The face of the scabbard is ornamented with the favourite Buddhist *Omega* Symbol of *Tri-ratna*, or the triple gem. The sword belt, after being passed through a ring attached to the side of the scabbard, appears to be twice crossed over the

---

[1] See Plate XIV., inner face of pillar, and Plate XVIII., upper bas-relief.
[2] Vit. Alexand., VIII. 9, "Capita linteis vinciunt."   [3] Geograph, XV. 1, 71.
[4] See Plate XXXII. fig. 1.

scabbard downwards, and then fastened to a ring at the tip, below which the broad ends hang down like the ends of a scarf.

In person the figure of the soldier is rather stouter and broader than a native of India, while a very thick neck, with flat features and short curly hair, seem to indicate a negro. But as the same flat features are found even amongst the female figures, I conclude that they have resulted chiefly from the sculptors' practice of carving down from a perfectly flat surface in a stone of adamantine hardness.

The soldier's tunic, which I have just described, would appear from the account of Strabo to have been a regular kind of uniform furnished by the king. As Strabo's account is taken direct from Megasthenes, who actually resided at Pâtaliputra, the Court of Asoka's grandfather, the testimony is unimpeachable. According to him " the fifth " class consists of fighting men, who pass the time not employed in the field in idleness " and drinking, and are maintained at the charge of the king. They are ready whenever " they are wanted to march on an expedition, for *they bring nothing of their own with them* " *except their bodies*."[1] In another place he says " there is also a royal magazine of arms, " for the *soldier returns his arms* to the armoury."[2] As to their arms we have the description of Arrian, which was taken either from Megasthenes or from Nearchus. " All wear swords of a *vast breadth*, though scarce exceeding three cubits in length. " These, when they engage in close fight . . . they grasp with both their hands, " that their blow may be the stronger."[3]

From these extracts we learn the curious fact that the Maurya kings maintained a regular standing army, as they seem to have provided their soldiers with arms and uniform, as well as pay.

5. FEMALE DRESS AND ORNAMENTS.

The best specimens of the women's costume are exhibited in the life-size busts of two queens on the bosses of the rails, and in the nearly life-size figures of Yakshinis and Devatâs on no less than seven of the pillars.[4] In six of these examples the upper part of the body appears to be quite naked, but in the seventh, that of the Yakshini Chandâ, there are very perceptible marks of the folds or creases of a light muslin wrapper under the right breast. I think it probable, therefore, that an upper garment of a light material is intended to be shown by the sculptor, and that for the sake of displaying the different necklaces, and collars, and girdles, he has purposely omitted the folds and traces of the muslin wrapper. In the smaller figure of Mâya Devi there is not the slightest trace of any upper garment; but as she is sleeping amongst her women attendants, the *Chaddar* may have been laid aside. It is quite certain, however, that the women did wear an upper wrapper, as some of the courtesan Apsarases, when they wished to tempt Sâkya Sinha, are said to have half uncovered their bosoms, whilst others appeared naked in transparent garments.[5]

About the lower garment there can be no mistake, as every female, high and low, is represented as wearing a *dhoti*, exactly the same as that of the men. At the present

---

[1] Strabo. Geog., XV. 1, 47.   [2] Strabo. Geog., XV. 1, 52.   [3] Arrian Indica, XVI.

[4] See Plate XXIV. figs. 5 and 6, for the two Queens; and Plates XXII. and XXIII. for the Yakshini Chandâ, and the Devatâs Chulakoka and Sirimâ.

[5] Lalita Vistara, translated from the Tibetan by Foucaux, p. 307.

day the sheet of cloth, which forms the common *Sári* of Hindu women, is simply an unsewn petticoat reaching from the waist to the ancles. In the Bharhut Sculptures it reaches very little below the knees, and the outer edge is gathered together in a continuous succession of equal sized stiff and formal folds. In Central India, including Bharhut, as well as in the Maharatha country, the *Sári* is still worn as a *dhoti* by most of the women, although the gathered ends are often let down, when the garment at once becomes the Hindu petticoat.

The heads of the women are always covered by elaborately worked veils or *Chaddars*, of which two very fine specimens are given in the two accompanying plates of the Yakshini *Chandá*, and the Devatá *Chulakoka*.[1] In the latter example the covering seems to be a simple veil, which falls backwards over the shoulders down to the waist. But in the former the thin flowered cloth is passed twice over the head crosswise, and the parallel creases seen under the right breast are probably intended to show that the *chaddar* was wrapped round the body. These veils appear to have been very richly and elaborately ornamented; and judging from the pattern of the border of Chandás veil I believe the work is intended to represent gold embroidery. Strabo mentions "garments embroidered and interwoven with gold" as being carried in processions.[2] These were probably intended for presents, just as brocades and shawls are now carried in separate trays at Darbárs for the same purpose.

The hair was parted in the middle, and always appears just under the front edge of the veil. In the bust of the Queen either the hair or the head-dress comes to a point at the top of the head. But in all the others the embroidered scarf takes the shape of the head, and the mass of the hair is gathered together at the back, and plaited into one or two long rolls which hang down as low as the waist, or twisted and tied into a large knot which half covers the back. The former arrangement is well shown in the figure of Chandá Yakshini and in the fine broken bust of another figure, the name of which is lost, and also in the attendants on Máyá Devi.[3]

ORNAMENTS.

The richness and profusion of the ornaments worn by most of the figures in the Bharhut Sculptures, both male and female, are very remarkable.

This taste of the ancient Indians was duly noticed by the Greeks, as Strabo remarks, "in contrast to their parsimony in other things, *they indulge* in ornament."[4] The two sexes have in common earrings and necklaces, as well as armlets and bracelets, and embroidered belts. The women alone use forehead ornaments, long collars, garlands, zones or girdles, and anklets. There are no noserings; and I may note here that I have not observed the use of this hideous disfigurement in any ancient sculptures. I will now describe each of these varieties of ornament in the order in which I have named them, taking due note of any special differences between the male and female specimens.

Forehead Ornaments.—These appear to be worn by every female just below the parting of the hair on the top of the forehead. There are several varieties of them; but the commonest form is that of a star, upwards of an inch in diameter. Eight different

---

[1] See Plates XXII. and XXIII.   [3] See Plates XXIII., LII., and XXVII. fig. 2.
[2] Geograph., XV. 1, 69.   [4] Geograph., XV. 1, 54.

kinds are shown in the accompanying plate.[1] Similar ornaments are worn at the present day. They are generally thin plates of gold or silver stamped into various patterns, amongst which the star shape is common, and the ornament is then called simply *Sitâra*, or the "star," but the common name is *bena*; and when the pieces are very small they are called simply *bindi*, or "spots." The old Sanskrit names are *lalâtika*, or "forehead piece," and *patrpâsyâ*, or "the fastened leaf," the ornaments being sometimes formed of a piece of gold-leaf stuck on the forehead.[2] I have not noticed any reference to these forehead ornaments in the Buddhist books.

Earrings.—These ornaments would seem to have been almost universally worn, both by men and women. The only exception which I have noticed is that of the soldier, whose ears are not even bored. The general name for an earring is *Karnika*, from *Karna*, an "ear," but the ornament takes almost as great a variety of names as it has shapes. If it is simply a ring or circle it is called *Kundal*; if a circular plate fixed outside the lobe it is called *dehri*; but if worked like a flower it becomes *karn-phul*, or the "ear flower." The pendant attached to these has also different names according to its shape as *Jhumka*, or the "bell pendant." In the accompanying Plate, fig. 12, is a *dehri*, and fig. 10 is a *Jhumka*. In this case it is not only bell-shaped itself, but it has two rows of small bells attached below.[3] Fig. 11 is a form peculiar to the Buddhists. It is the symbol of the famous *Tri-ratna*, or "triple gem," of the Buddhist Triad, *Buddha*, *Dharmma*, and *Sangha*, and was therefore a very favourite ornament. In the Bharhut Sculptures it is of very frequent use either as an earring or part of a necklace. It is also placed on the soldiers' scabbard, and on the top of a standard, and I have found it amongst the small collection of Buddhist terra-cottas which I discovered at Kosâmbi. In these it forms the woman's earring, and the central ornament of a king's necklace. These terra-cottas seem to belong to the period of Indo Scythian rule in Upper India, about the beginning of the Christian era.

But the most remarkable earrings are shown in figs. 13 and 14 of full size.[4] These are worn by males as well as females, and they are by far the most common kind of earrings. They are worn by the Yakshas and Yakshinis, by the Devatâs, and by the Nâga Rajas and Nâgnis, as well as by most of the human figures. I examined all the large examples very closely, and I am satisfied that the middle portion was formed of a spiral tube, and that the whole ornament, though very large, was most probably not very heavy. The flanged end was always worn outwards, and the square flowered end inwards touching the cheek. They were no doubt placed in position by pushing outwards the flanged end through the long slit in the lobe of the ear, and then two complete turns of the spiral would place the ornament in the position shown in figs. 13 and 14, with the square end touching the cheek.

In all these representations I take the small circles and dots to represent precious stones, with which wealthy Indians have always been fond of enriching their golden ornaments. Strabo, indeed, says that their dresses were worked with gold and precious

---

[1] See Plate XLIX. figs. 1 to 9.

[2] Colebrooke's *Amara Kosha*, in voce.

[3] See Plate XLIX. fig. 10. This curious form is found hanging from a tree in the representation of the *Kukkura Jâtaka*, or "Cock" birth.

[4] See Plate XLIX. for all the different kinds of earrings.

stones, and that their vessels of gold, large basins and goblets, &c. were set with " emeralds, beryls, and Indian carbuncles."[1]

Necklaces are worn by all the figures, both male and female, who are represented in the Bharhut Sculptures, with the single exception of the soldier. They are of two kinds, short and long; which for the sake of distinction I will call necklaces and collars. The former were named *Kantha-búshá*, or " throat ornaments," or simply *Kanthí* and *Kantha*, which names they still retain, although these are now confined to the short necklaces worn by men. The longer necklaces or collars were named *Lambanam* or " long," and also *lalántika* or " *dalliers*," because they dallied between the breasts of the women. For the same reason they are also known as *Mohanmálá*, or the " bewitching garland;" but the common name for all these long collars is *hár*. In the Bharhut Sculptures nearly all the short necklaces which go round the throat are broad and flat, of the kind now called *pátiyá*, or " broad." These are generally made of plain gold; but they may be also inlaid with precious stones. Other necklaces are named after the number of strings of which they are composed as *pachlari*, and *satlari*, or the " five-strings " and " seven-strings;" and amongst the Bharhut Sculptures may be seen many examples of all kinds from three to seven strings.

In the accompanying Plate of Necklaces,[2] I have given examples of all the richer kinds taken either from the larger figures or from the separate representations of the ornaments themselves on the copings of the Railing. There is a broken statue of a female which offers specimens of both the long and the short necklaces.[3] The short one is a *cháu-lari*, or " four-string " necklace, each string of which we may suppose to have been formed of pearls increasing in size towards the central gem, which was probably an emerald. A specimen of a three-string necklace, *tilari*, is given in fig. 1 of Plate L., in which the central stones are shown with several faces instead of being flat. Fig. 7 is another specimen of the short necklace taken from the figure of Chandá Yakshini. This is a *Sat-lari* or " seven-string " necklace, with flat stones at various intervals, and some new devices in the upper row consisting of two leaves, two elephant-goads, and a symbol; all of which would have been made of gold. Fig. 7 is also a short necklace, which would appear to be formed of a succession of semi-circular plates overlapping from the centre towards each end. It would have been made of gold alone, or with an inlaid flower of precious stones on each separate plate.

The remaining specimens in the Plate, with one exception, are all long necklaces or *lalántikas*. Nos. 5 and 6 are taken from the separate representations of the copings. No. 8 is part of the long collar of a large female figure on a pillar at Batanmára, which was carried away from Bharhut.[4] Its chief ornament is the *ankus*, or elephant-goad. No. 3 is part of the long necklace of the statue of *Sirimá Devatá*. The main feature in all these specimens of the long necklace is the very effective use of the favourite symbol of the *Tri-ratna*, or " Triple Gem," of Buddha, Dharmma, and Sangha, as the principal ornament. In these collars the symbol is never used alone, but always in pairs. Mr. Beal calls this " the sacred symbol of the *Mani*, or ' three-fold gem,' indicating the all supreme Buddha." Its adoption as an ornament by the Buddhists is therefore quite analogous with the use of the cross as an ornament by Christians.

----

[1] Geograph., XV. 1–54, and 69.	[3] See Plate LII. fig. 1.
[2] See Plate L.	[4] See Plate XXI., middle figure.

Armlets, or bracelets on the upper arm, are worn by all, both males and females.[1] Figs. 15 and 16 are taken from the large statues of the two goddesses named *Chulakoka* and *Sirimâ*, and No. 18 from the large statues of the *Yaksha Kupiro*, the *Nâga Raja Chakavâko* and an unnamed figure. No. 27 belongs to another unnamed female figure. All these specimens would appear to have been bands of gold set with precious stones. Armlets are now called *bâju*, and are usually made of gold or silver beads. When set with precious stones they are named *navaratna*, or the " nine gems," and when formed as a circle they are called *ananta*, or the " endless," *i.e.*, the circular.

Bracelets are worn by all the figures, both male and female, whether human, as King Magha Deva and his attendants and the Queen Mâyâ Devi and her attendants, or semi-devine as the Yakshas, Devatâs, Nâgas, and Apsarases. The most common form appears to be a succession of strings and beads either square or round. Thus the Yaksha *King Kupiro* has six rings of square beads, and the Nâga Raja Chakavâko has five rings of the same. The goddess Chulakoka has eight rings and Sirimâ Devatâ no less than 13, the former being apparently formed of round beads, while the latter looks like a spiral coil of 13 twists. But by far the most elaborate specimens are the bracelets of Chandâ Yakshini, of which an enlarged sketch is given in the accompanying Plate.[2] These undoubtedly consist of spirals of 10 coils each, with a jewelled plate on the outside of the wrist, and on the inside a curious arrangement of four perpendicular wires attached to a loop, apparently for the purpose of keeping the spiral closed.

As well as I can judge from the sculptured representations, these bracelets would have been made of gold. All bracelets are known by the general name of *Kangkan* or *Kangan*; but they have also received different names according to the different material of which they are made; or if they form successive rings, according to the position which they hold on the wrist.

Girdles or *Zones*.—The most remarkable of all the ornaments of ancient India are the elaborate girdles or zones which were worn by the women. There is no female without a belt of several strings of beads, in addition to a broad embroidered belt, which is also worn by the men. This girdle is known by several names, and is frequently alluded to in the Buddhist writings. In the Amara Kosha these names are *Mekhalâ*, *Kânchi*, *Saptaki*, *Rasanâ*, and *Sârasanâ*; on which Colebrooke remarks that though given as synonymous these terms " signify belts of various kinds, differing in the number of " rows or strings." Other names are *Sakkari*, *Kakshâ*, *Kati-Sutra*, *Katitra*, &c. Of these names the most common is *Mekhalâ*, which not only includes a woman's *girdle* and a soldier's belt, but is also applied to the *janeo*, or sacrificial string, worn by these upper classes. *Kati* means the hips or loins, so *Kati-Sutra* means the " loin cords," or as we should say in English the waist-belt. *Saptaki* means a girdle of " seven strings." Of *Rasanâ* and *Sârasana* I do not know the meaning; but Wilson says that the latter is the name of a woman's zone of 25 strings, as well as of a military belt. *Rasanâ* is the term used by Kâlidâsa,[3] for the tinkling girdle of the *Vesyas* or dancing girls. Colonel Ouvry translates the sloka very literally. " *The Vesyas*, whose girdles tinkle as they " dance, &c."

---

[1] See all the Plates of large figures, and Plate XLIX. figs. 15, 16, 17, and 18.
[2] See Plate LI. fig. 1. Other specimens of bracelets may be seen on the figures specified by name.
[3] *Megha-duta*, or " the Cloud Messenger," sloka 37.

The other terms *Kánchi* and *Kakshá*, which mean respectively the plant and seed of the Abrus precatorius, or *Gunja*, seem to me to point to a time when the girdle was made of strings of its brilliant red seed, *Kakshá*, more generally known as *rati* or *raktika*, or the "red seed." In the course of time these would have been gradually superseded by gold and silver beads amongst the richer classes. These again would naturally have been expanded into larger beads of various shapes, square, round, or oval, according to the fancy of the wearer. After these would have followed chains of gold and silver, to which bells were added by the dancing girls. In this way I suppose that the Indian lady's girdle gradually assumed the elaborate and costly form of five, six, and seven strings of gold beads, such as we see worn by all the females in the Bharhut Sculptures.

In the Lalita Vistara the Apsarases, who are described as having exhausted all their blandishments in their temptation of Sákya Sinha, are said to have displayed the "golden zones" which girded their figures, some by their transparent scarves, and others by suddenly dropping their garments.[1] Others are said to have *shaken* their golden girdles, from which I have no doubt tiny bells were suspended. All these devices are practised by dancing girls of the present day, whose girdles, however, are generally limited to two or three silver chains. A brief description of a similar scene is given in the Pali *Attakatha*, or Commentaries on the *Maháwanso*, where the most beautiful dancing girls display their charms with the intent of diverting Prince Siddhártha from becoming an ascetic.[2]

Of the female zone very fine specimens will be found in the accompanying plates on the figures of Chandá Yakshini and Chulakoka Devata.[3] But the most elaborate specimen is that of the goddess Sirimá, of which I have given a sketch on a large scale for the clearer understanding of this costly ornament.[4] The broad flat belt, marked A, I take to be an embroidered girdle of cloth of gold, for the manufacture of which the Indians have always been conspicuous. The two small bead-girdles of two strings each, marked B and C, are what I take to be the early imitations of the strings of the red *rati* seeds in gold or hard stones, such as agate, jasper, carnelian, lapis-lazuli, jade, and others. The remaining strings, which I have numbered consecutively, form a rich example of the *Saptaki* or *Kánchi* of "seven strings." Of these the two outside strings consist of square beads, next which comes a string of round beads, and then another of square beads on each side, the middle line being either a chain or a string of oval beads. Many of the girdles were provided with small bunches of bells, which sounded as the wearer moved. A specimen of this musical ornament is given in Plate LI., fig. 3, one half of the original size.

In the extracts which I have given from the Lalita Vistara these girdles are spoken of simply as "golden zones," but in the *Attakathá* on the *Maháwanso* the *Mekhalá* is described as being "set with gems in newly burnished gold and silver."[5] It is most probable, therefore, that the flowers figured on the beads of Sirimá Devatá's *Mekhalá* are intended to represent inlaid stones. With these specimens before us, we can more readily believe Strabo's account of the Indian indulgence in ornament.[6]

---

[1] Lalita Vistara, translated by M. Foucaux, from Tibetan, p. 307.
[2] Turnour, in Bengal Asiatic Society's Journal, VII. 806.   [3] See Plates XXII. and XXIII.
[4] See Plate LI. fig. 2.   [5] Turnour, in Bengal Asiatic Society's Journal, VIII. 806.
[6] Geograph., XV. 1, 54.

The belt of the men, as represented on the figures of the Yaksha Kupiro and the Nâga Raja Ohakavâko, might perhaps be more appropriately called a sash, as after encircling the waist it is tied in a long bow just below the navel, with the two ends hanging down to the knees. I infer from the fact of tying, that the male belt must necessarily have been of cloth, although it was no doubt richly embroidered with gold.

The soldier's sword-belt is quite plain, and was most probably made of leather.

Anklets are worn by all the female figures, but there is not much variety in them. In the accompanying Plate, I have given three selected specimens from different figures.[1] All of them appear to be formed either of spiral coils or of consecutive circles of gold, piled one over the other, the upper and lower rings being more or less ornamented. Fig. 5 has apparently two rows of chains. Fig. 4 gives a specimen of a separate anklet, with a row of bells, such as was worn by Apsarases and dancing girls. In the temptation of Prince Siddhârtha some of the Apsarases are said to have "tinkled the bells on their feet."[2] Similar anklets are worn by dancing girls even in the present day. The plain circular ring is now called *Karâ*, the thick chain *Sânkla*, and the ornamented circle with a row of small bells is named *ghûngru*.

Thumb-rings and *Finger-rings* are also worn by all the women, but I have not noticed any particular forms. They are generally plain rings crowded together on the *middle joints* of the fingers.

6. TATTOOING.

The practice of ornamenting the face and body with tattoo marks is common to all the aboriginal races of India. Amongst the Kols, the Saurs, the Uraons, and the Gonds, it is universal, no female being without some marks, while most of the women are rather profusely decorated. Now, it is a curious fact that not only are all the females in the Bharhut Sculptures more or less ornamented with tattoo marks, but they are all dressed in the same short *dhoti-petticoat* of the present inhabitants, which reaches down to the knees. I conclude, therefore, that as the mass of the modern population about Bharhut is of Kol descent, it is most probable that the great bulk of the people in this part of the country must have been Kols in the time of Asoka.

The practice of tattooing is called *godna*, and the art is entirely confined to women, who make periodical visits to all the villages in their neighbourhood. From two of these women I obtained the modern tattoo marks given in Plate LII., with the name and price of each separate pattern. The smaller ones are confined to the fingers, cheeks, arms, and breasts. The larger ones are confined to the body and the thighs. I was disappointed at the small number of these modern marks which appear amongst the ancient sculptures. I had hoped to have found many of the old marks still surviving, but most of them would seem to have fallen into disuse.

Amongst the ancient tattoo marks I notice the sun and moon on the cheek-bones of the Yakshini Chandâ, who has also several small flowers on her cheeks and chin. Two other statues, and one of the female busts, have their decorations limited to a single mark of the *ankus* or elephant-goad on one of the cheeks. The statue of Sirima Devata also has only a single star or flower on her left cheek-bone. But others are much more

---

[1] See Plate LI. figs. 4, 5, and 6.
[2] Foucaux, Lalita Vistara, French translation from Tibetan, p. 307.

profusely ornamented, as shown in the accompanying Plate.[1] Here No. 1 figure will be seen to have a small bird or trisul above each breast, and another on the upper arm, also an *ankus* with two straight lines and a small flower on each cheek-*bone*, besides two elaborate cheek ornaments. A similar style is shown in No. 2, which is just one half of the original size. Here the cheek-bones are decorated with the sun and moon, while each cheek is literally covered with a dense mass of small ornaments which might be called a female cheek piece. Similar cheek ornaments may be observed in numberless examples, as for instance :

The female standing beside Sákya Muni's Bodhi Tree - - - XIII. 1.
The female standing with bird in hand - - - - XIV. 2.
The two Nágas before the sacred tree - - - - XIV. 3.
The Apsarases dancing and playing - - - - XV. I.
The seated female holding a flower - - - - XV. 2.
The female attendants of Ajátasatru - - - - XVI. 3.

In modern practice, which is most probably much the same as that of Asoka's days, the punctures are made with a needle, guarded by a coil of thread to within one-eighth of an inch of its point. Sometimes two needles are fastened together when parallel lines are required. The operation is always a painful one and brings on more or less fever, so that only a limited amount of tattooing can be performed at one time. The colouring matter is either lamp black or indigo. The following list gives the names of each of the modern figures with the part of the person on which it is usually punctured. The prices vary from one paisa to one anna each, or from about one farthing to three-halfpence :—

No.					
1. The Clove - - - - -					on the fingers.
„ 2. The Scorpion - - - -					hand.
„ 3. The Sieve - - - - -					arm.
„ 4. The Shell - - - - -					leg.
„ 5. The Stool - - - - -					lower arm.
„ 6. The Bird - - - - -					stomach.
„ 7. The Parrot - - - - -					legs.
„ 8. The Duck - - - - -					ditto.
„ 9. Pair of Geese - - - -					upper arm.
„ 10. Peacocks - - - - -					side of leg.
„ 11. Elephants - - - - -					upper arms.
„ 12. City of Jhansi - - - -					back of hand.
„ 13. Ditto - - - - -					ditto.
„ 14. City of Urcha - - - -					hand.
„ 15. Garden - - - - -					upper arm or legs.
„ 16. Ditto - - - - -					ditto.
„ 17. Regiment (or Rám and Lakshman) - -					ditto.
„ 18. Sita's Kitchen - - - -					upper arms.

There are of course many little varieties in the details of these rude figures, as may be seen in Nos. 1 and 2, Nos. 12 and 13, and Nos. 15 and 16, where I have given the variant examples of my two informants. My figures are about one half the size of the original sketches made for me by the two practitioners themselves.

---

[1] Plate LII. fig. 1.

C.—ANIMALS.

The animals represented in the Bharhut Sculptures are of two classes, the Natural and the Fabulous. The latter, however, are limited to three varieties, an Elephant with a fish-tail, a Crocodile with a fish-tail, and a winged Horse; while the former comprises no less than 14 Quadrupeds, 6 Birds, 1 Snake, 1 Fish, 1 Insect, 1 Crocodile, 2 Tortoises, 1 Lizard, and 1 Frog. The quadrupeds include the Lion, Elephant, Horse, Rhinoceros, Wild Boar, Bull, Deer, Wolf, Monkey, Cat, Dog, Sheep, Hare, and Squirrel. The birds comprise the Cock, Parrot, Peacock, Goose, Wild Duck, and the Quail. The Snakes and Fishes appear to be of only one kind each; and the solitary Insect is beyond all doubt a Flesh-fly.

The *Lion* is represented in several of the small scenes on the coping of the Rail, where he is at once distinguishable by his mane. A large figure of a Lion was placed as the first stone of the coping at each entrance facing the in-going visitor. Portions of three of these Lions have been found, but the head is unfortunately missing in two of the examples. The remains of these figures are shown in the accompanying Plate of Copings.[1] The single head is boldly designed, but the mane is both stiff and formal. The mouth shows much spirit. The feet are perfect and correctly delineated. The general pose of the body shows considerable freedom of design as well as more truthfulness of execution than is generally found in Indian sculpture. The tail is rather too long and its tuft is very much exaggerated.

The *Elephant* seems to have been a favourite subject with the ancient Indian artists, and in my judgment a very successful one. No doubt the small scale on which they are sculptured has helped to diminish any faults of execution; but the outlines of the bulky figures are generally very correctly rendered, and the action in many cases is natural and spirited. The animal is represented in almost every possible position, as standing, walking, running, sitting down, eating, drinking, throwing water over his back, and, lastly, kneeling down in reverence before the holy Bodhi Tree. He is also represented in full front view, half front, and full side.

The sitting Elephant is found on the beginning of all the copings with a figured housing (*Jhúl*) on his back, and an undulating line issuing from his mouth, which encloses a separate scene within each of its progressive undulations.[2] These figures are all executed with much spirit and considerable accuracy. Another sitting Elephant is shown in the well-known scene of Máyá Devi's dream,[3] but the hindlegs of this figure are weakly drawn, and it is altogether inferior to most of the other elephants of these sculptures.

On the first pillar of the Eastern Gate there is a large Elephant full face who is carrying a royal rider in charge of a relic-casket.[4] The Elephant's head is encircled by a string of pearls with pendent symbols, and the rider carries the *ankus*, or elephant-goad, which he rests on the forehead of the animal just as we see the Mahauts do at the present day.

In the bas-relief of the *Nága loka* one half of the medallion is occupied by six elephants in various postures. As Nága means an "Elephant" as well as a "Snake," I

---

[1] See Plate XXXIX.
[2] See Plates XI., XII., and XXXIX.
H 255.

[3] See Plate XXVIII. fig. 2.
[4] See Plate XII., corner Pillar with Relic bearer.

G

infer that the artist intended by their insertion to represent their native land, as well as that of the Serpent.[1] Of the six animals here sculptured the one at the bottom is shown in the act of plucking a sheaf of corn; the next above him is throwing his trunk backwards over his head; the third is filling his trunk with water from a stone bowl; the fourth is pouring the water from his trunk down his throat; the fifth has thrown his trunk back over his head like the second; and the sixth, a large tusker, stands full to the front, his ears extended. The attitudes of some of these figures are well conceived and fairly executed, and altogether the scene is both natural and animated.

The bas-relief of Bodhi-worship also presents the figures of six Elephants; but there the attitudes are limited to the two reverential acts of presenting garlands and bowing before the Tree.[2] The figure of the larger Elephant in the act of bowing, with his hogged back, and his forelegs bent backwards beneath his body, is sketched with equal spirit and accuracy.

In the *Latuwá Játaka*, or " Birth as a Latuwá—bird," the Elephant is represented under three different aspects :[3] first, as being attacked by a bird and an insect; second, as running away; and third, as plunging down a precipice. In the second figure, where the passion represented is fear, I notice that the animal's tail is placed between his legs; and in the third, where madness is intended to be shown, the tail is swung violently backwards; while in the first scene, before he is roused to passion, his tail hangs down unmoved.[4] These differences show that the artist was not unobservant of the character of the animal, although the drawing and execution of the figures are inferior to those of the sitting Elephants on the coping.

The *Horse* is more rarely represented in the Bharhut Sculptures than would have been expected. The principal examples are the two chargers of the male and female standard bearers at the East and South Gates; a caparisoned Horse on one of the pillars of the South-west Quadrant, and the Chariot Horses of Raja Prasenajita and of the Mugapakka Játaka.[5]

Arrian relates, apparently on the authority of Nearchus, that the Indians "have " neither saddles nor bridles for their horses, like those the Grecians or Keltœ make use " of, but instead of bridles they bind a piece of raw bullock's hide round the lower part " of their horse's jaws, to the inner part of which the meaner sort fix spikes of brass or " iron, not very sharp, but richer ones have theirs of ivory. Within the horse's mouth " is a piece of iron like a dart, to which the reins are fastened. When, therefore, they " draw the reins, the bit stops the horse, and the short spikes thereto fixed make him " subservient to the rider's will."[6]

An examination of the Bharhut Sculptures shows distinctly that the Indians had no saddle, while they certainly used a bridle. Of course it is quite possible that the bridle may have been introduced between the time of Alexander and that of Asoka. Instead of a saddle there is a thickly-wadded pad, with ornaments at the four corners. The

---

[1] See Plate XXVIII. fig. 1.   [2] See Plate XXX. fig. 2.   [3] See Plate XXVI. fig. 1.

[4] In Hardy's Manual of Buddhism, p. 178, a frightened elephant is thus described : The " Elephant Girimekhalo, fell upon his knees, trembled with fear, . . . curled up his trunk, and thrust the end into his mouth, *put his tail between his legs*, growled fiercely, &c., and fled away."

[5] See Plate XXXII, for the standard bearers, and Plates XIII. and XXV. for the four-horse chariots.

[6] See Arrian Indica, XVI.

bridle, which is made of a twisted cord, is fastened to the head-gear over each side of the horse's mouth. The head-stall itself has the usual band passing over the top of the head behind the ears, and a second band down the face. These are connected by three horizontal bands, the lowest being level with the mouth, the middle one passing under the cheek, and the upper one above the cheek. A broad horizontal band, ornamented with flowers or rosettes at regular distances, passes right round the horse from chest to tail. As to the horses themselves they are all round-barrelled animals with short thick necks and thick legs.

The Chariot Horses of Râjâ Prasenajita have plaited manes, and plumes on their heads. The crossbar of the chariot pole rests on the necks of the two middle horses. The Raja is driven by a charioteer.

The *Ass* is perhaps represented in one of the half-medallions, as the tail is much too long for any animal of the Deer kind, but the beast has long ears and a hairless tail.[1]

The *Bull* is represented only on a small scale in the bas-reliefs of the coping. The chief scene is that of the *Sujâta Jâtaka*, where according to the legend the animal should be represented as dead. But the design in the bas-relief is not happily rendered, as the bull appears to be sitting up. On the Pillars and Rail-bars there are larger figures, but they are rather clumsily drawn. All of them have humps.[2]

The *Rhinoceros* (or an animal very like one) is represented only once in the half-medallion at the top of one of the North-east Pillars.[3] The long snout approaches that of the Tapir, but from the appearance of a horn on the top of the head I am inclined to believe that the artist really intended to represent a Rhinoceros. The bulky legs are in favour of this identification. The sculptor's sketch must certainly have been made from memory, as the tail is quite a fancy one of the most preposterous length.

The *Deer* is frequently represented. No less than six specimens, both male and female, appear in the *Miga Jâtaka*, or "Deer birth," and a single buck is shown in the *Isi-Miga Jâtaka*.[4] But the largest and best figures of the Deer are in the half-medallion at the top of one of the South-east Pillars.[5] They are true Deer with Antlers, and not Antelopes. The Antelope is also represented as well as the spotted Deer or *Pârâ*,[6] and the bas-reliefs show that the artist was quite familiar with the forms of these animals.

The *Monkey* was evidently a favourite subject with the Buddhist Sculptors, as he is represented in several scenes and in various aspects, both serious and humorous. He appears in the *Bhisa-haraniya Jâtaka* as an important personage, seated on the ground and energetically addressing the chief person in the scene.[7] A second scene seems to be intended for a fight between men and monkeys. About one half of it is lost, but there is so much life and variety in the figures which remain that the loss of the rest is very much to be regretted.[8] As the whole of the monkey scenes will be separately described in another place, I will only refer here to the spirit and freedom of the drawing which most of these bas-reliefs display, and to the real humour shown in the two scenes exhibiting an Elephant taken captive by Monkeys.

---

[1] See Plate XXXV. fig. 4.
[2] See Plate XXXIV. fig. 1, Plate XVII. fig. 10, and Plate LVII.
[3] See Plate XXXVI. fig. 4.
[4] See Plate XXV. fig. 1, and Plate XLIII. fig. 2.
[5] See Plate XXXVI. fig. 3.
[6] See Plate XLIV. fig. 8, for the spotted Deer.
[7] See Plate XLVIII. fig. 7.
[8] See Plate XXXIII. fig. 5.

The *Cat* is represented only thrice, and each time of so small a size that the execution offers no point for remark. In the *Birála Játaka*, or "Cat birth," the Cat appears watching a Cock seated in a tree.[1] In the *Uda Játaka* two Cats appear to be quarrelling over some Fish.[2]

The *Dog* is represented five times; but thrice under the same disadvantageous condition of a small scale. Two Dogs appear in the *Uda Játaka* along with the Cats. One is apparently walking off with a bone, while the other is taking his disappointment quietly in a sitting posture.[3] In the third representation the Dog is also sitting, with his mouth open and showing his teeth, as if snarling. The legs are gone.[4] The other specimens are luckily on a larger scale, where two Dogs are represented attacking a Boar. They are like the present hill dogs, with straight ears and bushy tails that curl over on to their backs.[5]

The *Sheep* is only once represented, as a Ram butting at the upraised knee of a man who is lying on the ground. The *Hare* is twice represented in the border above the Rhinoceros. There is no possibility of mistaking the animal, although his forelegs are made longer than his hind legs.[6] The *Squirrel* is also represented twice on the sides of a Pillar below the centre medallion. The animal is the common striped Squirrel called *galeri*, which is so well known. It is appropriately represented eating fruit while holding on to the small branch of a tree.

The *Cock* is only once represented in the *Kukkuta Játaka*, or "Cock birth." The *Parrot* is several times given on the sides of the Pillars just below the medallions. He is always shown hanging from a spray and pecking at the fruit. He is distinguished by his hooked bill and long tail. The *Peacock* is known by his expanded tail. He is thus represented on the sides of the Pillars on a small scale, and he forms the sole figure of one of the medallions on a large scale. He is also seen in the *Hansa Játaka*, or "Goose-birth," as the suitor for the Goose's daughter—but this bas-relief is unfortunately broken.[7] The Peacock is an easy subject for a sketch, as his expanded tail with its large round spots cannot be mistaken.

The *Goose* occurs only in the *Hansa Játaka*. The legs and hinder part of the body are gone, but the head and fore part remain, which are readily recognizable as belonging to a Goose, without the aid of the accompanying label. The Wild Duck, or some other fishing bird like it, is represented in the *Nága Játaka* in the act of swallowing a Fish.[8] The *Latuwá*, or Quail, is found only in the Latuwá Játaka. It is represented with a long tail and a sharp bill.[9]

All the representations of *Snakes* belong to the superhuman Nágas, whose heads are always of the Cobra species.

The single specimen of an *Insect* in the Bharhut Sculptures is that of a Flesh-fly in the Latuwá Játaka. The Insect is of the size of life, and on the wing, attacking an Elephant in the eye. In the same scene there is a *Frog* sitting on a rock above, who by his wide open mouth seems to be croaking his loudest to assist in distracting the Elephant.

---

[1] See Plate XLVII. fig. 5.
[2] See Plate XLVI. fig. 2.
[3] See Plate XLVI. fig. 2.
[4] See Plate XXVII. fig. 14.
[5] See Plate XXXIV. fig. 1.

[6] See Plate XXXVI. fig. 4.
[7] See the Hansa Játaka in Plate XXVII. fig. 11.
[8] See Plate XXV. fig. 2.
[9] See Plate XXVI. fig. 1.

The representations of all these animals, with the single exception of that of the Rhinoceros, are generally correct and spirited, although the legs of the Deer and Horses are often clumsy and much too thick for beauty. To my eye the Elephants are the most successfully treated, which is perhaps due to their bulky bodies and massive legs, in which a slight departure from nature would not be so perceptible as in the more slender limbs of the Horse and Deer. There is considerable truth also in the heads of the Crocodiles on the ends of the Toran beams. But the most spirited of all the animals are the Monkeys, with whose attitudes and figures the artists have been generally very successful.

D.—TREES AND FRUITS.

The Trees represented in the Bharhut Sculptures are as numerous and varied as the Animals, but partly as I believe from want of skill in the sculpture, and partly I fear from my own ignorance, there are a considerable number of them that still remain unidentified. Some of the trees can be recognized at a glance, such as the Banian Tree with its pendent roots, the Mango Tree with its peculiarly shaped fruit, the Bambu with its joints, and the Tár Tree with its fan-like leaves. Others, again, have been luckily labelled by the sculptors as the Bodhi Trees of particular Buddhas, as the "Bodhi of "Vipaswi," which was the Pátali or Trumpet Flower-tree, the "Bodhi of Viswabhu," which was the Sál Tree, or Shorea Robusta, &c., &c. In a few instances the fruits only have been sculptured; such as the Mango, the Jack Fruit, and the Custard Apple.

The following brief notice of the principal Trees and Fruits will be sufficient to direct the attention of botanists to the sculptures in which they are represented :—

1. The *Banian Tree*, or *Ficus Indica*.—One of the best specimens of this Tree is in the scene of the Chhadantiya Játak'a,[1] where the Tree can be recognized by its pendent roots. But as we learn also from the legend that the famous Chhadantiya Elephant was accustomed to stand under a great Banian Tree, we have a direct proof that the Tree must be intended for a Banian. Another excellent representation of this Tree will be found on Prasenajita's Pillar, in the scene where a number of Elephants are placing garlands at the foot of a Tree.[2] Here, again, the Tree is known by its pendent roots; but the identification is placed beyond all doubt by the accompanying label, which reads *bahu hathiko nigodhe*, where *bahu hathiko* alludes to the herd of Elephants, and *Nigodhe* to the *Nyagrodha*, or Banian Tree. In a third representation of the Bodhi Tree of Kásyapa Buddha, we are equally certain of the identification, as the Banian Tree was his Bodhi.[3] In this the pendent roots have been omitted—to make room, as I suppose, for a number of garlands—but the leaves and berries are a sufficient proof that the Tree is a Fig Tree.

2. The *Pippal*, or *Ficus Religiosa*.—The identification of this Tree is certain, as it was the Bodhi Tree of Sakya Muni.[4] It is correctly represented with long pointed single leaves, but the inscription of

Bhagavato Saka Munino Bodhi—

leaves no doubt whatever that the Tree is intended for the Holy Pippal of the Buddha Sakya Muni.

3. The *Udumbara*, or *Ficus Glomerata*, is recognized by the label giving the name of

---

[1] See Plate XXVI. fig. 2.
[2] See Plate XV. fig. 3.
[3] See Plate XXX. fig. 1.
[4] See Plate XIII. fig. 1, and Plate XXX. fig. 3,

the Buddha Kanaka Muni whose Bodhi Tree it was.[1] The peculiar Fig-tree leaf is well marked, but I see no other peculiar point that would lead to its identification.

4. The *Páṭali*, or *Bignonia Suaveolens.*—This was the Bodhi Tree of the Buddha Vipaswi, whose name is inscribed above the medallion—

Bhagavato Vipasino Bodhi—

The Tree is in flower, but as the flower is represented in full front view, the peculiar shape which gave it the name of *Páṭali*, or the "Trumpet-flower," is not seen.[2]

5. The *Sál Tree*, or *Shorea Robusta*, is frequently represented in Buddhist Sculptures, as Máyá Devi gave birth to the infant Sákya Muni when standing under a *Sála*. It was also the Bodhi Tree of the Buddha Viswabhu, and his name is inscribed below the representation of his Tree.[3] Unfortunately this bas-relief has been much injured; but in the same Plate I have given a fragment of one of the broken statues, in which the hand of a female is grasping the flower and leaf of a Sál Tree. In the upper part of the same a portion of the fruit is also visible. The representation of the flower is somewhat conventional, but it is sufficiently true to the general form and appearance to have been recognized by several of my native followers.

6. The *Sirisa*, or *Acacia Sirisa.*—This was the Bodhi Tree of the Buddha Krakuchanda, and his name forms part of the label inscribed above the Tree[4]—

Bhagavato Kakusadhasa Bodhi—

The lower part of the sculpture has been lost, but the whole of the Tree is in good preservation. Its small leaves and large bunches of flowers are characteristic of the Acacia Sirisa.

7. The *Mango*, or *Mangifera Indica*—This well-known Tree occurs frequently amongst the sculptures, and is easily recognizable by its peculiarly shaped fruit. In the bas-relief of the Jetavana Monastery there is a holy Mango Tree surrounded by a Railing, the story of which I have already given.[5] There is another specimen in the scene representing the visit of Raja Ajátasatru to Buddha, which took place in the *Mango* garden of Jivaka at Rajagriha.[6] A third specimen occurs in the Sankisa Ladder scene; and a fourth in the bas-relief of the Asadrisa Játaka.[7] In all these examples the Tree is small, and the fruit is very minute, but throughout the bas-reliefs of the coping large bunches of the Mango fruit form a common ornament.[8]

8. The *Jambu*, or *Eugenia Jambu.*—The Tree here identified was recognized by my native followers. It is apparently a holy Tree, as it has a throne beneath it surrounded by a number of spotted deer.[9]

9. The *Kachnár*, or *Bauhinia variegata.*—This Tree also was recognized by my native followers, but I am not satisfied as to the accuracy of their identification.

10. The *Bambu*, or *Bambusa.*—The Bambu, being a favourite food of the Elephant, is appropriately added to several scenes in which he appears. One of the best specimens of Bambu occurs on the middle beam of the East Gateway. A second specimen with

---

[1] See Plate XXIX. fig. 4.
[2] See Plate XXIX. fig. 1.
[3] See Plate XXIX. fig. 2.
[4] See Plate XXIX. fig. 8.
[5] See Plate XXVIII. fig. 3.
[6] See Plate XVI. fig. 3, Le Lotus de la Bonne Loi, p. 451.

[7] See Plate XVII. fig. 2, and Plate XXVII. fig. 13.
[8] See Plate XLIII. 6; Plate XLVI. 1; and Plate XLVII. 9.
[9] See Plate XLIV. fig. 8.

Elephants browsing, and a third amongst rocks will be found amongst the bas-reliefs of the copings.[1] In all of these the knotty joints and the long plumy branches of the Bambu with their numerous leaves are characteristically rendered.

11. The *Tár Tree*, or *Borassus flabelliformis.*—This is the well-known Fan-palm, whose spreading pointed leaves are successfully represented in one of the broken medallions. The peculiar appearance of the trunk of the Tree is also happily hit off.[2]

12. The *Khajur*, or *Phœnix silvestris.*—This is the wild date tree of India. Its identification is perhaps doubtful; but I cannot recall any tree which would agree half so well as the Khajur with the Sculpture.[3] The Khajur is also represented on a large scale on the Prasenajit Pillar where the trunks are placed at the angles of the Pillar so as to form frames for the bas-reliefs. Both leaves and fruit are shown in these specimens.

13. The *Khatahal*, or *Artocarpus integri folia.*—The Jack Tree with its huge fruit is too well known to need description. In some of the scenes I think that I can distinguish the Jack Tree with its fruit, but there is no doubt about the identification of the fruit itself in many of the bas-reliefs of the coping.[4]

14. The *Sitá-phal*, or *Annona Squamosa*—the Custard Apple.—My identification of this fruit amongst the Mathura Sculptures has been contested on the ground that the tree was first introduced into India by the Portuguese. I do not dispute the fact that the Portuguese brought the Custard Apple to India, as I am aware that the East India Company imported hundreds of grindstones into the sandstone fort of Chunár, as if for the purpose of illustrating the proverb about carrying coals to Newcastle. I have now travelled over a great part of India, and I have found such extensive and such widely distant tracts covered with the *wild* Custard Apple that I cannot help suspecting the tree to be indigenous. I can now appeal to one of the Bharhut Sculptures for a very exact representation of the fruit and leaves of the Custard Apple.[5] In a second sculpture a Monkey is represented on a branch of a Custard Apple Tree eating one of the fruits.[6] On a third a striped Squirrel is so represented. The common Hindi name is *Ata*, or simply *át*, from the Sanskrit *átripya.*

15. The *Plantain* Tree with its broad straight leaves appears to be represented in Plate XLIV. fig. 6.

16. The *Lotus* flower is extensively used in the ornamentation of the basses of medallions of the Pillars and Rails. It forms also the sole decoration of the outside of the coping, where the long continuous row of large many-leaved flowers with a few buds and stalks striking and rich line of ornament. The Plant itself with its buds and blossoms is found on a large scale in one of the Játaka medallions.[7]

17. The *Wheat* is represented standing in one of the bas-reliefs of the coping, where it is being cut by a female.[8]

18. The *Siris* Tree, or *Acacia Sirisa*, is represented in the scene of "Elápatra Nága worshipping Buddha" whose throne is placed under one of a group of six *Siris* Trees.

---

[1] See Plate VIII., Plate XLVI. 6, and Plate XLVIII. 9.

[2] See Plate XXX. fig. 4.

[3] See Plate XV. fig. 3, and Plate XIII. 1, 2, 3.

[4] See Plate XIV. 1, XLI. 4, XLII. 8, XLIII. 1.

[5] See Plate XLVII. fig. 2.

[6] See Plate XXXIII. fig. 6.

[7] See Plate XL. fig. 1, for the coping flower, and Plate XXVII. fig. 10, for the plant.

[8] See Plate XL. fig. 1.

E.—SCULPTURED SCENES.

1. JÂTAKAS, OR PREVIOUS BIRTHS OF BUDDHA.

The *Jâtakas*, or "Births," are legends of Buddha's previous existences, which he related at various times to his hearers, in illustration of his doctrine that good actions secure a higher and better position in the next birth, while bad actions entail a lower position, in consequence of which the attainment of Nirvâna is still longer deferred. These legends would appear to have been very popular everywhere, as they form many of the most conspicuous subjects of the Buddhist Sculptures of Bharhut, Sânchi, Mathura, and Gândhâra. They are still very popular both in Ceylon and in Burma, where they are best known in a work called *Pansiya-panas Jâtaka pota*, or "Book of the five hundred and fifty births." . . . "The Singhalesæ," adds Spence Hardy, "will listen the " night through to recitations from this work without any apparent weariness, and a " great number of the Jâtakas are familiar even to the women."[1]

In India proper amongst the Nepalese collection formed by Hodgson only one work has been found which contains a collection of Jâtakas. This is appropriately named *Jâtaka mâla*, or the "Garland of Births."[2] According to Burnouf, who examined the Nepalese collection, the work contains an account of the various meritorious acts of Sâkya prior to the time when he became a Buddha.

The following is Spence Hardy's account of the Ceylonese collection of the 550 Jâtakas:—[3]

"It is named *Jâtaka Gâtha*, or 'Birth Stanzas,' although a large proportion of them " has no reference (independent of the comment) to any birth, being general maxims " or miscellaneous observations. Each of the first one hundred Jâtakas consists of a " single verse of four lines ; but some of the remainder, being histories, are much longer, " the last one, or history of King Wessantara, occupying 40 pages. The comment " comprises :—1. The occasion upon which the verse was spoken. 2. A story illustrating " it, affirmed to have been related at the time by Buddha, detailing circumstances which " occurred to him and the parties respecting whom the verse was spoken, in a previous " birth. 3. A philological explanation of the words and sense of the stanza, the verses " being mostly inserted at length."

Spence Hardy gives a list of the number of times in which Buddha appeared in particular states of existence as recorded in the Jâtakas ; but the list as he himself observes is imperfect, as the details amount to only 506 different births out of the 550.[4] Upham professes to give the complete list ; but many of his names are given more than once. His spelling of the names too is so corrupt, as to make their identification generally difficult, and in some cases perhaps impossible.[5] But in addition to this he has given the story of the Hansa Jâtaka under the wrong title of Nada Jâtaka. The Buddhist Jâtakas are acknowledged to be the originals from which many of the tales of the Buddhist Panchatantra and of the Brahmanical Hitopadesa have been derived. It is true that great differences exist in the details of these stories, but M. Fausböll is of

---

[1] Hardy's Manual of Buddhism, p. 99.
[2] Introduction à l'Histoire du Buddhisme Indien, p. 61.
[3] Manual of Buddhism, p. 99.   [4] Ibid, p. 100.
[5] Sacred and Historical Books of Ceylon, III. 269.

opinion that if an old manuscript of the Panchatantra could be found, "the similarity "between the Singhalese (Pali) and the continental (Sanskrit) fables would appear greater, "the Panchatantra being originally, as Professor Benfey has clearly shown, a Buddhistic "work."[1] Now in the Bharhut Sculptures we have a "continental" edition of about a score of the Jâtakas, which is not only several centuries older than the Panchatantra, but is also much more ancient than the Pali version of Ceylon. And herein lies the great value of the Bharhut bas-reliefs, that they form by far the oldest collection of the Buddhist Jâtakas that has yet been brought to light. A comparison between them and the Singhalese and Panchatantra versions will prove which of the two, the Singhalese or the continental Sanskrit, has departed farthest from the original.

The following extract will show very clearly to what extent the fables of the Hitopadesa are indebted to the old Buddhist Jâtakas:—

"Baka Jâtaka.[2]

"An artful Cormorant (Crane) addressing himself to some Fish who were living in a "very shallow tank, offered his services to convey them to another, in which he assured "them there was abundance of water. The simple Fish, seduced by this tempting offer, "permitted the Cormorant (Crane) to take them out in succession—but instead of conveying "them to the promised tank he had no sooner got them out of the sight of their com- "panions then he fell to and devoured them. One day he happened to address himself "to a Crab, who resided in the same tank, and who readily accepted the offer, but proposed "as the most convenient mode of transporting him, that he should cling about the "Cormorant's neck. The Cormorant consenting to this arrangement, they proceeded on "their journey. After having gone some distance the Crab, looking round and discovering "no appearance of a tank, suspected the intention of the cormorant, and seizing him fast "by the neck, threatened him with instant death, unless he went back immediately to the "tank they had quitted. The Cormorant, not daring to refuse, returned accordingly with "the Crab, who just as he was entering into the water, with his piercing claws nipped off "the cormorant's neck, in the same manner as the stem of a lotus is cut in two by a pair "of sharp scissors. Bodhisat, then a Tree-god, observing what had passed proclaimed "aloud the mischief of deceit, and the just punishment by which in this case it was "followed."[3]

This simple tale, which reads very much like one of Æsop's fables, has not been improved by the Brahmanical Author of the Hitopadesa, but the alterations are very slight. As his version is fortunately very short I give it here in full:—[4]

"The Crane and the Crab.

"A silly crane after devouring many fine inferior and middle-sized fishes, perished "under the gripe of a crab, for his excessive gluttony.

"How, asked Chitravana, was that?

"The Minister related.

"In the county of Malwa is a pool called *Padma-garbha* (Lotus bearing), where an "old crane deprived of strength, stood feigning himself troubled in mind; and on being

[1] Sacred and Historical Books of Ceylon, III. 269.

[2] two Jâtakas, in Royal Asiatic Society's Journal, New Series, Vol. V. p. 1.

[3] Upham, "Sacred and Historical Books of Ceylon," Vol. III. pp. 293–94.—*Baka* or *Vaka* is the common name for a *Crane*, and not a *Cormorant*.   [4] Johnson's Hitopadesa, p. 103.

" asked by a certain Crab at a distance, ' How is it you stand here renouncing food.? '   He
" replied, ' My means of living are fish ; and the talk of the fisherman outside the town, that
" the fish here are inevitably about to be killed by the fishermen, has been heard.
" Judging therefore, that for want of subsistence from this quarter, my death is near, I
" have lost all regard for food.'   Then all the Fishes thought amongst themselves, ' On this
" ' occasion at least he appears our benefactor ; let him therefore be consulted how we
" ' are to act.   For thus it is said :

            " ' An alliance should be formed with a foe
            " ' who benefits, not with an injurious friend ;[1]
            " ' for kindness or injury is the characteristic
            " ' mark of both.'

" The Fishes said, ' O Crane, where are the means of our safety ? '   ' Means of safety
" there are,' said the Crane ; ' another pool ; thither I will carry you one by one.'   The
" Fishes said, through fear, ' Be it so.'   The treacherous Crane then having taken the
" Fishes one by one, and eaten them in a certain spot, returned and said, ' They have been
" ' placed by me in another pool.'   At length a Crab, said to him, ' O Crane, take me there
" too.'   The Crane, longing for the delicate flesh of the Crab, respectfully conveyed him
" and set him on the ground ; but the Crab, seeing the ground strewed with fish bones
" thought ' Alas ! I am undone, unfortunate that I am !   Well, I must now act suitably to
" the emergency, for :—

            " ' We ought to fear danger only so long
            " ' as it is distant ; but when we see
            " ' danger near, we ought to fight like
            " ' those who are not afraid !

" Moreover—

            " ' When a wise man being attacked, can
            " ' see no safety for himself, he then
            " ' dies fighting with the foe.'

" With this resolution the Crab tore the throat of the Crane so that he perished."

The following list gives the names of all the Játakas which are represented in a
sculptured form amongst the Bharhut bas-reliefs.   No less than 18 of these scenes
have their names inscribed either above or below them.   While the stories of three
others, which have lost their inscriptions, are so clearly told, as to leave no doubt
whatever as to their identification.   These three are Nos. 9, 13, and 14.

No.

1. Miga Játaka   -   -   -   - or Deer Birth.
2. Nága Játaka   -   -   -   - or Elephant Birth.
3. Yava Majhakiya Játaka   -   - or ?
4. Muga Pakaya Játaka   -   -   - or ?
5. Latuwa Játaka   -   -   - or Quail Birth.
6. Chhadantiya Játaka   -   -   - or Chhadanta Elephant Birth.
7. Isi Singiya Játaka[2]   -   -   - or Rishi Sringi Birth.
8. Yambumano Avayesi Játaka[3]   -   - or ?

---

[1] This is more concisely stated in our English proverb—"Better an open foe than a treacherous friend."
[2] Called Nálini Játaka in Ceylon.   [3] Called Andhabhuta Játaka in Ceylon.

1. MIGA JÂTAKA.

The subject of this Jâtaka has not yet been identified with certainty; but it seems probable that it may represent the *Miga Jâtaka* of the Pali Books of Ceylon. According to Spence Hardy, Buddha had been a Deer no less than ten times; and I have got the names of several of these Jâtakas, but they have all got some qualifying epithet to distinguish them from the simply named *Miga Jâtaka* or "Deer Birth." Thus there are the *Nigrodha Miga*, the *Vata Miga*, the *Tipallatha Miga*, the *Kurunga Miga*, the *Nandiya Miga*, and others; but only one of the Jâtakas is distinguished by the simpler title of *Miga Jâtaka*. It seems probable, therefore, that this should be the subject of the Bharhut bas-relief which bears the same title. I must confess, however, that I cannot trace any of the Jâtaka scenes in the sculpture,[1] but as the story is a short one I will here give the outline of it from Subhuti's translation, in the hope that others may be more fortunate than myself:—

"In days of yore there reigned a king in Rajagriha, the capital of Magadha. At
"that time the great Bodhisatta had been born a Deer, and was the king of one
"thousand other Deer. He had two Fawns named Lakshanaya and Kalaya,—to whom
"when he grew old he gave up his sovereignty. Then followed a famine, when all the
"wild animals suffered severely from the scarcity of food, as the people set snares and
"traps to catch the Deer which ate their corn, so that many of them were killed. Then
"Bodhisat addressed his two successors and advised them to withdraw with their herds to
"the foot of mount Aramira during the reaping season, after which they might return to
"the old forest. Now the Royal Deer named Kala was foolish, and he conducted his herd
"near villages during the day time, so that many of them were killed before he reached
"the mountain. But the Royal Deer named Lakshana was wise—and led his herd far
"away from the villages during the night time—so that he reached the mountain in

---

[1] See Plate XXV.

H 2

" safety. At the end of four months Lakshana returned to the forest with his 500
" followers, while his brother Kala, having lost all his followers, returned alone. So the
" former was received with joy, but the latter with disgrace. The Monk Sâriputra, who
" now leads his followers in the right path of religion and virtue was then the Royal Deer
" Lakshana, and the Monk Devadatta, who now perverts all his followers, was then the
" Royal Deer Kala."

As well as I can judge there is no portion of this legend represented in the Bharhut
sculpture. If the human figures were omitted the Roebuck with his five Does might be
taken for the wise Lakshana, and the solitary Roe swimming the river would be the
foolish Roe Kâla. But the presence of the human figures seems to me altogether to
preclude this identification.

The *Miga Jâtaka* is also mentioned by Bishop Bigandet, in the following terms.[1] " He
" (Buddha) related to them the *Dsat Miga*, by which he showed to them that during
" former existences Râhula had distinguished himself, in a conspicuous manner, by his
" excellent and admirable disposition. As a reward for his good behaviour and high
" mental qualifications he was made Patzin (*Pratyeka*). His mind continuing to expand
" in a manner almost miraculous he became a Rahanda with millions of *Nats* (Devas)."

2. NÂGA JÂTAKA.

In this scene the principal actors are an Elephant and a Crab which has seized the
Elephant by the right hind leg.[2] Two other Elephants appear behind, and there is a
pond full of fish from which the Crab has just issued. The legend here represented is the
Nâga Jâtaka, or " Elephant birth," but in Ceylon it is better known by the name of
Karkataka Jâtaka, or the " Crab birth." The former, however, is the correct name, as in
the legend here represented Buddha is the King of the Elephants, and therefore the
Jâtaka, or Birth, must of necessity have been named after him. For this identification I
am indebted to the learned Buddhist priest Subhûti of Vaskaduve in Ceylon, who has
also kindly furnished me with an English translation of the Jâtaka, of which the following
is a pretty full summary :—

" In times past when Raja Brahmadatta reigned in Benares there lived in a certain
" pond a gigantic Crab. Near this pond, which was named after the Crab, there lived a
" herd of Elephants under a king or leader of their own. Whenever the herd went
" down to the pond to feed on the roots of the Lotus, the great Crab would seize one of
" them by the hind leg, and hold it fast until it died from exhaustion, when the Crab
" would feed on the carcass at his leisure. Now it happened at this time that Bodhisat
" was conceived in the womb of the Queen Elephant, who retired to a secluded part of
" the forest and in due course gave birth to the ' Discoverer of Truth.' When Bodhisat
" grew up he chose a large female Elephant for his mate, and taking with him his mother
" and his mate he proceeded to the neighbourhood of the crab pond to pay a visit to his
" father. When Bodhisat heard that the Crab was in the habit of killing many of the
" Elephants that went down to the pond, he said to his parent, ' Father, charge me with
" ' the work of destroying this Crab.' But his father replied, ' Son, do not ask this—
" ' that Crab has killed many Elephants, therefore you must not go near the pond.' But

---

[1] Legend of the Burmese Buddha, p, 176,   [2] See Plate XXV.

" arrogating to himself the dangerous task of killing the Crab, Bodhisat led a herd of
" Elephants down to the bank of the pond and going into the water they all fed on the
" roots of the Lotus. On leaving the pond Bodhisat brought up the rear when the great
" Crab seized him by the hind leg, and dragged him towards his hole. Then Bodhisat
" cried out for his life—and the herd of Elephants roared, too, through fear and fled away
" from the pond. Then Bodhisat cried out to his mate, ' O meritorious spouse-loving
" ' she-elephant, the big and bold-eyed Crab, who lives in this pond has seized me by one
" ' of the hind legs, why therefore do you leave me?' Hearing this the female
" Elephant drew near to him and said, ' Keep up your courage, for even if I were
" ' offered ten thousand *yojanas* of (land in) Dambadiwa, I would not forsake thee.'
" Then turning to the Crab she said, ' O gold coloured one of great size, the King and
" ' Chief of all Crabs, I pray thee to let go my husband, the King of Elephants.' Then
" the Crab, moved by her words, and ignorant of danger, loosened his hold on Bodhisat,
" who no sooner felt himself free than he set his foot on the back of the Crab and
" crushed him. So the Crab died and Bodhisat roared with delight—and the rest of the
" herd trampling on the Crab his body was crushed to pieces. But the two big claws
" still remained in the pond, from whence they were carried into the Ganges. Here one
" claw was caught by the Dasabâ Princes, who made it into a drum to be used at their
" festive gathering; while the other claw was carried down to the Ocean, where it was
" seized by the Asuras who made it into a drum to be played at their festivals."

3. YAVA-MAJHAKIYA JÂTAKA.

The title of this Jâtaka is not to be found in the Ceylon list of Buddha's 550
previous births, neither has the story yet been identified by Subhûti. But I have myself
been fortunate enough to recognise in it a very striking representation of the legend of
Upakosâ, the young wife of Vararuchi, as told in the *Vrihat Katha* of Kshemendra, and in
the *Katha Saritsâgara* of Soma Deva. Subhûti suggests that *Majhakiya* is the name of a
country, which is likely enough, but it has not yet been of any assistance in identifying
the Bharhut sculpture with any one of the Pali Jâtakas of Ceylon. Perhaps the title
may simply mean the " Young woman Jâtaka."

The story of Upakosâ, as told by Kshemendra in the Vrihat Katha has been translated by Dr. Bühler, and as it would be spoilt by curtailment, I now give it at full
length.[1] On comparing the sculpture with the story the principal figures can be
recognized at once. In the midst is King Nanda seated on the throne; to the right is
the young wife Upakosâ, pointing to the open baskets; and in the foreground are the
four baskets containing her four lovers. Three of the baskets have been opened, thus
exposing the lovers faces, while the fourth has just arrived on the shoulders of two
porters. I wish to draw particular attention to the baskets, as the word used by
Kshemendra is *Manjûsha*, which means a " basket " and not a box :—

From the Vrihat-katha.

" Having heard this (story of the origin of Pâtaliputra), and having received all
" sciences from my teacher, I (Vararuchi) who dwelt at my ease, obtained in marriage
" the daughter of Guru Upavarsha, called Upakosâ. After I married Upakosâ whose
" eyes resembled blue lotuses, I became the empire over which Cupid rules and vessel

---

" of all happiness. Whilst I, living in the company of Vyâdi and Indradatta, acquired
" the fame of omniscience, a pupil of Varsha, Pânini by name, who was formerly a
" blockhead, obtained by virtue of his austerities, keeping his senses in subjection, a new
" grammar from Siva. Disputing with me for eight days he proved himself an opponent
" of equal force. When I conquered him at the end of that period, Hara, bewildering
" me by a growl, bereft me, through anger, of the recollection of Indra's grammar.
" After I had suddenly forgotten that work I resolved to perform austerities in order
" to obtain the sight of Bharga, who is the destroyer of Cupid, and the wish-fulfilling
" husband of Parvati, and I placed money for the household expenses in the hands of a
" neighbour, a Vâniyâ called Hiranyagupta. After I was gone my faithful Upakosâ,
" though left alone in the beauty of her fresh youth, being versed in the Vedas,
" performed the vow which is becoming for wives whose husbands are absent. Time
" passed on, and once the young *foujdar* of the King, the *domestic priest*, and the *minister*
" saw that beauty with the swan-like gait, who bathed daily, and played with the thick
" spray, which had the appearance of a thin and transparent garment, whose broad hips
" resembled sand-banks, who was dark blue in colour, whose eyes had the appearance of
" newly-opened lotuses, and who was a bud of Cupid, going like Yamuna to the Ganges.
" Gazing at her all three fell in love with her and apart from each other. First amongst
" them the son of the Minister said to her, ' Love me.' She who had finished bathing,
" seeing that night had come, became afraid and spoke to him. ' Be it so, on the third
" day at night-fall I will meet you secretly.' Speaking thus to him she went. After
" leaving him she addressed the domestic priest to this effect, ' On the third day hence,
" in the second watch of the night I shall be at your disposal.' Turning away from him
" she said to the Foujdar, ' On the third day hence, in the third watch of the night I am
" ready to do your will.' After she had made this assignation, he let her go, and she
" went home, filling as it were, by her frightened glances the sky with lotuses."

        " Being in want of her husband's money she tried to remedy its concealment (by
" the banker). But Hiranyagupta asked her for an assignation in her house. She said
" to him, ' On the third day hence, at the end of the night, I will obey thee, what harm
" ' is there (in my doing it) ? ' She told that story to her domestics. When the third
" day had come, the excellent minister, trembling and having lost all control over
" himself, entered in the night her house, where the lamps had been extinguished.
" Upakosâ called him by his name, and said, ' On you I have placed my affection.' At
" her order he entered a dark room in the interior of the house."

        " There the servant maids smeared for a long time the limbs of the lover with the
" soft unguent consisting of oil lamp soot. But when in the second watch of the night
" the domestic priest came in haste, Upakosâ showed to the (first lover) an open
" wooden box, said ' Enter quickly here comes the master of the house,' and made him
" enter it. Closing it with an iron bolt, she said to the domestic priest, ' You must not
" ' touch me without having bathed.' He also was treated in the same manner (as the
" first lover). When he had been anointed with oil and soot the third also came.
" Forsooth, who escapes being deceived and made a fool of by the rogue Cupid. After
" the priest, overwhelmed with fear, had been disposed of in the same box (as the first
" lover) the third also, in his turn, was made to resemble a goblin. At the end of the
" night the excellent Vâniyâ, Hiranyagupta arrived, and the Foujdâr was concealed
" likewise in the wooden box. Then Upakosâ facing the box spoke to the Vâniyâ, who

" was sitting at his ease on an excellent seat, 'Give me the deposit.' Hiranyagupta
" replied 'Love me, sweet smiling one, I have the money, fair-browed one, which
" 'your husband deposited with me?' Hearing this she exclaimed in a loud voice,
" 'Hear ye deities of the house, be witnesses ye goblins; he has my property.'
" Speaking thus she defaced him also with lamp soot. Then she said, 'The night
" 'has passed, go.' Quickly the Vâniâ went forth, covering his face from fear of the
" people who are about early. Bereft of his garments, he was hooted on the road by the
" people. Wise Upakosâ who had thus protected her virtue, after his departure,
" started early for the audience hall of King Nanda. The King was informed that the
" daughter of Upavarsha, the faithful wife of Vararuchi had come, and he honoured her
" there. She said, 'O King, the Vâniyâ Hiranyagupta conceals great wealth which
" 'my husband deposited with him. It is now for you, Lord, to give orders.' After
" that, when that liar had been summoned and came, Upakosâ said, 'Lord, at home I
" 'have witnesses; order my household gods to be brought, who are kept in a box;
" 'they will declare the truth.' The basket box was brought at the King's command
" and placed by the bearers in the midst of the assembly. Then the faithful wife spoke
" again. 'Ho ye deities, who are worthy of constant worship, tell the truth for my
" 'sake. If you remain silent in this matter of evidence, I shall quickly burn the
" 'basket.' Hearing this, they said, full of fear, 'Forsooth, thy property is in the hands
" 'of Hiranyagupta, we three are witnesses to that.' All present in the assembly who
" heard this miraculous answer were astonished, they opened the basket and saw the
" naked men smeared with soot. When the King had been informed of the circum-
" stances of the case, he punished them by a fine and honoured Upakosâ as his
" spiritual sister. About this time I (Vararuchi), by the grace of Sambhu, remembered
" the grammar learned with joy the news about my house and went to visit my teacher.
" The story of Upakosâ."

The version of the legend given by Somadeva in the *Katha Saritságara* is almost the
same as that of Kshemendra—as will be seen by the following summary :[1]—" During the
" absence of her husband Upakosâ became the object of the addresses of the King's
" family priest, the commander of the guards, the Prince's tutor, and her husband's
" banker. She made appointments with them all to come to her house on the same
" night. At the expiration of the first watch of the night the preceptor of the Prince
" arrived. Upakosâ affected to receive him with great delight; and, after some conver-
" sation, desired him to take a bath, which her handmaidens had prepared. The
" preceptor made no objection; the bath was placed in a dark room, his own clothes
" were taken away, and in their place he was supplied with sheets, smeared with lamp-
" black oil and perfumes. When sufficiently rubbed, the women exclaimed, 'Alas, here
" 'arrives our master's particular friend.' Thereupon they hurried the poor man into a
" basket, well fastened by a bolt outside, and, in the same way, they disposed of the
" priest and commander of the guard. From the banker Upakosâ demanded her
" husband's money, and leading him near the closed basket, spoke aloud, and made him
" promise that she should have it. A bath was then proposed, but before it could be
" enjoyed, daylight appeared, and the banker was glad to depart."

---

[1] Ancient and Mediæval India, by Mrs. Manning, II. 316. Her abstract is taken from H. H. Wilson,
Works, Vol. III.

" Next day, Upasoká presented a petition to King Nanda, saying that the banker
" sought to appropriate property entrusted to him by her absent husband, Vararuchi.
" The banker was then summoned into court, and Upasoká said that the household gods
" which her husband had left in baskets could give witness. The King having sent for
" the baskets, Upasoká said, 'Speak, gods, and declare what you have overheard this
" 'banker say in our dwelling. If you are silent, I will unhouse you in this presence.'
" The men in the baskets acknowledged that they had heard the banker admit that he
" possessed wealth belonging to the husband of Upasoká. The court was amazed, and
" the terrified banker promised restitution. The King now begged for a sight of these
" household gods, and out came the culprits like lumps of darkness; and being recog-
" nized, they were not only exposed to ridicule, but banished as criminals from the
" kingdom, whilst Upasoká excited the admiration and esteem of the whole city."[1]

A much more modern version of the same legend may be found in the *Bahár-dánish*,
in the story of the merchant Hasan and Gauhar, daughter of a Pársá or (Devotee), of
which the following is an abridgment:—

A merchant named Hasan, when out hunting met a very beautiful girl, when the
two at once fell in love with each other. As she was the daughter of a devotee, Hasan
was in despair; but by her instructions he became a very assiduous attendant at prayers,
and so managed to obtain the father's consent to their marriage. Shortly afterwards
Hasan became poor, and his wife, who was named Gauhar, or the "Pearl," having
embroidered a piece of cloth, he took it to the bazaar for sale. When the Kotwál saw
this fine piece of embroidery he accused the merchant of having stolen it, and hearing
that Hasan's wife was very beautiful, he seized her also, and sent them both to the Vazir,
who put them in prison. At night they were released by the Kotwál's servant, who had
fallen in love with Gauhar.

After various adventures they settled in another city, where Hasan was soon afterwards imprisoned on a false accusation. His wife went at once to the Kotwál to demand
justice, but the Kotwál fell in love with her, and told her that her husband could only
be released by her acceding to his wishes. Feigning consent, she pointed out her house
to him, and fixed that very night for his visit. She then went to the court of the Kázi
to complain of the Kotwál's conduct; but the one was no better than the other, for the
Kázi having also fallen in love with her would only agree to release her husband on the
same terms as proposed by the Kotwál. Again she feigned consent, and fixed that night
for his visit, but a little later than the time appointed for the Kotwál.

On her way home Gauhar bought two bottles of wine for the entertainment of her
guests. When the Kotwál arrived, she proposed that as the whole night was before them
for enjoyment he had better begin the evening with wine. So the Kotwál drank, and
gradually became tipsy. Then there was a cry that the Kázi is coming, and the Kotwál
being frightened, begged Gauhar to hide him. Unfortunately there was no accessible
place for concealment, except a large earthen vessel, which stood in the room. So the
Kotwál was squeezed into this vessel, and its mouth was securely fastened by Gauhar.

The Kázi then came in and was treated to wine in the same way as the Kotwal, and
he was nearly tipsy, when he heard a loud knocking at the door, and a cry of the " Vazir

---

[1] It will be observed that the lady's name, which was Upakosá in the Vrihat-Kathá has been changed by
transposition to Upasoká in the Kathá Saritságara.

is coming." Being frightened he begged the lady to conceal him somewhere, so she put him in a large gunny bag, and fastened the mouth of it securely.

Gauhar then went to sleep, and in the morning she hired coolies to carry the earthen jar and the sack, and took them before the King, from whom she demanded justice. Then the jar and the sack being opened, the Kotwāl and the Kāzi were dragged out and sentenced to be beheaded, and the merchant Hasan was released from prison, and returned home to his faithful wife Gauhar the "Pearl."

A similar story still lingers amongst the people in other places, as may be seen in the following legend of Dinājpur, entitled the Touchstone, of which only the latter part need be quoted.[1] "As the Kotwāl was going round the city he saw the girl on the roof, "and said to the garland maker, 'I will come and see your sister to-night.' She said, "'My sister has made a vow that no one shall come and visit her unless he presents "'her with a touchstone.' The Kotwāl promised it, and went away. After this the "King's councillor saw the girl, and said to the garland maker, 'I will come and visit "your sister to-night.' By the girl's order the garland maker agreed, and he said he "would come at one watch of the night. After this the prime minister came, and, "having made an arrangement that he should come at the second watch in the night, "he went away. And at last the King himself came out to enjoy the air, and when he "saw the girl on the roof, he said he would come at the last watch of the night. When "the girl heard they were all coming, she prepared a large pot, and mixed in it two "seers of milk and one seer of water, and put it on the fire, and also brought some grass "and a jar of water, and placed them ready, and when it was evening she put a stool "near the fire for herself, and another stool for the other people to sit on, and proceeded "to mix the milk and water. In the meantime the Kotwāl come, bringing the touch-"stone with him; so the girl took it and invited him to drink the milk and water which "she had prepared, and they talked together until the first watch of the night had "passed away. At that time, according to previous arrangement, the councillor came, "and when he knocked at the door the Kotwāl asked the girl who it was, and was very "much frightened to hear it was the King's councillor, and asked where he could hide "himself. She then smeared him all over with molasses, and poured water on him, and "covered the whole of his body with cotton wool, and fastened him in the window. "After that the councillor came in and sat down and began to talk, and she gave him "some milk and water, and so the second watch of the night passed. After that "the King's prime minister came and knocked at the door, and the councillor asked the "girl who it was, and when she told him, he was exceedingly alarmed and asked where "he could hide. She told him she had placed the Kotwāl in the window and covered "him with cotton wool, and made a frightful object of him; and then she covered the "councillor with the mat, and opened the door to the prime minister. He came into the "house and sat down on the stool, and, as before, the girl talked with him, and so the "third watch of the night passed away. Then the King himself came and knocked at "the door, and the prime minister inquired who it was, and as soon as he heard he was "very much frightened and asked where he could hide, as he was in danger of his life; "so the girl took him near the frightful looking Kotwāl and put him under a screen of "bamboo, and then opened the door to the King. The King came in and talked to the

---

[1] See the Indian Antiquary, vol. II. p. 359, by G. H. Damant, C.S.

" girl and meantime the councillor from beneath his mat, and prime minister from
" behind his screen, seeing the hideous form of the Kotwâl, became excessively frightened.
" Just at that moment the King happened to be looking round on every side of the
" house, and seeing the Kotwâl he said ' What is that fastened there ?' The girl replied,
" ' Oh, there is a young Râkshara tied there.' As soon as the Kotwâl heard that he
" leaped out, and the King seeing him thought, ' He will eat me ;' the councillor thought,
" ' He will eat me ;' the prime minister thought. ' He will eat me ;' so they all, one
" after the other ran away to their own houses, and the Kotwâl also went to his house."

4. MUGHA PAKKHA JÂTAKA.

The Pillar on which this scene is sculptured was removed from Bharhut to
Batanmâra seven generations back along with several other Pillars and some portions
of the Eastern Gateway. The present Thâkur of Batanmâra very kindly allowed me to
examine the whole of his castle where these remains of the Bharhut Railing were
inserted some two hundred years ago. Unfortunately this Jâtaka Pillar was laid flat in
the floor of the arcade, where it had been trodden over daily, but luckily only by bare feet,
otherwise the inscription, which is engraved on the raised edge of the medallion, would
have disappeared altogether. The sculpture itself has suffered very little, owing partly
to the flinty hardness of the stone and partly to its being sunk below the surrounding
rim. But the inscription has been worn away at the edges so that the letters are not
very distinct. I read it as *Mugaphakaya Jâtaka* or *Muga pakaya Jâtaka*, which I take
to be the same title as the *Muga pakkha Jâtaka* of the Ceylonese list. Unfortunately
I have not received any translation of this Jâtaka, as my respected friend Subhûti was
under the impression that the scene belonged to the famous Wessantara Jâtaka. But this
can hardly be the case, as the story of the Prince Wessantara requires his wife
as well as his two children to appear on the scene. Besides which on the right hand
of the sculpture there is a seated Rishi, who is apparently addressing a royal personage
standing before him with clasped hands.[1] Now there is no Rishi in the story of Prince
Wessantara. So that the sculptured scenes appear to me to offer no points in common
with his history save a chariot standing in the foreground.

5. LAṬUWA JÂTAKA.

In Ceylon this legend is called the *Laṭukîka Jâtaka*.[2] When I first saw the Bharhut
sculpture I recognised the story as one which I had heard in Kashmir as long ago as
1839. I have lately received both the text and a translation of the Jâtaka from my
good friend Subhûti, the learned Buddhist priest of Ceylon. As the scenes represented
in the Bharhut bas-reliefs agree in almost every minute detail with the Singhalese Pali
version of the legend, I will here give the latter at some length from Subhûti's version :—

" In days of yore when Brahmadatta was Raja of Benares, Bodhisatta was born as
" an Elephant, and was the leader of 80,000 other Elephants, it happened that a *Laṭukîka*
" built her nest on a certain pathway, and laid her eggs in it. One day when she was
" sitting in her nest watching her young ones who were still unable to fly, she was
" frightened by the appearance of Bodhisatta attended by his herd of 80,000 Elephants.
" Seeing the imminent danger to which her young brood were exposed she straightway

---

[1] See Plate XXV. [2] Latukika, " The diminutive Indian Quail," Childers, Pali Dictionary, in voce.

" flew towards the leading Elephant Bodhisatta and besought him to save her young
" ones from being crushed under the huge feet of his herd. Moved by the earnest
" appeal of the mother bird, Bodhisatta stood over her nest until all the Elephants had
" passed by. He then left himself, first warning the bird that a *Solitary* Elephant of
" savage temper would shortly come by this way, and might do her little ones some
" harm. As one danger often succeeds another, the poor Laṭukika was not yet relieved
" from her fears, but was still dreading the approach of an enemy whom no entreaties
" might move. Then seeing the Solitary Elephant approaching she flew towards him.
" ' O noble Elephant who livest in the forest, I adore thee with my two wings, and
" ' humbly beseech thee to spare my young ones who have only just escaped from a
" ' threatening danger.' But her prayer was in vain, for the savage Elephant unmoved
" by her entreaties answered, ' What can a poor thing like you do if I should harm your
" young ones?" And trampled them to death with his left foot.

" Then the heart-broken Laṭukika alighting on the branch of a tree and brooding on
" revenge exclaimed, ' You shall see what a weak little bird can do against thy boasted
" strength.' So she then became assiduous in her attentions to a Crow, who when he heard
" her story promised to peck the eyes of the Elephant as a reward for her services. In a
" similar way she secured the services of a Flesh-fly and a Frog. Then the Crow pecked
" at the eyes of the Elephant, and the Flesh-fly laid her eggs in the wounds, which soon
" made him blind. Lastly, the Frog, who had taken up his position on a hill, allured the
" Elephant by his croaking to believe that water was near. Then descending the hill he
" croaked again, and the Elephant attempting to follow him fell headlong down the rocks
" and was killed. Then the Laṭukika seeing the Elephant lying dead at the foot of the
" hill, alighted on his body and walked to and fro, and being fully satisfied with the
" completion of her revenge flew away."

The close agreement between the scenes of the Bharhut Sculpture and the Sinhalese
version of the legend is very remarkable. In the medallion we see :—1st. The Bird's
nest with the young ones lying on the ground beneath the Elephant's foot. 2nd. The
Bird sitting on the tree and brooding over her revenge. 3rd. The attack of the Crow
and the Flesh-fly, the former on the Elephant's head the latter on his eye. 4th. The
Elephant running away frightened with his tail between his legs. 5th. The Frog seated
on the rocky mount ; and 6th. The fall of the Elephant down the rocky cliff.

I have not the means of referring to the collections of tales preserved in the *Katha
Saritsagara*, but I have no doubt that this tale of the *Laṭukika* and the *Solitary Elephant*
was included in one or both of them, as the version of the legend as told to me in
Kashmir in 1839 by a Muhammadan accords generally with the story of the Buddhist
Jâtaka, and has even preserved some of its petty details with wonderful exactness.
Such are the sitting of the bereaved Bird on the branch of a tree after the death of her
young ones, when she meditates on revenge, and the death of the Elephant by falling
down the rocks, although the Frog is omitted. This late Kashmiri version I venture to
give in the words in which I embodied it in Kashmir in 1839, to show the strong vitality
of a popular story. The story was told to me by a Muhammadan, who had only just
heard it himself, and who was much struck by the punishment of the Elephant by such
apparently insignificant means :—

The Elephant and the Thrush.

Written in Kashmir, 1839.

Once a Thrush, in search of food,
Guardless left her nestled brood
Hanging o'er a streamlet's brim
From a young tree, tall and slim,
Backwards, forwards, to and fro,
Swinging as the wind did blow.

Led by hunger to this spray,
Chanced an Elephant to stray,
And the delicate green stem
To a mouthful tempted him.
So his trunk he gently wound
Firmly that young branch around,
Pulling with a quiet stress,
Used when certain of success,
Broke the branch, while with a scream,
Nest and brood fell in the stream,
Which soon swept them all away,
While the Elephant did stay,
Witless of the harm he'd done
Slowly, quietly munching on—
Still he munched, and still he stayed,
Revelling in the leafy shade; [munched
Still he munched, and munched, and
Till he'd comfortably lunched.

When the Thrush came back anon
And saw her little ones were gone,
With a painful scream and shrill,
All the food dropped from her bill;
On a tree she sate hard by
Wailing in her agony.   [she,
" Who hath wrought their death?" thought
" Who hath done this wrong to me
" I that ne'er hurt living form?"
(But the Thrush forgot the worm
Proving birds like men are prone
To forget sins of their own—)
When the Elephant espying
Who was still the branches eyeing,
Came conviction unto her
That he was the murderer—
But the thought gave no relief,
Adding only to her grief,

For upon so great a foe,
How could she avenge her woe.

Then afresh her shrilly scream
Startled the rushing mountain stream.
Silent next she thought upon
All her friends; but there was none
Able 'gainst a foe so strong
To avenge her cruel wrong—
Then she thought her of all those
Who by nature are his foes;—
Tiger fierce, Rhinoceros,—
Buffalo that dares to toss
His wide horns with fearless aim
'Gainst that adamantine frame,
But tiny birds these monsters knew not,
And her petty wrongs would rue not—
Aping mankind to a tittle,
Just as great men shun the little.
—Then her shrilly scream once more
Pierced the sullen torrent's roar—
But when sorrow's clouds are highest
Then the Heaven of Hope is nighest—
Just when her sad heart had failed her
Sure relief that moment hailed her
And away she joyous flew
For the Queen Bee's aid to sue
And the quick Musquito's too.

" Sister," said the Great Queen Bee,
" Thou shalt have such aid from me
" As my subjects can afford "—
And the Queen Bee kept her word.
The Musquitoes, small but able,
To annoy most irritable,
Promised also their assistance.
And, though dwelling at a distance,
Likewise spake the mountain flood
He would do all that he could—
In remembrance of the song
She had sung to him so long.

These allies were nothing slack
To begin their planned attack ;
On they came, as still as death,

Holding in their little breath ;
First with weapons sharp and thin,
Small Musquitoes pierced his skin,
For their lighter armed stings
Fitted them for skirmishings.
In the rear the great Queen Bee
Marshalled all her chivalry.

On all sides Musquitoes charge
For the enemy was large,
And displayed a warlike front
Fit the boldest heart to daunt—
Round they wheel, advance, pursue,
As expertest horsemen do,
With a sharp envenomed sting
Still for ever harassing—
Charge and wound, retire, and then,
To the charge come back again—
For these cunning little elves,
Who have warred with men themselves,
Are most swift upon the wing,
Skilled in all manœuvreing—
Hovering round their enemy,
Now they charge, and now they fly ;
Pierce, and prick, and sting, until
Their revenge hath had its fill.

Now the labouring Elephant,
Tired with fight begins to pant ;
Mad with pain, his trunk he rears,
Swings his tail, and flaps his ears ;
From his quick trunk frequent throws
Clouds of dust upon his foes—
Still the tireless little flies,
Buzzing round his winking eyes,
Keep him swinging, flapping ever,
In a fruitless vain endeavour,
To break through their wings or centres,
And get rid of his tormentors ;—
Thousands in its angry tosses

Slew he with his quick proboscis ;
Thousands slain, if slain were any
What are thousands 'mongst so many ?
He was big and powerful too,
But alone what could he do ?
He fought well, but they fought better,
He was great, their odds were greater—
So hatchets small, with many a blow,
Lay the forest giant low ;
So numerous droppings wear a stone,
So life's in many minutes gone.
Still the tireless little fellows
Blew their buzzing trumpet bellows,
Sounds of war, at midnight heard,
Much by sleepy people feared—
Still they pricked, and pierced, and stang,
Till with his roars the forest rang—
When finding fruitless all his slaughter,
Off the mad beast rushed for water.

Then advanced the Bee reserve,
Troops of mettle and tried nerve,
With their longer, stronger lances,
To his eyes made quick advances,
Piercing twixt his eyelids, they
Made him blind unto his way,
On he rushed not seeing whither
And they all rushed on together.

Then was heard the mountain torrent
Swelling with a mighty current
Craggy rocks and boulders o'er
Like the sullen thunders' roar
In the chasmous dell beneath,
Hearing which the Elephant
Down that perilous descent
Madly plunging met his death.
And the Thrush soon saw the Crow
Feeding on her giant foe.

6. Chhadantiya Jâtaka.

This bas-relief was broken into two pieces at least 150 years ago, when the lower half was carried away to Pathora by the Jâgirdar along with many other sculptures. The upper half was first found at Barhut, but the lower half was only discovered 10 months later by Babu Jamna Shankar at Pathora, seven miles distant, where it was

in daily use by a washerman, who beat his clothes upon it.[1] The story of the Chhadanta
Elephant is one of the best known of the Buddhist Jâtakas. The later form of the
legend is thus told by Hwen Thsang.[2] "When Buddha was a king of the Elephants
" with six tusks, a hunter who wished to make a prize of those precious teeth disguised
" himself in a *Kashâya*, or religious dress, and stringing his bow watched for his prey.
" The king of the Elephants, out of reverence for the *Kashâya*, immediately tore out his
" tusks and presented them to the hunter." The scene of this legend is placed by Hwen
Thsang in the neighbourhood of the *Mrigadâva* near Benâres.

        The legend is also alluded to in the Dathavansa, or History of the Tooth-relic of
Gotama Buddha.[3] "Of that Tathâgata, who, being once an Elephant of the Chhadanta
" tribe, though from being shot by a poisoned arrow, he had his body smeared with blood,
" (yet) cut off his tusks, lustrous with six coloured rays, (and) gave them to the hunter
" (who pursued him)." In this brief notice there is no allusion to the *six* tusks, which
I had always supposed to be the invention of a much later period. But the discovery of
the lower half of the Bharhut bas-relief shows that the six-tusked Elephant was known
at least as early as the time of Asoka. There is, however, no allusion to the *six* tusks in
the Pali version of Ceylon, but only to a single pair of tusks from which issued rays of
six different colours.

        The Jâtaka of the Chhadantiya Elephant is extremely curious and interesting, but
it is much too long to be given in full. I will therefore give only a short summary
compiled from Subhûti's translation of the legend :—

        Long ago a herd of 8,000 Chhadanta Elephants who had the power of passing
through the air lived close by a lake named Chhadanta, not far from the rock Himâlaya.
At that time Bodhisat was the king of the Elephants. His body was white, and his
mouth and feet were red. His tusks possessed the power of shedding rays of six
different colours. He lived in a cave with the two Queen Elephants Mahâsubhadra and
Chulla Subhadra.

        The lake Chhadanta was square, with waters blue as sapphire. It was surrounded
by seven ranges of rocks, named respectively *Suvarna*, *Mane*, *Surya*, *Chandra*, *Udaka*,
Mahakâla, and *Chullakâla*. To the North-east there was a large Banian tree. One day
the King Elephant having shaken a tree under which his two Queens were standing,
the flower dust fell on the Elder Queen Mahâsubhadra. Whilst only dry sticks, leaves,
and ants fell on the younger Queen Chulla Subhadra, who from that time cherished a
hatred of the King on account of his supposed preference for Mahâsubhadra. Shortly
after Chulla Subhadra having seen the King Elephant present sweet fruits, honey, and
lotus roots to 500 Pase Buddhas, made a similar gift herself, at the same time wishing
that after her death she might be born as the daughter of the king of *Madu*, be named
Subhadra, and when grown up she might become the wife of the king of Benares ; that
she should then please her husband so much as to prevail on him to send a hunter to
shoot the King Elephant with a poisoned arrow, and to cut off his tusks, which emitted
rays of six different colours.

        All happens according to her wish, and a huntsman named Sonuttara is sent to kill
the king of the Chhadanta Elephants, and to bring back his tusks. The Queen describes

---

[1] See Plate XXVI.   [2] Julien's Hwen Thsang, II. 360.
[3] Dathavansa by Mutu Coomara Swamy, p. 5, c. III. V. 31.

to him the route he is to follow until he reaches the crest of the seventh rocky ridge named Suvarna, which surrounds the Chhadanta lake. From this rock he will see the huge Banian tree under which lives the king of Chhadanta Elephants. The hunter accordingly started on his journey, and having reached the crest of the Suvarna ridge he beheld the king standing under the great Banian tree surrounded by his herd of 8,000 Chhadanta Elephants. Here he stayed some time to watch the king, and having observed that he always retired to the same spot after bathing he dug a pit there, and covered it carefully over, leaving only one small hole in the middle for his arrow to go through. In this pit he hid himself, dressed in a yellow robe like a priest, and when the Chhadanta king after his bath retired to his favourite spot, the Hunter drew his bow and shot his arrow straight into the navel of the Elephant. The pain was so great that the king roared, and trumpeted three times, and the whole of 8,000 Elephants then roared, and dispersed in all directions to seek for the shooter. His Queen Mahâsubhadra, who was supporting him, alone remained. Then reasoning with himself the king of the Elephants understood that the arrow had come from the earth beneath, and sending Subhadra away he quickly tore up the ground, and lifting the planks began to feel the sides of the pit with his trunk. The artful huntsman then placed the yellow robe of the priesthood in the Elephant's trunk, and the pacified animal at once drew him out unhurt, and thus addressed him: "If a man who is still corrupted by passion, who has " not given up worldly passions, or who does not speak the truth puts on the yellow " robe he is like a monkey covered with a lion's skin; if a man suppresses his passions, " practices all the moral virtues, spends his time in religious meditation, and speaks the " truth, he is fit to wear the yellow robe which is the dress of the Buddhas."

Being unwilling to kill him in spite of his baseness, the royal Elephant asked the Hunter why he had shot him whether on his own account or for another. Then the Hunter told him everything, and the Elephant, recognising all the facts of the story, thus addressed him: " Chulla Subhadra cherishing a hatred against me for a mere trifle has " sent you to kill me, and to carry off my tusks. They will, however, be of no use to " her, but you may cut them off before I die." The Hunter being unable to reach the Elephant's tusks on account of his great height, the animal told him to place the saw in his trunk, when this was done he quickly cut off his own tusks, and holding them out with his trunk, said, "Friend Hunter, I offer you these tusks not because I am tired of " them, nor because I hope to become either Sakra or Brahma after my death, but " because I expect to become a Buddha which is millions of times more valuable than " they are." The king of the Elephants shortly after died, and the herd burned his body on a funeral pile, while innumerable Buddhas standing around chaunted his praises.

The Hunter Sonuttara, guided by the light of the six-coloured rays of the tusks, reached Benares in seven days. Then laying the tusks before the Queen he said, "Respected Queen, in your previous birth having cherished hatred against your husband, " the king of the Chhadanta Elephants, you wished to kill him. Accordingly I have " killed him and here are his tusks." But the Queen then began to reflect that in causing the death of such a noble animal she had committed a very cruel deed; and remembering all the virtues of the Elephant king, such a deep sorrow came upon her that she died the same day of a broken heart.

The Bharhut Sculpture agrees generally with the Sinhalese Jâtaka; but there is one important difference between them which seems to me, to point to an earlier origin for the Bharhut version. In the Pali account the Elephant is a huge animal, so lofty that the Hunter cannot reach his tusks and accordingly the royal animal kindly cuts off his own tusks and presents them to Hunter. This also is the version of the legend as heard by the Chinese pilgrim Hwen Thsang in the seventh century. But in the Bharhut Sculpture the Elephant is of the natural size, and is represented as kneeling down to enable the Hunter to cut off his tusks with greater ease.

Another version of this Jâtaka is given by Mr. Beal from the Chinese.[1] In this version the young Chhadanta Elephant, who is described as of a white colour, and with six tusks, was captured by a Hunter by command of Brahmadatta Raja of Benares. But when the king heard that the young Elephant had been the support of his old parents, he gave him his liberty, saying:

> Go and welcome thou faithful Elephant Nâga
> Nourish and cherish thy parents as in duty bound,
> I would rather lose my life, and end it now,
> Than cause thee and them the grief of separation.

7. Isi-Singiya Jâtaka.

The story represented in this Sculpture is known in Ceylon as the *Nâlini Jâtaka*, from the name of the heroine who plays a principal part in the legend.[2] The title of *Isi-Singiya Jâtaka*, or the "Rishi Sringa Birth," is altogether unknown in Ceylon; but the subject was at once recognised by M. Minayeff when I showed him the photograph, and afterwards by Subhûti, who has kindly furnished me with a full translation of the legend. As the subject is not a delicate one, a very short summary of the story will be sufficient:—

In days gone by when Brahmadatta was Raja of Benares, our great Bodhisat was born as a Brahman, who in due time became a *joshi* and retired to the Himâla forest, where he perfected himself in knowledge and piety. It happened that a Doe having grazed over the spot where Bodhisat had made water, became pregnant, and in due time gave birth to a boy who was brought up by the ascetics under the name of *Isi Singe*, or Rishi Sringa. They clad him in the dress of a recluse, and taught him all the rules observed by the ascetics. So that in a short time he became a very learned and a very pious Rishi. As his piety and religious merit increased with his years, he acquired such power that the marble throne of Sakra king of the Heavens became too hot for him to sit upon. Sakra sought for the cause and soon discovered that his throne was threatened by the overwhelming piety and religious merit of the Rishi Sringa. He accordingly thought of a stratagem to vitiate the purity of the Rishi, and caused a drought throughout the country of Benares so that no rain fell there for three whole years.

The Raja of Benares attempted to stop the drought by performing meritorious acts in person, but they were of no avail; and he was beginning to despair when the god Sakra (Indra) appeared to him in a dream and informed him that the drought was caused by the prevailing merits of the young ascetic Sringi Rishi, and that it could be stopped only by corrupting his purity, which might be accomplished by the Raja's daughter Nâlini.

---

[1] Romantic History of Buddha, p. 366.   [2] See Plate XXVI.

The Princess Nálini accordingly departs for the forest near the Himála mountains, where she adopts the dress of an ascetic, and during the absence of Bodhisatta succeeds in corrupting the merits of Sringi Rishi, who had never seen a woman. The Princess then departed, and the young Rishi became sick with longing for his friend, and entreated Bodhisatta to take him to the monastery to which the supposed monk had retired. The great Bodhisatta having heard the entreaties of the young monk, perceived that his merits had been clouded by some woman, gave him a long address on the dangers of intercourse with women, and wound up by telling him that it was very fortunate the she-demon had left him without devouring him.

The young monk trembled at the words of Bodhisatta and besought his forgiveness, saying that he would not leave his monastery to go after the woman. He then applied himself so assiduously to his religious duties that he acquired a second time the powers of a holy Rishi, and when he died, received a new birth in the Brahmaloka.

In the Bharhut bas-relief there is only a portion of the legend represented in the birth of the young Rishi, who is taken up by Bodhisatta himself in the presence of other Rishis. The peculiar dress of the Rishis, who were fire worshippers, and the simple style of their dwelling form the only interesting parts of this curious but repulsive legend.

The Sringi Rishi would seem to have been rather prone to temptation, as Hwen Thsang records the temptation and fall of the Rishi Ekasringa.[1]

8. YAMBUMANE AVAYESI JÁTAKA.

In the Páli books of Ceylon this legend is known as the *Andhabhuta Játaka*, or "Blind-man Birth." This identification is due to the kindness of Subhúti who also furnished me with a translation of the Játaka from which I have made the following summary :—

In days of yore there was a virtuous Raja in Benares named Brahmadatta. By his Queen he had a son who was comely in person, and well versed in every branch of science. But he was an inveterate gambler, and when playing the gold dice on the silver board with his minister he would recite the following verse :—

> *Sabbá nadi wankayatá,*
> *Sabbe katthamayo waná,*
> *Sabbittho karopápa*
> *Labhamánáte wátake.*

> Like as rivers all meander,
> Like as forests teem with wood,
> So would every woman wander
> From the right way if she could.

The minister finding his wealth nearly exhausted began to think that his want of success must be due to the truth of the king's stanza, and he resolved to test it by taking to wife a woman who had never seen a man. So he procured a newly-born female child and had her brought up in a secluded house where she saw none but women. As she grew up very beautiful the minister married her, and when he next went to gamble,

---

[1] Julien's Hwen Thsang, II. 124.

no sooner had the king repeated his customary stanza than the minister added "my wife excepted." As the king continued to lose from that day he got angry, and determined to corrupt the minister's wife. So he employed a young man of handsome appearance to open a shop near the minister's house. Here the shopkeeper having observed an old woman who went out and came back again daily with a basket, one day rushed suddenly before her and embraced her, and declared himself her long lost son. So they became friends, and the shopkeeper prevailed on his new mother to take all the goods required for the house from him without payment. Some months had passed in this way when the shopkeeper pretended to be very sick, and when the old woman inquired what was the matter with him he told her that he had heard so much of the beauty of her young mistress that he had become sick from love and could get no rest, and that he was sure he would not recover until he had seen her face. So the old woman arranged that he should be carried into the house in her basket, and when the minister's wife saw him she was so fascinated that she kept him for two days in her private apartments. After some time the young shopkeeper obtained such influence over her that she made no opposition when her lover proposed to knock the minister on the head. Accordingly when her husband returned the young wife asked him to play the harp blindfolded so that she might dance in his presence unabashed, and further that she might be allowed to give him a knock on the head. To this the fond old minister consented. No sooner was he blindfolded than the shopkeeper appeared on the scene and the two lovers danced together while the blindfolded minister played on the harp. Suddenly the young shopkeeper gave him such a tremendous blow on the head that "his deep-sunken eyeballs were almost thrown out of their sockets," and before he recovered from the blow the lover had gone back in the basket to his shop.

From the day that his wife had proved untrue the minister's good luck had forsaken him, and when the king told him of the faithless conduct of his wife, he returned to his house quite dejected and accused her of incontinence. But the cunning woman protested her innocence, and declared that she would cast herself into the fire as a proof of her virtue. Having sent timely notice to her lover, when the day appointed for the ordeal arrived, and the wife was ready to cast herself into the fire, the shopkeeper suddenly rushed on the scene, and seizing her by the hand, exclaimed, "Why does this hard-" hearted Brahman thus treat this innocent young woman?" On which the wife at once cried out, "I am willing to take my oath, and to undergo this trial by fire, that except " this young shopkeeper who has just stopped me from entering the fire, no other man " but my husband the minister has ever touched me." But the minister perceived her cunning, and the young woman was turned out of his house.

The Bharhut sculpture represents the principal scene of the legend where the blind-folded husband plays the harp while his wife and her lover dance before him. As the scene is said to have taken place in the minister's house, the building in the bas-relief must represent an Indian private house of the better sort shortly after the time of Asoka. The Sinhalese name of *Andhabhuta Játaka*, or the "Blind-man Birth," is perhaps only a popular description of the scene derived from the principal figure. Of the title inscribed above the Bharhut sculpture,

Yambumane avayesi Játakam,

I am unable to offer any explanation.

The Pillar on which the scene is represented is now at Pathora, seven miles distant from Bharhut, from whence it was carried away four generations back, when the ancestors of the present *Jágirdar* received his estate from the reigning *Raja*. A portion of each side of the Pillar, as far as the curved sockets for the rails extended, has been cut away to make it fit into its present position as a stone beam in a recently erected cenotaph outside the village of Pathora. The medallion face of the Pillar has luckily been placed inside the building, but it is of course placed sideways, and was thickly coated with whitewash. Much of the whitewash was removed with acetic acid, but enough of it still remains to spoil any attempt at making a perfect photograph. The accompanying photograph is, however, sufficiently good to show all the details of the dresses as well as all the letters of the inscription.[1]

9. KURUNGA MIGA JĀTAKA.

The bas-relief representing this curious legend was found in its present condition in a small village one mile and a half from Bharhut. This and the following sculpture once formed the bosses or medallions of a single bar of the Railing. The stone was carried off long ago, and afterwards split down the middle so as to separate the two sculptured scenes. All the side portions of the bar, including its inscription, were cut away.[1] But the story is too clearly told in the sculpture to require a label, and the instant I saw it I recognized it as the *Kurunga-miga Játaka*, or "Kurunga-Deer Birth." This legend has been fortunate in being translated by the eminent Pali scholar Mr. V. Fausböll. I possess also a translation by the learned Buddhist priest Subhúti. I here annex Mr. Fausböll's version:—[2]

" In times past, while Brahmadatta reigned in Bárânasi, Bodhisatta having become
" a Kurunga-deer, took up his abode in the wood, in a thicket not far from a lake.
" At the top of a tree not far from that lake sat a Woodpecker, and in the lake there
" lived a Tortoise. Thus those three companions lived pleasantly together. Then a
" Deer-hunter, roaming in the wood, having seen Bodhisatta's footmarks near a water-
" pool, (and) having placed a trap made of leather (thongs, and as strong) as an iron
" chain, went (his way). Bodhisatta, having come to drink water, (and being) caught
" in the trap during the first watch (of the night) shrieked (frantically) as a prisoner.
" At his shriek the Woodpecker, coming down from the top of the tree, and the Tortoise
" out of the water, consulted (together, saying) What is to be done ? Then the Wood-
" pecker, addressing the Tortoise (said), Friend, you have teeth, cut this trap; I will
" go and manage (it so) that he shall not come; thus by the efforts made by us our
" companion will obtain life; (and) explaining this matter (he) pronounced the first
" stanza:—

> 1. " Therefore the leathern trap
> Cut with thy teeth, O Tortoise,
> I will manage (it) so
> That the Hunter shall not come."

The Tortoise began to gnaw at the leather thongs. The Woodpecker went to the village where the Hunter dwelt. The Hunter at dawn, having taken (his) hunting knife,

---

[1] See Plate XXVI.　　　[2] In Royal Asiatic Society's Journal, N. S., Vol. V. p. 10.

K 2

went out. The Bird perceiving that he was about to go out, shrieked aloud, shaking (his) wings, and struck him in the face when he was going out at the front door. The Hunter (said to himself), " I have been struck by a bird of bad omen," (and) so (saying) he returned, lay down a little (while), and then got up again and took (his) knife. The Bird (thought), " this (man) went out the first (time) by the front door, now he will go out by the back door," (and) seeing this he went and sat down at the back door. But the Hunter thought, " when I went out by the front door I saw a bird of bad omen, now I will go out at the back door," (and) so (thinking) he went out by the back door. The Bird again shrieking aloud went and struck (him) in the face. The Hunter, again struck by the bird of bad omen, (thought,) " this (bird) will not allow me to go out," (and) so returning he lay down until daybreak, and (then) at the dawn of morning took his knife and went out. The Bird went away hastily and told Bodhisatta that the Hunter was coming. At this moment, with exception of one thong, the other thongs had been cut by the Tortoise. But his teeth looked as if they were going to fall out, (and his) mouth was soiled with blood. Bodhisatta, seeing that the Hunter had taken (his) knife, and was coming on with the speed of lightning, burst that thong and entered the wood. The Bird (now) set himself on the top of a tree. But the Tortoise from weakness lay down there. The Hunter, after throwing the Tortoise into (his) bag, fastened (it) to a post. Bodhisatta, on (his) return, seeing (what had taken place) and knowing that the Tortoise had been caught, (thought,) " I will preserve (my) companion's life," (and) so, feigning to be weak, he appeared before the Hunter. He (thought), " this (deer) must be weak, I will kill him," (and) so, taking (his) knife, he followed (him). Bodhisatta, neither going very far (away) nor very near, entered the wood, taking him (with him). (But) when he knew that he had gone a great distance he changed his pace and went (back) with the rapidity of the wind another way, (and) when he had thrown up the bag into the air, with (his) horn, and let it fall and be torn on the ground, he drew out the Tortoise. The Woodpecker descended from the tree. (Then) Bodhisatta said admonishingly to the two (others) " I got life through you ; by " you has been done unto me what ought to be done to a companion ; now when the " Hunter comes he will seize you, therefore, friend Woodpecker ! take your children " and get to another (place), and you, friend Tortoise ! go into the water." They did so. The Master having become enlightened, pronounced the second stanza :—

" The Tortoise went into the water,
The Deer entered the wood,
The Woodpecker from the top of the tree
Carried (his) children far away."

The Hunter coming (back) to that place, (and) not seeing anyone, took (his) torn sack and went to his house, seized with distress.

The three companions, on the other hand, without breaking off (their mutual) confidence during life (at last) passed (away) according to (their) deeds.

The Master having given this moral instruction wound up the Játaka thus : " At " that time the Hunter was Devadatta, the Woodpecker Sáriputta, the Tortoise Moggallâna, " but the Kurunga-deer (was) myself." The " Kurunga-Deer Birth."

10. (BULL AND WOLF.)

The subject of this bas-relief is unknown to me, and Subhúti tells me that he is
unable to identify it. There are only three actors in the scene, a humped Bull standing
in a pond of water, and two Wolves, one of which is seated on the bank of the pond,
while the other has been caught in a snare and is hanging by one of his hind legs from
the top of a pole.[1] I call the animals wolves and not tigers, as the one seated on the
bank would seem to be afraid of entering the water. Now this is a trait of a
wolf, and not of a tiger, who takes to the water freely. In fact I have myself seen a
tiger swim across the Irawadi River, and also three lions swim over the Sutlej on two
different occasions. I think, therefore, that the snared animal as well as the other on the
bank of the pool must be wolves. The shortness of their tails is also in favour of this
identification.

The snare represented in the bas-relief is one well known in India, where it is used
for catching any large beasts of prey including tigers. A description and sketch of one
now used in Arakan will be found in the Journal of the Bengal Asiatic Society.[2]

11. HANSA JÁTAKA.

This sculpture is very much broken, the whole of the lower half and portions of both
sides being lost. Enough, however, remains in the head and neck of a Goose (hansa) and
in the head and outspread tail of a Peacock to identify the story, even without the
accompanying label, as the *Hansa Játaka*, or "Goose Birth."[3] The only version of the
legend that I have been able to find is given by Upham, under the title of *Nada Játaka*.
As his abstract is a short one, it may be quoted entire :[4]—"In this *Játaka* is related the
" story of the royal *Hansa*, the king of the Birds, who assembled all his subjects in
" an extensive plain, in order that his daughter might choose a husband from amongst
" them. She singled out the Peacock, who vain at the preference, immediately began to
" dance, and spreading out his tail, displayed to the company those parts which ought
" never to be exposed to view, at which indelicacy his Majesty was so much shocked
" that he instantly broke off the match."

12. KINARA JÁTAKA.

This small bas-relief is unfortunately broken, so that the lower halves of the three
figures are wanting; but there can be no doubt that the two standing figures are
intended for Kinnaras, male and female, in accordance with the title of the Játaka. The
Kinnara was a fabulous being, the upper half of whose body was human, and lower half
that of a bird, and the big leaves or feathers which go round the bodies of the two
standing figures, must have separated their human bodies from their bird legs.[5]

In a list of the 550 Játakas of Ceylon, kindly furnished to me by Subhúti, there is only
one in which the name of Kinnara occurs. This is the *Chandra Kinara Játaka*, which
agrees with the Bharhut bas-relief in limiting its actors to a Raja and a pair of Kinnaras,
male and female. The following is a brief summary of the story made from Subhúti's
translation of the Játaka :—

---

[1] See Plate XXVII.   [2] See Vol. IV. Plate IV.   [3] See Plate XXVII.
[4] Sacred and Historical Books of Ceylon, III. 289.   [5] See Plate XXVII.

"In the days of yore when Brahmadatta was Raja of Benares, the great Bodhisatta
"was born as a Chandana Kinnara in the Himála forest where he lived with his wife
"Chandrika on the silver mountain. It happened that the Raja of Benares went out
"deer shooting towards the Himála forest during the hot season when the Chandana
"Kinnaras leave the Silver Mountain for the banks of a river. Then anointed with
"Sandal wood (Chandana) and other perfumes and decked with garlands of flowers,
"they danced on the bank of the stream, or bathed in its waters, or seated on beds of
"flowers, they sang songs to the sound of the bambu flute. There danced the Kinnara
"Queen accompanied by song, when the Raja of Benares attracted by the sweet voice
"drew near and beheld the scene. Allured by her beauty the Raja thought to obtain
"possession of her by killing her husband, whom he instantly shot with an arrow. The
"Raja then tried to soothe the Queen by making her his chief wife, and the head of
"sixteen thousand women. But the Queen fled to the Silver Mountain cursing the
"Raja. 'O cruel Raja, who hast slain my husband, the pain and sorrow which thou hast
"'caused me shall be the lot of thy wife. Thy mother shall become mad, frequenting
"'graveyards, and thy daughter shall be childless.'
"When the Raja had gone, the Queen descended the Silver Mountain towards the
"body of her husband. Then carrying the corpse to the top of the hill she placed the
"head on her lap and invoked the Devas to restore her husband to life. The appeal was
"heard by Indra, who, descending to the earth in the form of an old Brahman, raised the
"dead Kinnara king to life. The loving couple then retired to the Silver Mountain, and
"lived happily ever afterwards."

If this is the same story as is represented in the Bharhut bas-relief, then the sculptured version differs from the Pali legend of Ceylon in making the pair of Kinnaras dance
before the Raja of Benares while he is seated on a chair or throne.

13. ASADRISA JÁTAKA.

This sculpture is unfortunately much broken, and any inscription which it may have
had is lost; but the story of Prince Asadrisa, the great Archer, is too clearly told to
leave any doubt as to its identification.[1] This Játaka is one of those given by Spence
Hardy, from whose work the following translation is extracted:—[2]

"In this birth, Bodhisat was the son of Brahmadatta, king of Benares, and was
"called Asadrisa. He had a younger brother, Brahmadatta. On arriving at a proper
"age, he received all necessary instructions from a learned preceptor; and the king at
"his death commanded that the kingdom should be given to Asadrisa, and the vazirship
"to his brother. The nobles were willing that the royal command should be obeyed;
"but as Bodhisat positively refused the kingdom, it was given to his younger brother,
"and he became vazir, or inferior king. A certain noble afterwards insinuated to the
"king that Asadrisa was plotting against his life; on hearing which he became enraged,
"and commanded that the traitor should be apprehended. But Bodhisat received
"warning of the danger in which he was placed, and fled to the City of Sámáya. On
"arriving at the gate of the city, he sent to inform the king that a famous archer had
"arrived in his dominions. The king gave orders that he should be admitted into the
"royal presence, and asked what wages he would require; and when he was answered
"that a thousand masurans would be a reasonable salary, he gave his promise that this

---

[1] See Plate XXVII.　　　　[2] Manual of Buddhism, p. 114.

" sum should be allowed. The king's former archers were naturally envious that a mere
" stranger should receive an allowance so much superior to their own. One day the king
" having entered the royal garden, commanded that a couch should be placed, and a
" cloth spread, at the foot of a mango tree. When seated, he espied a mango fruit at
" the very uppermost part of the tree ; and as it was impossible that any one could get
" it by climbing, he intimated that the archers should be called, who were to bring it
" down by an arrow. The archers of course gave way to the man of the thousand
" *masurans;* and the king repeated his command to Asadrisa, who requested that the
" royal couch might be removed from under the tree. The archers perceiving that the
" Bodhisat had neither bow nor arrow in his hand, resolved among themselves, that if
" he were to request their assistance, they would refuse him the use of their weapons.
" Bodhisat then laid aside his usual garment, arrayed himself in a splendid robe, girt his
" sword by his side, and his quiver upon his shoulder ; and putting together a bow that
" was made of separate pieces, jointed, with a coral necklace as the bow-string, he
" approached the king, and inquired whether the fruit was to be felled by the arrow
" as it went up or as it returned. The king replied that it would be the greater
" wonder if the fruit were brought down by the returning arrow. Bodhisat gave notice
" that as the arrow would proceed right into the firmament, it would be necessary to
" wait for its return with a little patience. An arrow was then shot, which cleft a small
" portion from the mango, then went to the other world, and was seized by the Devas.
" Another arrow was shot, and after some time, there was a noise in the air, thrum,
" thrum, thrum, at which the people were afraid. Bodhisat told them it was the sound
" of the arrow ; and they were then more fearful, as each one thought it might fall
" upon his own body. The arrow, as it returned, divided the mango from the tree ; and
" Bodhisat going to the place, caught the fruit in one hand and the arrow in the other.
" At the sight of this, the people a thousand times shouted in triumph, a thousand
" times clapped their hands, and a thousand times waved their kerchiefs round their
" heads and danced ; and the king gave Asadrisa countless treasures.

      " At this time seven kings, having heard that Asadrisa was dead, surrounded the
" City of Benares, and gave the king his choice, either to fight or to deliver up his
" kingdom. Brahmadatta sighed for the assistance of his brother, and having received
" information of his place of retreat, sent a noble to invite him to return. Asadrisa at
" once took leave of Sámaya, and on arriving near Benares, he ascended a scaffold, from
" which he shot an arrow, with an epistle attached to the following effect : ' This is the
" ' first arrow from the hand of Asadrisa ; if the second should be sent, you will all be
" ' slain.' The arrow fell upon a dish from which the seven kings were eating rice, and
" as they thought within themselves that the threat would certainly be accomplished,
" they fled to their own cities. Thus Bodhisat conquered the seven kings, without the
" shedding of a single drop of blood. Brahmadatta now offered to resign the kingdom,
" but Bodhisat again refused it, and going to the forest of Himála, by strict asceticism,
" he gained supernatural power, and afterwards passed away to the highest of the
" celestial regions."

14. DASARATHA JÁTAKA.

      This scene has also lost its label from a break in the stone, but the story is so
distinctly indicated by the figures and accessories as to be recognizable at the first
glance. As the Buddhist story of Dasaratha differs in several particulars from the

Brahmanical version, I venture to give it in full from the translation of Mr. Fausböll.[1] The bas-relief illustrates the interview between Ráma and his brother Bharata, when the former refuses to return, and gives his straw shoes to Bharata, telling him, Well then, until my return these shoes shall reign."[2]

" In times past there lived in Báránasi a great king, Dasaratha by name, (who) after " abandoning a reckless life reigned with justice. His queen (who was) the head wife " of 16,000 women bore (unto him) two sons and one daughter. The elder son was the " sage Ráma by name, the second the Prince Lakkhana, the daughter the Princess Sita " by name. Afterwards the queen died. The king, when she was dead, after having " for a long time given way to the sway of sorrow (was at length) brought to reason by " (his) ministers, (and) when he had performed the necessary funeral ceremonies he set " another in the place of queen. She became dear (and) pleasing to the king. She " afterwards having conceived, and having gone through the ceremonies (on occasion) " of her conception, bore a son. They named him Prince Bharata. From love to (this) " son the king said, '(My) dear, I grant thee a boon, accept it.' She having accepted " (it but) leaving it in abeyance (for a while), at the time, when the prince was (about) " seven (or) eight years (old) went to the king and said, 'Lord, a boon was conferred " 'by you upon my son; now grant it him.' 'Take (it my) dear.' 'Lord, give the " 'kingdom to my son.' The king snapping his fingers (angrily at her) reprimanded " her (saying), 'Wretched outcast, my two sons shine like masses of fire, thou askest " ' (me to give) the kingdom to thy son after having put them both to death.' She " (was at first) terrified (and) entered the inner apartment, (but) on subsequent days " she again and again asked the king for the kingdom. The king, however, not granting " her the boon, thought, 'Women as (well) known, are ungrateful (and) treacherous ; " ' this one, either by writing false letters or by resorting to mean bribery, will have my " ' sons killed,' (and) so having summoned (his) sons (and) told them the matter (he " said), '(My) dears, if you (continue to) live here, there may be obstacles (in your " ' way), go (therefore) to a neighbouring kingdom, or to the forest ; come back at the " ' time of my funeral pyre and seize upon the paternal kingdom,' (and) so having said, " after again calling the astrologers and asking (them) the limit of his life, and hearing " that another 12 years would pass (before his death), he said, ' (My) dears, after the " ' lapse of 12 years (hence) return and raise the (royal) umbrella.' They said, ' Well ;' " bowed to (their) father, and descended from the palace weeping. The Princess Sítá " (saying), 'I too will go away with my dear brothers,' bowed to her father and went " out weeping. These three having gone out surrounded by a multitude (of people), " and having, after sending back the multitude, gradually entered the Himávanta, built " a hermitage in a region abounding with water (and) where various kinds of fruits " were easily to be had, and resided (there) subsisting on fruits. The sage Lakkhana, " however, and Sítá demanding of the sage Ráma (said), 'You stand in our father's " ' place, therefore do you stay at the hermitage, we will bring fruits and nourish you,' " and so they took (his) promise. From that (moment) the sage Ráma remains there. " The others brought fruits and watched over him. (While) they were residing (there), " living on fruits, the great Dasaratha ended his days from sorrow for his sons in the " ninth year (after their departure). Having finished the funeral rites over him the " Queen said, 'Raise the umbrella for my son, Prince Bharata.' But the ministers

---

[1] Dasaratha Játaka, p. 13.   [2] See Plate XXVII.

" (said): ' the masters of the umbrella live in the forest,' (and) so (they) did not allow
" it. The Prince Bharata (saying to himself): ' I will bring my brother the sage Râma
" ' from the forest and raise the umbrella (for him),' took the five royal insignia, reached
" with a fourfold army his dwelling-place, and after halting the army at a short distance
" entered the hermitage with a few attendants at a time, when the sage Lakkhana and
" Sitâ had gone to the forest. Having approached the sage Râma, who was sitting at
" ease and without desires at the door of the hermitage like a fixed golden statue, and
" having bowed (to him) and, while standing apart, told the tidings of the king's (death),
" he fell down at (his) feet, together with the attendants, and wept. The sage Râma
" neither grieved nor wept, there was not even the slightest commotion of his senses.
" While Bharata was thus sitting weeping, the other two at the evening time came
" back bringing (with them) various kinds of fruits. (Then) the sage Râma thought:
" ' These are young, they have no discriminative understanding, as I have; if on a
" ' sudden they are told, "Your father is dead," they will not be able to bear the
" ' sorrow, (but) their hearts will break; by some means I will get them to go down
" ' into the water, and (then) I will tell (them) these tidings.' Then showing them a
" pool in front of them (he said): ' At length you have come, this be your punishment,
" ' go down into this water and stay (there,' and) so (having said) he at the same time
" pronounced the first half stanza:—

" 1a. Come Lakkhana and Sitâ

" both go down into the water.

" They, at (his) mere call, went down and stayed (there). Then telling them those
" tidings, he pronounced the (other) half stanza:—

" 1b. Thus says this Bharata:

" ' The king Dasaratha is dead.'

" Hearing the tidings of (their) father's death they became insensible. He again
" told them, (and) they again became insensible. Thus for the third time having
" become insensible, the attendants raised them up, took (them) out of the water and
" comforted (them). They all sat mutually crying and lamenting. Then Prince Bharata
" thought: ' My brother Prince Lakkhana and (my sister Princess Sitâ, having heard
" ' the tidings of (their) father's death, are not able to restrain their sorrow, but the sage
" ' Râma mourns not (and) laments not, what can be the reason of his not mourning? I
" ' will ask him,' (and) so asking him he pronounced the second stanza:—

" 2. ' By what strength (of mind,) O Râma,

" ' dost thou not mourn what is to be mourned?

" ' having heard (that thy) father (is) dead

" ' pain does not overwhelm thee.'

" Then the sage Râma, telling him the reason of his not mourning, (said):—

" ' What cannot be preserved

" ' by man, even if much bewailed

" ' for such a thing's sake why should the

" ' intelligent (and) wise (man) distress himself?' "

(Here follow nine other stanzas.)

" Thus by these stanzas be elucidated the uncertainty (of all things). The assembly
" having heard this religious discourse of the sage Râma, elucidating the uncertainty
" (of all things) became free from sorrow. Then Prince Bharata bowing to the sage

" Râma, said : ' Accept the kingdom of Bârânasi ' ' (My) dear, take Lakkhana and the
" ' Princess Sîtâ and go and rule the kingdom.' ' But you, Lord ? ' ' (My) dear, my
" ' father said to me, " After the lapse of twelve years then come and rule," if I go now I
" ' shall not fulfil his words, but having passed three years more (here) I will come,'
" ' Who shall reign during that time ? ' ' Do you reign ? ' ' We shall not.' ' Well then,
" ' until my return these shoes shall reign,' so (saying) he took off his straw shoes
" and gave (them) to (Bharata). Those three persons, having taken the shoes and
" bowed to the sage Râma, went to Bârânasi, surrounded by a multitude (of people).
" For three years the shoes reigned. The ministers, after placing the straw-shoes on
" the royal couch, consider the case ; if it be badly considered the shoes strike against
" each other. (Taking warning) by this sign they again consider (the case). At the
" time when the case is duly considered, the shoes sit together noiselessly. The sage
" Râma at the end of three years went out of the forest, and on reaching the city of
" Bârânasi entered the Park. Having learned his arrival, the princes, surrounded by
" ministers, went to the Park, and after making Sîtâ queen, they anointed them both.
" Thus having received the (royal) unction, Mahâsatta standing on a chariot, entered the
" city with a large retinue, and after a reverential salutation having ascended the upper
" story of the magnificent palace Suchandaka, he from that time reigned with justice
" during 16,000 years, and (then) went to heaven.

<blockquote>
" During ten thousand years
" and sixty centuries
" the fine-necked and great-armed
" Râma reigned."
</blockquote>

" This stanza by him who possessed universal knowledge illustrates the matter."

In the Brahmanical account of this scene, the interview with Bharata takes place at
the mountain of Chitrakuta, to which Râma and Sîtâ had retired after his father's
declaration that he had given the throne of Ayodhya to his younger brother Bharata.
The latter refused the throne, and followed his brother to Chitrakuta, and urged him to
return to Ayodhya. This Râma persistently refused. "Bharata then took a pair of
" new shoes, adorned with gold, and turned to his brother Râma and said :—' Put on
" ' these shoes, I pray you, and they shall furnish the means of securing the good of all.'
" The heroic Râma then put on the shoes, and returned them to the magnanimous
" Bharata. And Bharata bowed to him, and said to Râma : ' O Râma, I will for
" ' fourteen years assume the matted hair—and the habit of a devotee, and subsist on
" ' fruits and roots—waiting your return, I will commit the management of the Râj to
" ' your shoes, and reside without the city ; and unless you return to Ayodhya within five
" ' days of the completion of the fourteenth year, I will enter the fire.' "[1]

This is the scene which is believed to be represented in the sculpture,[2] where we
see Bharata standing in front of Râma and Sîtâ, and holding in his right hand an
umbrella and a pair of shoes. In his left hand he holds a pole which rests on his
shoulder. Something which was attached to the pole has been lost by the breaking of
the sculpture. In mid-front is a dog, which apparently belongs to Râma, as it sits at his
feet facing Bharata.

---

[1] See Wheeler's Râmâyana.   [2] See Plate XXVII.

On his return to Ayodhya, Bharata said to his assembled subjects, "Bring hither " the state Umbrella! By these shoes of my elder brother is justice established in the " Ráj." The umbrella was therefore an essential part of the installation of the shoes, as shown in the bas-relief. The story ends with a description of the usual transaction of business under the new rule of Ráma's shoes: "Himself (Bharata) holding the royal " umbrella over the shoes, while the *Chámara* (or *Chauri*) was taken by Satrughna, and " all the affairs of the government were transacted under the authority of the shoes. " The fortunate Bharata installed with the shoes of his elder brother, and paying " homage to them, thus governed the Ráj. All the presents that were brought, and all " the business of state which occurred he first laid before the shoes, and afterwards did " as occasion required."

15. Isi-Migo Játaka.

The small scene labelled as the *Isi-migo Játaka* or " Rishi-deer Birth," is represented in one of the panels of the coping.[1] It contains two figures, one a man, apparently a royal huntsman by his costume, and deer, with a tree in the background. The whole scene I believe is intended to represent the famous meeting between the Raja of Benáres and the King of the Deer (Buddha in a former birth) in the Deer-park (Mrigadáva) at Isi-pattana. The name of *Isi-migo* I take to be an abbreviation of *Isi-pattana-migo* or *Rishi-pattana-migo*.[2] The legend, which is told at length by Hwen Thsang, is briefly as follows:[3]—In a previous existence when Buddha was King of the Deer, the Raja of Benáres was a zealous hunter, and caused great loss amongst the Deer as much by setting fire to the grass as by his arrows. One day therefore the King of the Deer boldly advanced towards the Raja, and proposed that he should give up hunting, in return for which he should receive one Deer daily. The Raja agreed to the proposal. This is the scene which I suppose to be represented in the Bharhut sculpture. In the more interesting sequel of the legend, the subsequent interview between the Rája and the King of the Deer takes place in the palace, and as no building is represented in the bas-relief I conclude that the subject of the sculpture is the first interview in the *Mrigadáva*, or Deer-park.

16. Uda Játaka.

The actors in this scene are a holy Rishi with a pair of dogs and a pair of cats.[4] The simple title of *Uda Játaka* does not occur in the long list of the 550 Játakas of Ceylon; but there is an *Udasa Játaka* or *Udachani Játaka*, and an *Uddala Játaka*, one of which may possibly be the subject of the Bharhut sculpture. The Rishi is seated on the ground with his water bowl and a basket of food near him. Before him is a pool of water stocked with fish. On the bank a pair of cats are quarrelling over the head and tail of a fish, and beyond them are two dogs, one trotting joyfully off with a bone, and the other sitting down disappointed, with his back turned to his luckier rival.

This story ought to be identified at once by any one possessing a complete copy of the 550 Játakas. The title of *Uda Játaka* means simply the " *Water-birth*," but I suspect that the name has been unintentionally shortened by the sculptor.

---

[1] See Plate XLIII. fig. 2.   [2] So in another Játaka we have *Kurunga Miga* for a Kurunga Deer.
[3] Julien's Hwen Thsang, II. 361.   [4] See Plate XLVI. fig. 2.

17. Sechha Jâtaka.

The name of this *Jâtaka* is not found among the 550 previous births of Buddha preserved in the Pali books of Ceylon. The actors are two men and two monkeys. One of the monkeys standing in a tree is being addressed by one of the men who carries a pair of water vessels on a pole.[1] The other monkey is standing on the ground and receiving in his hands a drink of water poured from a vessel by the other man. Both of the men's right shoulders are bare, and their heads unshaved, from which it may be concluded that they are monks.

18. Sujâto Gahuto Jâtaka.

The following account of this Jâtaka is taken entire from Spence Hardy's abstract:[2]—

" It came to pass that whilst Gotama Buddha resided in the Vihâra called Jetavana,
" near the city of Sewet, he related the following Jâtaka, an account of an ascetic who
" had lost his father. In what way? Buddha having perceived that an ascetic who had
" lost his father endured great affliction in consequence, and knowing by what means he
" could point out the way of relief, took with him a large retinue of priests, and
" proceeded to the dwelling of the ascetic. Being honorably seated, he inquired,
" 'Why are you thus sorrowful, ascetic?' To which the bereaved son replied, 'I am
" 'thus sorrowful on account of the death of my father.' On hearing this Buddha said,
" 'It is to no purpose to weep for the thing that is past and gone.' In what manner?
" That which follows is the relation. In a former age, when Brahmadatta was King of
" Benares, Bodhisat was born of a wealthy family, and was called Sujâta. The
" grandfather of Sujâta sickened and died, at which his father was exceedingly
" sorrowful; indeed his sorrow was so great, that he removed the bones from their
" burial-place, and deposited them in a place covered with earth near his own house,
" whither he went thrice a day to weep. The sorrow almost overcome him; he ate not,
" neither did he drink. Bodhisat thought within himself that it was proper to attempt
" the assuaging of his father's grief; and therefore, going to the spot where there was
" a dead buffalo, he put grass and water to its mouth, and cried out, 'Oh Buffalo, eat
" 'and drink!' The people perceived his folly and said, 'What is this, Sujâta? Can a
" 'dead buffalo eat grass or drink water?' But without paying any attention to their
" interference, he still cried out, 'Oh Buffalo, eat and drink!' The people concluded
" that he was out of his mind and went to inform his father; who forgetting his parent
" from his affection for his son, went to the place where he was, and inquired the reason
" of his conduct. Sujâta replied, 'There are the feet and tail, and all the interior parts
" 'of the buffalo, entire; if it be foolish in me to give grass and water to a buffalo dead,
" 'but not decayed, why do you, father, weep for my grandfather, when there is no part
" 'of him whatever to be seen?' The father then said, 'True my son, what you say is like
" 'the throwing of a vessel of water upon fire; it has extinguished my sorrow!' and
" thus saying he returned many thanks to Sujâta."

" I Buddha am the person who was then born as the youth Sujâta."

I have quoted the account of this Jâtaka at length because it shows very clearly the
way in which Buddha introduced these stories of his previous births into his common

---

[1] Plate XLVI. fig. 8.   [2] Manual of Buddhism, pp. 107, 108.

discourse. In the present legend the only difference between the Ceylonese version and the sculptured representation is in the substitution of a buffalo for the humped bull of the bas-relief.[1] In the sculpture a young man is represented offering food to a dead bull, while a more elderly person is standing by looking on. The bas-relief occupies one of the small panels of a coping stone—and is duly labelled above:

Sujâto-Gahuto Jâtaka,

which I interpret doubtfully; " Birth as Sujâta the Bull-inviter "—by taking gahuto as a compound word, made up of go or gav a bull, and huto, from the root hwe to " call, invite, or summons." This title of Sujâta is fully borne out by the Singhalese version of the legend in which he repeatedly summons or " invites " the dead animal by calling out " O Buffalo, eat and drink."

19. BIDALA JÂTAKA, OR KUKUṬA JÂTAKA.

The subject of this bas-relief is the well-known fable of the Cat and the Cock, which is here doubly labelled as the Biḍâla Jâtaka, or " Cat-birth," and the Kukuṭa Jâtaka, or " Cock-birth." The general scope of the story is sufficiently clear from the sculpture which represents a Cat looking up at a Cock seated in a tree.[2] For the following account of the legend I am again indebted to the friendly aid of Subhûti:—

" Whilst the most kind Lord Buddha was residing in the monastery of Jetavana " this Jâtaka was recited by him an account of a monk who had fallen deeply in love " with a certain woman. When he was taken before Buddha, and questioned as to his " being in love with a woman, he answered in the affirmative. Then Buddha said, ' O " ' priest it is a fault to be in love with a woman. By their fascinations women conquer " ' men, and cause them misery. It is like the endeavour of a Cat to ensnare a Cock; in " illustration of which he related a story of one of his previous births.

" In days long past when Brahmadatta reigned in Benares, Bodhisatta was a cock " living in the forest with a large brood of fowls. At the same time a she-Cat was living " close by who had already eaten many of the fowls, and was now intent on getting hold " of Bodhisatta himself. It struck her that the readiest way of seizing the Cock was to " offer herself as his wife. So she went towards the village near which the fowls lived " and tried to persuade Bodhisatta to take her as his wife, saying, ' O king of fowls, with " ' strong wings and red comb, I wish to become your wife.' But the Cock suspecting " treachery replied, ' We are birds and you are a quadruped; every one should take a " ' wife from his own kind.' Then the Cat rejoined, ' You must not say so. I will serve " ' only you, and if you still doubt me let the contract be made before all the people of " ' Benares.' But Bodhisatta said, ' Your wish is not to serve us, but to get hold of my " ' fowls and myself.' Then addressing the priest, Buddha said, ' O priest, had that Cock " ' fallen in love with and lived with her, his death would have followed. In like manner " ' if a man falls into the hands of a woman his life will be in danger. But if he escapes " ' the fascination of woman, like the Cock who got rid of the Puss, his fate will be " ' happy. At that time I Bodhisatta was the Cock.' "

Under the tree in which the Cock is sitting the sculptor has placed the ornamental bunch of small bells worn by dancing girls. I notice this point, as it seems probable

---

[1] See Plate XLVII. fig. 3.   [2] See Plate XLVII. fig. 5, and Plate LIII. inscription 6, copings.

that the artist may have placed it there intentionally to indicate the watchfulness of
the Cock.

The story of the Cock and the Cat is similar to Æsop's Fable of the Dog, the Cock,
and the Fox, which, as it is short, may here be quoted in full :—[1]

"A Dog and a Cock having struck up an acquaintance went out on their travels
"together. Nightfall found them in a forest; so the Cock flying up on a tree perched
"among the branches, while the Dog dozed below at the foot. As the night passed
"away and the day dawned, the Cock, according to his custom, set up a shrill
"crowing. A Fox hearing him, and thinking to make a meal of him, came and stood
"under the tree and thus addressed him : 'Thou art a good little bird, and most useful
" ' to thy fellow creatures. Come down, then, that we may sing our matins and rejoice
" ' together.' The Cock replied, ' Go, my good friend, to the foot of the tree, and call
" ' the sacristan to toll the bell.' But as the Fox went to call him, the Dog jumped out
"in a moment and seized the Fox and made an end of him."

20. MAGHA DEVA JÁTAKA.

Magha Deva was an ancient Raja who reigned in the city of Miyulu. He was the
first mortal whose hair turned grey. This did not happen until he had reigned 252,000
years, and although he had 84,000 years still to live, he was so penetrated with the
instability of human existence that he resigned his kingdom to his son, and became an
ascetic in a forest which afterwards bore his name.[1] Spence Hardy adds that "there
"were 84,000 princes of this race, all of whom when they saw the first grey hair,
"resigned the kingdom and became ascetics." In the Maháwanso and other Pali books
his name is written *Makhadewa;* but the story shows that he is the same person as the
Magha Deva of the Bharhut Sculptures.[3]

The bas-relief containing this legend is one of the small panels of a coping stone.[4]
The story is well told, but the subject is a difficult one for sculpture, which cannot well
represent grey hair. The Raja is seated between two attendants, with his left hand
resting on his knees and his right hand raised before his face, holding something small
between his forefinger and thumb. The attendant on his right is leaning forward, and
apparently drawing the Raja's attention to a similar object, which he also holds up
between the forefinger and thumb of his right hand. In the sculpture itself I could not
perceive what the object was. That it was something exceedingly small was quite clear,
and I was inclined to think, from the king's pensive appearance, that it must be a pill
and that the attendant already noticed was the physician holding up another pill.
Mr. Beglar also thought that this figure was a physician, whose action seemed to be that
of feeling the finger of the Raja. The two hands, however, do not touch, although they are
placed very close together, and may perhaps be holding the same grey hair. The third
person is merely an attendant, who stands to the left of the king, with his hands joined
upon his breast in an attitude of respect. When once the name of the subject is known,
the spirit of the scene is evident, and the story is perhaps as well told as such a subject

---

[1] Æsop's Fables, by James, Fable 32, p. 22.
[2] Hardy, Manual of Buddhism, pp. 129, 130, 134.
[3] Tournour's Mahawanso, pp. 8, 9 ; and Upham's Sacred and Historical Books of Ceylon, III. 283.
[4] See Plate XLVII. fig. 2.

could be in sculpture. Fortunately the artist has inscribed the title of the scene at the top of his work as

Magha Deviya Jâtakam,

that is the "Magha Deva birth" of Buddha or his previous existence as King Magha Deva.

21. BHISA HARANIYA JÂTAKA.

The name of this Jâtaka is not found amongst the 550 Jâtakas of Ceylon, and I feel doubtful as to its meaning. There are five actors in the scene, a Rishi, or male ascetic, a female ascetic, a layman, an elephant, and a monkey. The Rishi and the monkey are both seated and are both speaking. The female ascetic, whose right shoulder is bare, is addressing the Rishi, and the layman is making an offering of a bundle of lotus stalks. Behind the Rishi is his hut.[1] It seems probable that the presentation of the lotus stalks has been the origin of the title of the Jâtaka, as *bhisa* is one of the names for the lotus, while *harniya* means either bringing, or seizing, or stealing. The meaning of the name may therefore be simply the "Lotus offering Jâtaka."

22. VITURA PUNAKAYA JÂTAKA.

Amongst the 550 *Jâtakas* preserved in Ceylon there is one called the *Vidhura* Jâtaka, which is thus alluded to in the Dathavansa :[2]—" Who, as Vidhûra by name, possessed of " a keen intellect, subdued, on the summit of Kâlagiri, the devil Punnaka, a cruel foe, " endowed with great supernatural powers, and addicted to sensuous appetites." Judging from the rocky background of the middle bas-relief of the corner pillar of the North Gate, the scene may be supposed to represent the summit of Mount Kâlagiri, while the figure suspended by his heels must be the "Devil *Punnaka*."[3] The inscription engraved immediately below this scene reads *Vitura Punakâya Jâtakam,* which must refer also to the scene below, in which the principal figure and his horse re-appear. I presume that the name of the principal actor should be *Vidhûra* "the wise," as he is described in the Dathavansa above quoted as "possessed of a keen intellect."

Owing to the difference in the spelling of the names the subject of the *Vitura* Jâtaka was not recognised either by Professor Childers or by my learned friend Subhûti. But as soon as I saw the above-quoted verse of the Dathavansa in which the two actors are *Vidhura* and *Punnaka*, I at once recognised the *Vitura Punakaya Jâtaka* of the Bharhut Sculptures. On referring Subhûti to this verse of the Dathavansa, he kindly furnished me with the following translation of the Vidhûra Jâtaka, which with some few alterations is given in his own words:—

" One day while the supreme Buddha was residing at the Monastery of Jetavana, " near the city of Sâvathi, and his disciples were assembled together at the Lecture " Hall, conversing about the extraordinary wisdom of their Teacher, it happened that " Buddha himself arrived there and inquired of them, 'O Disciples, on what subject have " ' you been conversing?' They answered, 'My Lord, it was on your Lordship's " ' wisdom.' And he rejoined, 'O Disciples, it is not only now that I am wise, but in

---

[1] See Plate XLVIII. fig. 7.
[2] Dathavansa by Muta Coomâra Swâmy, p. 51.
[3] See Plate XVIII., middle bas-relief.

" ' former births also I acted with wisdom;' and then to demonstrate the veracity of
" this assertion he related the *Vidhúra Játaka* as follows :—

"   " In former times there reigned a king named Dhanajaya Korava, in the city of
" Indapatta in the country of Kuru. He had a minister named Vidhûra Pandit who
" advised him on all matters. This Pandit was famed for his wisdom, and won the
" hearts of all the kings of Dambadíva (ancient India) and many of their subjects, by his
" lectures on the Righteous Law (Sudharma).

"   " At that time four men of the city of Kâlachampâ in the country of Anga having
" each supported an ascetic obtained by the efficacy of that religious entertainment
" rewards such as each desired. One of them was born as the son of Dhananjaya Korava,
" the second became Indra, King of the Gods, the third was King of the Nâga world,
" and the last was Garuda, King of the Garuda world. The first born as the son of
" Dhananjaya the Korava king, succeeded his father on the throne. Afterwards all
" four happening to come to a certain grove for the purpose of performing *Sila* (or
" religious observances), accidentally met each other. Then there arose among them a
" controversy which they referred to Vidhúra Pandit, who having admonished them,
" decided their contention to the entire satisfaction of all the four, and they were so
" pleased with his decision of their controversy that each of them gave him a valuable
" present, that of the Nâga king being his throat gem.

"   " When the Nâga king had returned to the Nâga world, his wife Queen Vimala,
" missing the famous gem, inquired of him about it. Then he related to her all the
" extraordinary virtues of the Pandit and about his wonderful preaching, and told her
" that he was so satisfied with his counsel that he had presented the gem to the Pandit.
" This created a great desire in the mind of Queen Vimala to see the Pandit and to hear
" his preaching. To accomplish this object she pretended to be sick, and told the Nâga
" king that she would not live unless she should get the heart of Vidhûra Pandit. The
" king, being very fond of her, was willing to meet her wishes, but as he could not think
" of any means of carrying out his purpose, he became very sorrowful. Then his
" daughter, the Nâga maiden named Irandati, approached her father and inquired of
" him why he was so dejected. The king replied, ' My daughter, if you wish that your
" ' mother should live, you should seek for a lover who is able to bring to her the
" ' heart of the Pandit Vidhûra.' His daughter consoled him by saying, ' You need
" ' not grieve any more about this.'

"   " Then she adorned her person most beautifully and repaired to the Kâlagiri moun-
" tain in the Himâlaya range, and began to play most sweetly on a musical instrument
" for the purpose of attracting a lover who should be able to accomplish her object.
" Then Purnaka Yaksha, an officer of the Yaksha armies, and a nephew of Vaisravana,
" King of the Yakshas, having seen the Nâga maiden, fell in love with her, and, having
" learned her object, went with her to wait upon her father. Then the Nâga king
" promised that if he would bring the Pandit Vidhûra into the Nâga world, the Nâga
" maiden should be given to him in marriage.

"   " Then Pûrnaka mounted his aërial horse of the Savindhava race, and went straight
" to the Vipulla rock from whence he took a wonderful and valuable gem, thinking to
" gamble with Dhananjaya, the Korava king, who was very fond of play, so that he
" might defeat the king and win from him the Pandit to carry back to the Nâga world.
" He then proceeded direct to the city of Indrapatta in the county of Kuru. There he

" took the form of a man, and having showed the wonderful gem to the Korava king
" he induced him to gamble with him, so that he won from him the Pandit Vidhûra.
" When Pûrnaka Yaksha announced that he intended to take the Pandit away with him,
" the king and all the people of the country became very sorrowful and were very loth
" to part with him. Pûrnaka however took no notice of this unwillingness, but referred
" the matter to the Pandit himself, who decided in favour of Pûrnaka Yaksha. As the
" Pandita said this the king was silent; but when Pûrnaka was preparing to take
" Vidhûra away he begged that the Pandit might be spared for three days for the pur-
" pose of advising his family as well as the king himself and the people of the country.
" When this was done the Pandit made himself ready for the journey, and Pûrnaka said
" to him, " As this horse travels ' through the air, you must hold fast by his tail and
" ' be carried along hanging behind him.' So the Pandit took hold of the horse's tail
" and hung on by it. Now Pûrnaka himself sate upon the horse, and rode through the
" air intending to kill the Pandit by banging him against the rocks and trees in the
" Himâlaya forest. But he escaped quite uninjured owing to the influence of his merits
" and to his great wisdom. So when Pûrnaka saw this he carried him to the top of the
" mountain peak called *Kâlagiri*, and there seizing the Pandit by the feet he dashed him
" on the rocks. But as the Pandit still remained uninjured the Yaksha thought to seize
" him again and to hurl him head foremost from the summit of the mountain. But the
" Pandit perceiving what he was about, suddenly asked Pûrnaka, without shewing any
" symptoms of fear, what was the object which he wished to accomplish; then Pûrnaka
" related to him the whole matter. But the Pandit knew that although the Yaksha was
" told to kill him and to carry his heart to the Nâga Queen Vimala, yet that was not
" her real object, which was simply to hear his discourse. He therefore decided that he
" would first instruct Pûrnaka Yaksha, and then each of them would be able to
" accomplish his respective object. So he thus addressed Pûrnaka: 'Yaksha, I know a
" ' very good science called *Sudharma;* do thou in the first place hear of that science
" ' from me, and after that kill me and take my heart to the Queen.' Then the Yaksha,
" being curious to hear this science of the Pandit, placed him upon his feet on the top of
" the mountain and listened to his discourse, with which he was so pleased that he
" proposed to take him back to the city of Indrapatta. But the Pandit persuaded the
" Yaksha to carry him to the Nâga world, where he preached the law (of Buddha) to
" the Queen Vimala and to the Nâga king. They were so pleased with his teaching that
" they gave their daughter Irandati in marriage to Pûrnaka Yaksha; and then Pûrnaka
" presented his wonderful gem to the Pandit, and carried him back to the city of
" Indrapatta in the country of Kuru."

" Thus the Supreme Buddha preached this Jâtaka, and pointing to himself, said,
" ' That Vidhûra Pandit was myself.' "

On turning to the photographs of the Bharhut Pillar on which this Jâtaka is
sculptured, I found that several of the scenes of the legend were represented in a very
clear and unmistakeable manner. The Pillar is unfortunately much broken, but the only
scene which has suffered any serious loss is that forming the lower compartment, of which
about one third has been altogether lost.[1] The following are the particular scenes of the
Vidhûra Jâtaka which I have been able to identify.

---

[1] See Plate XVIII. figs. A, B, and C.

Uppermost scene, marked A. 1. in the Plate.—Here two figures, a male and a female, are represented standing amidst rocks. These I take to be the Yaksha Púrnaka listening to the music of the Nâga maiden Irandati on the top of the Kâlagiri mountain. The head of a Bear is seen peeping out of a cave in the rocks.

Second scene, marked A. 2.—In this bas-relief two male figures are represented standing before the King and Queen of the Nâgas, who are both seated. The king is known by his five-headed snake canopy, while the queen has only one snake over her head. The principal standing figure, who has his hands crossed over his breast in an attitude of respect, I take to be the Yaksha Púrnaka who has come to ask the snake king's permission to marry his daughter Irandati. The Nâga king himself is addressing the Yaksha as shown by his upraised right hand. The place of meeting is the interior of the king's palace in the Nâga-loka. To the left is seen the outer gate of the palace, with the back of a man who is going inside.

Lowermost scene, marked C.—This bas-relief is unfortunately incomplete, but I have little hesitation in suggesting that it is intended to present the Yaksha Púrnaka gambling with Dhananjaya, Raja of Indrapatta or Delhi, for the possession of the wise Pandit Vidhûra. The figure of the Yaksha is known by his costume and ornaments, as well as by the presence of his aërial steed immediately behind him. As the Yaksha is represented seated with a table in front of him, I conclude that King Dhananjaya must have been seated opposite to him. The gateway of the Raja's palace is seen to the left with a man coming out. It is similar in all respects to the gateway of the palace in the Nâgaloka.

Middle scene, marked B.—In this large bas-relief I believe that several portions of the story are represented in continuous action. In the lower right corner the Yaksha appears just beginning his aërial journey, which is continued further to the left where the Pandit Vidhûra is seen holding on by the tail of the flying steed, which is rapidly approaching the rocks and forest of the Himâlaya. In the upper right corner the Yaksha has seized the Pandit by the feet and is dashing his head on the rocks, and in the upper left corner the Pandit is seen standing by the side of the Yaksha, and teaching him the *Sudharma*, or "Excellent Law" of Buddha, the precepts of which he enforces with his upraised hand.

With this scene the sculptured illustrations of the Vidhûra Jâtaka come to an end, as the bas-reliefs of the adjacent face of the Pillar refer to some other legend. But with the conversion of the Yaksha the real story of the Jâtaka also ends, as the marriage of the Nâga princess to Púrnaka, and the return of the wise Pandit Vidhûra to Indapatta, are only the natural results of the previous incidents, all of which have been clearly, although somewhat rudely, represented in these Bharhut bas-reliefs.

E. 2.—HISTORICAL SCENES.

Besides the *Jâtakas*, there is a large number of other curious scenes, several of which are labelled. Amongst them are some of the greatest historical interest, as they refer directly to events, either true or supposed, in the actual career of Sâkya Muni himself. Of these, six have their names inscribed over them, and a seventh is recognized by its subject. These are as follows:—

1. Tikutiko Chakamo.
2. Maya Devi's dream.
3. The Jetavana Monastery.
4. Indra Sâla-guha.
5. Visit of Ajâtasatru to Buddha.
6. Visit of Prasenajita to Buddha.
7. The Sankisa Ladder.

1. Tikutiko Chakamo.

When I first saw this scene, I took it to be a representation of the Nâga-loka, which the Hindu Cosmogonies, both Buddhistical and Brahmanical, place at the foot of the *Trikutika* Rocks. The presence of no less than seven Elephants (or Nâgas), and of one great three-headed Serpent (or Nâga) seemed to confirm this identification. But it has been objected that the presence of two Lions is fatal to this attribution.

2. Dream of Mâyâ Devi.

The dream of Mâyâ Devi, the mother of Sâkya Muni, is one of the commonest subjects of Buddhist Sculpture. A white Elephant of the *Chhadanta* breed approached the princess in her sleep, and appeared to enter into her womb by her right side. In the Tibetan version of the Lalita Vistara the term *Chhadanta* is translated into six tusks.[1] According to the Burmese account it was a " young white Elephant," and in his trunk he carried a white lily.[2] The Ceylonese, whose account should be the same as the Burmese, as both were derived from a common source, are altogether silent about the Elephant, and simply state that Bodhisat appeared to Mâyâ Devi " like a cloud in the moonlight " coming from the North, and in his hand holding a lotus."[3] This is Spence Hardy's account, which I do not clearly understand, as it seems difficult to imagine a cloud with a hand, even in the brightest moonlight.

In the Bharhut Sculpture the Elephant has only two tusks, but they are marked to represent three tusks each. There can be no doubt, therefore, that the name of Chhadanta was supposed to refer to " six tusks" as early, at least, as the time of Asoka. But Chhadanta is also said to be the name of a country.[4]

The Bharhut medallion representing the dream of Mâyâ Devi is on the inner face of one of the Railing pillars close to the Eastern Gate. Above it in large characters is inscribed *Bhagavato rukdanta*, which may perhaps be translated by " Buddha as the " sounding elephant," from *ru*, " to sound," to make a particular sort of sound, as the Burmese account of the dream describes that ." his voice occasionally resounding through " the air could be heard distinctly by the inmates of the grotto, and indicated his " approach."[2] In corroboration of this reading, I may quote the parallel account of the Jains of the first object seen by Queen Trisalâ in her dream. This is described as an " elephant with four tusks, looking like radiant drops of dew, or a heap of pearls, or the

---

[1] Foucaux's translation from the Tibetan, pp. 61–83. Csoma de Körös gives "six trunks," but this is perhaps a misprint. See Transactions Bengal Asiatic Society, XX. p. 287.
[2] Bigandet, " Legend of the Burmese Buddha," p. 16.
[3] Manual of Buddhism, p. 142.
[4] Turnour's Mahawanso, pp. 22 and 134.

" sea of milk, possessing a radiance like the moon, huge as the silvery mountain
" *Vaitâdhya*, while from his temples oozed out the sweet liquid that attracts the swarms
" of bees. Such was the incomparably stately elephant, equal to Airâvat himself, which
" Queen Trisalâ saw, *while uttering a fine deep sound, with his trunk filled with water, like*
" *thunder*."[1]

In the Bharhut Sculpture the Princess is represented in the centre of the medallion
sleeping quietly on her couch, with her right hand under her head, and her left hand by
her side. The position leaves her right side exposed. The time is night, as a lamp is
burning at the foot of the bed, on an ornamental stand. Three women are seated in
attendance by the bed, one of whom is waving the cow-tail *chauri* to keep off insects.
The second has her arms extended, but for what purpose is not clear. The third with
joined hands sits in an attitude of devotion. Mâyâ Devi is in full costume, with earrings,
necklace, bracelets, and anklets, and numerous girdles, all complete. The Elephant has
an ornamental cloth, covering the top of his head,[2] but he carries no flower in his trunk,
as in the Burmese account of his appearance before the Princess.

There are a few representations of this scene amongst the Buddhist Sculptures from
the Yusafzai districts, now in the Lahore Museum, and there is a single bas-relief of the
same scene from the Dipaldinna Stûpa at Amaravati on the Kistna River, which is now
in the Calcutta Museum. In none of these has the Elephant got more than two tusks,
nor does he carry a flower. The Bharhut Sculpture is in a very fine state of preservation,
but the workmanship is coarse, and the position of Mâyâ Devi is stiff and formal.

3. JETAVANA MONASTERY.

The view of the celebrated Jetavana Monastery is preserved in the circular medallion
of one of the Pillars.[3] The following inscription, which is placed immediately below the
sculpture, gives the name of the monastery, as well as that of the munificent builder
Anâtha-pindika :—[4]

Jetavana Anâdhapeḍiko deti Koṭisanthatena Keṭâ,

which Mr. Childers thus translates—[5]

" Anâthapiṇḍiko presents Jetavana, (having
become) its purchaser for a layer of koṭis."

Before giving the legend itself regarding the layer of Koṭis (of gold coins) which
Anâthapiṇḍika spread over the garden of Prince Jeta as the purchase money, I think it
best to quote the very interesting and apt illustration which Mr. Childers has given of
the inscription :[6] " I had long been anxious to find the Pali version of the story of
" Anâthapiṇḍika, in order to ascertain whether its language bears out that of the Bharhut
" inscription. It occurred to me this morning that the story might be found in
" Buddhaghosa's Introduction (*Nidâna*) to the Buddhist Jâtaka. I at once examined
" that work, and found, to my great delight, not only the story of Anâthapiṇḍika, but

---

[1] Dr. Stevenson's Kalpa Sutra, p. 42.
[2] In the Lalita Vistara translated from Tibetan by Foucaux, p. 83, the Elephant with six tusks is described
as being "bién parés d'or et de perles, et revêtus d'un reseau d'or."
[3] See Plate XXVIII. fig. 3 ; No. XV., Pillar, S. E. quadrant ; also Plate LVII. for a large view.
[4] See Plate LIII., Pillar XV. No. 20, for this inscription.
[5] See "The Academy" for 28th Nov. 1874, p. 586.
[6] See "The Academy" for 5th Dec. 1874, p. 612.

" the very expression a ' layer of Koṭis,' which is a crucial one in the inscription. The
" passage is as follows :—

" ' Tasmim samaye *Anâthapiṇḍiko* gahapati . . . *Jetavanam Koṭisantharena*
" ' attharasahiraññakotihi Kinitva navakammam patthapesi. So majjhe Dasabalassa
" ' *Gandhakuṭim* kâresi,' which means, ' At that time the householder Anâthapiṇḍiko,
" ' having purchased the garden of Jeta for a layer of koṭis, for 18 koṭis of gold, began
" ' to build (*lit.* set on foot the new works). In the midst he built Buddha's pavilion.'

" I have placed in italics the words which this passage has in common with the
" inscription, and it will be seen that every word of the inscription is found in the
" passage except deti, which, however, occurs further on. The words santhatena and
" santharena are exact synonymes, and kinitavâ, ' having purchased,' corresponds to
" keṭâ, ' purchaser.' The text distinctly states that Buddha's house was on the Jetavana
" grounds, and sure enough there it is in the bas-relief."

" After a brief enumeration of the monastic buildings erected by Anâthapiṇḍiko at
" Jetavana, the narrative proceeds to describe the triumphal progress of Gautama from
" Râjagaha to Sâvatthi, and the pomp with which the wealthy Setthi went forth to meet
" him. Then we read :—

" ' Bhagava imam upâsakaparisam purato katvâ mahâbhikkusanghaparivuto * *
" ' * * Jetavanavihâram pavisi. Atha nam Anâthapiṇḍiko pucchi. Kathâham bhante
" ' imasmim vihâre patipajjâmîti ? Tenahi gahapati imam vihâram âgatânâgatassa
" ' bhikkhusanghassa dehîti. Sâdhu bhante ti makâsetthi suvannabhinkâram âdâya
" ' Dasabalassa hatthi udakam pâtetvâ, imam Jetavanavihâram âgatânâgatassa, Buddha-
" ' pamukhassa sanghassa dammîti adâsi.'

" The Blessed One, preceded by this procession of devout laymen and followed by
" a great company of monks, entered the Monastery of Jetavana. Then Anâthapiṇḍiko
" asked him, ' Lord, how am I to proceed in the matter of this monastery?' ' Since you
" ' ask me, householder, bestow this monastery upon the Buddhist clergy, present and
" ' to come.' And the great Setthi replying, ' It is well,' the Lord took a golden ewer,
" and pouring water upon Buddha's hand, made the donation with these words: ' This
" monastery of Jetavana I give to the clergy, present and to come, in all parts of the
" ' world, with the Buddha at their head.' Here we have the only remaining word
" unaccounted for in the inscription, for *adâsi* in the text answers to *deti*, and we have
" no difficulty in identifying the ' golden ewer' with the vessel which Anâthapiṇḍiko
" in the picture is holding in his hands."

In the curious scenes just described the sculptor has apparently aimed at giving a
view of the great Buddhist Vihâra of Jetavana, whilst illustrating the story of its
establishment by *Anâthapiṇḍika.* Thus we know that the holy tree surrounded with a
Buddhist railing, and the two Temples respectively labelled *Gandha-kuṭi* and *Kosamba-
kuṭi,* did not form any part of the original garden of Prince Jeta. There are, however,
four other trees which are no doubt intended to represent the garden, or most probably
only the Sandal-wood trees, which alone were left standing, while the rest of the scene
illustrates the famous story of the purchase of the garden for as many gold *masurans* as
would suffice to cover its surface. The story is a favourite one with Buddhists, and has
been told at length by Spence Hardy, from whom I quote the following passage :—[1]

_____

[1] Manual of Buddhism, pp. 218, 219.

" When Anepiḍu (or Anâthapiṇḍiko) returned to Sewet (or Srâvasti) he examined
" carefully the suburbs of the city, that he might find a suitable place for the erection
" of the Vihâra, not too near nor too distant. At last he found a place of this des-
" cription belonging to the Prince Jeta. But when he asked the prince to dispose of
" it, he replied that he would not let him have it, unless he were to cover it over with
" golden *masurans*. . 'It is a bargain,' replied Anepiḍu, 'upon these conditions the
" 'garden is mine.' When the prince saw that he was serious, he was unwilling to
" abide by what he had said; and as Anepiḍu would not give up his right, the matter
" was referred to a court of justice, and decided against the prince. Jeta then reflected.
" 'My garden is a thousand cubits in length and breadth; no one has wealth enough
" 'to be able to cover it with gold; it is therefore yet mine, though the case is decided
" 'against me.' The prince and Anepiḍu went together to the garden, and saw that all
" the useful trees were cut down, only such trees as sandal and mango being permitted
" to remain; and the whole place was made perfectly level. Then Anepiḍu called his
" treasurer, and commanded that his stores of wealth should be entered, as many
" *masurans* brought out as would be necessary. The treasurer accordingly emptied
" seven stores, and measured the golden *masurans* as if they had been grain. The
" *masurans* were measured to the extent of 90 *yalas*, and were then brought and thrown
" down in the garden; and a thousand men, each taking up a bundle of money, began
" to cover the garden. Anepiḍu commanded his servants to measure the space occupied
" by the standing trees, and to give as many *masurans* as would have been required if
" they had not been there, that he might lose no part of the merit he hoped to gain.
" When he saw that the entrance was not covered, he commanded his treasurer to break
" open another of the stores, and bring a further supply, though he knew by the plates
" of copper on which his wealth was numbered, that the store preserved by his fore-
" father in the seventh generation backward had been opened, and that the whole sum
" disposed of amounted to 18 *koṭis* of *masurans*. But when Jeta saw that although
" Anepiḍu had already given so much he was equally ready to give more, he reflected
" that it would be well for him also to partake in the merit, and declared that the sum
" he had received was sufficient. After this was concluded Anepiḍu began the erection
" of the Vihâra. Around it were houses for the priests; offices that were suitable for
" the day, and others for the night; an ambulatory; tanks and gardens of fruit and
" flower trees; and around the whole, extending 4,000 cubits, was a wall 18 cubits
" high. The whole of these erections cost 18 koṭis of *masurans*. In addition, Anepiḍu
" had many friends who assisted him, some by their personal labour, and others by
" their wealth. Jeta also said, 'What has a prince to do with money procured from a
" 'merchant?' So he expended the whole of the 18 koṭis he had received in building
" a palace seven stories high at each of the four sides of the garden."

The Chinese pilgrim Hwen Thsang repeats the same story in a very concise form,
adding that Prince Jeta's demand, for as much gold as would cover the surface of the
garden, was only said in jest.[1] Fa Hian also mentions the Jetavana as "the plot of
" ground which the nobleman Sudatta bought after covering it with gold coins."[2]

I have given the above extracts with the view of making my description of the
Bharhut Sculpture more readily intelligible. I have already mentioned the two temples,

---

[1] Julien's Hwen Thsang, II. 297.

[2] Beal's Fa Hian, p. 79. Sudatta is only another name for Anâthapiṇḍiko.

and the four trees which represent the garden. To the right of the *Kosamba-kuṭi* and below the *Gandha-kuṭi* there is a single mango tree surrounded by a Buddhist railing, which is without doubt intended for the holy mango tree, the stone of which was planted by Ananda according to Buddha's instructions. According to the Burmese account,[1] " A gardener gave him, in present, a large mango fruit. Ananda prepared the fruit " and Buddha ate it. When this was done, the stone was handed to Ananda, with an " injunction to plant it in a place prepared to receive it. When planted, Budda washed " his hands over it, and on a sudden there sprung up a beautiful white mango tree, " 50 cubits high, with large branches loaded with blossoms and fruit. To prevent its " being destroyed, a guard was set near it, by the king's order. Dismayed at such a " wonderful sign, the heretics fled in every direction, to conceal their shame and " confusion."

In the foreground there is a bullock cart, with the bullocks unyoked sitting beside it, and with the yoke tilted up in the air to show that the cart has been unloaded. In front are two men, each holding a very small object between his thumb and forefinger. These two I take to be Anâthapiṇḍika himself, and his treasurer, counting out the gold pieces brought in the cart. Above them are two other figures seated, and busily engaged in covering the surface of the garden with the gold coins, which are here represented as square pieces touching one another. If these squares were intended for a pavement of any kind they would have broken bond, instead of which they are laid out just like the squares of a chess board. From this arrangement I infer without hesitation that they are intended for the gold coins with which Anâthapiṇḍika engaged to cover the whole area of the garden as the price of its purchase. To the left are six other figures, whom I take to be Prince Jeta and his friends; and in the very middle of the composition there is Anâthapiṇḍika himself carrying a vessel, just like a tea kettle, in both hands, for the purpose of pouring water over Buddha's hands as a pledge of the completion of his gift.

The story is sufficiently well told by the sculptor, who has wisely limited his work to a few of its leading features, such as the largeness of the sum of money which required a cart for its conveyance, the counting of the coins, and the spreading of the gold pieces over the whole surface of the garden. But to me the chief interest of the scene lies in the two temples, which I take to be actual representations of the two buildings bearing the respective names of *Gandha-kuṭi* and *Kosamba-kuṭi*. It is true that their insertion in the scene is an anachronism, as the temples could not have been built until after the purchase of the garden. If they had been mere buildings without names they might perhaps have been looked upon as simple garden houses; but with the significant names that are attached to them, I have no doubt whatever that they are faithful representations of the two temples which bore those titles, as far as the powers of the artist enabled him to reproduce them. The *Kosamba-kuṭi* is also mentioned in an old inscription which I dug up within the precincts of the Jetavana monastery itself early in 1864.[2] This temple was, therefore, still in existence when the inscription was recorded in the first century B.C. A comparison of the alphabetical characters of this record with those of the Bharhut bas-relief will show at a glance how great a change had taken place in the Indian letters within the short space of two centuries.

---

[1] Bigandet, Legend of the Burmese Buddha, p. 205.
[2] Royal Asiatic Society's Journal, New Series, Vol. V. p. 192, and accompanying Plate XXXII.

4. Indra-Sála Guha.

It is unfortunate that the bas-relief of the famous cave in which Buddha was living when Indra paid him a visit to propound his 42 questions has been injured by the cutting away of both sides of the circular medallion to fit the pillar as an architrave in one of the cenotaphs at Batanmára. But the whole of the middle part is still in excellent preservation, and the inscribed label is in perfect order. The words are simply *Indra-sála-guha*, or "Indra's Hall Cave." This is the name by which the cave is known in the Pali books of Ceylon; but the Chinese pilgrim Hwen Thsang calls it *Indra-saila-guha*, or *Indra-sila-guha*, and the latter form is found in the Buddhist inscription from Ghosráwa in Bihár.[1] I have identified this cave with the Cave of Gidhadwár in the South face of the double-peaked mountain above Giryek. This cave is also mentioned by Fa Hian, but without giving its name.[2] Hwen Thsang's notice is almost equally brief, and the only detailed account of Indra's visit to Buddha that I have been able to find is that given by Spence Hardy.[3] This account I now give in full for comparison with the Bharhut Sculpture.

" At one time Buddha resided in the cave called Indrasála, in the rock Wedi, at the
" North side of the Brahman village Ambasanda, on the east of Rajagaha. Sakra was
" long desirous of paying a visit to the teacher of the three worlds, but on account of
" the multitude of affairs that required his attention, he did not meet with a proper
" opportunity. When he thought about his death, he was greatly afraid, as he knew
" that he must then leave all his power and treasures. This made him look about, to
" see if there was any being in the three worlds who could assist him and take away
" his fear, when he perceived it was in the power of Buddha alone to render him the
" aid he required. Accordingly he issued his command that the Déwas should accom-
" pany him to the residence of Buddha. There was a reason for this command. On a
" former occasion, when Buddha was residing in Jetávana Vihára, Sakra went alone to
" see him and hear bána; but as the sage foresaw that if he obliged him to come again
" he would then be accompanied by 80,000 Déwas, who would thereby be enabled to
" enter the paths, he did not permit him to come into his presence, and he had to return
" to his loka without accomplishing the object of his visit. It was because he thought
" if he again went alone he would meet with a similar reception, that he now called
" the Déwas to accompany him. In a moment's time the whole company came from
" the déwa-loka to the rock Wedi, and rested upon it like a thousand suns. It was now
" evening, and the people were sitting at their doors, either playing with their children
" or eating their food. When they perceived the light upon the rock they said that
" some great Déwa or Brahma must have come to pay honour to Buddha."

To announce his arrival to the sage Sakra sent forward the Déwa Panchasikha, who took with him his harp, 12 miles in length; and having worshipped Buddha he began to sing certain stanzas, which admitted of two interpretations, and might either be regarded as setting forth the honour of Buddha, or as speaking in the praise of Suriyawachasá, daughter of the Déwa Timbara. His voice was accompanied by the tones of the harp. In this manner the praises of the pure being and the praises of evil were mingled

---

[1] Journal of Bengal Asiatic Society, 1848, p. 495, "beautiful as the peak of the Mount Indra Sila."
[2] Beal's Fa Hian, CXXVIII.; Julien's Hwen Thsang, III. 58.
[3] Manual of Buddhism, p. 288.

together, like ambrosia and poison in the same vessel. Buddha said to the Dêwa, "Thy "music and thy song are in harmony," and he commanded that Sakra should be admitted, lest he should be tired with waiting and go away, whereby great loss would be sustained by him and his followers. From the delay, Sakra had begun to think that the dancer was forgetting his errand and speaking about his own matters to the sage; and he therefore sent to tell him not to talk so much, but to procure his permission to enter the honourable presence. The years appointed to Sakra being nearly ended, Buddha knew that it would not be right to say to him on entering, in the usual manner, "May your age be multiplied!" and he therefore addressed him and the others collectively; but by this salutation, three kotis and 60,000 years were added to his life, as the ruler of the Dêwa-loka of which he was then chief. Buddha and Sakra alone knew of this result.

On comparing this account with the Bharhut Sculpture, I notice that Indra's harper, the Dêwa Panchasikha is represented on the left side with harp in hand. The seated figures in the middle of the bas-relief I take to be Indra and his companions, as Buddha is nowhere represented in person amongst the Bharhut Sculptures. His invisible presence is indicated by the throne canopied by an umbrella. The rocky nature of the mountain is shown by piles of rock above the cave.

5. VISIT OF AJÂTASATRU TO BUDDHA.

The visit of Ajâtasatru to Buddha is represented on one of the corner pillars of the Western Gateway.[1] The story is told at length in the *Sâmanna-phala-sutta*, which has been translated by Burnouf, and in a more concise form by Spence Hardy, from the Pali books of Ceylon.[2] After the murder of his father, the king had been unable to sleep, and he sought the presence of Buddha, by the advice of his physician Jivaka, in the hope that the great Teacher might be able to ease his troubled mind. The Râja left his palace at night by torchlight, mounted on an elephant, and accompanied by 500 women, also on elephants, and a still greater number on foot. This part of the scene is represented in the lower part of the Bharhut Sculpture, where the Râja, driving his elephant with his own hand, is followed by several women on elephants, while an attendant carries an umbrella over his head. In this small sculpture there is no room for the representation of any of the city gates of Rajâgriha,—and of the garden of Jivaka under the *Gridhra kuta*, or mountain of the Vulture peak, there is only one trace shown. But within the narrow limits of a very small bas-relief the sculptor has contrived to represent three different phases of the story. First we have the king's procession to the garden; then his dismounting from the Elephant near the dwelling place of Buddha; and lastly, his devotion at the *Bodhimanda*, or throne of Buddha, which is the symbol of Buddha, as the sage himself is nowhere represented in any of the Bharhut Sculptures.

In the Ceylonese version the women, who were mounted on elephants, are said to have carried "weapons in their hands." In the present sculpture, however, they carry only elephants' goads, and these were perhaps the only arms of the original story, which were afterwards converted into weapons. In the second portion of the scene, the dismounted Râja stands with his right hand raised in the attitude of addressing his

[1] See Plate XVI. fig. 3.   [2] Le Lotus de la bonne Loi, p. 449.

H 255.   N

followers. No doubt this is intended to represent Ajâtasatru putting the question to Jivaka, " Where is the Buddha ?" or " Which is Buddha ?"[1] In both the Indian and the Ceylonese versions Buddha is described as being seated near the middle pillars of the Vihâra. But in the Bharhut Sculpture Buddha himself is not represented at all ; and accordingly only his footprints are seen on the step or footstool in front of the *Bodhimanda* throne. On the right-hand pillar, which serves as part of the frame to this interesting scene, there is the following short inscription :—

Ajâtasatru Bhagavato vandaté ;

that is, " Ajâtasatru worships (the footprints) of Buddha."[2]

6. VISIT OF PRASENAJITA TO BUDDHA.

The visit of Prasenajita Râja of Kosala to the *Punya-Sâla* of Buddha is represented on one of the broken pillars of the South Gate.[3] The label inscribed upon it, in two short lines, reads simply—

Râja Pasenaji
Kosalo.[4]

When the Chinese pilgrim Hwen Thsang visited Srâvasti, the Punya Sâla of Prasenajit was already a complete ruin, on the top of which the people had built a small Stûpa.[5] But in this ancient sculpture of Bharhut we have placed before us a detailed representation of the famous building which I think we] may accept, without any great stretch of probability, as an actual view of the Punya Sâla which Râja Prasenajita erected in the city of Srâvasti for the use of Buddha.

The building itself will be described in detail in another place, but I may mention here that it is a two-storied edifice, the lower part being apparently an open-pillared room for the establishment of a large wheel, which occupies the middle of the front. This is appropriately labelled—

Bhagavato dhama Chakam,[6]

that is, " Buddha's Dharma Chakra," or " Wheel of the Law," a symbol which here takes the place of Buddha himself. It is, I believe, intended as a type of the advancement of the Buddhist faith by preaching, and thus becomes an emblem of Buddha the Teacher, in the same way that the *Bodhimanda*, or seat on which Sâkya Muni sat for six years in meditation, is used as a symbol of Buddha the Ascetic in all the Bharhut Sculptures, where the figure of Buddha himself is never represented. The Wheel has a garland hanging from its axle, and is surmounted by an umbrella figured with garlands, On each side stands a worshipper, with both hands joined upon his breast in an attitude of devotion.

The *Punya Sâla*, or " Hall of Religious Merit," occupies all the upper portion of the bas-relief, save a narrow strip on each side. In these strips we have the head and tail of the procession, the whole of the lower half being occupied with the main body, and the

---

[1] See Burnouf, Le Lotus de la bonne Loi, p. 461, "ami Jevaka, on est donc Bhagavat," and Hardy's Manual of Buddhism.

[2] See Plate LIV., No. 62 inscription.　　　　　[3] See Plate XIII. fig. 3.

[4] See Plate LIV. No. 14, for a copy of the inscription. This would appear to have been his usual appellation, as the Ceylon books call him *Pasenadi Kosala*, and the Burmese books *Pathanadi Kosala*.

[5] Julien's Hwen Thsang, II. 294.　　　　　[6] See Plate LIV. fig. 13, for this inscription.

gateway of the palace through which the Râja has just passed. The leader of the procession is apparently a footman, who is closely followed by a horseman, whose back only is represented together with the hind part of his horse. Next comes another footman. All these who have turned upwards to the left are closely followed by Râja Prasenajita in a chariot drawn by four horses abreast. The horses are gaily caparisoned with lofty plumes and plaited manes. The Râja is attended by three servants, of whom one carries the Indian *Chauri*, and a second holds an umbrella over his head. The third is the charioteer, although the art of driving chariots as well as elephants was in those early times part of the usual education of a young prince, as we learn from the curious account of the bringing up of Sâkya himself.[1] Behind the chariot is the palace gateway, through which three followers are passing. Unfortunately only their heads now remain, as the whole of the lower right corner of the sculpture, including the horses' legs and the greater portion of the chariot wheels, has been broken off. Behind the gateway, and advancing towards it, are two other followers mounted on elephants, who close the procession.

The interest of this remarkable scene is divided between the great Râja Prasenajita and the famous Buddhist symbol of the Dharma Chakra. In the other scene, which I have lately described, Ajâtasatru's visit to Buddha, the Râja is mounted on an elephant. The Bharhut Sculptures have thus fortunately presented us with two of the principal scenes of royal life in ancient India : one Râja riding his elephant, and another riding in his chariot. And these scenes become still more interesting when we remember that Buddhist history specially mentions that Ajâtasatru paid his visit to Buddha mounted on an elephant, while Prasenajita rode in a chariot. The account of the latter Râja's visit is given by Burnouf from a Buddhist Sûtra, in which the Râja is made to call for his chariot, as he wished to show honour to Buddha.[2] " Alors Prasenâjit dit à unde ses " gens: va, et attele promptement un bon char ; j'y monterai pour aller voir aujourd' " hui même Bhagavat, afin de lui faire honneur. Alors Prasênadjit, roi du Kôçala, " étant monté sur ce bon char, sortit de Crâvastî et se dirigea vers Bhagavat, dans " l'intention de le voir, afin de lui honneur."

A second specimen of a four-horse chariot was found by Mr. Beglar on a pillar in the Thakur's private residence at Batanmâra. It is the *Mugapakka Jâtakam*.

7. THE SANKISA LADDER.

Another scene about which there can be no mistake is that of the great Ladder by which Buddha descended at Sankisa from the Trayastrinsas heavens.[3] This bas-relief is on the same corner pillar as that last described, and is in excellent preservation. The Ladder is represented as a triple flight of solid stone steps, similar in all respects to the single flight of steps which was found at the Western Gateway of the Stûpa. The legend of the Sankisa Ladder is related by both of the Chinese pilgrims, as well as by the Pali annalists of Ceylon. But the earliest notice that I have yet discovered is that of the Asoka Avadana translated by Burnouf.[4] The main points of the legend are the same in

---

[1] Lalita Vistara, translated by Foucaux from Tibetan, p. 150, " l'equitation sur le cou de l'éléphant, sur le dos du cheval, la conduite des chars."

[2] Introduction à l'Histoire du Buddhisme Indien, p. 169.

[3] See Plate XVII., central compartment.

[4] Introduction à l'Histoire du Buddhisme Indien, p. 398.

all the accounts, but there are many differences in the details. According to Spence
Hardy, Buddha visited the Trayastrinsas heavens to preach his doctrine to the Devas[1] as
well as to his mother Máyá Devi. At the end of three months, his purpose having been
accomplished, he determined to visit the earth at the city of Sakaspura, that is, Sankassa
or Sankisa in Pali, and Sankasya in Sanskrit. Then " Sakra (Indra) reflected that he
" (Buddha) had come from the earth at three steps, but that it would be right to
" celebrate his departure with special honours. He therefore caused a Ladder of gold
" to extend from Mahámeru to Sakaspura. At the right side of this Ladder there was
" another, also of gold, upon which the *Devas* appeared, with instruments of music ; and
" on the left there was another of silver upon which the *Brahma* appeared holding
" canopies of umbrellas. These Ladders were more than 80,000 *yojanas* in length.
" The steps in the Ladder of Buddha were alternately of gold, silver, coral, ruby, emerald,
" and other gems, and it was beautifully ornamented. The whole appeared to the people
" of the earth like three rainbows."[2]

The account of Fa Hian thus describes the scene of the triple Ladder.[3] " When
" Buddha went up to the Trayastrinsas heavens to say *bána* for the sake of his mother,
" after three months he descended at this place (Sankisa)," . . . " At the appointed
" time the Mahárájas of the eight kingdoms, and all the ministers and people, not having
" seen Buddha for so long, greatly desired to meet him. They flocked, therefore, in great
" crowds to this country to await the return of the world-honoured one. Then the
" Bhikshuni Utpala began to think thus with herself, ' To-day the king, ministers, and
" ' people are all going to meet Buddha and render homage to him, but I, a woman, how
" ' can I contrive to get the first sight of him ? ' Buddha immediately by his divine
" power changed her into a holy Chakravarti Rája, and in that capacity she was
" the first to reverence Buddha on his return. Buddha was now about to descend from
" the Trayastrinsas heavens. At this time there appeared a threefold precious Ladder.
" Buddha standing above the middle Ladder, which was made of the seven precious sub-
" stances, began to descend. Then the king of the *Brahma-kayikas* (*i.e.* Brahmá) caused
" a silver Ladder to appear, and took his place on the right hand, holding a white *Chauri*
" in his hand ; whilst the divine *Sakra* (Indra) caused a bright golden Ladder to appear,
" and took his place on the left hand, holding a precious Parasol in his hand. Innumer-
" able Devas were in attendance while Buddha descended. After he had accomplished
" his return the three Ladders all disappeared in the earth, except seven steps which still
" continued visible."

The account of the later pilgrim Hwen Thsang is substantially the same as that of
Fa Hian, but as it is brief, and differs in some of the details, it is better to give it entire.[4]
" Indra, the king of heaven, exerting his supernatural powers, set up three precious
" Ladders. The middle one was of gold, that on the left side was of crystal, and on the
" right of silver. Buddha having left the *punya sála*, accompanied by a crowd of Devas,
" descended by the middle Ladder. Mahá Brahmá, carrying a white *Chauri*, came down
" by the silver Ladder, and Indra, the lord of heaven, carrying a gem-adorned parasol,
" came down by the crystal Ladder on the left. The crowd of Devas springing into the
" air scattered a shower of flowers." The pilgrim adds, " That the three original Ladders

1 Manual of Buddhism, p. 296.   3 Hardy's Manual of Buddhism, pp. 300–301.
3 Beal's Fa Hian, p. 62.   4 Julien's Hwen Thsang, II. 238.

" had completely disappeared, but that the people had set up three others, similar to
" them, made of stone and brick, over which they had erected a *Vihára*, containing a
" stone statue of Buddha, with statues of Indra and Brahmá standing on the steps to the
" left and right, as if about to descend."

At Kúrkihár in Bihár I have seen a statue of Buddha attended by Indra and Brahmá
holding respectively a Parasol and a Chauri, but the date of the sculpture could not be
older than the ninth or tenth century. In the Bharhut Sculptures, where Buddha is never
represented in person, we could not expect to see either Indra or Brahmá. But we have
three flying figures, who no doubt represent the crowd of Devas, carrying flowers and
garlands. The triple Ladder occupies the middle of the scene with a *Bodhi tree* and a
Vajrásan at its foot. There is one footprint on the top step and a second footprint on
the bottom step of the middle Ladder. These are, of course, intended for the footprints
of Buddha, and in his absence they form the invisible objects of reverence. A number of
spectators on all sides is intended to represent the crowd of kings, ministers, and people,
who, according to Fa Hian, flocked to Sankisa to await the return of Buddha. The scene
is clearly the same; and although Buddha is never represented in person in the Bharhut
Sculptures, the triple Ladder shows that as early at least as the time of Asoka the legend
had already appropriated the Brahmanical gods Indra and Brahmá as the attendants of
Buddha's descent from heaven.

I have since obtained a small seal of burnt clay from the Bihár mound near Sankisa,
on which the triple Ladder is represented surmounted by a Buddhist Railing. Above each
there is a single letter of the Gupta alphabet, that on the left of the seal being *Ba* for
Brahmá, and that on the right *Sa* for Sakra, or Indra, the two Devas who accompanied
Buddha on his descent from the Triyastrinsas heavens. The seal was originally coated
with a light blue glaze, of which a great part still remains, but very much faded in
colour.

E. 3.—MISCELLANEOUS SCENES.

INSCRIBED.

Besides the Játakas and the quasi-historical scenes, there is a great number of
other scenes, both labelled and unlabelled, several of which are extremely curious and
interesting, although few of the stories have yet been made out either fully or satisfactorily. Ten of these scenes are inscribed, and as they would seem to offer the best
chance of identification I will begin with them.

1. *Jatila Sabhá.*—This sculpture is unfortunately broken, which is the more to be
regretted as the scene would have been one of the most interesting subjects of the
whole series.[1] The only portions now remaining are a tree with rocks, and half of the
head and upper part of the body of a man. But there can be little doubt that the
original scene represented the "Assembly of the Jatilians," *Jatila Sabhá*, who were the
followers of Uruvilva Kásyapa.[2] The Mahawanso states that he had 1,000 disciples,
but Spence Hardy gives him only 500 followers. This Kásyapa and his two brothers
were fire-worshippers, and as such they are represented both in the Sánchi and in the
Gándhára Sculptures. It is, therefore, very unfortunate that this still earlier represen-

---

[1] See Plate LIII. Copings V. 13, for the inscription. [2] Turnour's Mahawanso, p. 2.

tation of the Assembly of the Jatilian fire-worshippers should have been so seriously mutilated. The name is said to have been derived from *jatan assa attithi*, " he who has " a top-knot of matted hair." This seems to be the peculiar headdress of the fire-worshippers in all these sculptures. It is curious, and perhaps not accidental, that the present peculiar cap of the Parsis has precisely the same shape and backward slope as the matted hair of these fire-worshippers of ancient India.

2. *Migasamadika Chetiya.*[1]—This scene occupies one of the small panels of the coping. In the middle of the bas-reliefs there is a tree, which must be the *Chaitya* mentioned in the label. Seated around are two Lions and six Deer living most amicably together. This is the subject which I suppose to be alluded' to in the inscription, where I take *Samadika* to mean the " eating together" of the Lions and Deer under the tree, which was accordingly named the " *Chaitya* under which Lions and Deer ate together."

3. *Ambode Chetiyam.*[2]—This is another small bas-relief from the coping. In the centre stands a tree to which three Elephants are paying reverence. The tree is the *Amb*, or mango, and must therefore be the *Ambode Chetiya*, or " Chaitya mango tree" mentioned in the label.

4. *Dadani-kamo-chakamo.*[3]—In this very curious scene an altar or throne occupies the middle place, behind which are four Lions with gaping mouths, and to the right five men standing in front of a sixth, who sits on the ground to the left in a contemplative attitude, with his head leaning on his left hand. In front are two gigantic human heads, with a human hand between them, and towards the throne or altar a bundle of faggots burning. I conjecture that this scene represents one of the 16 Buddhist hells, or places of punishment. This seems to be borne out by the inscription, which I would render as the place (*chakamo* or *chakra*) of punishing (*dadani* or *dandani*) works (*kamo* or *karma*) that is the division of the kosmos in which works (*karma*) received their reward, or in other words " hell."

5. *Chitu-páda-sila.*[4]—As the chief feature in this scene is a " Split rock," I think that *Chitu* may be intended for *Chhitu*, " splitting," of the rock (sila); but I am unable to explain *páda*. The scene represented in the sculpture shows two parties of two men each seated on a broad-topped rock, and playing at some game like draughts. A square space on the surface of the rock is divided into 36 small squares, and beside the square are several small square pieces, with marks on the top, which have evidently been used in playing the game. They are exactly the same as the coins used for paving the Jetavana. But lo! the rock has suddenly split between the two parties, and the two men on the right side are sinking downwards with the smaller half of the rock, which is already in a very slanting position. I have not succeeded in discovering this legend; but there is a story of a Raja named *Chétiya*, who is saddled with the ill repute of having told the first lie ever spoken in the world, which illustrates the chief point in this scene, and which may possibly be a different version of the same legend.[5] " When " *Chétiya*, the son of Upachara, began to reign, he appointed as his principal minister

---

[1] See Plate XLIII. fig. 4, and Plate LIII., Copings III. 10, for the inscription.
[2] See Plate XLVII. fig. 7, and Plate LIII., Copings II. 4, for the inscription.
[3] See Plate XLVIII. fig. 6, and Plate LIII., Copings III., for the inscription.
[4] See Plate XLV. fig. 9, and Plate LIII., Copings VIII. 21, for the inscription.
[5] Hardy, Manual of Buddhism, p. 128.

" Korakatamba, with whom he had been brought up, like two students attending the
" same schools, saying that he was senior to Kapila his elder brother. This was the
" first untruth ever uttered amongst men, and when the citizens were informed that the
" king had told a lie, they inquired what colour it was, whether it was white, or black,
" or blue. Notwithstanding the entreaties of Kapila, the king persisted in the untruth,
" and in consequence his person lost its glorious appearance, *the earth opened*, and he went
" to hell, the city in which he resided being destroyed." The version here given appears
to belong to the *Chétiya Játaka*.

In the Bharhut Sculpture perhaps the point of the story may have been the first
occurrence of cheating, and the consequent punishment of the offender. The two figures,
who are apparently descending into hell along with the sinking rock, would be the party
guilty of cheating, while the principal figure of the opposite party, who still remains
seated on the main rock looking on with wonder and amazement, would be Buddha
himself in a previous existence.

6. *Raja Janaka and Sivald Devi.*—In [this scene there are three figures, each with a
label overhead giving the name. The chief figure is of a royal personage seated to the
left, and before him stand two others, a male and a female.[1] The name of the seated
figure on the left is lost, but the first letter would appear to have been U, or perhaps B.
The name in the middle is *Janako Raja*, and that to the right *Sivald Devi*.

In Burma this story of Janaka is included amongst the *Játakas*, but it does not
occur, under this name at least, in the list of Ceylonese Játakas furnished to me by
Subhúti. This legend is given by Bishop Bigandet,[2] from which I have taken the
following brief outline. When Arita Janaka, Raja of Alithita, was slain in battle, his
queen, who was with child, took refuge in Champa, where she gave birth to a beautiful
child resembling a statue of gold, to whom was given the name of *Janaka*. When grown
up Janaka devoted himself to trade, that he might obtain the means of returning to his
native country. When at sea on his way to Kámawatara his ship was wrecked, but he
was saved by a daughter of the Devas, who taking him in her arms carried him to Mithila
and placed him on the table stone of his ancestors. Here he fell asleep. On that very
day his uncle the Raja of Mithila had died, leaving an only daughter named *Sivali*.
Before his death the Raja had charged his ministers to select for the husband of his
daughter " a man remarkable for beauty and strength, as well as for ability." He was to
be able to bend and unbend an enormous bow, a feat which one thousand could scarcely
achieve. On the seventh day after the Raja's death the ministers resolved to leave the
selection of a husband to chance. So " they sent out a charmed chariot " believing that
its inherent virtue would point out the fortunate man who was to be the husband of the
princess. Accordingly the chariot proceeded straight towards the stone on which Janaka
was sleeping. As the Brahmans perceived on the hands and feet of the stranger unmistakable signs foreshowing his elevation to the royal dignity, Janaka was awoke
and taken to the palace in the charmed chariot. Here he performed the required feats of
bending and unbending the great bow, and was "duly united to the beautiful and
youthful Sivali."

The Bharhut bas-relief apparently represents this last scene.

---

[1] See Plate XLIV. fig. 2, and Plate LIII., Copings VIII., 20, for the inscription.
[2] Legend of the Burmese Buddha, 2nd Edit., p. 412, under the title of *Dzanecka* or Janaka.

7. There is a long label descriptive of this scene, which I am unable to make out. The letters seem plain enough,[1]—

Asadâvadhususâne Sigâlanyeti.

In the foreground a man is lying down apparently either dead or asleep, and quite unnoticed by three *Jackals* who are watching a female sitting in a tree, to which she is clinging with both hands. As the inscription appears to allude to the young girl (*Vadhu*), and the jackals (*sigâla*) in a cemetery (*Susâna*), the man lying on the ground is probably a corpse.

The story here represented agrees pretty closely with that of Râma, Raja of Benâres, and the Princess Priyâ, the eldest sister of four Sâkya brothers who founded Kapilavastu, excepting only the relative positions of the Raja and the Princess, which are exactly reversed. But as the sculpture is certainly older than the Pali books of Ceylon, and as there is an indication in the Singhalese account of the story that the Raja was to have lived in a cave,[2] I accept this as the original version of the legend, which is thus told by Spence Hardy :—

" The queen-mother Priyâ (of whom we have spoken in connexion with the " founding of Kapilavastu), was seized with the disease called *Sweta Kushta*, or ' white " leprosy,' on account of which she was obliged to reside in a separate habitation ; and her " whole body became white like the flower of the mountain ebony, *Kobalila*. This disease " was so infectious that even those who merely looked at her might catch it; and as the " princes themselves were in danger of taking the infection, they took her to a forest " near a river, at a distance from the city, in a chariot with drawn curtains. A hole was " dug of sufficient size to afford every necessary accommodation for the princess. It so " happened that Rama, the king of Benares, was seized by the same disorder, and the " disease was so malignant in its type that neither the queen nor his concubines could " approach him lest they should be defiled. As the king was thus put to shame, he gave " the kingdom to his son, and retired into the forest, thinking to die in some lonely cave. " After walking about some time he was overcome by hunger, and ate of the root, leaves, " fruit, and bark of a certain tree; but these acted medicinally, and his whole body " became free from disease, pure as a statue of gold. He then sought for a proper tree " in which to dwell, and seeing a *kolom* with a hollow trunk he thought it would be a " secure refuge from the tigers. Accordingly he made a ladder sixteen cubits high, by " which he ascended the tree, and cutting a hole in the side for a window, he constructed " a frame on which to repose, and a small platform on which to cook his food. At night " he heard the fearful roaring of wild beasts around; but his life was supported by the " offal left by the lions and tigers after they had eaten their prey. One morning a tiger " that was prowling about for food came near the place where the princess was con- " cealed, and having got the scent of human flesh he scraped with his paw until the " earth that covered the cave was removed, when he saw the princess and uttered a loud " roar. The princess trembled with fear at the sight of the tiger, and began to cry. As " all creatures are afraid of the human cry, the tiger slunk away without doing her any " injury. The cry was heard by Râma as well ; and when he went to see from whom it

---

[1] See Plate XLVII. fig. 9, and Plate LIII., Copings, III. 8, for the inscription.
[2] Hardy's Manual of Buddhism, p. 134, "he gave the kingdom to his son, and retired to the forest, thinking to die in some lonely *cave*."

" proceeded, he beheld the princess. The king asked who she was, and she said that she
" had been brought there that she might not defile her relatives. Râma then said to her,
" ' I am Râma, king of Benares; our meeting together is like that of the waters of the
" ' rain and river; ascend, therefore, from the cave to the light.' But Priya replied, ' I
" ' cannot ascend from the cave; I am afflicted with the white leprosy.' Then said the
" king, ' I came to the forest on account of the same disease, but was cured by the eating
" ' of certain medicinal herbs: in the same way you may be cured; therefore at once
" ' come hither.' To assist her in ascending, Râma made her a ladder, and taking her to
" the tree in which he lived he applied the medicine, and in a little time she was perfectly
" free from disease."

The king and princess had a numerous family, and became the founders of the city
of *Koli*, in the neighbourhood of Kapilavastu, which was so-called from the *kolom* tree in
which the king (or the princess) had taken refuge.

8. *Dighatapasisise anusdsati*, the label inscribed above this scene, seems to refer to the
well-known *Tirthika* apponent of Buddhism named *Dirgha-tapasa*, or " long penance,"
who was a follower of the famous *Nigantha Nâtha*, or chief of the Nirgranthas.[1] His
conversion to Buddhism is told at great length by Spence Hardy.[2] After holding a
controversy with Buddha he returned to his master Nigantha Nâtha, when he was
surrounded by his disciples, amongst whom was one named Upâli. " Nirgrantha Nâtha
" enquired of Dirgha-tapasa whence he came, and when he told him that he had been
" speaking to Gotama, and repeated the conversation that had taken place, he told
" his disciple that he had answered discreetly. Upâli, on hearing what had passed, said
" that he also would go and hold a controversy with Gotama; ' I will hold him,' said
" he, ' as a man seizes a sheep by its long hair, and it kicks and struggles but cannot
" ' get away; or as a toddy-drawer who takes the reticulated substance he uses to strain
" ' his liquor, knocking it on the ground that it may be free from dirt; or as a flax
" ' dresser who takes his flax, soaks it in water for three days, and then tosses it about
" ' right and left, that it may be suited to his purpose; or as an elephant sporting in
" ' a tank, that sends the water out of his trunk in all directions.' Nigantha Nâtha said
" it was a matter of little consequence who went to argue with Gotama, as any one
" of them would be able to subdue him. *Dirgha*, however, warned Upâli of the danger
" he would incur by conversing with Gotama, as he knew his artful method of gaining
" over persons to his opinion; and though their teacher ridiculed his fears, he thrice
" entreated Upâli not to go. The warning was given in vain, as Upâli went to the
" Vihâra and made obeisance to Buddha," by whom he was soon converted.

This story has no connexion with the subject of the Bharhut Sculpture, and I have
quoted it only to show the high position which Dirgha-tapasa held in the Buddhist
Church. To the left, on a raised platform, is seated the great ascetic, with his long
matted hair and scanty clothing. In front of him are seated four female disciples, one
of whom appears to be earnestly addressing the chief, who is replying to her. The label
inscribed above seems to refer to these females as Rishis. I read it *Dighatapasisise
anusdsati*, which I take to mean " *Dirghatapas* instructs the female Rishis " (*Isise*).

---

[1] See Plate XLVIII. fig. 4; and Plate LIII., Copings II. 3, for inscription.
[2] Manual of Buddhism, pp. 266 to 271.

9. This curious scene has a long label inscribed above it which I cannot make out.[1] To the right are some large rocks, and to the left is an ornamented bag or skin suspended from two pegs. In the middle is a man seated in front of the bag, the ends of which he holds as if he was in the act of milking. This action seems to be alluded to in the label,—

Vadukokatha dohati nadode pavate,

where I read *dohati* as "milks." *Pavate* is perhaps the Sanskrit *pravritti*, a "continuous flow or stream."

10. In this sculpture we have a companion scene to the last. Here a man is receiving both meat and drink from two hands which project from the trunk of a tree.[2] In one hand is a bowl filled with solid food, and in the other a water vessel with handle and spout like a teakettle. The scene is labelled :—

Jabu nadode pavate.

I take *Jabu* as the equivalent of the *Jambu* tree, which here perhaps stands for the fabulous *kalpa drûm*, or "wishing tree" of Indra's heaven, that produced whatever was desired. I have since discovered a large sculpture of the *kalpa drûm*, which forms the apex of the capital of one of Asoka's pillars in the ruins of Besnagar, at the junction of the Bes and Betwanti Rivers.

E. 4.—MISCELLANEOUS SCENES.

NOT INSCRIBED.

1. Plate XL. figs. 2, 3, 4, 5.—I have grouped these four coping panels together, as I think it probable that they belong to one continuous story. They are placed together on the coping, and they occupy four contiguous panels, contrary to the usual arrangement of alternate scenes and ornaments. If, however, these four panels do not present a single story, it is quite certain that the two scenes on the left hand belong to one story, and the two on the right hand to a second story.

The first scene on the left shows a tall tree between two women. The woman to the left, apparently a servant, is cutting some standing corn, while the other to the right, her mistress I presume, is seated on the ground beside a large vessel, which is raised upon a common earthen *Chûla*, or fireplace. The purport of the scene seems to be that the one woman is cutting corn for the other woman to cook.

In the next scene to the right, the woman whom I suppose to be the mistress is seated on the ground beside a man, both engaged in eating some broad flat cakes (*Chapâtis?*), which are being presented to them by a female servant, who is most probably the corn cutter of the first scene.

In the third scene to the right there are four actors, a man and woman, and a boy and girl. In the middle stands a tree, with large garlands hanging on all sides of it. The boy and girl are lying on mattrasses spread on the ground. The man and woman are standing and bending forward, the former towards the girl and the latter towards the boy. Unfortunately, their action is not quite clear. At first I thought that they were pulling out the tongues of the children with long pincers; but I am now rather inclined to think that they are administering poison to them with long spoons.

---

[1] See Plate XLVIII. fig. 9; and Plate LIII., Copings VIII. 18, for the inscription.
[2] See Plate XLVIII. fig. 11; and Plate LIII., Copings VIII. 19, for the inscription.

The fourth scene on the right hand shows two gigantic birds carrying off two dead human beings, male and female, by the hair of their heads. I call them dead because their bodies are naked, while their arms are hanging idly by their sides. Connecting this scene with the previous one, I conjecture that the two bodies which are being carried off in this scene are those of the man and woman of the former scene, and that this is their punishment for having tortured the children.

This manner of carrying the dead is noted by Spence Hardy as peculiar to the square-faced inhabitants of Uttarakuru.[1] When they " die they are wrapped in a fine " kind of cloth, procured from the tree, far more exquisite in its fabric than anything " ever made by man. As there is no wood of which to form a pyre, they are taken to " the cemetery, and there left. There are birds, more powerful than elephants, which " convey the bodies to the *Yugandhara* rocks, and as they sometimes let them fall when " flying over Jambudwipa, these precious cloths are occasionally found by men."

2. Plate XLI. figs. 1, 3.—I have joined these two scenes together, as the actors are the same in both, and the latter scene seems to be the completion of the former. The actors are a Rishi carrying two baskets slung from the ends of a Banghi pole, a Shepherd, and a Ram. In the first scene the Rishi is seen approaching the Ram, who has already begun to incline his head downwards as if intending to butt. The Shepherd is apparently warning the holy man not to come too near the Ram. The result is seen in the second sculpture, where the Rishi is on the ground with his right knee raised to receive the Ram's butt. His Banghi load lies behind him, while the Shepherd, with his forefinger raised, is apparently addressing him in the familiar formula, " I told you so."

3. Plate XLI. fig. 5.—Here a man and woman are standing beside a house, engaged in earnest conversation. Behind the house another man is seated. There is nothing to indicate the nature of the story. But I have a suspicion that the seated figure is Râma, and the other two Sita and Lakshana.

4. Plate XLII. fig. 1.—A Rishi, seated in front of his hut, is engaged in addressing a five-headed snake who is coiled up in front of him. I am ignorant of the story.

5. Plate XLII. fig. 5.—Unfortunately this sculpture is much broken, and the fragments could not be found. Three Rishis are represented flying through the air carrying their alms bowls in their left hands. There were probably five of them when the bas-relief was complete, as there would be room for two more on the right. Beneath is a fire altar, which is the only part now remaining of the lower half of the composition. I think it probable that this bas-relief represents the famous ploughing match which arrested the progress of five Rishis flying from the South towards the North. The story is told by Beal as follows:—[2]

" At this time there happened to be five Rishis flying, by means of their spiritual " powers, through the air, possessed of great energies, and thoroughly versed in the " Shasters and Vedas. They were going from the South towards the North, and when " they arrived just over the Jambu tree in the garden aforesaid, wishing to go onwards, " suddenly they found themselves arrested in their course. Then they said one to " another, ' How is it that we, who have in former times found no difficulty in flying " ' through space and reaching even beyond Sumeru to the Palace of Vaisravana, and even " ' to the City of Arkavanta, and beyond that even to the abode of the Yakshas, yet now

[1] Manual of Buddhism, p. 15.   [2] Romantic History of Buddha, p. 74.

" ' find our flight impeded in passing over this tree ? By what influence is it that to-day
" ' we have lost our spiritual power ? '

" Then the Rishis, looking downwards, beheld the prince underneath the tree, sitting
" with his legs crossed, his whole person so bright with glory that they could with
" difficulty behold him. Then these Rishis began to consider : ' Who can this be ? Is it
" ' Brahma, Lord of the world ? or is it Krishna Deva, Lord of the Kâma Loka ? or is it
" ' Sakra ? or is it Vaisravana, the Lord of the Treasuries ? or is it Chandradeva ? or is it
" ' Suriya Deva ? or is it some Chakravartin Raja ? or is it possible that this is the person
" ' of a Buddha born into the world ?"

At this time the Guardian Deva of the wood addressed the Rishis as follows :—
" Great Rishis all! this is not Brahma Deva, Lord of the world, nor Krishna, Lord of
" the Kâma heavens, nor Sakra, nor Vaisravana, Lord of the Treasuries, nor Chandradeva,
" nor Suriya Deva ; but this is the Prince Royal, called Siddhârtha, born of Suddhôdana
" Râja, belonging to the Sâkya race. The glory which proceeds from one pore of his
" body is greater by sixteen times than all the glory proceeding from the bodies of all
" those forenamed Devas! and on this account your spiritual power of flight failed you
" as soon as you came above this tree ! "

6. Plate XLII. fig. 7.—The same three figures seem to be represented in this sculpture as those described in No. 3. Here the woman and one of the men are standing
together in a courtyard surrounded on three sides by houses. The woman is holding out
a flat basket or tray, into which the man is emptying the contents of a round basket. The
second man is standing outside the house to the right, with his *banghi* load of two baskets
placed on the ground. As the arrangement of the houses in this sculpture agrees with
Valmiki's description of Ráma's dwelling-place at Panchavati on the Godâvari, we have
an additional argument in favour of the connexion of this scene with the Râmâyna
legend. " Then Râma showed his brother a beautiful spot facing the river Godâvari, and
" there was a sheet of water near it, as bright as the sun, and frangrant with lilies, and
" in the distance were high mountains abounding with glens, and vocal with peacocks.
" In this charming neighbourhood Lakshmana built a large hut on a high floor of earth,
" with firm posts of bambus wrought together with wicker-work, and he covered it and
" roofed it with branches of trees, and tied it with strong cords, and thatched it with
" grass and leaves, and *he divided it into four rooms*."[1]

This division into four rooms I take to be the arrangement of the four rooms or
separate huts, to form four sides of a square, so as to enclose a courtyard. In early times
this disposition of the rooms must have been almost universally adopted as a protection
against wild beasts.

7. Plate XLII. fig. 9.—In this sculpture there are four men, two seated and two
standing. The former are dressed in the usual costume of most of the Bharhut figures ;
but the latter two have peculiar flat caps on their heads, apparently ornamented with
feathers, and broad collars of large leaves round their necks ; I take these to be foreign
merchants who have come to deal with the two home merchants that are seated. In front
of the latter are two baskets and a number of objects which look like elephants' tusks and
the Chauri tails of the Yâk. The two foreign merchants are engaged in close conversation, the subject of which we may imagine to be the price of the tusks and *Chauri tails.*

---

[1] Wheeler's Râmâyana, pp. 257–58.

8. Plate XLIII. fig. 6.—This scene consists simply of two Elephants moving in opposite directions. The animal going to the right is carrying a garland to deposit, either at the foot of a Bodhi tree, or at the base of a Stûpa. His open mouth shows his fat tongue in a very natural manner.

9. Plate XLIII. fig. 8.—In this scene the actors are a Rishi, a hunter, or a shepherd, and an antelope in a forest near the Rishi's hermitage. The antelope is lying down with its head stretched out and resting on the ground, apparently as if bound, while the Rishi is about to plunge a knife into the back of its neck. The hunter, or whoever the other figure may be, has both his forefingers raised as if expostulating with the ascetic, who, from his dress, must be a fire worshipper.

10. Plate XLIV. fig. 4.—Here two men, one standing and one seated, are holding an earnest conversation, to which a woman is listening from a circular hole or opening in the roof of an adjacent house; both of the men are speaking together, and enforcing their arguments with their upraised forefingers. This scene may perhaps also refer to the history of Râma, Sita, and Lakshana.

11. Plate XLIV. fig. 6.—The subject of this scene is, I think, the well-known story of the appearance of the four exiled *Ikshwâka* princes before the sage Kapila, who gave up his residence to them for the site of their new city, which was accordingly named *Kapila-vastu*, or *Kapila-nagara*.[1] In the bas-relief the sage is seated with his right shoulder bare, and his long hair twisted and coiled into a massive *Jatâ* behind his head after the usual manner of ascetics, a fashion which has descended even down to the present time. The four princes stand and kneel before him with their hands joined in an attitude of respect.

As the story of the four exiled princes is intimately connected with the origin of the name of Sâkya, it has a special interest of its own, irrespective of the curious light which it throws on some of the social habits of the people. The following is a brief outline of its leading features taken from Spence Hardy's long account :—

The last Ikshwâku king had five wives and five sons, one by each wife. The mother of the youngest, five days after his birth, "arrayed him in a splendid robe, took him to " the king, and placing him in his arms told him to admire his beauty. The king on " seeing him was much delighted that she had borne him so beautiful a son in his old " age, and gave her permission to ask for anything she might desire. She of course " asked that her son might be declared heir to the throne, which was then refused." But not long afterwards, when the king was talking to her in a pleasant manner, she told him that it was wrong for princes to speak untruths, and asked him if he had never heard of the monarch who was taken to hell for the utterance of a lie.[2] By this allusion the king was put to shame. He then sent for his four eldest sons, and told them that his youngest son was to be his successor, and that they should take such treasures as they required, and as many people as would follow them, and seek another place for their abode. The four princes accordingly started from Benares with a large retinue. "When their five sisters heard of their departure, they thought that there " would be no one now to care for them, as their brothers were gone; so they resolved " to follow them, and joined them with such treasures as they could collect." In the

---

[1] This legend is given by Csoma de Körös in the Bengal Asiatic Society's Journal, Vol. II. p. 390; and by Hardy in his Manual of Buddhism, p. 130.
[2] This was king Chetiya, whose story has been already given.

course of their wanderings the princes arrived at the hermitage of the sage Kapila, to whom they paid due reverence, and when he asked them what they were doing in the forest, they told him their history. The sage then offered them the site of his own hermitage " for the building of their city, telling them that if even an outcast had been born " there, it would at some future period be honoured by the presence of a *chakravarti*, and " that from it a being would proceed who would be an assistance to all the intelligences " of the world. No other favour did the sage request in return, but that the princes " would call the city by his own name, Kapila."[1] It is this interview between Kapila and the four exiled princes which seems to me to form the subject of the Bharhut bas-relief.

" The princes then said to each other, ' If we send to any of the inferior kings to " ' ask their daughters in marriage, it will be a dishonour to the Okkáka race; and if " ' we give our sisters to their princes it will be an equal dishonour; it will therefore " ' be better to stain the purity of our relationship than that of our race!' The eldest " sister (named Priyá) was therefore appointed as the queen mother, and each of the " brothers took one of the other sisters as his wife." In the Tibetan version it is specially noted that the sisters also had different mothers, and that each of the brothers accordingly selected his half sister. In the course of time each of the queens had eight sons and eight daughters, " When their father heard in what manner the princes had acted, " he thrice exclaimed, ' *Saká wata bho rájakumára, paramá Saká wata bho rájakumáráye,*' " ' The princes are skilful in preserving the purity of our race, the princes are exceedingly " ' skilful in preserving the purity of our race.' On account of this exclamation of the " king, the Okkáka race was henceforth called *Ambatta-Sákya.*"

In the Tibetan account, when the king is informed that his four sons have " taken " their sisters for their wives, and have been much multiplied, he is much surprised, and " exclaims several times, ' *Shákya, Shákya,*' ' Is it possible, is it possible,' or, ' O daring ! " ' O daring !' and this is the origin of the Shákya name."

12. Plate XLIV. fig. 8.—The subject of this bas-relief is the reverence paid by a herd of Deer to a Bodhi tree, with the Bodhimanda, or Throne of Buddha, placed beneath it. There is nothing specially remarkable in the sculpture except that the animals are all spotted Deer.

13. Plate XLV. fig. 3.—This scene is in perfect order, but at present I see no clue to its identification. A sage, with his right shoulder bare, is seated on a *morha* with his right leg raised, in the Indian fashion, and his left foot resting on a footstool. In the middle stands a female, who is apparently arguing with the sage, as both have their right forefingers raised as if addressing each other. To the right a female is leaving the scene. There is nothing to attract special attention in this sculpture, save perhaps the simple dressing of the women's hair, which is merely combed down the back of the head and fastened in a knot behind the neck.

14. Plate XLV. fig. 5.—In this scene there are a man and two monkeys in the midst of a forest. One of the monkeys is carrying away a pair of water vessels slung from the ends of a Banghi pole. The other monkey is seated on the ground in front of the man, who is standing, and apparently addressing him. The action of the seated monkey is not quite clear. He holds some indistinct object in his hands, which I at first took to be a net.

---

[1] Hardy, Manual of Buddhism, p. 133.

15. Plate XLV. fig. 7.—The only actors in this scene are a pair of birds, like Doves, which are represented sitting on two different walls and apparently conversing. Between them is the round gable end of a house, to the right of which is a lower house with a door in the outer wall, and in the background a row of houses with a second round gable end. The subject of this bas-relief is quite unknown to me, but I have no doubt that it represents some well-known Buddhist story.

16. Plate XLVI. fig. 4.—This sculpture has probably some connexion with the scene represented in No. 10. The same two men and the same woman here appear standing before a seated ascetic. Behind the Rishi is his hermitage. The men are standing in a respectful attitude with their hands crossed on their breasts, while the woman is eagerly listening to the words of the sage, who is addressing them with his forefinger raised. It is possible that these two scenes may represent some well-known Buddhist legend; but I have a strong suspicion that they are connected with the story of the wanderings of Râma, Lakshana,[1] and Sîta. The present scene, for instance, in spite of the difference of dress, may perhaps be intended to picture the arrival of Râma, Sîta, and Lakshana, at the hermitage of the sage Bharadwâja, near the junction of the Ganges and Jumna at Prayâga, or at that of Válmiki near Chitrakuta. In the Râmâyana, the two brothers are represented as having assumed the bark dress and the matted hair of the ascetics before they left Ayodhya. If this early assumption of the ascetic dress really formed part of the original story of Rama, then these Bharhut Sculptures cannot have been intended for illustrations of the Râmâyana legend. But as both of the brothers are said to have been armed with swords and shields as well as with bows and arrows, there would seem to be some difficulty about the assumption of the ascetic's dress. Their dwelling is described as made of branches of trees and roofed with leaves. "It was adorned with a " large bow covered with gold, resembling the bow of Indra, and with a large quiver of " arrows, as bright as the rays of the sun, and as keen as the faces of the serpents in the " river Bhagavati. This hermitage* * * was likewise adorned with two cimitars wrapped " in cloth of gold, and with two shields which were studded with gold, and the guards for " the arms and the fingers were also covered with gold."[2] Now as all the real ascetics, such as Bharadwâja, Sutikshna, and Agastya, are described as being quite unarmed, it seems most probable that in the original story the two royal brothers were represented as simple exiles who carried their arms, and not as armed ascetics. For this reason I am tempted to suggest the possible connexion of these scenes with the Râmâyana legend.

Two other scenes of the same story are probably represented in Nos. 3, 6, and 10, which have been noticed already. That the story of Râma was a popular one even in the early Buddhist times we learn from Spence Hardy's quotation from the Singhalese Amawatura.[3] "This is just like the teaching of Tîrthakas, a thing without benefit, " *as useless as the tales called Bharata and Râma*, like the seeking for hard wood in the " plaintain, or rice in mere chaff."

17. Plate XLVI. fig. 6.—In this scene the actors are three Elephants in a Bambu forest. Apparently they are simply feeding on the Bambus; but their attitudes are very spirited, more particularly that of the animal on the left, who is represented in a three-quarter front view, with his great ears spread out, and with a bambu branch grasped in his upraised trunk.

---

[1] This is the Buddhist form of the name of Râma's brother Lakshmana.
[2] Wheeler's Râmâyana, pp. 126–127, 204.   [3] Manual of Buddhism, p. 271.

E. 5.—HUMOROUS SCENES.

The only scenes of humour amongst the Bharhut Sculptures are devoted to the actions of monkeys in contact with men and elephants. The few scenes of this kind are brought together in a separate Plate, for the sake of ready comparison with one another. Two of the scenes represent the capture of an elephant by monkeys, who lead him along in a sort of triumphal procession.

Scene 1.[1]—In this medallion four monkeys are employed in dragging along a captive elephant, who is carefully secured by stout ropes from doing any mischief. A billet of wood is fastened along the back of his trunk to restrain its action, while a rope tied to his tail is carried between his legs and passed round the root of his trunk. The leading monkey in front of the elephant has the end of the rope over his right arm, while he shoulders the *ankus*, or elephant goad, which is grasped with both hands. Three other monkeys drag separate ropes which are passed over their shoulders after the fashion of boatmen in towing a boat. From the end of the last monkey's rope hang the two bells, which had formerly dangled from the elephant's sides. In front of all are two monkey musicians, one playing a drum which is suspended from his neck, and the other sounding a shell which is attached to the end of a long pipe.

Scene 2.[2]—Represents the same story in a more advanced stage. The elephant is still seen marching along, but he is no longer dragged by his monkey captors, who, with the exception of the musicians, have all mounted on his back. The leading monkey with the *ankus* is now seated on the animal's neck, and is driving the goad with both hands into the back of his head. A second monkey stands on one of the elephant's tusks, facing the driver, whom he is energetically addressing. Two other monkeys are seated behind the driver, whilst a fifth holds on by his hands to the rope passing under the elephant's tail and fixes his feet on the animal's rump after the very common fashion of an elephant coolee. The drummer still trudges in front and the shell-blower alongside, but a third monkey has joined the musicians as a player of cymbals.

These two scenes are no doubt the work of the same sculptor, as they occupy the two opposite faces of the same Rail bar in the S.W. quadrant. Both designs are conceived with much spirit, but the workmanship is not equal to the intention. The left hind leg of each elephant is faulty, and there is too much sameness in the attitudes of the monkeys in the first scene. This was probably noticed by some of the artist's friends, as in the second scene all the five monkeys on the elephant's back are in different attitudes, and what is more, every one of the attitudes is a natural one. This attention to nature as well as to art in varying the attitudes shows that the old Indian sculptor had at least some of the instincts of a true artist.

Scene 3.—Is another circular medallion representing an elephant and monkeys, but with the addition of a giant, who is the principal figure in the composition.[3] I call the human figure a giant because he is just twice the height of the elephant. The giant is seated on a low-backed chair, with his feet on a footstool. He has the usual royal headdress, earrings, bracelets, and necklace, and is naked as far as the waist. His right arm hangs straight down by his side, but his left is extended towards a monkey seated on a

---

[1] See Plate XXXIII. fig. 1, Rail bar of S.W. quadrant.
[2] See Plate XXXIII. fig. 2, Rail bar of S.W. quadrant.
[3] See Plate XXXIII. fig. 3, from No. XV. Pillar, S.W. quadrant.

low stool in front, with the palm of the hand turned upwards, which the monkey is either cutting or pricking with a short pointed tool. A second monkey is pulling out one of the giant's teeth with a large forceps, which is secured to an elephant by a long rope. A third monkey is driving the goad into the back of the elephant's head to make him go quickly, whilst a fourth monkey is biting the animal's tail and beating him with a stick for the same purpose. Above there is a fifth monkey playing a drum, and below there is a sixth blowing a very large shell.

It is possible that this scene represents some well-known story with which I am not acquainted. From the stiff position of the giant I conclude that he is bound to his seat, but the cords are not apparent, unless the band round his stomach, which looks more like the usual girdle, should be a rope. Perhaps also the loose thick band round his neck, which looks very like a long necklace, may be another rope. There is much less spirit in this scene, than in those of the Captured Elephant just described. The same monkeys figure over again, but with less action, and the general effect is comparatively tame. The best figure is that of the monkey, who is piercing or cutting the giant's hand. His fixed and grave expression is certainly good; while his attitude, with the legs drawn in and resting on the toes, marks his eager attention to the work in hand. The figure of the giant is badly drawn, and his supine listlessness is suggestive rather of having his nose tickled than of having a tooth violently tugged by a forceps worked by an elephant. But there can be little doubt that ignorance of the story must take away much of the interest of this curious sculpture.

Scene 4 represents a fight between men and monkeys.[1] Unfortunately the whole of the lower half of this spirited scene is lost, and the only figures that now remain are those of two men and three monkeys. To the right a man is hurling a large stone at a monkey who clasps him by the legs. In the middle a monkey is trying to escape up a tree from a man who clings tenaciously to his back. The third monkey is lying along the branch of a tree, with his head facing downwards. His opponent is lost. The whole of these figures are very spirited both in design and in execution.

Scene 5 is of a peaceful kind, containing a row of trees, with one man and two monkeys.[2] The man stands on the left, with both hands raised, and forefingers elevated, and is evidently speaking earnestly to one of the monkeys who is seated on the ground, engaged in working a net, or some other object, with both hands. The second monkey is carrying off a pair of round vessels (gharás) fastened to the ends of a pole in *Banghí* fashion. No doubt this scene also represents some well-known story.

Scene 6 presents a tree filled with monkeys, with a man and monkey below seated on stools facing each other.[3] The man is evidently speaking, as his right hand is raised towards the monkey, who sits all attention, leaning slightly forward with both hands resting on his knees. Behind them stand two men who are holding out a rectangular object between them, which may perhaps be a mat to catch fruit falling from the tree. The monkeys are represented in various ways, as climbing, sitting, jumping, and eating the fruit of the tree. The bust of a man appears between the two seated figures with his hands crossed on his breast. A portion of the medallion on the left hand has been

---

[1] See Plate XXXIII. fig. 5, from a coping stone. [2] See Plate XLV. fig. 5, from a coping stone.
[3] See Plate XXXIII. fig. 4, from a pillar.

broken off, but not much is lost. The story of this animated scene is also unknown to me, but I suspect that it represents the interview between Râma and Sugriva, king of the monkeys.

To complete the series of monkey scenes I have added two small pieces, one of which represents a monkey seated on the bough of a mango tree, eating a fruit, and the other a monkey who has turned ascetic, and is seen sitting on a stool outside his hermitage.[1] This may be Sugriva himself.

To this short account I may add a notice of a single scene of grim humour, in which monkeys take no part. This is sculptured on a round medallion, which has been removed to Uchahara, where I found it buried under the walls of the fort. It represents a great marine monster, with mouth wide open, in the act of swallowing a boat with its crew of three men. A second boat is drifting towards the same fate stern foremost, while her crew of three men have given up rowing, in despair.[2] The waves are rough, and several small fishes appear between the sea monster and the second boat. This bas-relief is valuable as being the only Bharhut Sculpture which presents us with the view of the ancient Indian boat. Here we have two boats, with their zigzag-cut planks fastened by iron cramps, just like those of the present day. The oars also and rudder are the same as those now in use, the former being made of a simple bambu with a piece of flat wood tied to the end for a blade. The men in the second boat who have given up rowing have placed their right hands on their breasts, a mode of action which was probably understood to signify despair. The head of the leviathan is particularly stiff and clumsy, but as the animal has to swallow a boat the mouth is necessarily large. Altogether this is a very curious and interesting piece of sculpture.

F.—OBJECTS OF WORSHIP.

In the Bharhut Sculptures there is no trace of any Image worship, the only objects of reverence being *Stúpas, Wheels, Bodhi Trees, Buddha-padas,* or "Footprints," and the symbol of the *Triratna,* or "Triple-gem." In the pillar inscriptions of Asoka the *Aswatha,* or Pippal Tree, which was the Bodhi Tree of Sâkya Muni, is alone mentioned,[3] and in the contemporary sculptures of Bharhut the Nâga Raja Erâpatra pays his devotions to Buddha by kneeling with joined hands at the foot of the Sacred Tree. The bas-reliefs on the Buddhist Railings at Buddha-Gaya, which are also contemporary works, agree with those of Bharhut in making the Bodhi Tree, the Stûpa, and the Wheel the three great objects of Buddhist reverence.[4] In the edicts of Asoka veneration for the Holy Fig-tree (*Aswatha*) is strongly inculcated, and both benefit and pleasure are promised to the people who make offerings to it. But there is no mention of either *Stúpas* or *Wheels.*

According to a Buddhist legend, quoted by Spence Hardy,[5] Gotama Buddha declared to Ananda that the objects proper to be worshipped are of three kinds: 1. *Sarîrika;*

---

[1] See Plate XXXIII. figs. 6 and 7.   [2] See Plate XXXIV. fig. 2.
[3] Journal Asiatic Society of Bengal VI. p. 585; James Prinsep's Translation of the west edict on the Delhi-Siwâlik Pillar.
[4] See Archæological Survey of India, Vol. I. Plate IX., where all of these objects are shown.
[5] Eastern Monachism, pp. 212-216.

2. *Uddesika* ; 3. *Paribhogika*. The first class consists of bodily relics of Buddha, such as *bones* after burning, and also cuttings of *hair* and *nails*. "The second," according to Spence Hardy, "includes those things that have been erected on his account, or for his "sake, which the commentators say mean the *images* of his person," but which in ancient times would appear to have been limited to *Stúpas*, *Wheels*, and *Tri-Ratnas*, or "Triple-Gem Symbols." The third class includes the personal possessions of a Buddha, such as his *girdle*, his *alms-bowl*, his *bathing-robe*, his *drinking vessel*, and his *seat* or *throne*. In this last class are included the *Bodhi Trees* of the different Buddhas.

The worship of the Bodhi Tree was specially enjoined by Sâkya Muni himself, who directed Ananda to obtain a branch of the tree under which he had obtained Buddhahood, and to plant it in the court of the Vihâra at Srâvasti ; adding that " he who worships it " will receive the same reward as if he worshipped me in person."[1] Such being the recorded origin of the reverence paid to the Pippal Tree of the last Buddha Sâkya Sinha, it is not surprising that Tree worship was generally popular. In the Divya Avadâna it is related that the Bodhi Tree was the favourite object of Asoka's worship ;[2] and in the Bharhut Sculptures we find that the Nâga Raja pays his adorations to Buddha (Bhagavat) by kneeling down, with joined hands and bowed head, before the Sacred Tree. In none of the many sculptured scenes at Bharhut and Buddha-Gaya, all of which are contemporary with Asoka, is there any representation of Buddha himself. Even in the much later sculptures of Sânchi, which date from the end of the first century A.D., there is no representation of Buddha, and the sole objects of reverence are Stûpas, Wheels, and Trees. But it is quite certain that figures of Buddha had already been introduced as early as the first century B.C., as he is portrayed on some of the coins of Kanishka both sitting and standing with his right hand upraised in the act of "turning the wheel of the Law."[3] My excavations at Mathura also have brought to light many stone statues of the same age, both Jain and Buddhist, which were set up in the first century B.C., during the reigns of the Indo-Scythian princes Kanishka, Huvishka, and Vâsu Deva.[4] The numerous sculptures of the Indo-Scythian period also abound in figures of Buddha, who is everywhere represented as an object of worship with a halo round his head. As the attitudes and general treatment of the latter Indian statues agree with those of the Indo-Scythian Sculptures, I conclude that the practice of worshipping images of Buddha must have been introduced into India from the Panjâb, where it had no doubt been originated by the semi-Greek population.

The preference for the Bodhi Tree over the other *Paribhogika* objects of reverence, such as the girdle, alms-bowl, &c., would appear to have been chiefly due to its capacity of being multiplied, so that it was possible for all great kings and great cities to become possessors of scions of the holy tree, while the possession of the alms-bowl, the girdle, or any other specimen of personal property, must have been limited to one proprietor only. I believe also that the preference was partly due to the more decidedly marked distinctions between the Bodhi Trees of the different Buddhas, than between their alms-bowls, and

---

[1] Hardy's Eastern Monachism, p. 212..
[2] Burnouf, Introduction à l'Histoire du Buddhisme Indien.
[3] See Journal of Bengal Asiatic Society, Vol. III. Plate XXV. fig. 11, and Vol. XIV. p. 438, and Plate II. fig. 6, for the seated Buddha. See also Ariana Antiqua, Plate XIII. figs. 1, 2, and 3. The inscription is *Raga* • • *Saka M* • • which may be read with some certainty as *Bhagavata Saka Muni*.
[4] See Archæological Survey of India, Vol. III. pp. 30 to 34 of Mathura inscriptions.

girdles, and other personal possessions.[1] Each Buddha had his own separate Bodhi Tree; those of the last seven Buddhas being the following :

Vipaswi	-	-	*Pâtali Tree*, or Bignonia Suaveolens.
Sikhi, or Sikin	-	-	*Pundarika*, or White Lotus.
Viswabhu	-	-	*Sâla*, or Shorea robusta.
Krakuchhanda	-	-	*Sirisa*, or Acacia.
Kanaka Muni	-	-	*Udumbara*, or Ficus Glomerata.
Kâsyapa	-	-	*Nyagrodha*, or Ficus Indica.
Sâkya Muni	-	-	*Pippala*, or Ficus Religiosa.[2]

In the Bharhut Sculptures the Bodhi Trees belonging to six out of these seven Buddhas have been found, with the names attached to them, the missing name being that of Sikin. But there can be little doubt that his Bodhi Tree was also amongst the sculptures of the lost part of the Railing.

A reverence for certain trees has been held by the people of India from time immemorial. The oldest Hindu coins bear representations of holy Trees surrounded by railings; and on one coin we have the names of the two principal Trees, the Banian and the Pippal, joined together as *Vataswaka*, or the *Vata* and the *Aswatha*. The veneration for trees was noticed by the companions of Alexander, from whom Q. Curtius derived the fact that the Indians " reputed as gods whatever they held in reverence, especially " Trees, which it was death to injure."[3] In the story of the Nyagrodha Tree at Benares, by Mr. Beal, there is a very curious illustration of the antiquity of Tree worship.[4] " This " Tree was an object of veneration to all the people," &c.

According to Spence Hardy, all the different objects of Buddhist reverence were called *Chaityas*, " on account of the satisfaction or pleasure which they produce in the " mind of those by whom they are properly regarded."[5] But in the Bharhut Sculptures this term, in its Pali form of *Chetiya*, would seem to be confined to holy Trees, as in the only two instances in which it occurs, a Tree is the object of worship over which it is labelled.[6] Colebrooke translates the word as an " altar," but adds in a note that some interpret it as " a monument of wood or other materials placed in honour of a deceased " person." Wilson calls it a " *sacred tree;* a place of sacrifice or religious worship, an " altar, &c., a monument," &c. While Turnour makes it " an object of worship, whether " an image, a tree, an edifice, or a mountain."[7] As the word is derived from the root *Chit*, to think, or meditate, it would seem to include every object of veneration and worship, whether a bodily relic, such as a bone, or tooth ; a personal possession, such as a bowl, or a Bodhi Tree ; or a monument, such as a *Stûpa*, a Wheel, or an image. That Chaityas were in existence before the time of Sâkya Muni, we learn from his own mouth,

---

[1] The difference between the Banian Tree of Kâsyapa and the Pippal Tree of Sâkya Muni was patent to every one, while the difference between their alms-bowls, or other personal possessions, was most probably very slight.

[2] Turnour's Mahawanso, Introduction, p. XXX. ii.

[3] Vit. Alexand. Mag. VIII. 9. " Deos putant, quidquid colere ceperunt ; arbores maxime, quas violare capital est."

[4] Romantic History of Buddha, p. 258.   [5] Manual of Buddhism, p. 217.

[6] See Plate XLIII. fig. 4, and XLVIII. fig. 6.

[7] Colebrooke's Amara Kosha ; in voce *Chaitya*. Wilson's Sanskrit Dictionary in voce. Turnour's Mahawanso, Index in voce.

as he directed the people of Vaisâli " to maintain, respect, reverence, and make offerings
" to the *Chaityas*, and to keep up the ancient offerings without diminution."[1]

Regarding the worship of Trees Mr. Beal makes the following judicious remarks, " I
" would observe, however, that the worship is not offered to the Tree, as if it were the
" residence of a Tree-Deva, or Dryad, but simply as it suggests an association of mind
" with the complete emancipation of Buddha beneath its shade; hence, it will be seen,
" the Diamond Seat, or throne beneath the Tree, is a joint object of adoration. So again
" we see Devas and men rendering worship to the same objects, the throne being
" distinguished by the presence of the sacred symbol of the *Mani*, or threefold gem,
" indicating the all-supreme Buddha."

I.—SARIRIKA, OR BODILY RELICS.

1. *Chuḍa Mahâ*, or " Great Headdress," more usually known as *Chuḍa Mani*, or the
" Head Ornament," which comprised the *hair* as well as the headdress of Prince
Siddhârtha. This precious relic is thus described:[2] " One fold of the turban appeared
" like one thousand, and ten folds like ten thousand folds, offering the magical coup-d'œil
" of as many different pieces of cloth, arranged with the most consummate skill. The
" extremity of the turban, which crossed vertically the whole breadth of the countless
" folds, appeared covered with a profusion of shining rubies. The head of Siddhârtha
" was small, but the folds of the turban seemed numberless." When the prince had
reached the opposite bank of the Anauma River, he cut off his hair with a single stroke
of his sword, and holding his hair and headdress together, he exclaimed, " If I am
" destined to become a Buddha let my hair and headdress remain suspended in the air;
" if not, let them fall to the ground."[3] The relic was at once seized by a Deva, who
carried it up to the Trayastrinshas heavens, where a building was erected over it called
Dædi Dzula Mani, (Chaitya-Chuḍa Mani). This famous relic is faithfully represented in
one of the Bharhut Sculptures, on a corner Pillar of the West Gateway.[4] To the right
there is the palace of the Devas, which is duly labelled *Vijayanta Pasâde*, or the " Palace
of Victory," which was the actual name of the building in the Trayastrinshas heavens,
in which the Devas were said to live. Beside the palace there is a domed temple,
enshrining the Headdress Relic, which is the exact counterpart of the headdresses worn
by all royal personages in the Bharhut Sculptures. This building is also duly labelled
" *Sudhammâ Deva Sabhâ Bhagavato Chuḍa-Maho*," or the " Head ornament of Buddha in the
" holy assembly of the Devas." Below these the Apsarases, or Heavenly Nymphs, are
represented dancing and singing in honour of the holy relic.

The building itself which enshrines the relic would appear to be square, with a
domed roof supported on pillars. In the middle of the front there is a projection like a
portico, with an arched roof, and a semicircular hood moulding. But the great
peculiarity of this building is that the roof is formed by two domes, one over the other,
exactly in the same manner as those of the chapels and the other Buddhist buildings at
Takhti-Bahi and Jamâl-garhi in the Yusafzai district. The lower dome is quite flat on
the top, from which rises a low cylindrical neck supporting a hemispherical dome, which

[1] Turnour, in Bengal Asiatic Society Journal, VII. 994.
[2] Bigandet, Legend of the Burmese Buddha, p. 52. 63.
[3] Ibid., p. 60.   [4] See Plate XVI., upper bas-relief.

overlaps the neck all round. By this arrangement, the under dome forms a flat ceiling to the lower storey, and a level floor to the upper storey, like those of the Buddhist buildings in the Yusafzai district.

II.—UDDESIKA, OR MONUMENTS.

1. STÛPAS.

A Stûpa was originally only a mound of earth, or a pile of stones, heaped up over a dead body as a memorial monument, such as the great barrows at Lauriya to the north of Bettiah. But the Stûpa of the Buddhists was a structural monument of stone or brick, raised to enshrine the bodily relics of a Buddha, or of some holy Arhat, or of a *Chakra-vartti-Râjâ*, or powerful king. Thus in his last injunctions to his disciple Ananda, Buddha dwelt " on the merits to be acquired by building thupá over relics of " *Tathágata, Páche Buddhá*, and *Sáwaka*, or Buddhas Pratyekas, and *Srâwakas;* and he more particularly pointed out that they who prayed at the shrines that would be raised to him would be born in heaven. On another occasion he informed Ananda that over the remains of a *Chakravartti* Raja "they built the *thúpo* at a spot where four principal roads meet."[1]

The *Stûpas* represented in the Bharhut Sculptures are masonry structures of the same form, and are adorned with the same amount of umbrellas and garlands, as those in the bas-reliefs of the Sánchi Tope. One of these Stûpas is shown in the accompanying Plate.[2] There are three or four other representations of similar Stûpas, of which one only has the Buddhist Railing surrounding the base. In the specimen given in the plate two streamers are shown hanging from the edge of the umbrella. Two large flowers spring from the top of the square pedestal on which the umbrella rests, and two others from its base. The dome itself is ornamented with a long undulated garland suspended in loops from pegs. These garlands are still used in Burma, where they are made of coarse flowered or figured muslins, in the shape of long cylinders or pipes extended by rings of bambu. I have seen them of all sizes from 30 and 40 to 200 feet in length, and from 6 inches to 2 feet in diameter. They are carried in processions on holy days by numerous bearers, and are eventually hung up on pegs around the Stûpa, exactly as shown in the Bharhut Sculpture, or are suspended from holy Trees or pillars in the courtyard of the Stûpa.

2. WHEELS.

Of the *Wheel* symbol I observed only three specimens amongst the Bharhut Sculptures; but one of these is of special value, as it is labelled *Bhagavato dhamma Chakam*,[3] or " Wheel of the Law of Buddha." It is placed inside a temple as an object of worship, and is surmounted by an umbrella, and adorned with garlands. Beneath, in a four-horse chariot, the great Raja Prasenajit is approaching to pay his respects to the holy Symbol.

---

[1] Tournour's in Bengal Asiatic Society, Journal, VII. 1006.

[2] See Plate XIII., side bas-relief, and Plate XXXI. fig. 1, for two highly decorated representations of Stûpas

[3] Plate XIII., to right. At the foot of this sculpture there is another bas-relief, but unfortunately broken which represents the famous Raja Prasenajita in a four-horse chariot. See Plate XXXI. 2, and Plate XXIV. 4.

The inscription attached to this scene is of unusual interest, as it gives the name of Prasenajita, the great king of Srâvasti, who was a contemporary of Sâkya Muni. The inscription reads simply, "*Raja Pasenaji Kosalo.*" Now we learn from the Chinese pilgrim Hwen Thsang that *Prasenajit* had built a great "Salle de la loi" for the use of Buddha.[1] The original Indian name of this building must have been either *Punya Sâla*, or *Dharmma Sâla*.

The earlier pilgrim Fa Hian[2] also records that Prasenajit, during Buddha's absence in the Trayastrinshas heavens, set up an image of him in sandal wood on the throne of the Vihâr, which Buddha usually occupied. But as we have already seen that images of Buddha were not known in India in the time of Asoka, nor even down to a much later period, I think it nearly certain that the object which Prasenajita set up was the *Dharmma Chakra*, or Smybol of Buddha as the turner of the "Wheel of the Law." In after times an image would have been added, which would have supplanted the old Symbol of the Wheel. At any rate there can be no doubt about the object which appears in this representation of Prasenajita's *Punya Sâla* being the *Dharmma Chakra*, or "Wheel of the Law," as this title is engraved on the roof of the Vihâra or Temple which enshrines it.

A second specimen of the same Symbol is shown in the accompanying Plate as occupying the summit of a pillar.[3] This was also a favourite design with the ancient Buddhists, as a similar representation is found both at Buddha Gaya, and at Sânchi, whilst a pillar surmounted by a wheel was actually standing at Srâvasti at the time of Fa Hian's visit in the early part of the fifth century. In the present instance the Symbol is being worshipped by both men and women who are standing before it.

3. TRI-RATNA SYMBOL.

The principal Buddhist Symbol is the *Tri-Ratna*, or "Triple Gem" Symbol, which is found in all the countries wherever Buddhism has prevailed. Mr. Beal calls this "the "sacred Symbol of the *Mani*, or threefold gem, indicating the all supreme Buddha;" and in another place he describes the Symbol as "the triple object of their veneration, Buddha, the Law, and the Church."[4] This triple Symbol was a very favourite form of ornament for the pinnacle of a gateway, or the earrings of a lady, and for the point of a military standard, or the centre piece of a necklace.[5] In the Bharhut Sculptures the Tri-Ratna Symbol is placed above the thrones of the Buddhas Viswabhu, and Sâkya Muni.[6]

Considerable interest attaches to this Symbol of the *Tri-ratna*, as there can be no reasonable doubt that the three rude figures of Jagannâth, and his sister, and brother, now worshipped with so much fervour in Orissa, have been directly derived from three of these Symbols. I was first led to this opinion in 1851, by the discovery of three of these Symbols set up together in one of the Sânchi Sculptures.[7] Since then I have found that these same three rude Jagannâth figures are used in all the Native Almanacs of

[1] Julian's Hwen Thsang, IL 294.
[2] Beal's Fa Hian, pp. 75-76.
[3] See Bhilsa Topes, Plate XXXII., for examples of ornamentation.
[4] See Plate XXIX. and Plate XIII., left-hand bas-relief.
[5] See Bhilsa Topes, Plate XXXIII. figs. 22 and 23.
[3] See Plate XXXIV. fig. 4.
[4] Catena of Buddhist Scriptures, pp. 147-49.

Mathura and Banáras as the representative of Buddha in the Buddha Avatára of Vishnu. This last fact seems to me to be conclusive; but I may add that the Jagannáth figure in Orissa is universally believed to contain a *bone* of *Krishna*.[1] But as Bráhmans do not worship the relics of their gods, I conclude that this bone must be a relic of Buddha, and that the rude figure of Jagannáth in which it is contained is one of the old *Tri Ratnas*, or "Triple-gem" Symbols, of the Buddhist Triad. The able reviewer of Mr. Fergusson's "Tree and Serpent Worship" remarks that "one of General Cunningham's " happiest hits is his derivation of the three fetish-like figures of Jagannáth and his sister " and brother, from three of the combined emblems of the Buddhist Trinity, placed side " by side as at Sanchi."[2] "The resemblance," he adds, "is rude but unmistakable."

III.—PARIBHOGIKA, OR "PERSONAL POSSESSIONS."

1. THRONES.

The throne of each Buddha is represented under his Bodhi Tree, and the thrones of the last four Buddhas, which are often mentioned by the Chinese pilgrims are joined together in a single bas-relief on one of the Railing bars.[3] Sákya Muni's throne will also be found in the sculpture representing the Nága Elápatra's worship of Buddha, and in the bas-relief representing the visit of Ajátasatru.[4] In nearly every instance the throne is covered by an umbrella, with garlands hanging from its edge. The Vajrásan or Diamond Throne of Sákya Muni still exists under the Pipal Tree at Bodh Gaya; but it has been so altered by repeated repairs, that it no longer represents a seat, but simply a series of steps surrounding the Tree.

2. BUDDHA-PAD, OR "FOOTPRINTS" OF BUDDHA.

The *Buddha-pad*, or "Footprints of Buddha," was most probably an object of reverence from a very early period. It must certainly have been fully established before the building of the Bharhut Stúpa, as the well-known footprints are represented in two separate sculptures, in one of which they form the object of worship.[5] In the "Ladder scene" at Sankisa, the print of one foot is shown on the top step, and that of the other foot on the lowermost step of the middle line of steps by which Buddha descended from the Trayastrinshas heavens. In the first sculpture the footprints are placed on a throne or altar which is canopied by an umbrella hung with garlands. A royal personage is kneeling before the altar, and reverently touching the footprints with his hands. The second example is in the bas-relief representing the visit of Ajátasatru to Buddha. Here, as in all the other Bharhut Sculptures, Buddha does not appear in person, his presence being marked by his footprints on the step of the throne.[6] The Wheel Symbol, which was one of the 32 birth-marks of a child destined to become a Bodhisatwa, is duly marked on both footprints.[7] Perhaps the worship of the footprints may have sprung up

---

[1] Ward's Hindus, Vol. I. p. 206; and Journal of Bengal Asiatic Society, Vol. XVIII. p. 97.
[2] Mr. Healy, in the "Calcutta Review."
[3] See Plate XXXI. fig. 4, for the four thrones. Sákya Muni's throne will be found in Plate XIII., left-hand sculpture.
[4] See Plate XIV., right hand, and Plate XVI. right hand.
[5] See Plate XVI., middle bas-relief.   [6] See Plate XVI. 3.
[7] Lalita Vistara, translated by M. Foucaux from Tibetan, p. 108.

in imitation of the reverence shown by Mahâ Kâsyapa and the priesthood to the actual feet of Buddha, when his body was lying on the funeral pile. "Adjusting his robes " (so) as to leave one shoulder bare, and with clasped hands, having performed the " *paddkhinan* perambulation three times round the pile, he opened (the pile) at the feet, " reverentially bowed down his head at the feet of Bhagawa."[1] The 500 priests did the same, and when the whole were in the "act of bowing down in adoration the funeral " pile of Bhagawâ spontaneously ignited."

Another name for these "footprints" is *Sripáda*, which is the common term now in use in Ceylon.[2] According to Spence Hardy, Buddha "left an imprint of his foot on " the bank of the river (Narmada), in the midst of a sandy desert, on a spot that is " occasionally covered by the waves. This impression may still be seen in the *Yon* " country, at a place where the waves strike upon a sandhill, and they again retire. It " is only on the retiring of the waves that the mark of the foot can be seen. From the " river Gotama went to the rock Sachabadha, upon the summit of which at the request " of a priest of the same name, he made an impression of his foot in clay."[3] Hardy suggests that a town named *Siripala*, which is placed by Ptolemy on the Narmada River, where it is joined by the Mophis or Myhes, ought probably to be *Sripada*, or the "illustrious foot." This scene is accompanied by a long inscription which I am unable to translate, but the pith of it would appear to be in the last few words, *Bhagavato sâsani patisandhi*.[4]

3. BODHI TREES.

The *Bodhi Tree* is a very common subject in Buddhist Sculpture; but it is only at Bharhut that we find the important addition of the names of the Buddhas to whom the trees belonged. The names of six out of the last seven Buddhas have been found; but the Bodhi Tree of Krakuchanda is broken, although his name is quite intact. The five remaining trees are represented in the accompanying Plates, to which I have added a sixth, which is being worshipped by a herd of wild Elephants.

The earliest of the Buddhas whose Bodhi Tree has been found is Vipasin, whose tree has a Throne or Bodhimanda in front, before which two people are kneeling, whilst a crowd of others with joined hands are standing on each side of the tree. The sculpture is labelled *Bhagavato Vipasino Bodhi*, or "the Bodhi Tree of the Buddha *Vipasyin*.[5] His tree was the *Pátali*, or Trumpet Flower, *Bignonia Suaveolens*.

The Bodhi Tree of the next Buddha, named *Sikhin*, has not been found; but that of the third of the seven Buddhas, named *Viswabhu*, is in excellent order, and is duly labelled *Bhagavato Vesabhuno Bodhi Sâlo*, or "the Bodhi Sâl Tree of the Buddha Vis-wabhu."[6] His tree was the *Sâl* or Shorea Robusta. There is a Throne or Bodimanda in front, surmounted by the symbol which is so common in all Buddhist Sculptures and coins, and which is freely used as an ornament for earrings and necklaces. In shape it may be compared to the small Greek letter *Omega*, surmounting an *Omikron*, or circle.

[1] Turnour in Bengal Asiatic Society Journal, VII. 1012.   [2] Hardy, Eastern Monachism, p. 227.
[3] Hardy, Manual of Buddhism, pp. 209, 210.   [4] See Plate LIV. No. 65, for this inscription.
[5] See Plate XXIX. fig. 1. It is on No. 2 Pillar of the N.W. quadrant. The inscription is given in Plate LIII. fig. 67.
[6] Ibid., fig. 2. It is on No. 2 Pillar of S.E. quadrant. The inscription is given in Plate LIII. No. 2 Pillar fig. 3. I have given another specimen of Sâl Tree with its flowers in the same Plate.

The latter would appear to be the *Dharmma Chakra*, and the former is the *Tri-ratna*, or "Triple Gem," which has been already noticed. Numerous garlands are hanging from all the branches of the tree. Two figures, male and female, are kneeling beside the throne, and two others, also male and female, are standing under the tree. The former is offering a bowl, and the latter a garland.

The next Bodhi Tree is that of Krakuchanda, the first of the last four Buddhas, which was a *Sirisa* or Acacia. This sculpture is unfortunately broken, but the inscribed label is still perfect, *Bhagavato Kakusadhasa Bodhi*, or the "Bodhi Tree of the Buddha Krakuchanda."[1]

The Bodhi Tree of the next Buddha, Kanaka Muni was an *Udumbara*, or Ficus glomerata. It has a *Bodhimanda*, or throne in front, supported on pillars, with two kneeling females before it. Under the tree which has garlands on its branches, are two male figures offering respectively a bowl and a garland. The sculpture is duly labelled *Bhagavato Konigamenasa Bodhi*, or "the Bodhi Tree of the Buddha Konâgamena" (or Kanaka Muni).[2]

The bas-relief representing the Bodhi Tree of Kâsyapa Muni, the third Buddha, is similar to those already described, with the exception that one of the females is sitting on a *Morha* before the throne, instead of kneeling. The tree of this Buddha was the *Nyagrodha*, that is the Banian or Ficus Indica; but the treatment of the leaves, as far as I have noticed, does not appear to differ in any observable points from that of the *Udumbara*, or the *Pippala;* and I can see no trace of any of the distinctive downward offshoots of a Banian tree. Perhaps the garlands hanging above the throne may have interfered with the proper delineation of the Tree, as other examples have the distinctive pendent roots of the Banian Tree, of which I have given one specimen in the Plate. The sculpture is labelled *Bhagavato Kasapasa Bodhi*, or "the Bodhi Tree of Buddha Kasyapa."[3]

The Bodhi Tree of the last Buddha Sâkya Muni is much more elaborately treated than any of the others.[4] This was the Pippala, or *Ficus Religiosa.* The trunk is entirely surrounded by an open-pillared building with an upper storey, ornamented with niches containing umbrellas. Two umbrellas are placed in the top of the tree, and numerous streamers are hanging from the branches. In the two upper corners are flying figures with wings, bringing offerings of garlands. On each side there is a male figure raising a garland in his right hand, and holding the tip of his tongue with the thumb and forefinger of the left hand. This curious action is also seen in another sculpture, in which the worship of Sâkya Muni's Bodhi Tree is represented.[5] In the lower story of the building there is a throne in front of a tree surmounted by two specimens of the favourite Buddhist symbol, which has before appeared with the Bodhi Tree of Viswabhu. Two figures, male and female, are kneeling before the throne; while a female figure is standing to the left, and a Nâga Raja with his hands crossed on his breast to the right. This figure is distinguished by a triple Serpent crest, and his attitude of devotion is exactly

---

[1] See Plate XXIX. for the sculpture ; and Plate LIII. No. 71, for the inscription.

[2] See Plate XXIX. fig. 4, for the sculpture, which is on No. IX. Pillar of the S.E. quadrant. The inscription is given in Plate LIII. No. IX. Pillar, fig. 11.

[3] See Plate XXX. fig. 1, for the sculpture ; and Plate LIV. No. 49, for the inscription.

[4] See Plate XXX. fig. 3, for the sculpture ; which belongs to the South-west quadrant. The inscription is given in Plate LIV., Corner Pillar, S. Gateway, No. 28.

[5] See Plate XVII., lower compartment, right hand.

similar to that of the Nâga Raja Chakavâka on the corner pillar of the South Gate. To the extreme right there is an isolated pillar surmounted by an Elephant holding out a garland in his trunk. On the domed roof of the building is inscribed, *Bhagavato Saka Munino Bodhi*, or " the Bodhi Tree of the Buddha Sâkya Muni."

As a further illustration of Tree Worship I may refer to a very curious scene of a herd of wild Elephants paying their devotions to a Bodhi Tree. In this instance the tree is easily recognisable as a Banian by its long pendent shoots; and this identification is confirmed by the name of *Nyagrodha*, which occurs in the accompanying inscribed label. In front of the tree is the usual throne, or Bodhimanda, before which Elephants, old and young, are kneeling. To the right and left other Elephants are bringing garlands to hang on the branches of the tree. In the upper left corner there is a second tree, and to to the right, where the stone is broken, a male figure with joined hands overlooks the whole scene. There are two labels attached to this sculpture. The first, which is limited to *bahu-hathiko*, or " the great herd of Elephants," is inscribed on one of the small sculptured pillars of the Buddhist Railing, immediately below the throne. The other describes the scene *bahu hathika nigodha nadode*, which I am unable to translate satisfactorily.[1] *Nigodha* is the *Nyagrodha* or Banian, which was the Bodhi Tree of Kâsyapa Buddha, and is correctly represented in the sculpture. The last word *nadode* occurs again in two other inscribed labels.[2]

A similar scene is described by both of the Chinese pilgrims, Fa Hian and Hwen Thsang, but the object of reverence was the deserted Stûpa of Râmagrâma. According to the elder pilgrim, " ever and anon a herd of Elephants, carrying water in their trunks, piously watered the ground, and also brought all sorts of flowers and perfumes to pay religious worship at the Tower. Buddhist pilgrims from all countries come here to pay their vows, and worship at the shrine. On one occasion some of these (or one of these) met the Elephants, and being very much frightened concealed themselves amongst the trees. They then saw the Elephants perform their services according to the Law."[3]

The account of Hwen Thsang is much more brief, but it confirms Fa Hian's description of the herd of wild Elephants making offerings of flowers to the Stûpa of Râmagrâma.[4] I conclude that the scene shown in the Bharhut Sculpture is an old form of the legend as it existed in the time of Asoka. I think also that the single man standing to the right of the tree is intended to represent the frightened pilgrim who concealed himself amongst the trees, and thus beheld the spontaneous offerings made by the herd of wild Elephants. The whole scene in fact appears to me to be exactly the same as that described by the two Chinese pilgrims, with the single difference of the substitution of a Bodhi Tree for the Stûpa of Râmagrâma.

A very fine specimen of a Bodhi Tree occurs on a long Rail Bar of one of the Gateways. There is no label attached to it; but the foliage is so distinct from that of the Bodhi Trees of the last three Buddhas, that I feel certain it must be intended for the *Sirisa*, or Acacia, of their immediate predecessor *Krakuchhanda*. The trunk is surmounted by a two-storeyed building, with arched openings, and in the Courtyard there is an

---

[1] See Plate XV., right hand, for the sculpture, which belongs to a corner pillar of the S. Gate. The inscription is given in Plate LIV. No. 44.

[2] See the last two scenes in Plate XLVIII. Nos. 9 and 11, and the inscriptions in Plate LIII., Copings Nos. 18 and 19.

[3] Beal's Fa Hian, p. 91.

[4] Julien's Hwen Thsang, p. 91.

isolated pillar surmounted by an Elephant. All the details are quite different from those of the Bodhi Trée of Sâkya Muni, but the most marked difference is in the small delicate foliage, which I take to be intended for the *Sirisa* of Krakuchhanda.[1]

G.—DECORATIVE ORNAMENTS.

The purely decorative ornaments which fill more than a half of the full medallions, and nearly all the half medallions, may be divided into three classes, according to their prevailing subjects, as Animal, Flowered, and Geometrical.

Most of the animals occurring in these medallions have already been described, but as they are generally surrounded with flowered borders, some of the more striking amongst them will be noticed on account of their adjuncts. These flowered borders are by far the finest works of the kind that I have yet seen in India. In the five accompanying Plates I have given upwards of forty specimens of the medallions, which include examples of every kind yet found excepting those that represent Buddhist legends.[2] But most of these, as well as the Játakas and other scenes, have already been given in some of the preceding Plates.

There is only one example of a *Geometrical* pattern amongst all the numerous sculptured medallions at Bharhut. But even in this apparently simple pattern the guiding feature is the *Swastika*, or mystic cross, and the whole is only a repetition of the cross with its four arms extended, each of which meets one of the extended arms of another cross. The pattern is effective as a decoration.[3]

In the flowered medallions, the central portion is always a many-leaved lotus, of which there are some very striking representations. Except in a few rare instances the flowers are always full blown, with the different rows of leaves well displayed. The leaves are generally pointed with rounded sides; but in some instances, for the sake of variety, their edges are made straight, and in a few others the points are rounded.[4] In the few exceptional cases the inner leaves are represented as only just beginning to open, while the outer leaves are fully displayed.[5] The simple lotus flower, without borders or ornamental addition of any kind, forms a common and effective decoration.[6] But the favourite design would appear to have been the full-blown lotus, surrounded with a broad border. In these borders the artist has showed both fertility of design and delicacy of taste, and the result is a series of ornamental medallions of rare beauty. Sometimes the border is confined to another row of leaves, divided from the central flower by a circular band, either plain or ornamented.[7] But the more usual form is a border of a distinct design, either of animals, or of ornamental chains, or of geometrical figures, or of repetitions of small flowers, or of a continuous undulating stalk studded with leaves and flowers.

Of the first class of these borders there are only a few specimens, representing a succession of winged lions, and of serpents' heads.[8]

Of the second class there are two examples in the Plates, which I take to be intended for some of the elaborate neck chains worn by all the people of rank. One of them

---

[1] See Plate XXXI. fig. 3.
[2] See Plates XXXIV. to XXXVIII.
[3] See Plate XI., middle pillar, full medallion.
[4] See Plate XXXVI. fig. 8 for the former, and Plate XXXV. fig. 8, for the latter,

[5] See Plate XXXV. fig. 7.
[6] See Plate XXXVIII. figs. 5 and 10.
[7] See Plate XXXV. fig. 6.
[8] See Plate XXXVI. fig. 5; and Plate XXXVIII. figs. 4 and 11.

consists of five rows of beads or pearls, with a number of round and square ornaments placed at intervals to the different strings in position.[1] The second example given in fig. 9, Plate XXXVIII., is much simpler. Of the geometrical borders I have given two specimens. The first, composed of linked squares and circles, is found as an abacus ornament on one of Asoka's pillars, and the other, composed of a succession of curved figures, is clearly suggestive of the serpents' heads already noted.[2] The borders of continuous rows of small flowers are very numerous. Four examples will be found in the Plates, which I have selected as exhibiting the richness and variety of the Bharhut style of ornamentation.[3] In some medallions the row of flowers is changed for a succession of small sprigs of conventional forms, which has an equally rich effect, but is perhaps not so striking.[4] The borders, composed of undulating stalks studded with leaves and flowers, are of less common occurrence. The two examples given in the Plates are fine specimens of these rich borders, but in one of them, at least, the flowers are perhaps too much crowded.[5]

Of the full medallions represented in the Plates, fig. 1 of Plate XXXV. has already been noticed as offering the bust of a Queen. Fig. 1, Plate XXXVI., is considered by Mr. Beglar to have been altered " by cutting and mutilating the original figure," which had " no connexion with the Brahmanical Lakshmi." But the same subject appears in the middle of the Gateway architecture of No. 3 Stûpa at Bhilsa, the date of which is not known, but which is most probably of the same age as the other Sânchi Sculptures, or about A.D. 100. A very much earlier representation of this scene, however, occurs on a large silver coin of Azilises in my possession, whose date cannot be later than 70 B.C. But in this latter case there is no proof that the subject belongs more to Buddhism than to Brahmanism. In the Sânchi Sculpture, however, its prominent position would seem to show that it was clearly Buddhistical. The figure of the goddess Lakshmi, sitting on a lofty Lotus Throne, was also one of the visions of Queen Trisalâ, the mother of Mahavira, the last hierarch of the Jainas. She held a water lily in her hand, and beside her stood her guardian elephant, " bathing her with water from his trunk."[6] The Bharhut specimen has been much injured by repeated ointments of ghi and oil, and the present figure of the goddess has been re-cut by a village mason, the marks of whose chisel are still prominent. The subject is not an uncommon one with Brahmanical sculptors, but I am unable to give any Buddhistical explanation of it.

The fish-tailed Elephant seen in fig. 2, Plate XXXVI., occurs amongst the Buddhist Sculptures of Buddha Gaya, but of a later date. The Elephant is holding up a bunch of lotus flowers with his trunk.

The central symbol of fig. 1, Plate XXXVII., has already appeared in one of the half medallions.[7] Here it is surmounted by a full-blown lotus flower seen from the side, accompanied by two half-blown flowers and two buds. Below it is a half lotus.

Fig. 3, Plate XXXVII., is entirely a fanciful figure, rising from a lotus, with a winged animal on each side.

---

[1] See Plate XXXVI. fig. 6.
[2] See Plate XXXV. fig. 3, and Plate XXXVI. fig. 11.
[3] See Plate XXXVII. figs. 2, 6, 7; and Plate XXXVI. fig. 8.
[4] See Plate XXXVIII. figs. 6 and 7.
[5] See Plate XXXVII. figs. 8 and 9.
[6] Dr. Stevenson's Kalpa Sutra, pp. 44, 45.
[7] See Plate XXXV. fig. 4.

Figs. 1 and 3, Plate XXXVIII., are compositions of lotus flowers rising from vases, with birds standing on the flowers. The two halves of these medallions are not exactly alike, although they have much similarity. They will stand comparison with most compositions of the same kind of a much later date, even during the most flourishing period of the Mughal empire.

Fig. 2, Plate XXXVIII., contains the famous Buddhist symbol of the *Dharma Chakra*, or "Wheel of the Law," with its top ornament of the *Tri Ratna*, or "Three Gems," four times repeated, above, below, and at the two sides. The same quadrangle form is also found upon early Buddhist coins, and on one of the Pillars at Sonári, near Bhilsa.

H.—BUDDHIST BUILDINGS.

The number of buildings represented in the Bharhut Sculptures is not many, and as most of them are on a very small scale, they offer but few details. We get, however, the leading features of all the principal religious structures, such as Stûpas, Palaces (*Prâsâda*), Temples or Shrines (*Kuṭi* and *Punya Sâla*), Thrones of the Buddhas (*Bodhimanda* and *Vajrâsan*), and Pillars, both isolated and combined. There are also several representations of Ascetic Hermitages, as well as a few specimens of the common dwellings of the people. I will now give a short account of these different kinds of buildings, as far as I have been able to make them out from their small sculptured representations. The Stûpas have already been described and do not require any further notice in this place.

1. PALACES.

Of *Palaces* there is one specimen labelled *Vijayanta Prâsâda*, which was the name of the Palace of the Devas in the Trayastrinshas Heavens. It is a three-storeyed building, and the only one of that height represented in the Sculptures.[1] The basement storey appears to be an open-pillared hall, the lower third of its height being closed by a Buddhist Railing. The building is also divided into three portions perpendicularly, of which the middle portion is retired. The lower third of the second storey is also closed by a Buddhist Railing, above which rise three arched openings, one on each section of the building. Above these a broad band, probably of mouldings, runs the whole width of the temple. The third storey also has its Buddhist Railing, above which are two arched openings in the wings, the middle recessed portion being plain. This would seem to be the usual finish for the uppermost story of such buildings, as it is repeated in the Punya Sâla of Raja Prasenajita.[2] In the Vijayanta Prâsâda the roof is not fully displayed, owing to want of space in the panel; but as all the other buildings in the Bharhut Sculptures are covered with domes, I presume that this also had a domed roof. As it is here represented there is nothing but its size and its three storeys to distinguish this Prâsâda or Palace from the smaller buildings called *Kuṭi* and *Punya Sâla* as well as from the canopy buildings which covered the *Bodhimanda* thrones or seats of the Buddhas.

---

[1] See Plate XVI. fig. A, to left. The shrine of the *Chuḍa Maha*, or head ornament of Buddha, and the dance of the Apsarases below, are further proofs that the building labelled Vijayanta Prâsâda is a palace.

[2] See Plate XIII. fig. 3.

The *Kuṭi*, in the two specimens labelled as *Gandha Kuṭi* and *Kosâmbi Kuṭi*, was a single-storeyed building, enclosing an altar or throne with a garland hanging over it.[1] It has an arched doorway, which is surmounted by a second arch like a hood-moulding. The roof the *Kosâmbi Kuṭi* is a dome, with a small pinnacle on the top; but that of the *Gandha Kuṭi* has gable ends with a pinnacle at each end.

A building of similar outline to that of the Kuṭi is represented in the same panel with the Vijayanta Prâsâda. It has the same arched door with its semicircular hood moulding, and the same domed roof. But it appears to be an open-pillared hall with a throne in the middle, canopied by an umbrella hung with garlands. It is inscribed,—

Sudhamma Devasabhâ

Bhagavato Ohuḍamahâ,

from which it is certain that this was the Hall of Assembly (*Sabhâ*) in the midst of which was enshrined a relic of Buddha known as the *Chuḍâ Mahâ*, or head-dress of Buddha. The lower part is surmounted with a Buddhist Railing.[1]

2. PUNYA-SÂLAS OR RELIGIOUS HOUSES.

The Punya Sâla of Raja Prasenajita is a two-storeyed building which enshrines the *Dharma Chakra*, or "Wheel of the Law" as a symbol of Buddha.[3] The lower storey appears to be an open-pillared hall standing on a plinth or basement which is ornamented with a Buddhist Railing. The upper storey, like that of the Vijayanta Temple, as I have previously noticed, is divided into three portions, of which the middle one is slightly retired. The two wings are pierced with arched windows covered with semicircular hood-mouldings, and the wall of the centre portion is ornamented with a line of Buddhist Railing up to the springing of the hood-moulding. From this level also springs the semi-cylindrical domed roof with two gable ends, and a line of eight small pinnacles on the ridge.

3. VAJRÂSAN CANOPIES.

Of the *Bodhimandâ* shrines, or *Vajrâsan* canopies, there are several fine examples, more especially that of Sâkya Muni, and another without inscription. In both of these the building consists of two storeys. The simpler form, which, as I believe, canopies the Bodhimandâ and Sirisa Tree of Krakuchanda, has three arched openings in front, and was most probably a square building, with the same number of openings on all sides, somewhat similar to the present *Bâradari*, or twelve-door summer house.[4] The trunk of the Bodhi Tree with the Vajrâsan or Diamond Throne is seen in the middle opening, and pendent garlands in the side openings. The two storeys are separated by an ornamental band of Buddhist Railing. In the centre appears the upper part of the Bodhi Tree breaking through the roof, and on each side a small arched window, or niche, with a garland hanging inside. Garlands are also pendent from the branches of the tree. The style of roof is uncertain, but as the building has rounded ends it was most probably covered by a dome.

---

[1] See Plate XXVIII. fig. 3. Gandha Kuṭi is near the top of the medallion, with its name inscribed on the edge above; the Kosâmbi Kuṭi is to the left below, with its name on the left edge beside it.

[2] See Plate XVI. fig. 1.   [3] See Plate XIII. fig. 3.   [4] See Plate XXXI. fig. 3

The more ornate example of the Vajrásan canopy is that which enshrines the Bodhimandá of Sákya Muni, as inscribed on the roof of the building.[1] The sculpture presents an open-pillared hall with a broad projecting front, and retired wings to the right and left. From its appearance I conclude that the building was square, and that it presented a similar elevation on all four sides. We know that the Bodhimandá of a much later date was a square building,[2] and it seems probable that the more modern building would have preserved the shape of the original, however much it may have differed from it in size. In the bas-relief the human figures are represented on a much larger scale than either the Bhodi Tree or the buildings, the two figures standing on the upper storey being just one half of the height of the tree. But allowing the tree to have been 40 or 50 feet high, the building would have been from 20 to 30 feet in height, and from 30 to 40 feet square. The smaller dimensions are the more probable, as I observe that the front of the building is supported on two pillars only. But if the structure was of wood the larger dimensions are the more likely.

A broad band of Buddhist Railing rests directly on the pillars, and separates the two storeys of the building. The projecting front is pierced by two arched windows, or niches, covered by semi-circular hood-mouldings, and both of the wings have similar openings. An umbrella stands in each niche with pendant garlands; and the wings niches have a human figure standing on each side. The roof is rounded at the ends and appears to be a flat dome surmounted by three small pinnacles. The top of the roof just reaches the lowermost branches of the tree.

4. BODHIMANDÁ THRONES.

The *Vajrásan* or *Bodhimandá* Throne of Sákyá Muni is placed in the middle of the lower storey of the building, immediately in front of the trunk of the Bodhi Tree. This was the sacred Seat on which Sákya sat for six years in abstract meditation until he gained Buddhahood. The front only of the throne or seat is represented, but this is sufficient to show that it was a square plinth ornamented on each face with four small pillars. On the top, to the right and left of the tree, are placed two *Dharma Chakra* symbols, which here, as elsewhere throughout the Bharhut Sculptures, take the place of Buddha himself. There are two figures on each side of the throne, a man standing and a woman kneeling on the right, and a woman standing and a man kneeling on the left.

The whole scene is a very curious one, and if, as I suppose, the building be an actual representation of the shrine that surmounted the famous *Bodhimandá* at Bauldha Gaya, we have before us a very fine specimen of Indian architecture of the time of Asoka, and one of the most sacred objects of Buddhist worship. That the tree represented in the sculpture is the holy Bodhi Tree of Sákya Muni, is placed beyond all doubt by the following inscription on the roof of the building:

Bhagavato Sáka Munimo Bodhi:

" the Bodhi (Tree) of the Buddha Sákya Muni."

---

[1] See Plate XIII., outer face of pillar.
[2] Julien's Hwen Thsang, II. 460. The pilgrim speaks of the four corners of the building, and notes that it was about 100 paces in circuit, or upwards of 60 feet on each side.

In another Plate I have given a view of a large building, containing four seats, with garlands hanging over them, which I believe to be intended for the thrones of the four Buddhas.[1] I have already stated my conjecture that the human hands, which are here sculptured on the side of each throne, may be symbolical representatives of a crowd of human worshippers. The style of the building is similar to that of all the others, its main features being a large open hall supported on octagonal pillars with bell capitals, and an upper storey with three arched windows, the whole being covered by a long dome-shaped roof, surmounted by ten small pinnacles.

5. PILLARS.

The monolith Pillars sculptured in the Bharhut bas-reliefs are necessarily very small, but sufficient details are given to show that the shafts were usually octagonal, that they very rarely had any bases, and that the capitals were of the bell shape, so well known to us from Asoka's monoliths at Allahabad, Bakra, and Lauriya, but above the bell capitals there appears a second capital, which I was at first inclined to identify with the spreading bracket capitals of the Manikyâla Stûpa and other buildings in the western Panjab and Kabul valley. But when I found that no regular architraves were represented in any of the Bharhut Sculptures, I came to the conclusion that what appeared at first sight as an upper or bracket capital was perhaps only *the end* of a transverse architrave, after the fashion of the temples of Kashmir. In one of the examples, however, this does not appear to be the case, as the upper capitals are very much spread, and are most probably intended for actual brackets.[2]

There are two examples of isolated Pillars, or large monoliths, of which views will be found in the Plates.[3] In each case the pillar is surmounted by an elephant. Both have bell-shaped capitals, but their style of ornamentation is different; that of the pillar near Krackuchanda's Bodhi Tree being composed of large leaves as in all the examples of the six compartments of one of the corner pillars,[4] while that of the pillar near Sâkya Muni's Bodhi Tree is composed of festoons touching each other the same as we now see in all the existing specimens of Asoka's monoliths; the same festoon ornament is used for the capitals of the pillars in the bas-relief of the herd of wild elephants worshipping the Banian Tree of Kâsyapa Muni.[5] But as much larger specimens of both of these styles still exist in the four capitals surmounting the grouped octagonal shafts of the sole remaining pillar of the Eastern Gateway, we see that the sculptors of these bas-reliefs, even in their smallest works, adhered strictly to a correct delineation of actual forms. All the details of these capitals will be seen in the accompanying Plates.[6] I wish to direct special attention to the small height of the bell portion compared to its breadth, as I look upon this particular feature as a certain proof of the antiquity of the Pillar, and therefore of all the sculptures of the great Buddhist Railing to which it belongs.

The octagonal form of shaft, which is universal throughout all the different kinds of buildings in the Bharhut Sculptures, is departed from only in the two examples of

---

[1] See Plate XXXI. fig. 4, taken from one of the long Rail-bars.
[2] See Plate XXXI. fig. 2.
[3] See Plate XIII. outer face of pillar, and Plate XXXI. fig. 3.
[4] See Plate XVI. and XVII.
[5] See Plate XXX. fig. 3, and Plate XV. fig. 3.
[6] See Plates XXI. and XII. for three different views.

isolated Pillars, already noticed, both of which have round shafts. We know also that all the six existing monoliths of Asoka have round shafts, and that the bas-reliefs of the Buddhist Railings at Bauddha Gaya represent all the pillars of buildings as either octagonal or polygonal. It seems probable therefore that in the age of Asoka the use of the circular shaft was confined to the great isolated monoliths, such as he himself set up, and that the polygonal shaft was in general use for buildings of all kinds, both religious and civil. This conclusion seems only natural, when we remember the widespread diffusion of the one fixed type of pillar for a Buddhist Railing which was in common use throughout India for many centuries, from the banks of the Indus to the mouth of the Ganges, and from the Himálayas to the banks of the Kistna.

6. Ascetics—Hermitages.

The Hermits dwellings are all of one uniform pattern—consisting of a single circular room, with a hemispherical domed roof.[1] A narrow door is always represented; but there is nothing to show of what material these hermitages were constructed. I infer that they are not *parna sálas*, or "leaf houses," as there are no indications of leaves, such as we see in the Sánchi Sculptures, but simple round huts with mat walls and thatched roofs. In a single instance the roof is represented as divided into large squares breaking joint which must therefore be intended to represent either slates or large flat tiles.[2]

7. Dwelling-Houses.

There is some variety in the cottages of the people, but this affects only the distribution of the different buildings and not their form, which is of one stereotyped pattern,—consisting of a long room, with either a pointed or a semicylindrical domed roof, and a small opening in each gable to give air and light.[3] The ends of the longitudinal timbers are shown in the gables, which leaves no doubt that the roofs were thatched. The walls were almost certainly of unbaked bricks or sun-dried mud, as the wall of one of the quadrangles is represented with a coping on which a bird is sitting, while the opening in the house wall for the two-leaved door shows a deep recess, which would not have been the case with a mat wall.[4] The general arrangement of the private houses would appear to have been just the same as at the present. Three or four separate huts are so disposed as to form three or four sides of a square. With three huts the entrance is on the fourth side, which is closed by a wall. With four huts the entrance lies through one of the huts.

I have reserved to the last the question of what materials the religious buildings were made, whether of stone or of wood. Excepting in one solitary instance, there are no visible marks to declare the nature of the material, but in that one instance of the walls of the *Trikutika* or dwelling of the Nágas, the layers of masonry breaking bond are too plain and distinct to be mistaken. But the Stúpa itself was a mass of brick masonry, although there are no indications of masonry in the representations of Stúpas in the bas-reliefs. This may perhaps be explained by the fact that masonry walls were usually plastered over, and as the plaster presented a plain surface there were no marks to

---

[1] See Plates XLVIII. fig. 7; XXVI. fig. 3; and XLVI. fig. 4.
[2] See Plate XLII. fig. 7; and Plate XLV. fig. 7.
[3] See Plate XXVI. fig. 3.
[4] See Plate XLV. fig. 7.

represent. This explanation would also be a sufficient reason for the absence of masonry marks in the other religious buildings.

That wood was plentiful and in common use we learn from Megasthenes who states that the walls of Palibothra in the time of Chandra Gupta Maurya, the grandfather of Asoka, were of wood, pierced with openings for the discharge of arrows.[1] It may therefore be presumed that the 570 towers and 64 gates of Palibothra were likewise built of wood. But we learn also from the same authority that only the cities that were situated near the sea were built of wood, "for no buildings of brick would last long there, not " only because of the violence of the rains, but also of the rivers, which, overflowing " their banks, cause an annual inundation over all the flat country. But the cities which " are situated on an eminence, are frequently built with brick and mortar."[2] It is clear, therefore, that both modes of construction were in common use even before the age of Asoka, about whose time I fix the erection of the Bharhut Stûpa.

The account of Megasthenes will be more clearly understood by comparing it with the common practice at the present day in Burmah, which possesses all the conditions of " violent rains, overflowing river, and vicinity to the sea." There all the private dwelling-houses, as well as the monasteries, are without any exception built of wood, while the Stûpas are always, and the Temples are generally, built of brick. The houses of the people, which are placed along the banks of the rivers for the sake of convenience, are necessarily built of wood, as they are all raised upon piles so as to allow the flood waters to pass by unchecked. For a religious building some eminence is usually selected, and if the spot is beyond the reach of flood, bricks will certainly be used.

In the damp climate of Palibothra, with its broad wet ditch, it is easy to understand the preference given to a wooden stockade over a brick wall. But in the drier climates of upper and middle India, where stone is plentiful, and wood dear, it seems more probable that all buildings of any consequence would have been constructed of stone,— or partly of stone and partly of brick. I conclude, therefore, that all the great buildings in the Bharhut Sculptures are intended to represent structures of stone or brick, and not of wood. In one instance indeed, and that a most remarkable one, the great triple ladder, by which Buddha descended from the Trayastrinsha heavens, is represented as made of stone,[3] which I recognise at once as being of exactly the same form as that of the stone ladder discovered near the Western entrance of the Bharhut Stûpa.[4] Any wooden ladder would certainly have been of a much lighter form, and much more like a ladder than the solid staircase of the bas-relief.

With respect to the *Vihâras* or Temples, which were often very lofty buildings, it is not impossible that some of the upper storeys may have been made of wood. This was probably the case with the great Vihâr of the Jetavana Monastery at Srâvasti, which was no less than seven storeys in height. Its destruction by fire is thus described by Fa Hian."[5] " The monarchs of all the surrounding countries, and their inhabitants, vied " with each other in presenting religious offerings at this spot. They decked the place " with flags and silken canopies, and offered flowers and burnt incense, whilst the lamps

[1] Strabon-Geograph. XV. 1, 36. We have also a second testimony to the same effect in Euphorion, who was the librarian of Antiochus the Great. According to him " the Indian Morias (*Mauryas*) lived in wooden houses." See my " Coins of Indian Buddhist Satraps," in the Bengal Asiatic Society's Journal, Vol. XXIII. p. 680.

[2] Arrian, Indica X.

[3] See Plate XVII. fig. 2.

[4] See Plate V. bottom fig.

[5] Beal's Fa Hian, c. XX. p. 76.

" shone out after day with unfading splendour.   Unfortunately a rat, gnawing at the wicks
" of one of the lamps, caused it to set fire to one of the hanging canopies, and this resulted
" in a general conflagration, and the entire destruction of the seven storeys of the Vihâra."

In the above description I would suggest that instead of "canopies" we should read
" streamers or garlands," such as I have seen both in Ladâk and Burma, and which are
represented as attached to all the Religious Buildings of the Bharhut Sculptures.   If the
Jetavana Vihâra had been built entirely of brick, like the great Vihâras at Buddha Gaya
and Nâlanda, the ignition of dozens of these light gossamer streamers could not possibly
have done any damage to it.   But if, as I suppose, there was a staircase leading to the
uppermost story, which was supported on wooden beams instead of being vaulted, then
the conflagration and destruction of the building would be certain.

K.—MISCELLANEOUS OBJECTS.

As there still remain to be noticed a few important sculptures which could not well
be included under any of the previous headings, I will now briefly describe them under
the following divisions:—1. Vehicles; 2. Furniture; 3. Utensils; 4. Musical Instruments.

1. VEHICLES.

The only Vehicles that I have observed amongst all the varied scenes of the Bharhut
Sculptures are the Boat, the Horse Chariot, and the Bullock Cart.

Of the *Boat* there are two examples, but unfortunately they are both in the same
bas-relief, and that still lies buried under the walls of the Palace at Uchhahara.   I had it
dug up, and whilst it was above ground I had an impression made of it, which I pencilled
over on the spot, and from that impression the present sketch has been reduced.[1]   The
scene is a very curious one, Two Boats, each containing three men, are represented on
a rough sea.   A huge fish with open mouth is swallowing one of the Boats with its crew,
while the crew of the second Boat, who have stopped rowing, are evidently anticipating
the same fate.

The *Boats* themselves are of exactly the same build as the *Boat* in the Sânchi
Sculptures.   The Bharhut examples, however, are about three centuries older; but as the
very same pattern of boat and the same oars are still in use at the present day, this bas-
relief only affords us another example of the unchanging habits of the Hindus.   Such as
their Boat was in the days of Asoka, such it is now.   The planks are notched on their
edges to prevent their sliding, and they are fastened together by iron clamps.   The oars
are shaped somewhat like large spoons : each has a long bambu handle, with a flat piece
of wood at the end *to hold* the water.

Of the *Horse Chariots* there are also two examples.   One of them is the Royal Chariot
of Raja Prasenajit ; and the other is most probably a king's chariot also.

The Chariot of Prasenajit is a two-wheeled vehicle with a high ornamented front
and lower sides.[2]   It is of good size as it holds four people : the Raja himself standing
in mid front with the driver on his left hand, a *chauri bearer* on his right hand, and an
umbrella holder behind him.   The chariot is drawn by four horses with plumes on their

---

heads. Their long manes are plaited, and their long tails are tied up on one side to prevent the animals whisking them in the charioteer's face.

The other chariot occurs in the *Mugapaka* Jâtaka. It is empty but is exactly the same with the last, with the same four horses.[1]

Of the *Bullock Carts* there are likewise two specimens. One in the bas-relief of the Jetavana monastery, and the other filling the whole of the medallion of one of the Rail-bars. In both examples the Bullocks are unyoked.

The small Cart which took *Anâthapindika's* gold coins to the Jetavana garden appears to be very much the same as the common two-bullock cart of the present day. It has the same yoke with the same two pins to secure the neck of each bullock. Apparently there are no sides.[2] The large cart in the Rail medallion is a much more costly vehicle. It has only two wheels, but it has straight wooden sides, and a straight wooden back. There is also a roof placed on the ground beside the cart. From the shape of the roof it would appear that the cart must have been square. The driver is sitting on the ground with a cloth passed round his knees and loins; and in front the two Bullocks are sitting in the usual drowsy fashion.[3]

2. FURNITURE.

The chief articles of Furniture are Seats of different kinds, Bedsteads, and Lamps.

The Seats are of two kinds : *chairs* with backs and arms, and *morhas* or stools. The use of the former would seem to have been restricted to royal personages, as I find that King Nanda occupies one of the examples, and King Magha Deva another. There is a third specimen in the bas-relief of the Kinnara Jâtaka in which the king is seated with two Kinnaras before him.[4] Other people, including even the minister in the Andhabhuta Jâtaka, sit upon low stools or rocks.

Of *Bedsteads* there is only one example, but it is a good one as it is of large size, in the bas-relief of Mâyâ Devi's dreams.[5] It is a simple oblong frame supported on four round legs with club feet exactly like the common bedstead of the present day. It is entirely covered by a mattress.

The *Lamp* of Asoka's age is also represented in the same bas-relief to show that it was night when Mâyâ Devi had her dream of the White Elephant. The present example is a standing Lamp with a heavy base to keep it steady. A second example is a hanging Lamp, which is introduced into the bas-relief of Ajâtasatru's visit to Buddha to show that it was night.

3. UTENSILS.

The only Utensil that is specially noticeable in the Bharhut Sculptures is the water vessel, which plays an important part in many of the Buddhist legends, as a gift was made irrevocable by the donor pouring water over the hands of the donee. A specimen of the vessel stands beside the couch of Mâyâ Devi, from which she stayed her thirst in the night. The shape of the pot is always the same with a round handle on the top and a spout in front exactly like a modern tea kettle. In the bas-relief of Jetavana monastery

---

[1] See Plate XXV. fig. 4.
[2] See Plate XXVIII. fig. 3 ; and Plate LVII.
[3] See Plate XXXIV. fig. 1.
[4] See Plate XXV. 3 ; XLVIII. 2 ; and XXVII. 12.
[5] See Plate XXVIII. fig. 2.

the donor Anâthapindika stands with his water vessel in the midst of the garden ready to ratify his gift by pouring water over the hands of Buddha.[1] A similar vessel is held out by the Deva of a Tree to a man seated in front of the tree.[2]

Other utensils are the Bowl and the Plate or Platter. Both will be found in one of the bas-reliefs of the coping.[3]

4. MUSICAL INSTRUMENTS.

The musical instruments are not very numerous, the only specimens that I have observed being the Harp, the Drum, the Cymbals, and the Shell.

1. The *Harp* would appear to have been the most common instrument in ancient times, as it is found in many of the bas-reliefs where no other instrument is used. On one of the broken pillars of the S.E. quadrant there was a life-size statue of an Apsaras playing a harp of seven strings. A similar instrument is used by the Harper in the bas-relief of the *Indra-sála-guha*, and by the minister in the *Andabhuta* Jâtaka.[4] This kind of Harp was called *parivádini*, and was usually sounded with a plectrum (*pariváda*) held between the forefinger and thumb, and not with the hand itself. In the scene in the palace of the Devas where the Apsarases are dancing, the music consists of one Drum, two Harps, and a pair of Cymbals; and a similar proportion of the instruments is found in the great scene of the Apsarases, where the dancers have their names written beside them.[5] That the Harp was the principal instrument in the time of Buddha we learn from the legend of the *Indra-sála-guha*, where Indra sends his Harper *Pancha-Sikha* to play before Buddha. The same kind of harp remained in use down to the time of the Guptas, as we find Samudra Gupta himself represented on some of his gold coins playing the seven-stringed harp.[6]

2. The *Drum* was of two kinds: the small hand Drum which was beaten by the fingers, and the large Drum which was suspended from the neck and beaten by drumsticks. The former is found in both of the Apsarases scenes as an indoor instrument.[7]

3. The *Cymbals* are used in both of the Apsaras scenes.

4. The Shell is found only in the Monkey and Elephant scenes, in which it is fastened at the end of a pipe. The sound must have been like that of a shrill trumpet.

---

[1] See Plate XXVIII. fig. 3.
[2] See Plate XLVIII. fig. 11.
[3] See Plate XL. fig. 3.
[4] See Plate XXVIII. 4; and XXVI. 4.

[5] See Plate XVI. fig. 1; and XV. 1.
[6] See Journal Asiatic Society, IV. 637; and Plate XXXIX. fig. 26.
[7] See Plate XV. 1; and Plate XXXIII. 1, 2, 3.

III.—INSCRIPTIONS.

The inscriptions on the Railing of the Bharhut Stûpa are of the same character as those of the great Sânchi Stûpa near Bhilsa. They record the names of the donors of different parts of the Railing, as of a Pillar, a Rail-bar, or a piece of Coping. Some of them also give the calling or occupation of the donors, and several add the name of their native city, or place of residence. The Sânchi inscriptions are generally limited to these announcements. But at Bharhut we have a considerable number of inscriptions which are labels, or titles, of the sculptured scenes above which they are placed. Thus we have the visit of Raja Ajâtasatru to Buddha inscribed with the words—

Ajâtasatru Bhagavato vandate,

or, " Ajatasatru worships [the feet] of Buddha;" and also a large tree inscribed with—

Bhagavato Sâka Munino Bodhi,

or, the " Bodhi Tree of Buddha Sâkya Muni." These short records are quite invaluable, as they enable us to identify the different scenes to which they are attached with absolute certainty. We thus obtain the means of distinguishing one class of people from another with confidence, and of ascertaining what legends were current and most popular at the early period when this Stûpa was erected.

There is also another prominent difference between the Bharhut and Bhilsa Railings, which adds greatly to the value of the former. This is the representation of Yakshas and and Yakshinis, and of Nâga Rajas and Devatâs with their names duly attached to them, from which we learn that the old Indian cosmogony, as represented in Buddhist as well as Brahmanical books, with its *Nâga-loka,* and its Guardian Rajas of the four quarters of the universe, was all fully elaborated as early as the time of Asoka. These inscriptions also teach us that the curiously shaped gateways of the well known Sânchi Stûpa were called by the name of *Torana,* and that the Rail-bars were named *Suchi,* or " needles," no doubt because they seemed to *thread* all the pillars together.

The alphabetical characters of the inscriptions are precisely the same as those of Asoka's time on the Sânchi Stûpa, and of the other undoubted records of Asoka on rocks and pillars. None of the letters have any heads, as in the coin legends of Amogha-bhûti, Dâra-Ghosha, and Vâmika, and in the still later Mathura inscriptions of Sudâsa, Kanishka Huvishka, and Vasu Deva. These Bharhut records also preserve the simple style of *dânam,* which was used in the Asoka period, and which certainly belongs to an earlier age than the more elaborate phraseology of *Deya-dharmma,* which is the prevailing form of the Indo-Scythian inscriptions. The Bharhut records also are distinguished by the persistent use of the letter *r,* instead of changing it into *l,* as in *lája* for *râja,* of most of the Asoka edicts. That this was the actual pronunciation of the people of this part of the country is proved by the same use of *r* in the genuine Asoka edict engraved on the neighbouring rock of Rûpnath.

GATEWAYS.

No. 1. On Pillar of E. Gateway.

1.   Suganam raje rájno Gágí-putasa VISA-DEVASA
2.   pauteṇa, Gotiputasa AGA-RAJASA puteṇa
3.   Váchhi-putena DHANA-BHUTINA káritam toranam
4.   Sila kaṁmata cha upaṅna.

No. 2. Gateway Pillar at Batanmára.

Saganam Raja   .   .
Aga Rajna   .   .
toraṇam   .   .

No. 3. Gateway Pillar at Batanmára.

.   .   hena
.   .   toranamcha
.   .   kata.

Nos. 2 and 3 must be portions of different inscriptions, and from different Gateways, as the word *Torana* is mentioned in each of them. This is important, as it proves that there were *three* separate Toran Gateways; and if there were three we know that there must have been four, as the corner pillars of the Rail-way found at the four cardinal points show that there were four openings.

For the following translation I am indebted to the kindness of Babu Rajendra Lál, who suggests that the word *upanna*, is most probably *upána*, a "plinth," but this could hardly be applied to the pillars of the Gateway, which are baseless, and spring direct from the ground.[1]

"In the kingdom of Sugana (Srughna) this *Toran*, with its ornamented stonework and plinth, was caused to be made by king *Dhana-bhúti*, son of *Váchhi* and *Aga Raja* son of *Goti*, and grandson of *Visa Deva* son of *Gágí*."

Here it will be observed that there are three other names in addition to those of the three Rájas, namely *Gágí* or *Gárgeya*, *Goti* or *Kautseya*, and *Váchhi* or *Vátseya*, which Babu Rajendra Lál considered " to be feminine names or the *names of the mothers* of the different "persons they refer to." Now it so happens that these are also the names of three distinguished spiritual teachers, *Darga, Kautsa*, and *Vatsa*, who gave their names to the three schools of the *Gárggi-puttriyas Kautsi-puttriyas*, and *Vátsi-puttriyas*, which led me to suppose that possibly the three Rájas might have belonged to these three different schools. I therefore referred the inscription with my conjectures to Dr. Bühler, whose great acquirements as a Sanskrit scholar are only equalled by his willingness to impart his knowledge to others, and from him I received another translation of the inscription, with the following clear and satisfactory explanation of the feminine names, " I agree with " Rajendra about the meaning of *Gágí* (i.e. Gárgeyí) *putra*, &c. Philologically any other " interpretation is impossible. If the kings wanted to characterise themselves as adherents

---

[1] See Plates XI. and XII.

" of the schools of *Gárgiputra*, &c. they expressed themselves incorrectly. The usage of
" calling sons after their mothers was caused, not by polyandria, as some Sanskritists
" have suggested, but by the prevalence of polygamy, and it survives among the Rajputs
" to the present day. In private conversation I have often heard a *Kuwar* called the
" ' son of the *Solankani*,' or of the *Gohildni*, &c. Here you will observe the Rani is called
" according to her family name, not according to her proper name; and you will
" know, from intercourse with the Rajputs, that the Ranis are always mentioned in that
" manner."[1]

" Now all the metronymica of the ancient kings and teachers, both Buddhistic and
" Brahmanical, are formed by a female family name with the word *putra*. Thus we have
" *Vasishthiputra*, or *Vasithiputra*, *Sátakarni*, &c., and these names ought to be translated,
" ' son of the (wife) of the Vasishtha family,' &c. The name was just intended to
" distinguish the king or teacher from the other sons of his father by naming his mother
" according to her family name.

" There is another point connected with these metronymica which deserves attention ;
" viz. that the family names are all those of Brahmanical gotras. The explanation of
" this fact is that in accordance with the precepts of the Smriti, the Rajas were con-
" sidered members of the *gotras* of their *purohitas*, and called themselves after the latter."

" My last suggestion refers to the fourth line,

" *Sila kanhmatá cha upana*,

" which I translate into Sanskrit,

" *Sila karmatá cha utpanná*,

" and into English literally,

" ' And the state of one who [performs] works of piety [has been] produced ; '

" or more freely,

" ' And thereby spiritual merit has been gained.'

" *Upaná* is =*uppanná*, as these inscriptions do not note double letters, and *uppanná* is
" the regular Prákrit for *utpanná*. My translation of the whole is therefore—

" This ornamental gateway has been erected by the king of Srughna, *Dhanabhúti*,
" born of [the queen of] the Vatsa family, [and] son of *Aga-rája*, born of [the queen of]
" the Gota family, [and] grandson of king [*Visa Deva*], born of [the queen of] the
" Gágeya race, and spiritual merit has been gained [thereby]."

The genealogy of the Royal family of Srughna, according to this inscription, is as
follows :—

Father unknown ✕   Mother of the *Gárgeya* family.
1. Viswa-Deva   ✕   Queen of the *Kautsa* family.
2. Agni-Raja   ✕   Queen of the *Vatsa* family.
3. Dhanabhúti.

The Mathura inscription of the same family continues the genealogy for two more

---

[1] This is invariably the custom with the Rajputs; and I remember a Sati memorial stone in the fort of
Bhatner recording the burning of six wives of Dalpat Sinh of the Bikaner family, each of whom was designated
by her own family name, written beneath her sculptured figure, as *Bhattiyáni*, &c. But a similar custom was
also adopted by the Muhamadans, as in the names of the *Akbarábádi* Masjid and *Fatehpuri* Masjid at Delhi,
which were built respectively by *Akbarábádi Mahal* the Begam of Shah Jahan, and by *Fatehpuri Begum* his
daughter.

generations, of which the first is also named in one of the short Bharhut records, as the donor of a Rail-bar.[1] I read the Mathura inscription as follows :—

1. *kala . . . [Dhana]*
2. *bhútisa . . . Vátsi*
3. *putrasa [Vádha-Pá] lasa*
4. *Dhanabhútisa dánam Vediká*
5. *Toranánám cha Ratnagriha sa—*
6. *va Buddha pujáya sahá Mátu-pi—*
7. *ta haisáhara chata . . pariahi.*

The missing letters in the third line are exactly three, which I have supplied to complete the name of *Vádha Pála*, the son of Dhanabhúti. I have also supplied the former half of Dhanabhúti's name in the first line. These restorations are fully justified by the occurrence of the names of Vátsi-putra and Dhanabhúti in the second and fourth lines, which show that the record must belong to the royal family of Srughna. Now the letters of this Mathura inscription have already got small *mátras*, or heads, an innovation which places this record of Danabhúti II. about B.C. 180 to 160, or contemporary with Agnimitra and Apollodotus. His grandfather Dhanabhúti I., must therefore have reigned from about B.C. 240 to 220, or during the lifetime of Asoka.

ON COPING STONES.
No. I. COPING.

1. *Aya Nágadevasa dánam.*
   " Gift of the reverend Nága Deva."

No. II. COPING.

2. *Magha Deviya Játakam.*
   " The Magha Deva Birth."[2]
3. *Digha-tapasisise anusasati.*
   [Dirgha-tapas instructs his female disciples.]
4. *Abode Chetiya.*
   " The Mango-tree Chaitya." (?)
5. *Sujáto-gahuto Játaka.*
   " Birth (of Buddha) as Sujáta the Bull-inviter." [3] (?)
6. *Bidála Jatara.[4] Kukkuta Játaka.*
   " The Cat Birth."   " The Cock Birth."
7. *Dadani kamo chakamo.*
   " Punishment of Works Region " (?); that is, the place of punishment, or Hell.

No. III. COPING.

8. *Asadávadhususane Sigála ñati.*
   [Story unknown—*Sigála* means a Jackal.]

---

[1] See Plate LIII. No. 4, for the Mathura Inscription, and Plate LVI. No. 54, for the Bharhut record of Prince Vádha Pála, son of Dhanabhúti.
[2] See Plate XLVIII. fig. 2.   [3] See Plate XLVII. fig. 3.
[4] The cross stroke of the letter k has been omitted by the sculptor, which leaves only the upright stroke of *r*, as given above. See Plate XLVII. fig. 5.

No. IV. Coping.

9. *Isi-migo Jâtaka.*
   "Rishi-deer Birth."[1]
Buddha was born as a deer in the *Mrigadâva*, or "Deer Park," at *Isi-pattana* or *Rishi-pattana*, near Banâras.

10. *Miga Samâdaka chetiya.*
    "Deer and Lions eating together Chetiya." (?)

No. V. Coping.

11. *Hansa Jâtakam.*
    "The Goose Birth."[2]
12. *Kinara Jâtakam.*
    "The Kinnara Birth."[3]
13. *Jâtila Sabhâ.*
    "Assembly of the Jâtilians."

No. VII. Coping.

14. *Uda Jâtaka.*[4]
    [Story unknown.] The Uda Birth.
15. *Sechha Jâtaka.*[5]
    [Story unknown.] The Seeha Birth.

No. VIII. Coping.

16. *Karahakata Nigamasa dânam.*
    "Gift of Nigama of Karahakata."
17. *Bhisaharaniya Jâtaka.*
    "The Lotus-offering Birth." (?)[6]
18. *Vadukokatha dohati nadode pavate.*
    [Story unknown.]
19. *Jabu nadode pavate.*
I suppose that the tree in the bas-relief is intended for the *Jambu.*[7]

No. IX. Coping.

20. *Janako Râja Sivalâ Devi.*
    "Janako Râja (and) Sivalâ Devi."[8]
21. *Chitupâda Sila.*
The inscription seems to refer to the split (*Chitu*) in the rock (*sila*).[9]
22. *Dusito-giri dadati* . .
    [Story unknown.]

---

[1] See Plate XLIII. fig. 1.
[2] See Plate XXVII. fig. 11.
[3] See Plate XXVII. fig. 12.
[4] See Plate XLVI. fig. 2.
[5] See Plate XLVI. fig. 8.
[6] See Plate XLVIII. fig. 7.
[7] See Plate XLVIII. fig. 11.
[8] See Plate XLIV. fig. 2.
[9] See Plate XLV. fig. 9.

PILLARS S.E. QUADRANT.

No. I. PILLAR.

1. *Vedisá Chápa Deváyá Revati Mita bhariyáya pathama thabho dánam.*
   "The first Pillar-gift of Chápa Devá, wife of Revati Mitra of Vedisa."

Vedisa is the old name of *Besnagar*, a ruined city situated in the fork of the Bes or Vedisa River and the Betwa within two miles of Bhilsa. The inscription is engraved on the first Pillar of the Railing next to the Gateway.[1]

No. II. PILLAR.

2. *Bhadantasa Aya Bhúta Rakhitasa Khujati-dakhiyasa dánam.*
   "Gift of the lay brother (Bhadanta) the reverend Bhuta-rakshita of Khujati-dakhiya."
3. *Bhagavato-Vesabhuno-Bodhisálo.*
   "The Sála Bodhi Tree of the Buddha Viswabhu."
   The Bodhi Tree of this Buddha was a *Sála* or Shorea-robusta.[2]
4. *Aya Gorakhitasa dánam.*
   "Gift of the reverend Gorakshita."
5. *Aya-Panthakasa thabho dánam.*
   "Pillar-gift of the reverend Panthaka."
6. *Chulakoka Devatá.*
   "The goddess Chulakoka," (or Little Koka.)[3]

No. VI. PILLAR.

7. *Dabhinikáya Mahámukhisa Dhita-badhikaya Bhichuniya dánam.*
   "Gift of the Nun Dhritabadhiká, the Mahámukhi (?) of Dabhinika."

No. VII. PILLAR.

8. *Yániya dánam*
   Pátaliputa Nága Senaya Kodi.
   "Gift of Nága Sena of Pátaliputra, a descendant of Kaundinya." (?)

No. VIII. PILLAR.

9. *Samanáyá Bhikhuniyá Chúdathilikáyá dánam.*
   "Gift of the Nun Samaná of Chúdathilika."

No. IX. PILLAR.

10. *Bahadagajatiranatane Isá Rakhitaputasa Anandasa thabho (dánam).*
    "Gift of Ananda, son of Isi Rakshita, the . . (title unknown)."
11. *Bhagavato Konigamenasa Bodhi.*
    "Bodhi Tree of the Buddha Kanaka Muni."[4]

---

[1] See Plate XII. This Pillar has the Standard Bearer and Relic Bearer sculptured on its inward faces.
[2] See Plate XXIX. fig. 2.   [3] See Plate XXIII. fig. 3.   [4] See Plate XXIX. fig. 4.

No. X. Pillar.

12. *Bhojakaṭakáya Diganagaye Bhichhuniya dánam.*
    " Gift of the Nun Diganaga of Bhojakaṭaka."
13. *Nága Játaka.*
    " The Elephant Birth."[1]

No. XII. Pillar.

14. *Bibikána Dikiṭa Budhino Gahapatino dánam.*
    " Gift of Dikshiṭa Budhi, the householder of Bibikâna."

No. XIII. Pillar.

15. *Supávaso Yakho.*
    " The Yaksha Supravasu."
16. *Dhama Gutasa dánam thabho.*
    " Pillar-gift of Dharma Gupta."

No. XIV. Pillar.

17. *Bibikána Dikaṭi Suladhasa Asavárikasa dánam.*
    " Gift of Dikshiṭa Suladha, the Asavárika."
The term Asawárika is most probably intended for an *Aswár, Sawár,* or " horseman."

No. XV. Pillar.

18. *Pusasa thabho dánam.*
    " Pillar-gift of Pushya."
19. *Miga Játakam.*
    " The Deer Birth." [2]
20. *Jetavana Anádhapeḍiko deti koṭi santhatena keṭá.*
    " Anáthapiṇḍika presents Jetavana, (having become) its purchaser for a layer
    of Koṭis." [3]
Mr. Childers' remarks on this inscription will be found in the " Academy " for
5th December 1874.
21. *Kosambi Kuṭi.*
    " The Kosâmbi Temple."
22. *Gandha Kuṭi.*
    " The Gandha Temple."
These two inscriptions are attached to the buildings in the famous Jetavana garden
which is described in No. 20.

No. XVI. Pillar.

23. *Dhama Rakhitasa dánam.*
    " Gift of Dharma Rakshita."
24. *Chakaváko Nága Raja.*
    " Chakaváka, King of the Nâgas." [4]

---

[1] See Plate XXV. fig. 2. [3] See Plate XXVIII. fig. 3.
[2] See Plate XXV. fig. 1. [4] See Plate XXI. fig. 1,

25. *Virudako Yakho.*
    " The Yaksha Virudaka."
26. *Gangito Yakho.*
    " The Yaksha Gangita.[1]

PLATE LIV.

CORNER PILLARS—S. GATE.

27. *Aya Isadinasa Bhânakasa dânam.*
    " Gift of the reverend Isadina of Bhânaka."
28. *Bhagavato Sâka Munino Bodhi.*
    " The Bodhi Tree of the Buddha Sâkya Muni."
29. *Purathimapusasudha Vasa Deva.*
    [Unknown.]
30. *Utaram disatuni savatanisisa.*
    [Unknown.]
31. *Dakhini disa chhaki mavam cha rasahâsani.*
    [Unknown.]
32. *Sâdika Sammadan turam devânam.*

This inscription is placed immediately below a bas-relief representing the dance and song of the Apsarases, to which it directly refers in the words *Sadika devânam*, praises of the gods.

33. *Misakosa Achhará.*
34. *Subhada Achhará.*
35. *Padumávati Achhará.*
36. *Alambusa Achhará.*

These four inscriptions are separately engraved, one of them being placed behind each of the four dancers in the bas-relief of the dance of the Apsarases. The names are easily recognised as those of four of the most famous of the heavenly courtesans, namely, *Misrakesi, Subhadrá, Padmávatí,* and *Alambusha.* The last was the mother of Râja Visala, the founder of Vaisâli.

Here we see that the Sanskrit *ps* was changed to *chh* in Pâli, which was also the representative of *ts.*[1]

37. *Kadariki.*

This is inscribed between two standing figures, male and female, on Prasenajit's Pillar.[1]

38. *Vajapi Vijadharo.*
    [Unknown.]
39. *Bhagavato dharma chakam.*
    " The Dharma Chakra of Buddha."
40. *Râja Pasenaji Kosalo.*
    " The Raja Prasenajit of Kosala."[4]
41. *Erapato Nâja Râja.*
    " Erápata, king of the Nâgas."

---

[1] See Plate XXI. fig. 2.
   See Plate XV. fig. 1.

[1] See Plate XIV. fig. 2.
[4] See Plate XIII. fig. 1.

42. *Erapato Nága Rája Bhagavato vandate.*

" Erápata, king of the Nágas, worships [the invisible figure] of Bhagavat."

Here the king of the Nágas is kneeling before a flowering tree, beneath which is a throne.[1] The tree here represented is a *Sirisa*, or Acacia, beneath which Buddha is said to have received the salutation of the Nága king. The story is told in the commentary on V. 182 of the Dhammapada [see Academy, 5 April 1875], and also by the Chinese Pilgrim Hwen Thsang. The six *Sirisa* trees of the legend are all given in the sculpture.

43. *Bahu hathiko.*

44. *Bahu hathiko Nigodha nadode.*

The first of these short labels means simply " the herd of elephants," to which the second adds the name of the tree *Nigodha* (or Nyagrodha), the Banian, before which they are bowing down. I am ignorant of the exact meaning of *nadode.* The shorter label is on the railing beneath the scene; the longer one on the throne beneath the Banian Tree.[2]

45. *Susupálo koddyo vetiko Arámako.*

This inscription is engraved in the field of the Elephant bas-relief above mentioned—just behind the heads of two human figures, who must be the *Susupála* and *Kodra* of the label. The third word may also be read as *Veduko.*[2]

46. *Yasika* . .

[Imperfect.]

On Pillars of Railings—S. W. Quadrant.

47. *Snáya dánam thabho.*

" Pillar-gift of Soná."

48. *Chakulanam Sangha mitasa thabho dánam.*

" Pillar-gift of Sangha-mitra of Chakulana."

49. *Bhagavato Kásapasa Bodhi.*

" The Bodhi Tree of Buddha Kásyapa."[3]

50. *Nágaye bhichhuniye dánam.*

" Gift of the Nun Nágá."

51. *Bhadanta Valakasa Bhánakasa dánam thabho.*

" Pillar-gift of the lay brother Valaka of Bhánaka."

52. *Karahakata Chayabhutakasa thabho dánam.*

" Pillar-gift of Chayabhutaka of Karahakata."

53. *Kosambeyekaya bhikhuniya Venuvagámiyáya Dhama Rakhita.*

" Gift of the Nun Dharmma Rakshitá of Venuwagráma in Kosambi."

When I visited Kosam, the ancient Kosámbi, after leaving Bharhut, I made inquiries about the village of *Venuwagráma*, or "Bambu town." There is a *Ben púrva* still existing to the north-east of Kosam, where I found that some ancient brick foundations were being dug up by the zamindar.

54. *Tikotiko Chakamo.*

" The region of Trikuta."[4]

This name has been discussed in my account of the Nágas, where I have suggested that the bas-relief to which this inscription is attached may be a representation of the

---

1 See Plate XIV, fig. 3.
2 See Plate XV. fig. 3.
3 See Plate XXX. fig. 1.
4 See Plate XXVII. fig. 1.

Nága Loka region of Snakes and Elephants (both called Nága), which was situated under the *Trikuta* rocks which supported Mount Meru.

55. *Bhadanta Mahilasa thabho dánam.*

" Pillar-gift of the lay brother Mahila."

56. *Karahakaṭa Samikasa dánam thabho.*

" Pillar-gift of Samika of *Karahakaṭa.*"

The name of this place occurs also in No. 52. It may be read as *Karhakata,* and might possibly be the original form of the name *Karha,* near Mánikpur on the Ganges.

57. *Bhádanta Samakasa thabho dánam.*

" Pillar-gift of the lay brother Samaka."

58. *Yava-Majhakiyam Játakam.*

" The Yava-Majhakiya Birth."[1]

I have given the story of this bas-relief in my account of the *Játakas,* but it has not yet been identified with any of the published names of the Ceylonese Játakas.

59. *Sirimá Devata.*

" The godess Sri-ma."[2]

The title of *Srimá* was given to Máyá Devi, the mother of Sákya Muni. I presume that it is an abbreviation of *Sri-máta,* or the " fortunate mother "; although it may also be a contraction of *Sri Máyá.* The inscription is attached to a large female statue on one of the pillars of the South-west quadrant. It seems not impossible, however, that the statue may be that of *Sirima,* the beautiful sister of the physician Jivaka.

60. *Suchiloma-Yakho.*

" The Yaksha Suchiloma."[3]

This Yaksha has given his name to a discourse in the *Sutta Nipáta.*

61. . . . *ratá bhikhuniya thabho dánam.*

" Pillar-gift of the Nun . . . ratná."

CORNER PILLARS—W. GATE.

62. *Bhadantasa Aya Isipálitasa Bhánakasa Navakamikasa dánam.*

" Gift of the lay brother, the reverend Isipálita of Bhánaka (Nava-kamika must be his title).

63. *Ajátasata Bhagavato vandate.*

" Ajátasatru worships (the feet) of Buddha."

The footprints of Buddha are carved on the step of the throne.[4]

64. *Sudhamma Deva sabhá Bhagavato Chuḍa Maha.*

" The grand head-dress (relic) of Buddha, in the Assembly Hall of the Devas."[5]

I take *Chuḍa,* which means a " crest, or topknot of hair," to be the name of the object which occupies the place of worship on the throne or altar. This object is beyond all doubt intended for Buddha's hair and head-dress, which were carried to the Trayastrinshas Heavens by the Devas. When I first saw the small photograph of this bas-relief I read the words at the end of the first line as *Reva Sabha;* but when I saw the pillar itself I found that the true reading was *Deva Sabhá,* or the " Assembly of Devas." This correction I communicated to Mr. Childers on the 18th April 1875. The same correction

1 See Plate XXV. fig. 3.   2 See Plate XXIII. fig. 1.   3 See Plate XXII. fig. 2.
4 See Plate XVI. fig. 3.   5 See Plate XVI. fig. 1.

was published by him in the "Academy" for 1st May 1875, about ten days before the receipt of my letter.

65. *Vijayanto Pâsâde.*

"The Vijayanta Palace."

As this was the name of the Palace of the Gods in the Trayastrinshas Heavens, my identification of the object of worship in the *Deva Sabhâ* is confirmed.

66. *Mahâsâmâyikayam Arahaguto Devaputo dhakato Bhagavato visani paṭisandhi.*

The scene to which this label is attached represents the worship of Buddha's footprints.[1]

PILLARS OF RAILING—N.W. QUADRANT.

67. *Moragirihma Nâgilâyâ bhikhuniya dânam thabho.*

"Pillar-gift of the Nun Nâgilâ of Moragiri."

68. *Bhagavato Vipasino Bodhi.*

"The Bodhi Tree of the Buddha Vipaswin."[2]

69. *Vedisa Phagu Devasa dânam.*

"Gift of Phalgu Deva of Vedisa (Besnagar)."

70. *Dodapâpechema chharo.*

[Unknown.]

71. *Purikâya Dayakana dânam.*

"Gift of Dâyakana of Purika."

72. *Bhagavato Kakusadhasa Bodhi.*

"The Bodhi Tree of the Buddha Krakusandha."[3]

73. *Vedisa Anurâdhaya dânam.*

"Gift of Anurâdha of Vedisa (Besnagar)."

74. *Chadantiya Jâtakam.*

"Birth (of Buddha) as a Chhadanta Elephant."[4]

CORNER PILLARS—N. GATE.

75. *Vitura Punakiya Jâtakam.*

"The Vidhûra (and) Pûnnaka Birth."[5]

76. *Brahma Devomânavako.*

[Unknown.]

DISPLACED PILLARS.

77. *Bhadanta Kanadasa Bhânakasa thabho dânam Chikulaniyasa.*

"Pillar-gift of the lay brother Kanada Bhânaka of Chikulaniya."

78. *Yakhini Sudasana.*

"The Yakshini Sudarsana."

79. .   *naḍoda pâde chena chhako.* .   .

[Unknown.]

---

[1] See Plate XVI. fig. 2.   [2] See Plate XXIX. fig. 1.   [3] See Plate XXIX. fig. 3.
[4] See Plate XXVI. fig. 2.   [5] See Plate XVIII. fig. 2.

PLATE LV.

PILLARS OF RAILING—N.E. QUADRANT.

80. *Bhadanta Budha Rakhitasa Saṭupadanasa dánam thabo.*
  "Pillar-gift of the lay brother Budha Rakshita of Saṭupadana." (?)

81. *Chada Yakhi.*
  "The Yakshini Chandra."[1]

I read as above because I suppose that if the name Chaṇḍa were intended it would have been spelt with the cerebral ḍ.

82. *Kupiro Yakho.*
  "The Yaksha Kuvera."[2]

83. *Ajakálako Yakho.*
  "The Yaksha Ajakálaka."

84. *Moragirihma Pusáyá dánam thabho.*
  "Pillar-gift of Pushyá of Moragiri."

85. *Aya Chulasa Sutantikasa Bhoga vadhaniyasa dánam.*
  "Gift of the reverend Chula Sautrantika, the increaser of enjoyment." (?)

86. *Moragirihma Thupadásasa dánam thabho.*
  "Gift of Thupadása of Moragiri."

Thupadása, in Sanskrit *Stúpadása*, or "servant of the Stúpa," is in the inscription an actual name, and not a mere title.

87. *Násika Gorakhitaya thabho dánam Vasukasa bháriyáya.*
  "Pillar-gift of Gorakshitá of Násika, the wife of Vasuka."

88. *Maharasa Atevásino Aya Sámakasa thabho dánam.*
  "Pillar-gift of Mahara, the pupil of the reverend Sámika."

89. *Bhagavato Rukdanti.*
  "Buddha as Rukdanti."[3]

This inscription has been discussed in my account of the bas-relief of Máyá Devis' dream, where I have suggested that *ruk* may mean "sounding or trumpeting," from *ru*, to sound or make a particular sort of sound, which it is recorded the Chhadanta Elephant emitted as he approached the couch of Máyá Devi.

PILLARS AT BATANMÁRA.

90. *Sakáya thabho dánam.*
  "Pillar-gift of Saká."

91. *Nandagirino Bhánakasa Selapuraka thabho dánam.*
  "Pillar-gift of Bhánaka Selapuraka of Nandagiri (? Nander)."

92. *Ida Sála guha.*
  "The Cave Hall of Indra."

93. *Pusadataye Nagarikaye Bhichuniye.*
  "[Gift] of the Nun Pushyadattá of Nagarika."

94. *Mugaphakasa Játaka.*
  "The Mugaphaka Birth."

---

[1] See Plate XXII. fig. 3.   [2] See Plate XXII. fig. 1.   [3] See Plate XXVIII. fig. 2.

95. *Moragiri Jita mitasa dánam.*
 " Gift of Jita-mitra of Maragiri."
96. *Karahakaṭa Utara gidhikasa thabho dánam.*
 " Pillar-gift of Uttaragidhika of Karahakaṭa."

PILLARS AT PATAORA.

97. *Yambumano avayesí Játakam.*
This scene is called the *Andhabhuta Játaka,* or the " Blindman Birth " in Ceylon.
98. *Mahakoka Devatá.*
 " The goddess Mahákoka," or " Great Koka."
99. *Chuladhakasa Purikáya Bhatudesakasa dánam.*
 " Gift of Chuladhaka Puriká of Bhatudesaka."
100. *Vedisa Aya Máyá dánam.*
 " Gift of the reverend Máyá of Vedisa."

INSCRIPTIONS ON RAILS—S. W. QUADRANT.

1. *Sapa Gutaye bhikhuniye dánam.*
 " Gift of the Nun Sarpa Gupta."
2. *Páṭaliputa Kodiyániya Sakaja Deváyá dánam.*
 " Gift of Sakajá Devá, of the race of Kaundinya of Páṭaliputra."
3. *Kákandiya Somáya bhikhuniya dánam.*
 " Gift of the Nun Somá of Kákandi."
4. *Páṭaliputa Mahidasenasa dánam.*
 " Gift of Mahendra Sena of Páṭaliputra."
5. *Chudathílikáyá Nága Deváyá bhikhuniya. . .*
 " (Gift) of the Nun Nágá Devá of Chudathílika."
6. *Chudathílikáyá Kujaráyá dánam.*
 " Gift of Kunjará of Chudathílika."
7. *Dhama Guta mátu Pusa Devaya dánam.*
 " Gift of Pushya Deva, mother of Dharma Gupta."
8. *Yajhikiyá dánam.*
 " Gift of Yajhiki."
9. *Dhama Rakhitaya dánam Suchi.*
 " Rail-gift of Dharmma Rakshita."
This is the first occurrence of the term *Suchi,* which I have translated by Rail (or bar),
as it is found only in the Rail-bar inscriptions, where it takes the place of *thabho* or pillar,
in the Pillar inscriptions. Its literal meaning is " needle," and its application to the Rail-
bars was no doubt due to its needle-like function of threading all the pillars together.
10. *Ati Mutasa dánam.*
 " Gift of Atrimuta."
11. *Laṭuwá Játakam.*
 " The Laṭuwá (bird) Birth." [1]
12. *Nadutaraya dánam Suchi.*
 " Rail-gift of Nadutará."

---

[1] See Plate XXVI. fig. 1.

T 2

RAIL INSCRIPTIONS—S. GATE.

13. *Mudasa dánam.*
    " Gift of Mudra."
14. *Isánasa dánam.*
    " Gift of Isâna."
15. *Isidatasa dánam.*
    " Gift of Isidata (or Rishi datta)."
16. *Aya Punávasuno Suchi dánam.*
    " Rail-gift of the reverend Punarvasu."
17. *Gága-mitasa Suchi dánam.*
    " Rail-gift of Ganga Mitra (or Garga Mitra)."
18. *Kanhilasa Bhánakasa dánam.*
    " Gift of Kanhila of Bhânaka."

RAIL INSCRIPTIONS—S. W. QUADRANT.

19. *Deva Rakshitasa dánam.*
    " Gift of Deva Rakshita."
20. *Vedisá Tabhuta Rakhitasa dánam.*
    " Gift of Tabhuta Rakshita of Vedisa."
21. *Goldyá Párikiniyá dánam.*
    " Gift of Pârikini of Golâ."

PLATE LVI.

22. *Purikayá Ida Deváyá dánam.*
    " Gift of Indra Devâ of Purikâ."
23. *Purikáyá Setaka matu dánam.*
    " Gift of Setaka's mother of Purikâ."
24. *Purikáyá Sámáya dánam.*
    " Gift of Sâmâ of Purikâ."
25. *Budha Rakhitaye dánam bhichhuniya.*
    " Gift of Buddha Rakshitâ the Nun."
26. *Bhutaye bhichuniye dánam.*
    " Gift of Bhutâ the Nun."
27. *Aya Apikinakasa dánam.*
    " Gift of the reverend Apikinaka."
28. *Sanghilasa dánam Suchi.*
    " Rail-gift of Sanghila."
29. *Sangha Rakhitasa Máta pituna athaye dánam.*
    " Gift of Sangha Rakshita on account of his father and mother."
30. *Dhutasa Suchi dánam.*
    " Rail-gift of Dhuta."
31. *Yakhilasa Suchi dánam.*
    " Rail-gift of Yakhila."
32. *Sihasa Suchi dánam.*
    " Rail-gift of Sinha."

33. *Isi Rakhitusa dánam.*
  "Gift of Isi Rakshita."
34. *Sirimasa dánam.*
  "Gift of Sirimâ."
35. *Bhadanta Deva Senasa dánam.*
  "Gift of the lay brother Deva Sena."
36. . . . *kaya bhichhuniya dánam.*
  "Gift of the Nun . . . ka."
37. *Nadinagarikáyá Ida Devaya dánam.*
  "Gift of Indra Deva of Nandinagara (Nander)."
38. *Gopálasa mata (?) Gosálasa dánam.*
  "Gift of Gosâla (or Gopâla . . ."

This inscription is engraved twice on the same rail; first in thin and somewhat cursive letters, and second in thicker letters, as if the first record had been faulty, or disapproved. It might, however, be read as the "gift of Gosâla the mother of Gopâla."

39. *Kachulasa . . . . bháriyáya dánam.*
  "Gift of . . . . s' wife of Kachula."
40. *Jeta bharasa dánam.*
  "Gift of Jetabhara."
41. *Aya Játo Sepetakino Suchi dánam.*
  "Rail-gift of the reverend Jâta Sepetaki."

The term *Sepatiko* occurs in the Arian Pali inscription of Taxila, where, according to Professor Dowson, it is the name of some "building or establishment." It is probable, therefore, that *Sepetakino* is the title of the reverend Jâta, as keeper or guardian of the *Sepatiko.*

42. *Buddha Rakhitasa Rupakárakasa dánam.*
  "Gift of Buddha Rakshita, the sculptor."

Here we have the name of one of the sculptors of the Bharhut bas-reliefs. I believe that it will be possible to recognise other specimens of his chisel by some slight peculiarities which I noticed in the shapes of some of the letters of this inscription.

43. *Bhádantasa Mikasatha Rákutiyasa dánam.*
  "Gift of the lay brother Mikasatha of Rákutiya." (?)
44. *Sirisapada Isi Rakhitáya dánam.*
  "Gift of Isi Rakshitâ of Sirisapadâ."

The name of this place, *Sirisapadá,* was probably derived from the *Sirisa* tree or Acacia, as in the case of *Sirsa,* and of *Siris* Ghat on the Betwa between Jhansi and Lalitpur.

45. *Moragirimá Ghátila Máta dánam.*
  "Gift of Ghâtila's mother of Moragiri."
46. *Atankhatasa Bhojakatakasa Suchi dánam.*
  "Rail-gift of Bhojakataka of Atangkhata," or, "of Atangkhata of Bhojakatakâ."
47. *Samidatáya dánam.*
  "Gift of Samidattâ."
48. *Chulanasa dánam.*
  "Gift of Chulana."

49. *Avisanasa dánam.*
   "Gift of Avisana."
50. (A duplicate of the last.)
51. *Sangha Mitasa Bodhichakasa dánam.*
   "Gift of Sangha Mitra of Bodhi Chakra." Perhaps there may have been a
   Bodhi Chakra as well as a Dharmma Chakra.
52. *Bodhi Rakhitasa Panchanekáyákasa dánam.*
   "Gift of Bodhi Rakhitasa of Panchanekáyáka."
53. *Isi Rakhitasa Suchi dánam.*
   "Rail-gift of Isi Rakshita."
54. *Dhanabhútisa rájano putasa Kumárasa Vádha Pálasa* (dánam).
   "(Gift) of Rája Dhanabhúti's son the Prince Vádha Pála."

Rája Dhanabhúti was the donor of the Eastern Gateway:—See his inscription, No. 1.
The present inscription proves that the Railing and the Gateways were of the same age.

55. *Phagu Deváya bhichhuniya dánam.*
   "Gift of Phalgu Devá, the Nun."
56. *Kadáya Yakhiya dánam.*
   "Gift of Kanda Yakshi."
57. *Ghosáye dánam.*
   "Gift of Ghosá."
58. *Yamidasa sa . . .*
   "[Gift] of Yamida . . ."
59. *Siriya-putasa Bhárini Devasa dánam.*
   "Gift of Siri's son Bhárini Deva."
60. *Mita Devaye dánam.*
   "Gift of Mitra Deva."
61. *Padelakasa Pusakasa Suchi dánam.*
   "Gift of Pushyaka of Pandelaka."
62. *Asitamasáya Vala Mitasa dánam.*
   "Gift of Vala Mitra of Asitamasá."

Perhaps the place here mentioned may have been on the bank of the Tamasá, or
Tons River, which flows within two miles of Bharhut. Ptolemy has a town named
Tamasis. But *Asita* was also a proper name, and the town may have been called *Asita-
masa,* and not *Asitamasa.*

63. (*Pa*) *rakaṭikaya Sivimáyá dánam.*
   "Gift of Sirima of Parakaṭika."
64. *Vijitakasa Suchi dánam.*
   "Rail-gift of Vijita."
65. *. . . sa dánam Atená.*
   Charata . . .
66. *Tiranuti Migila Kuchimha Vasu Guto Machito Mahadevanam.*

This is inscribed on the Rail which bears the bas-relief of the great fish swallowing
two boats and their crews. *Machito* therefore may have reference to the fish.[1]

---

[1] See Plate **XXXIV.** fig. 2.

FRAGMENTS.

1. *Vedisa Vásithiya Velimi.* . . . .
   " Gift of Vâsistha (wife of) Velimi (tra.)"
2. *Aya Nanda.*
   " [Gift] of the reverend Nanda."
3. *Araha Guta Reva puta (sa dânam).*
   " Gift of Arahata Gupta, son of Reva."
4. *Avâsikâ.*
5. *Mahada* .
6. *Chandâ* . . .
7. *Satika* . . .
8. . . . *rakatayâyâ* . . .
9. . . *tu rajine adhi râjaka* . . *yata.*
10. . . . *tarasa* . .
11. . . *yasini sayâni* . .
12. (*san*) *gha mi* (tasa) . .
13. . . . . *sakusu* . .
14. . . . *niya Játaka.*
15. (Na) *n-dagerino dâ* (nam).
    " Gift of Nandagiri."
16. . . *yâyâ dânam.*
17. . . *pancha sana.*
18. . *dusito-giri datina.*
19. (Ba) *hu hathikasa âsana.*
    (*Bhaga*) *vato Maha Devasa.*

By supplying the initial letters of both lines I make out that this inscription refers to the scene under which it is engraved. This represents a throne (*âsana*) with a number of human hands (*bahu hathika*) carved on the front. Perhaps the hands are intended as symbols of worshippers.

LONDON:
Printed by GEORGE E. EYRE and WILLIAM SPOTTISWOODE,
Printers to the Queen's most Excellent Majesty.
For Her Majesty's Stationery Office.
[P 455.—250.—2/79.]

BHARHUT.

PLATE I

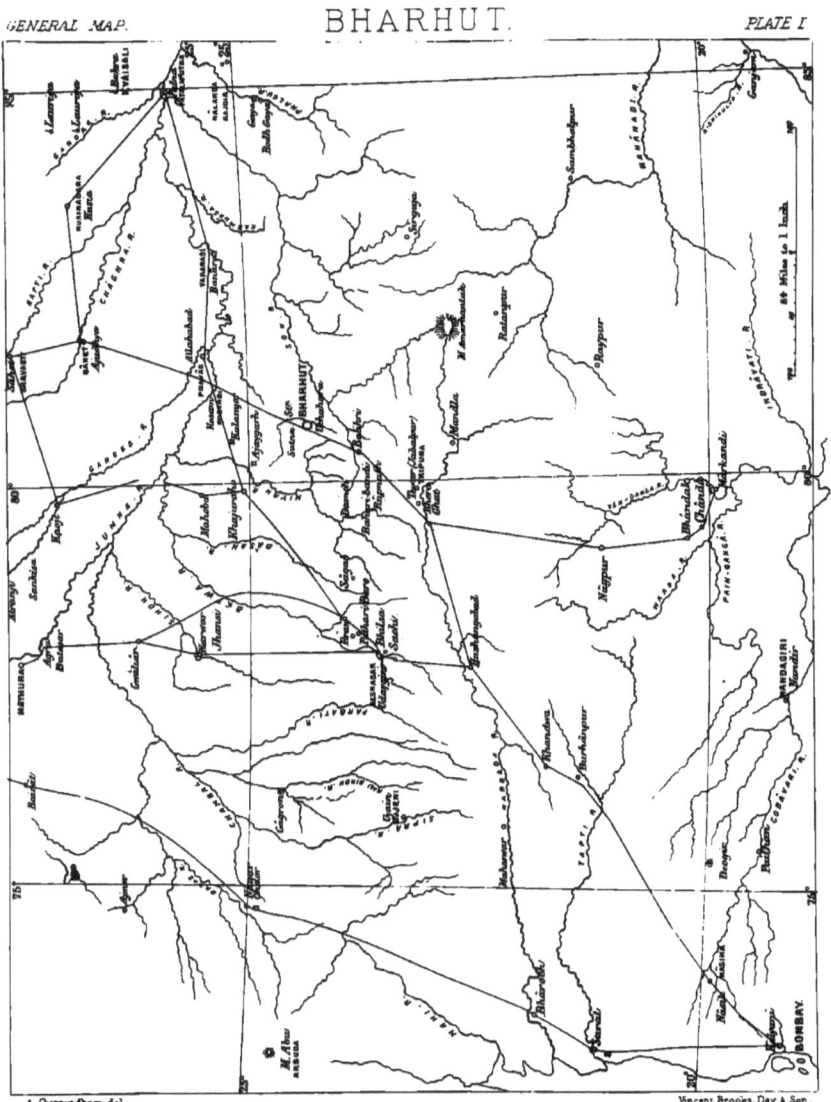

BHARHUT.

PLATE II.

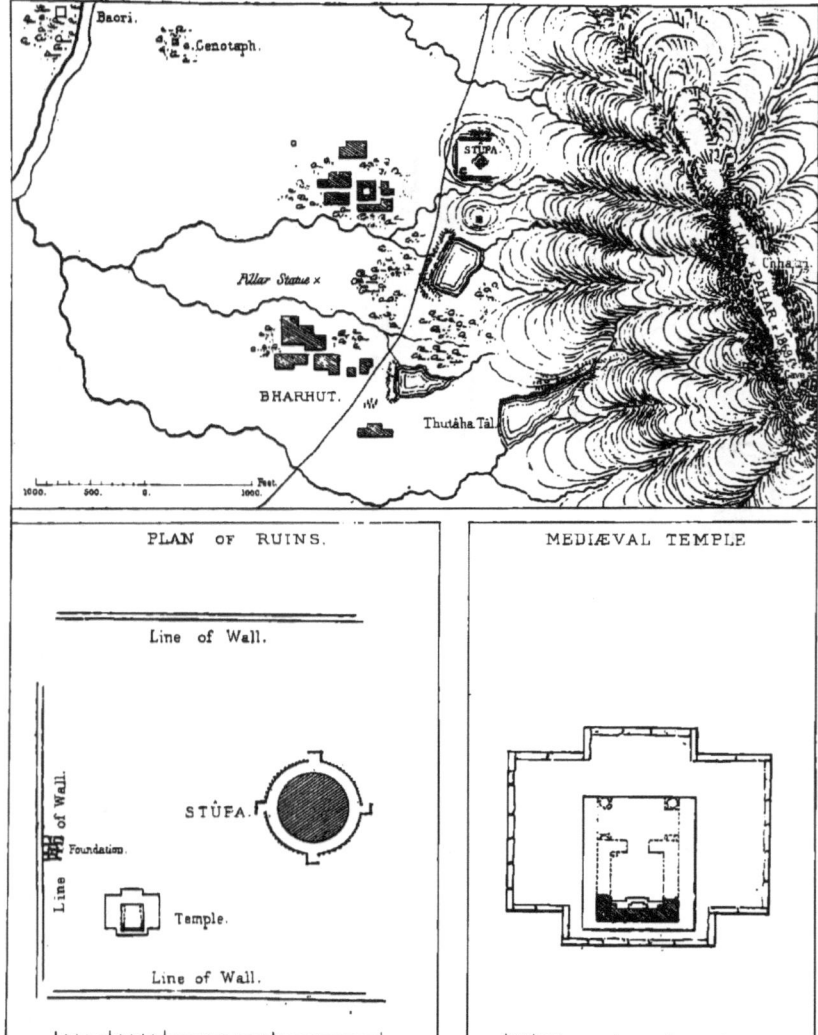

PLAN OF RUINS.

MEDIÆVAL TEMPLE

A Cunningham del.

Vincent Brooks, Day & Son

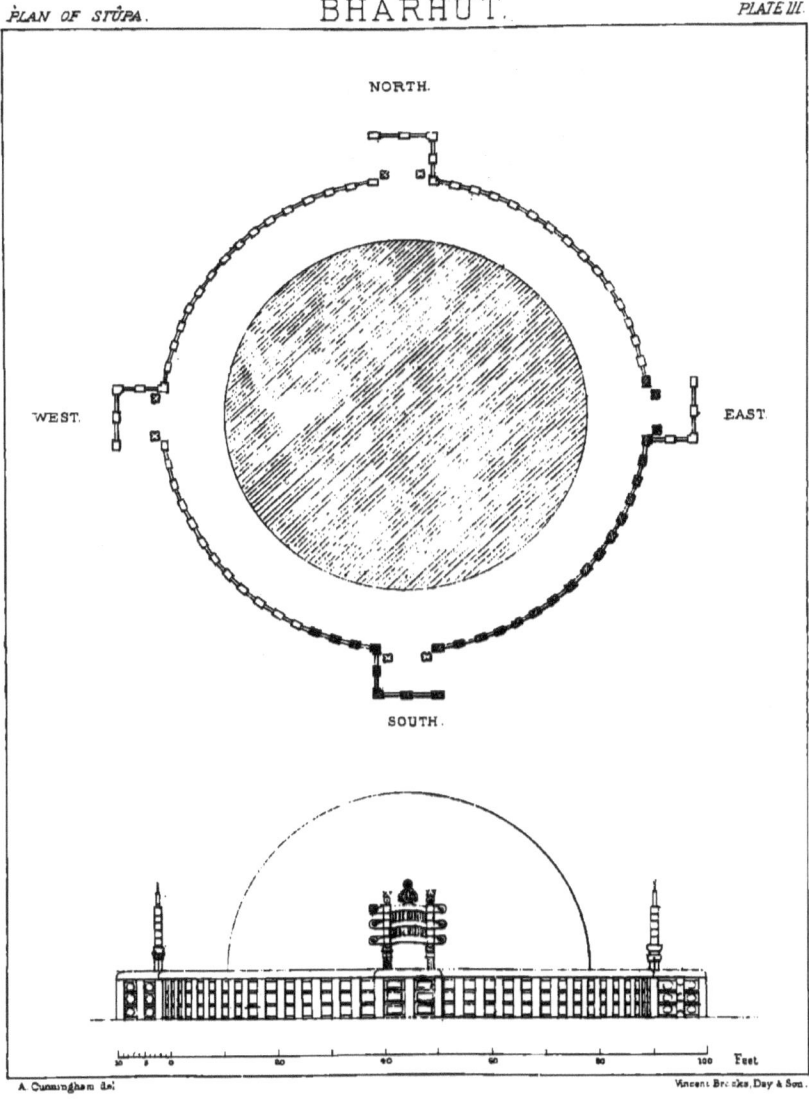

NORTH.

WEST.

EAST.

SOUTH.

A. Cunningham del.

Vincent Brooks, Day & Son.

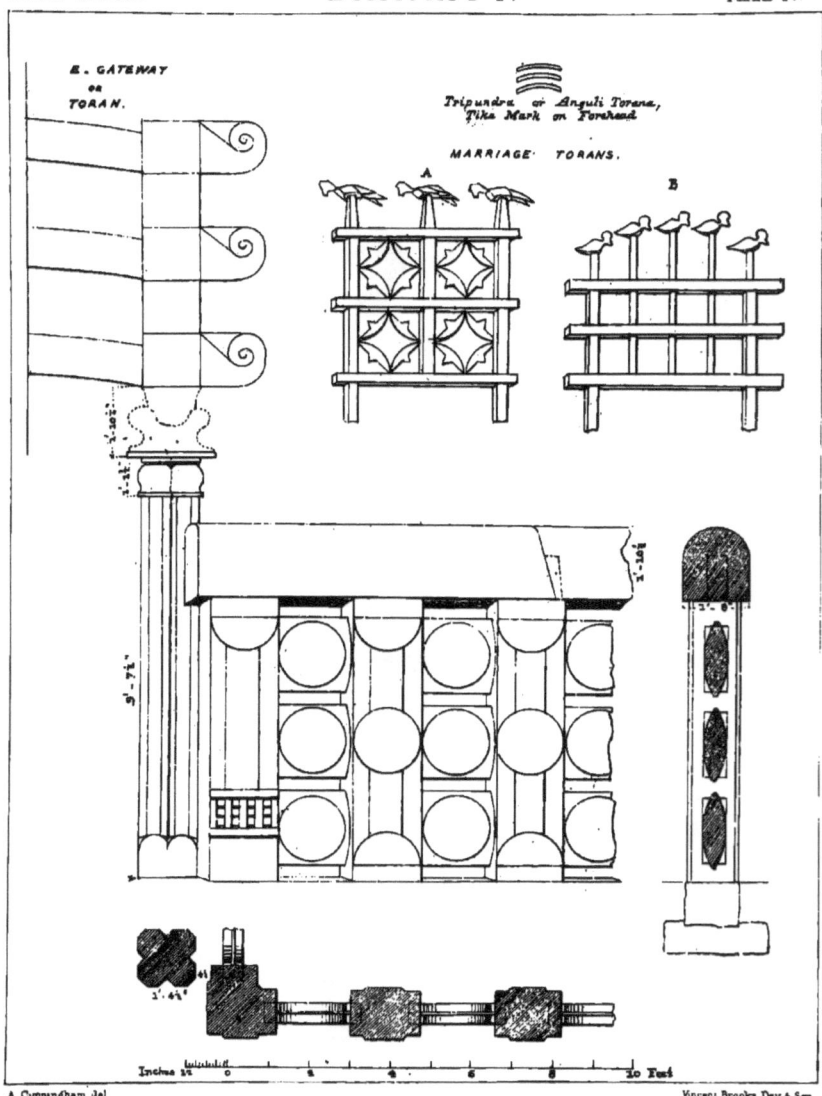

E. GATEWAY
or
TORAN.

Tripundra or Anguli Torana,
Tika Mark on Forehead

MARRIAGE TORANS.

A

B

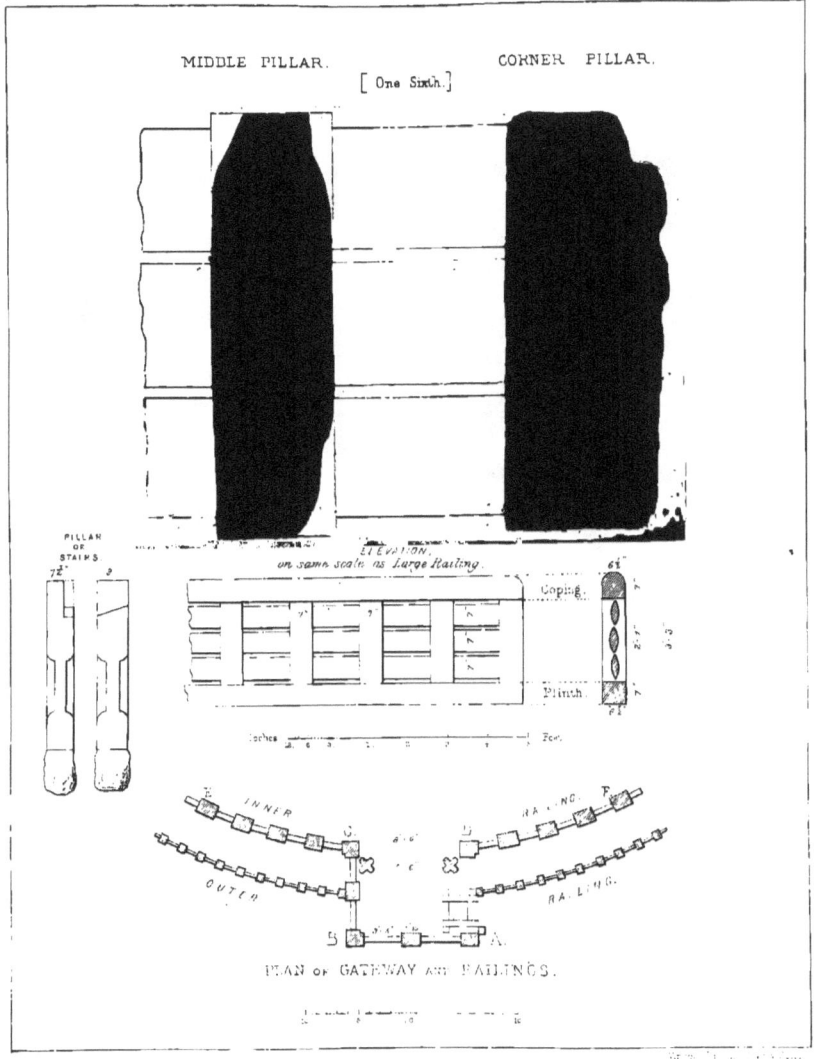

MIDDLE PILLAR.   CORNER PILLAR.

[One Sixth.]

PLAN OF GATEWAY AND RAILINGS.

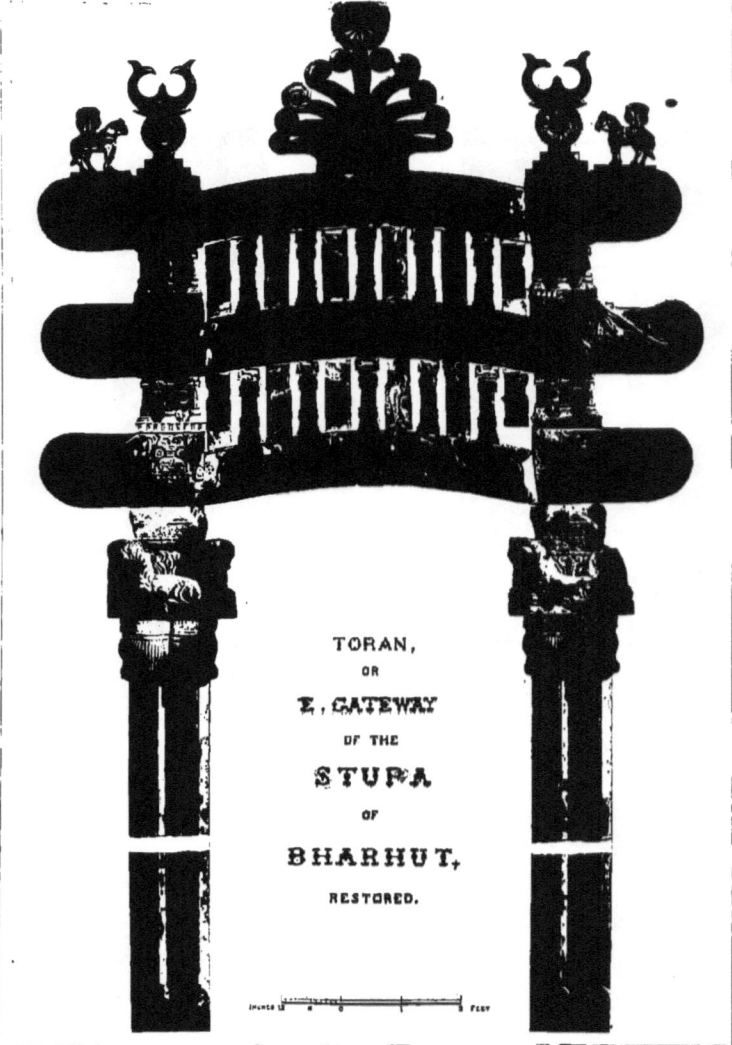

TORAN,

OR

E. GATEWAY

OF THE

STUPA

OF

BHARHUT,

RESTORED.

Vincent Brooks, Day & Son.

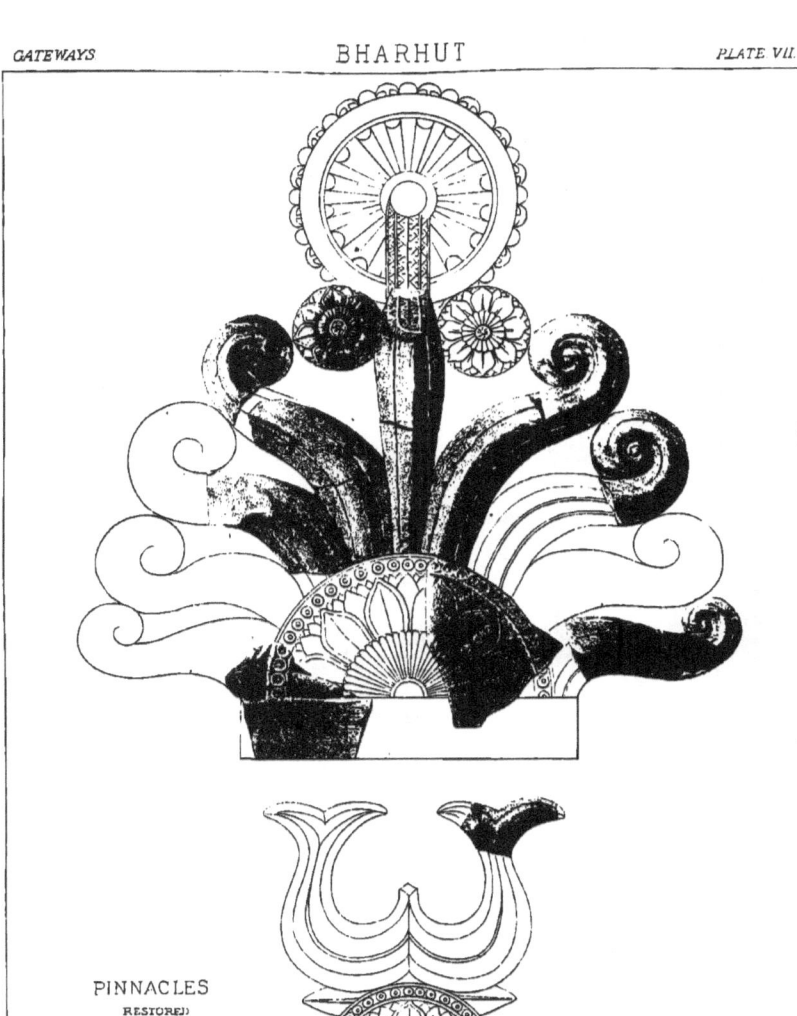

PINNACLES
RESTORED
FROM
EXISTING FRAGMENTS
(one sixth)

A. Cunningham. del.

REMAINS
· OF ·
TORAN
– OF –
E. GATEWAY.
(See Sixth

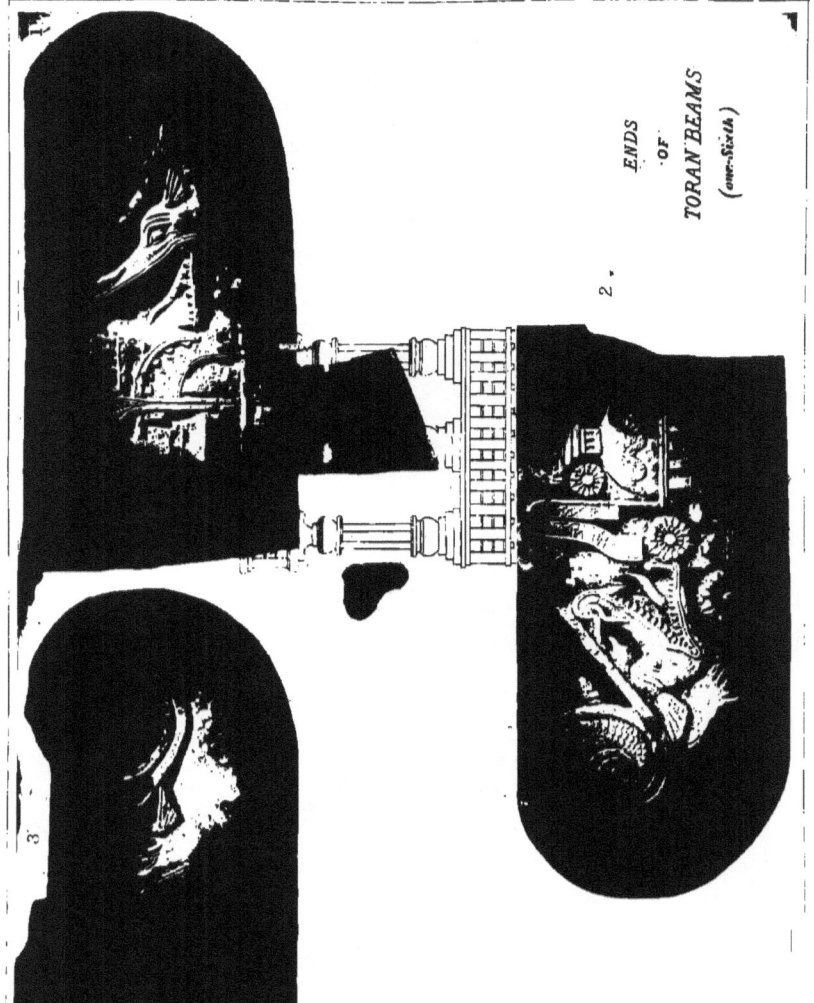

ENDS
OF
TORAN BEAMS
(one-Sixth)

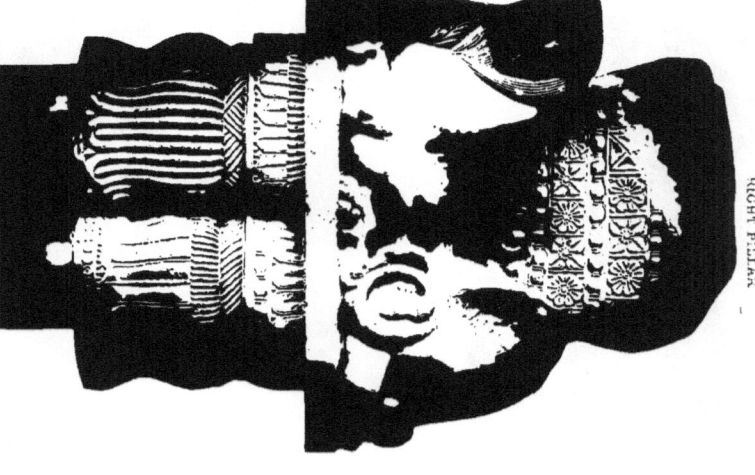

INNER VIEW OF E. GATEWAY.

Amant Brooks, Day & Son.

S. GATE

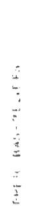

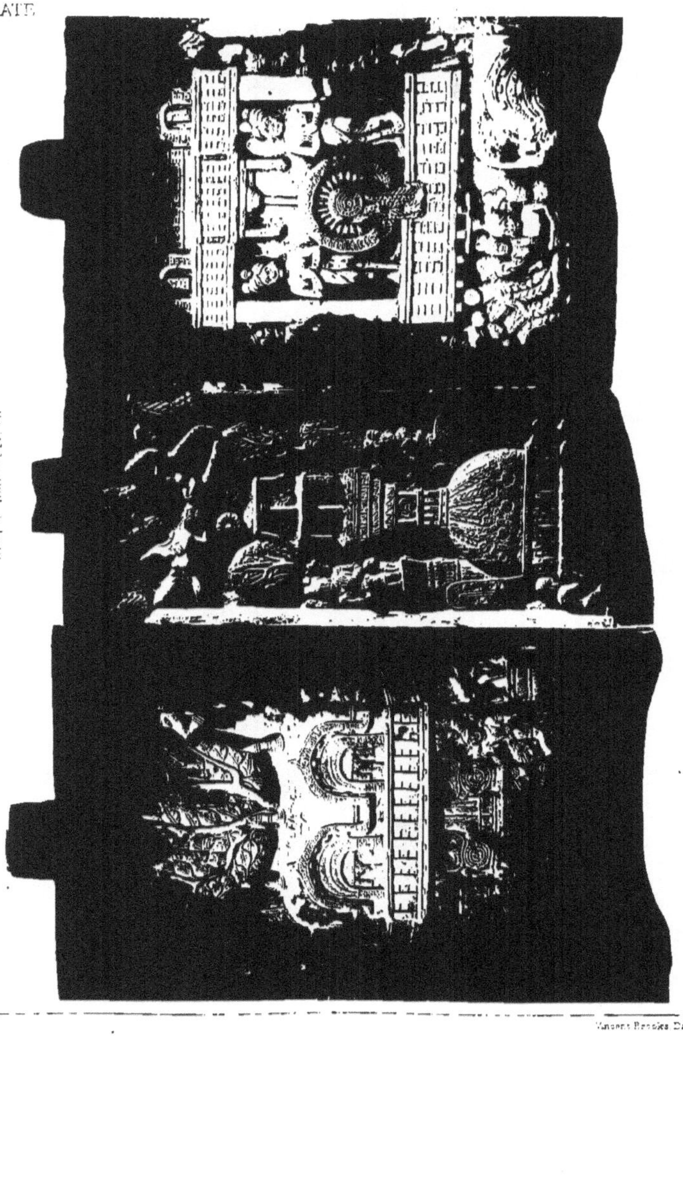

PRASENAJIT PILLAR

INNER BAS-RELIEFS

SIDE

OUTER FACE

Vincent Brooks, Day & Son

S GATE

PRASENAJIT PILLAR

MEDH. BAS-RELIEFS

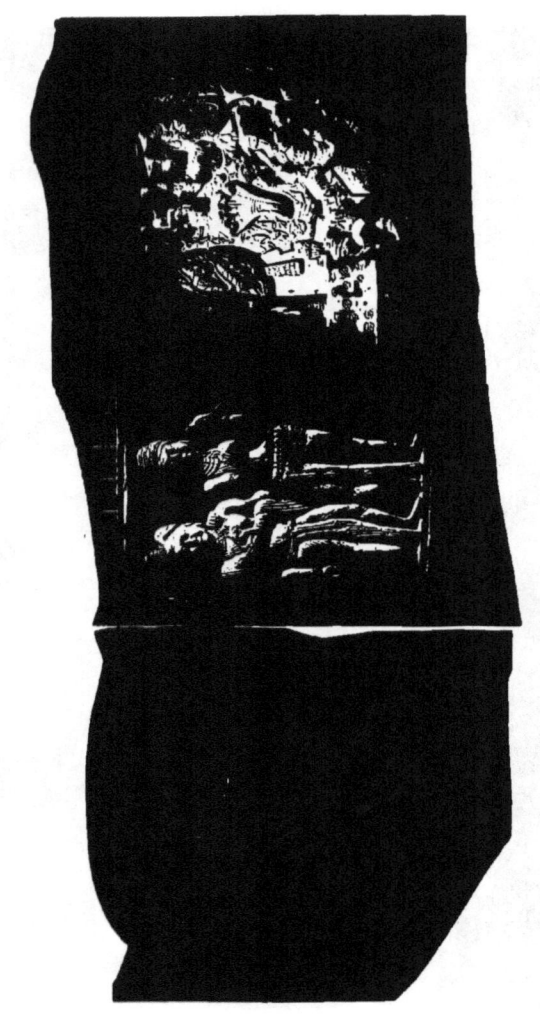

INNER FACE

SIDE

OUTER FACE

W. GATE.

CORNER PILLAR.

AJÁTASATRU PILLAR.

LEFT SIDE

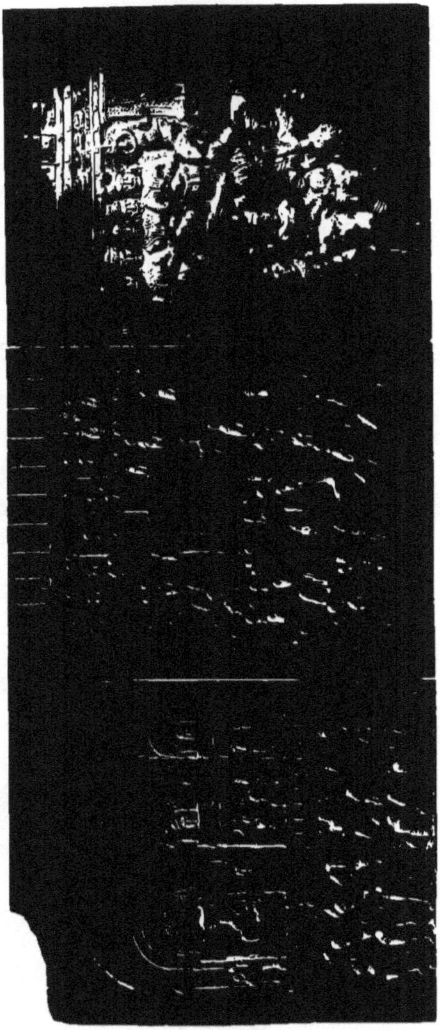

LOWER BASRELIEF

MIDDLE BASRELIEF

UPPER BASRELIEF

Vincent Brooks, Day & Son.

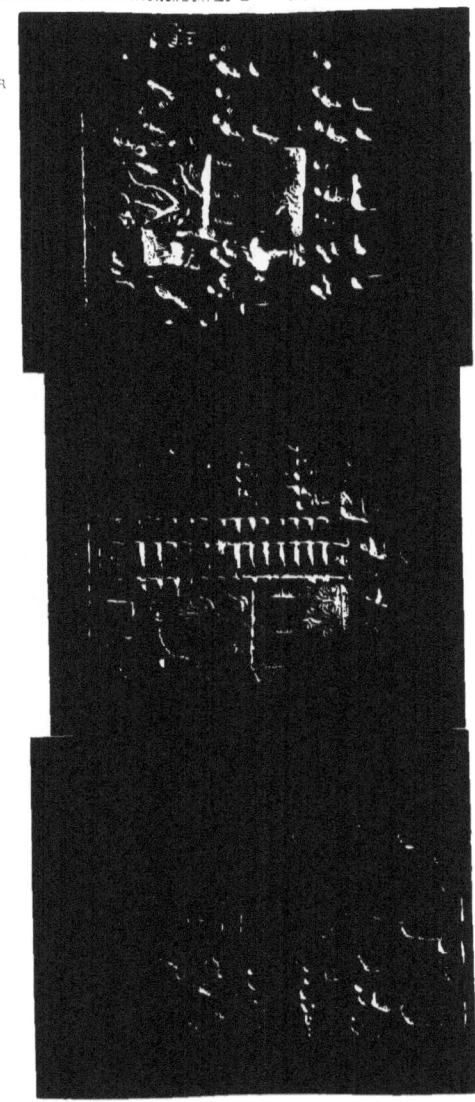

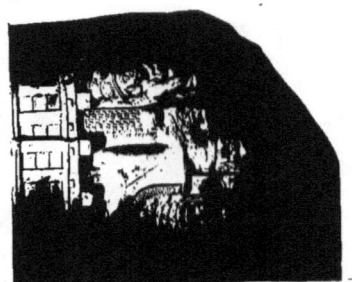

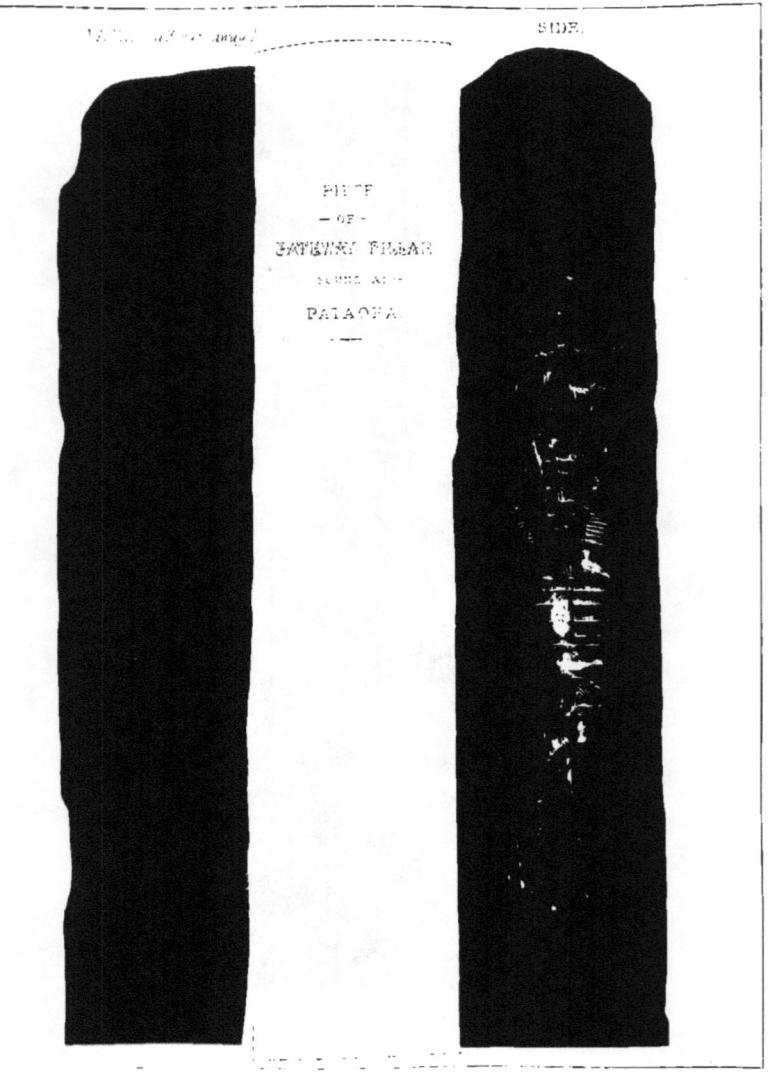

BAR HUT

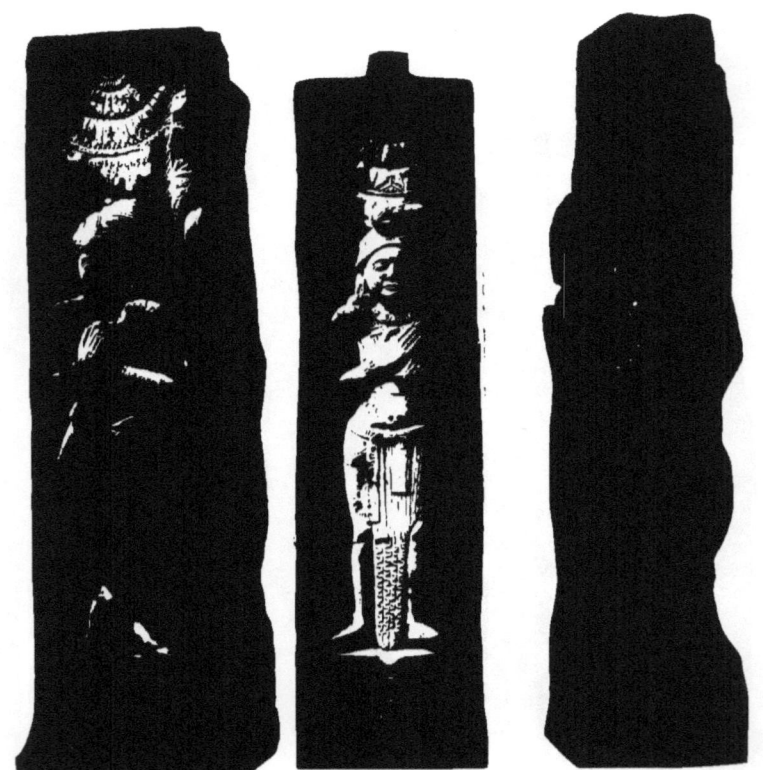

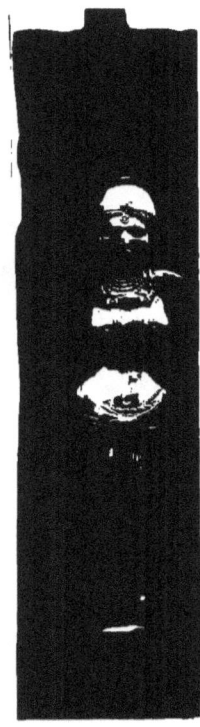

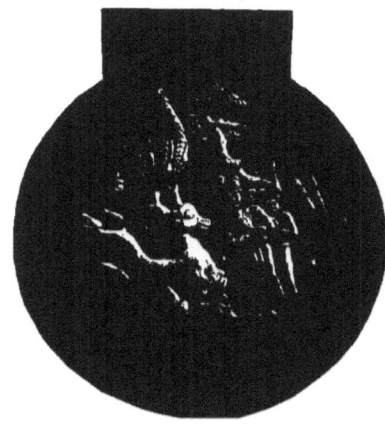
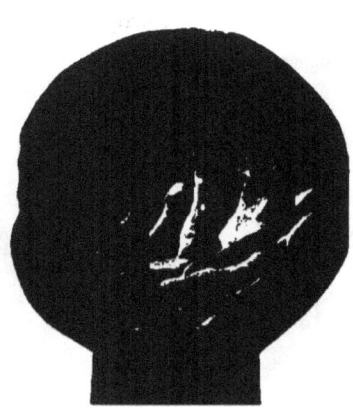

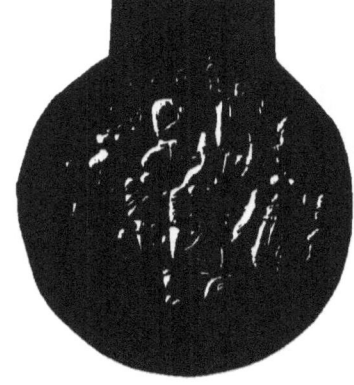

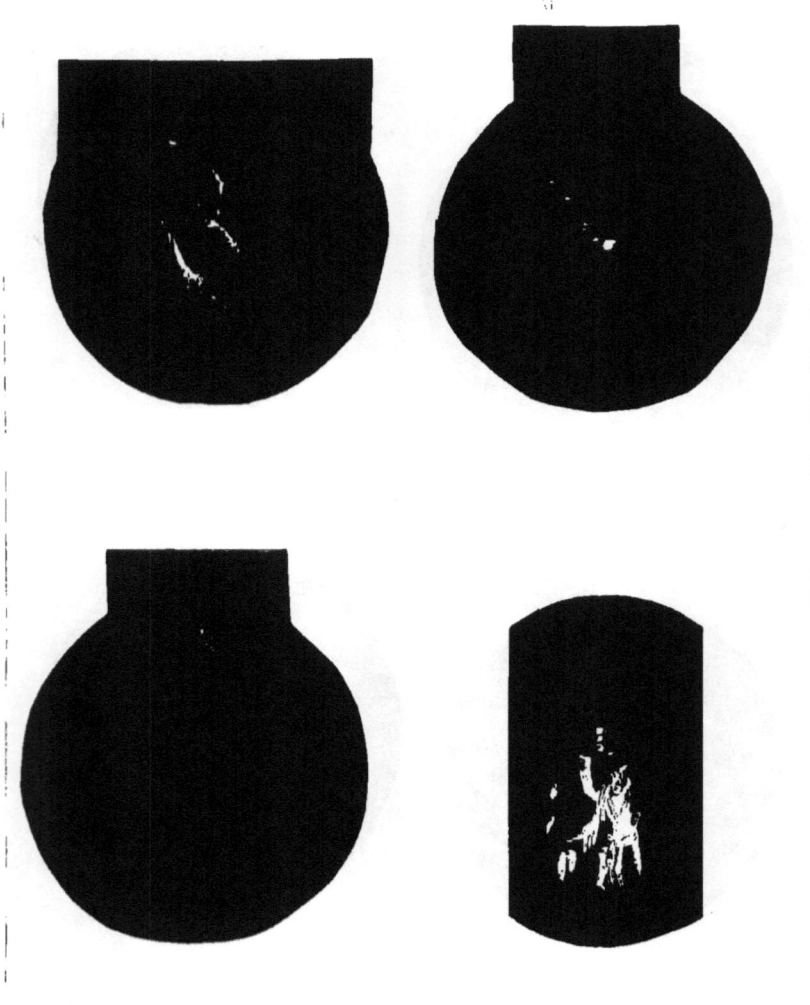

HANSA JATAKA

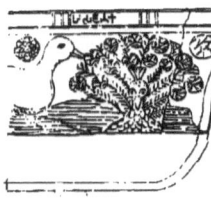

KINARA JATAKA

FRAGMENT

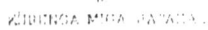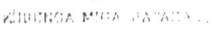

MRIGA JATAKA

BULL AND TIGER

JATAKA

NAGAPARHA JATAKA

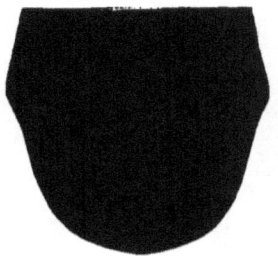

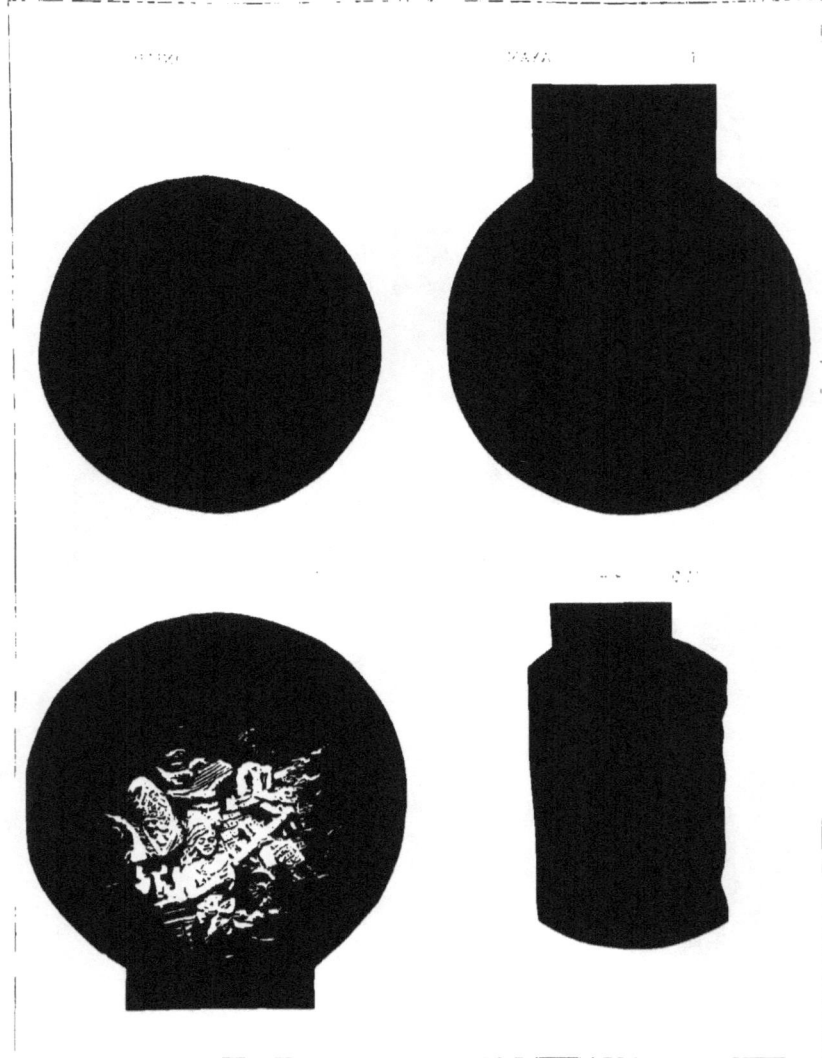

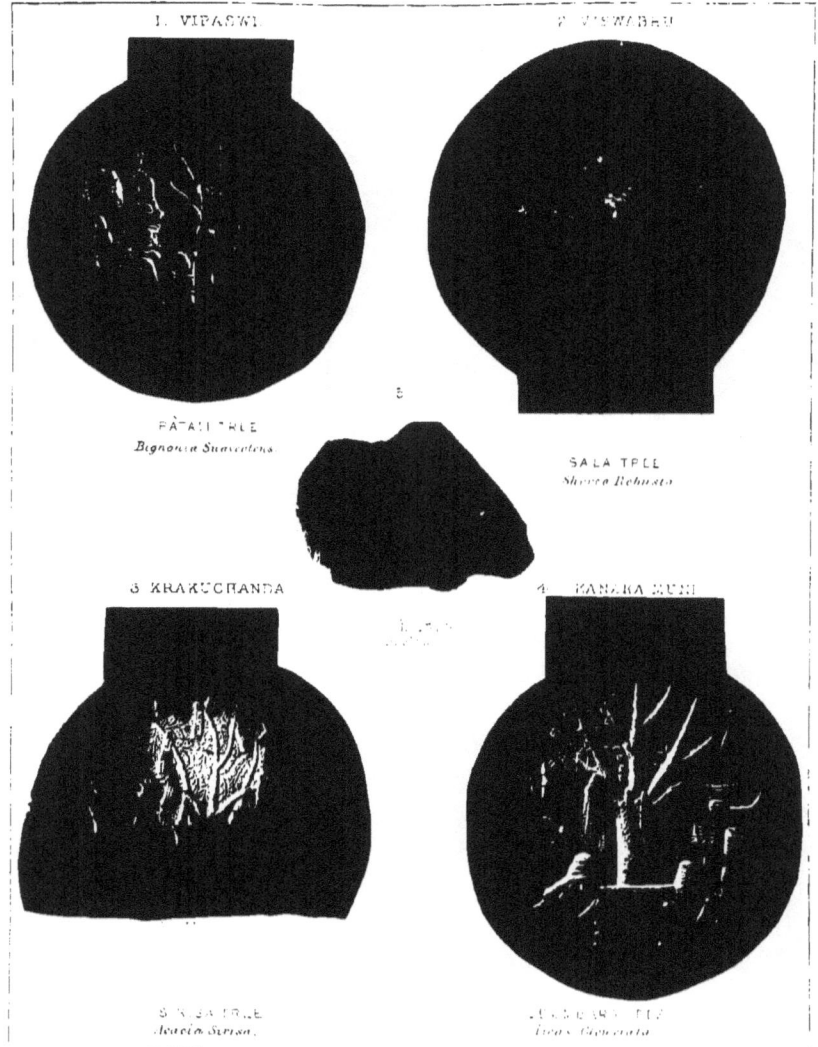

1. VIPASWI

2. VISWABHU

PÁTALI TREE
Bignonia Suaveolens

SALA TREE
Shorea Robusta

5

3. KRAKUCHANDA

4. KANAKA MUNI

SIRISA TREE
Acacia Sirisa

UDUMBARA TREE
Ficus Glomerata

KASYAPA
NYAGRODHA TREE. *Ficus Indica*

3 SAKYA MUNI. PIPPALA TREE.

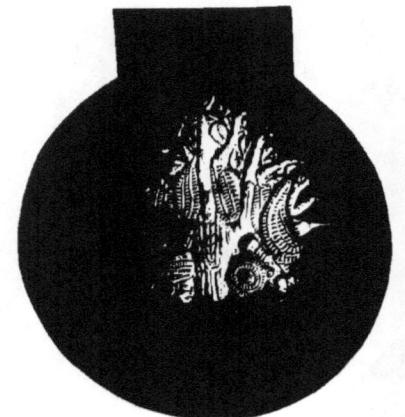

2 NYAGRODHA. *Ficus Indica*

4 TALA TREE. *Fan Palm.*

2. Dharma Chakra

4. Throne of the Four Buddhas.

1. Stupa.

3. Bodhi Tree.

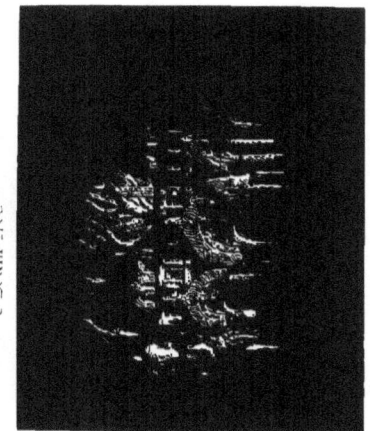

PLATE XXXII

6. 7. 5.

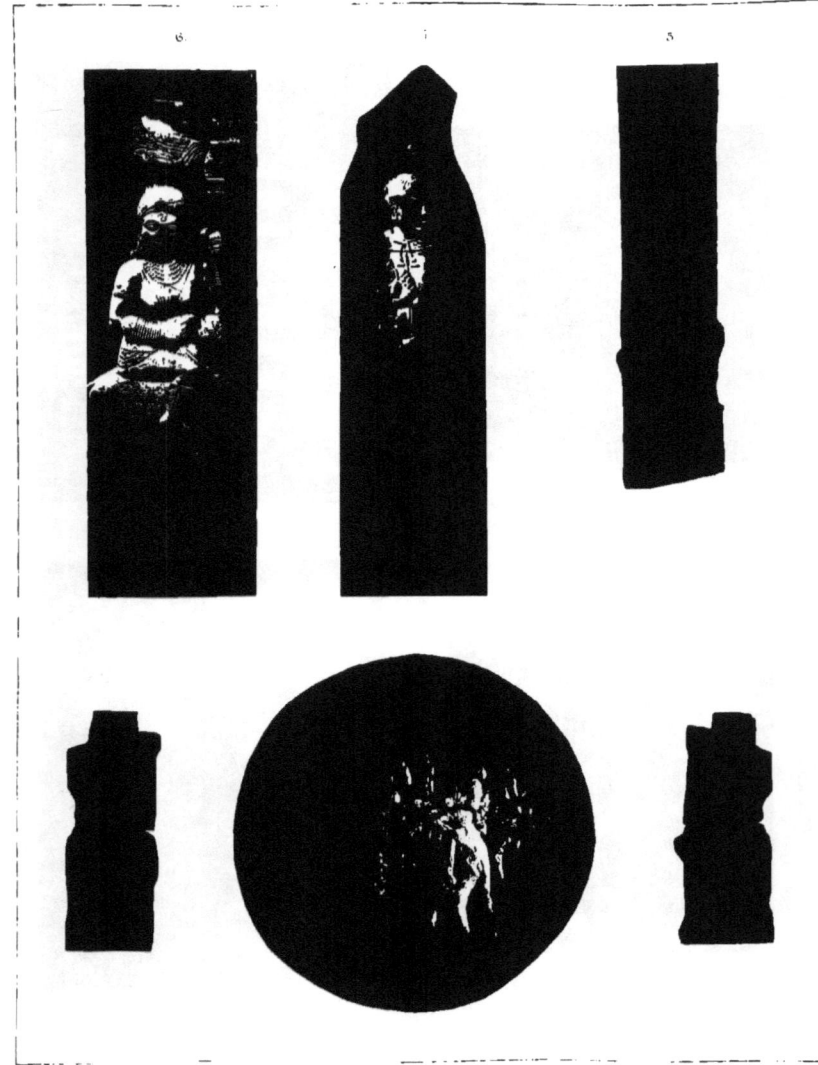

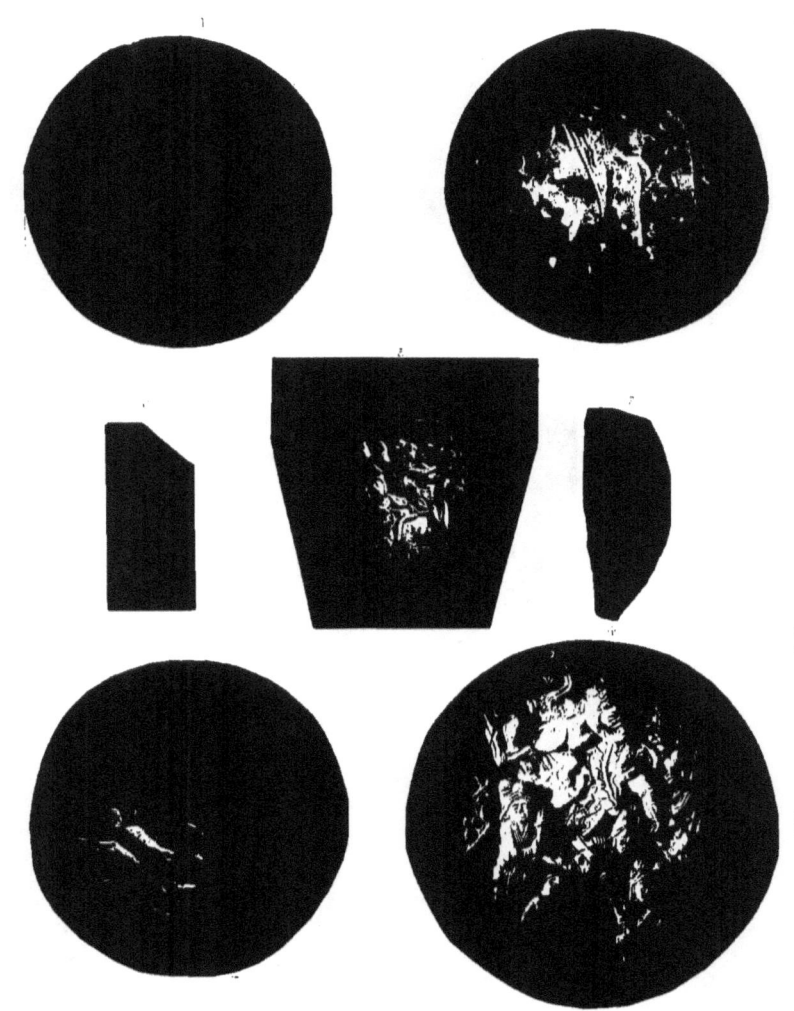

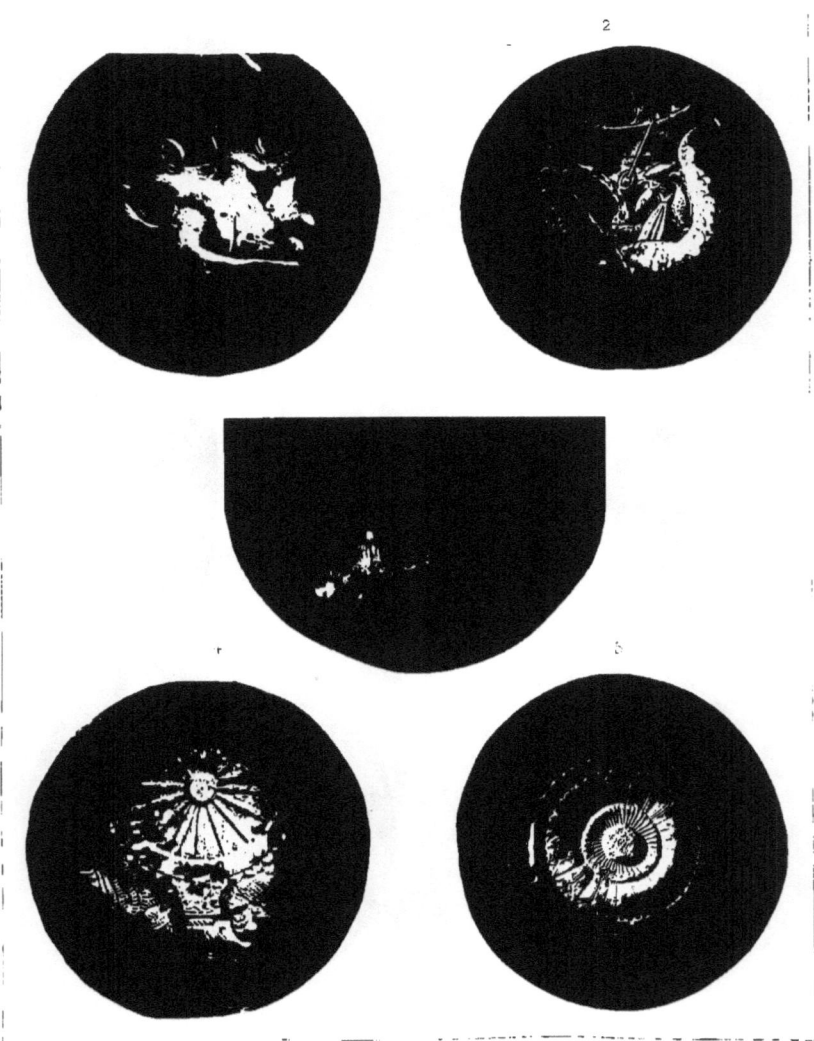

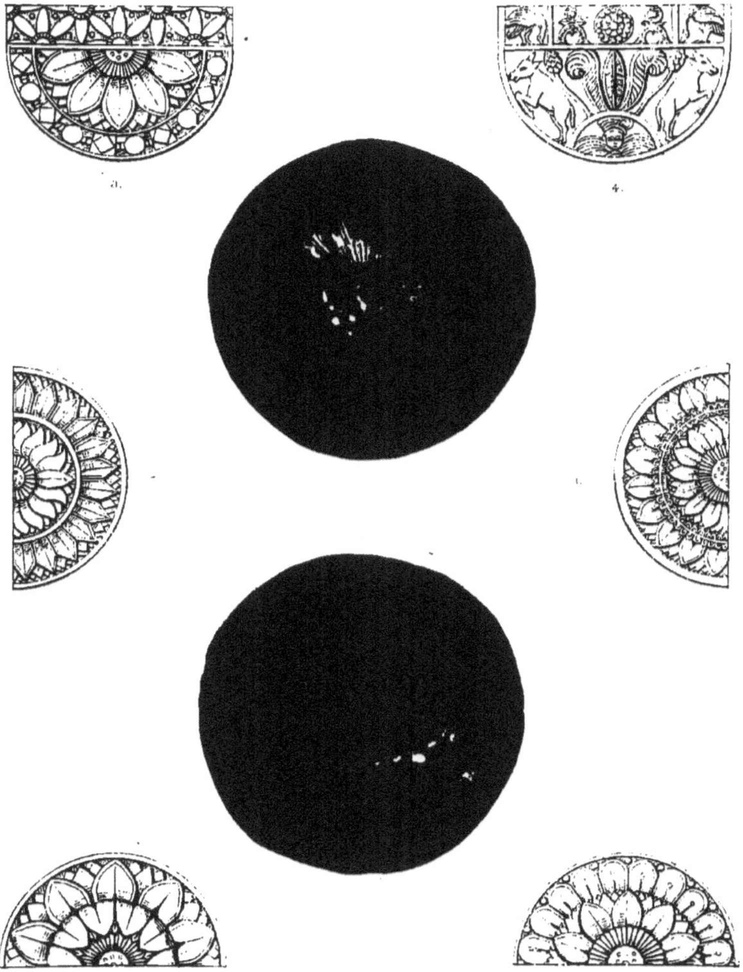

4.

5.

1.

6.

7.

2.

8.

9.

3.

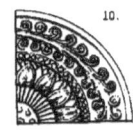

10.

11.

4.

1.

5.

7.

2.

7.

8.

3.

8.

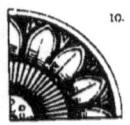

10.

11.

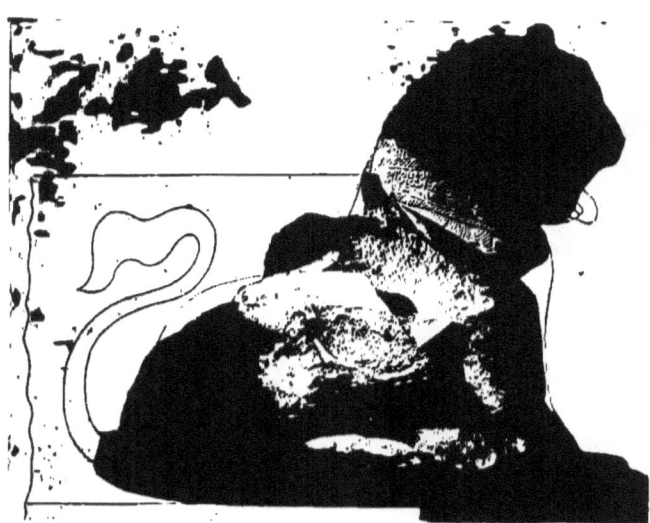

END OF COPING - INSIDE.

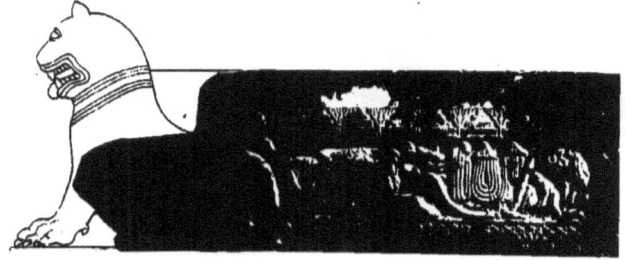

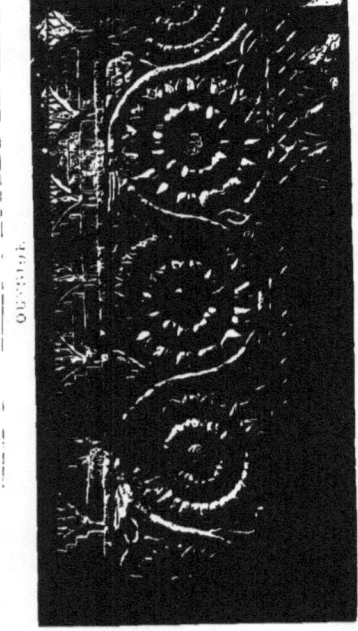

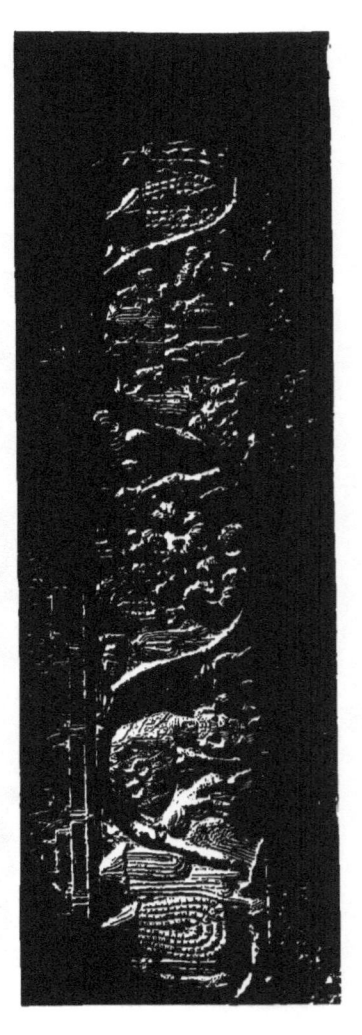

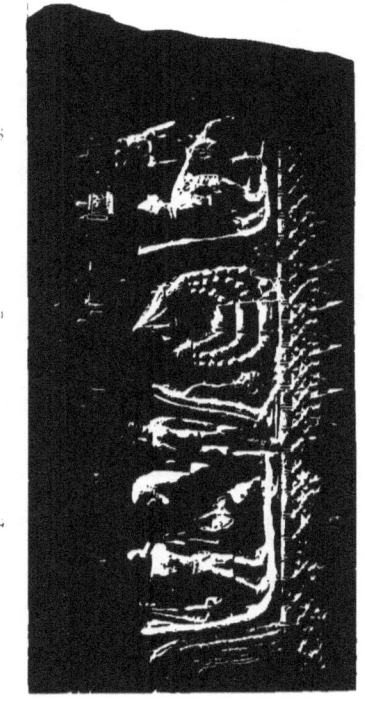

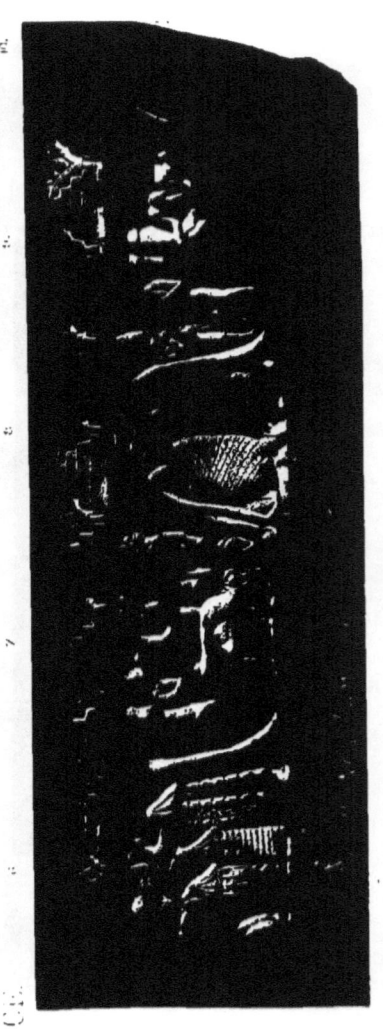

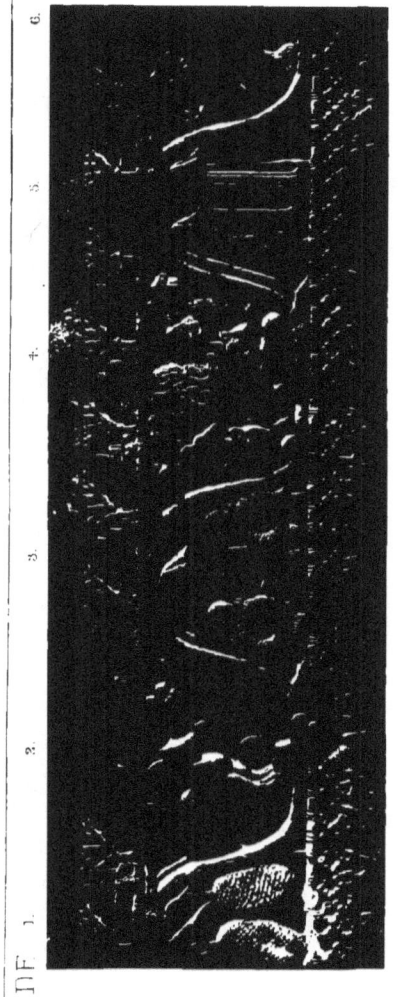

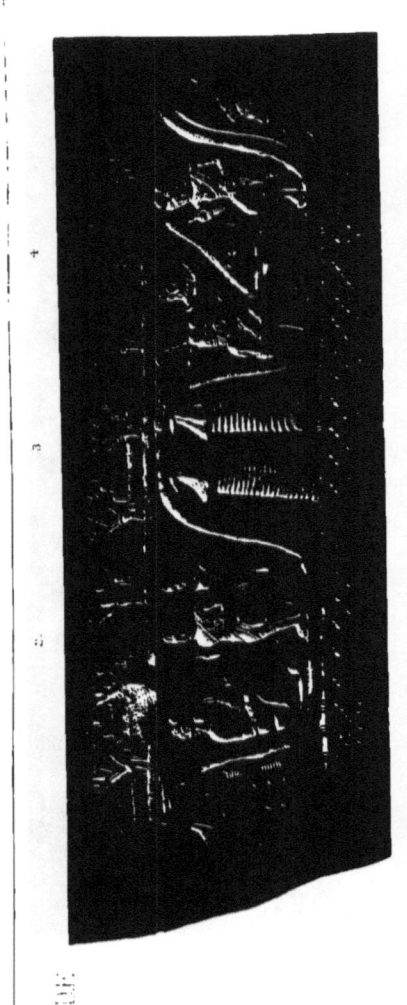

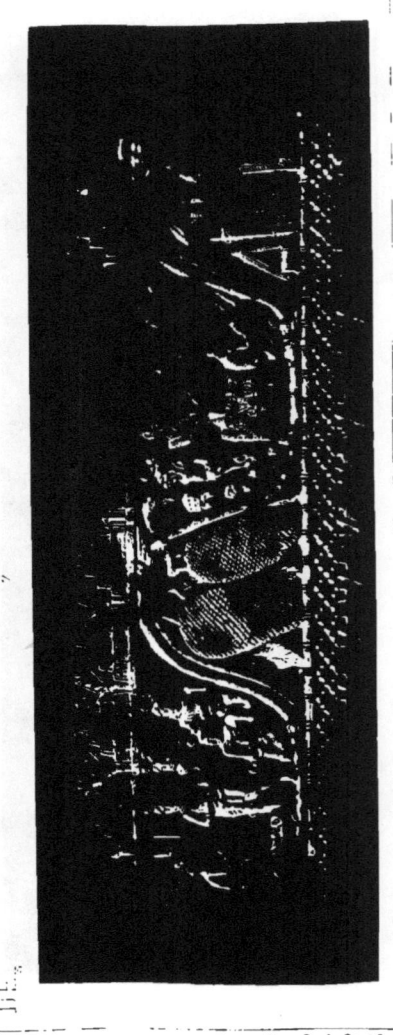

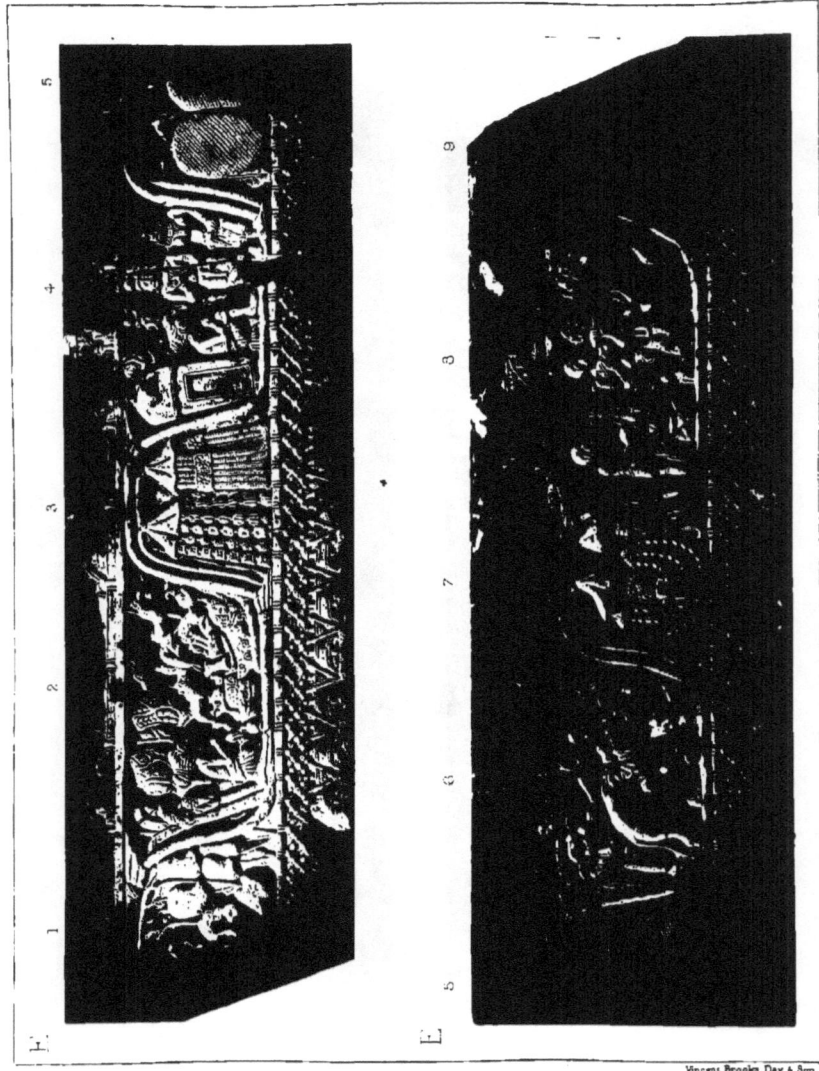

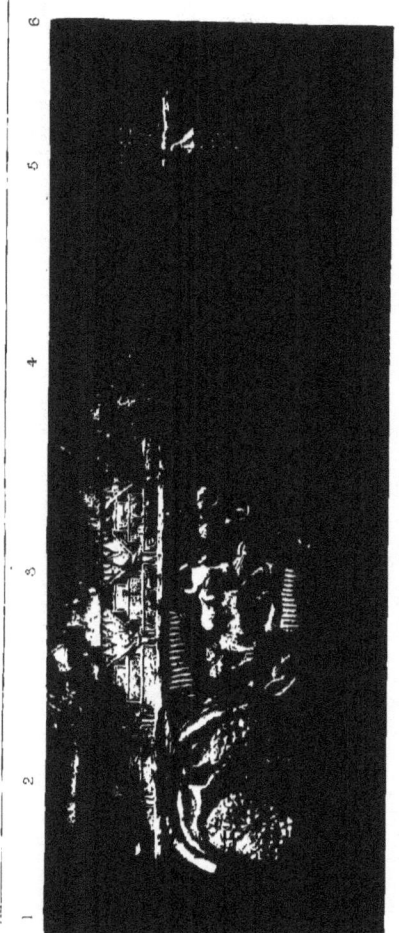

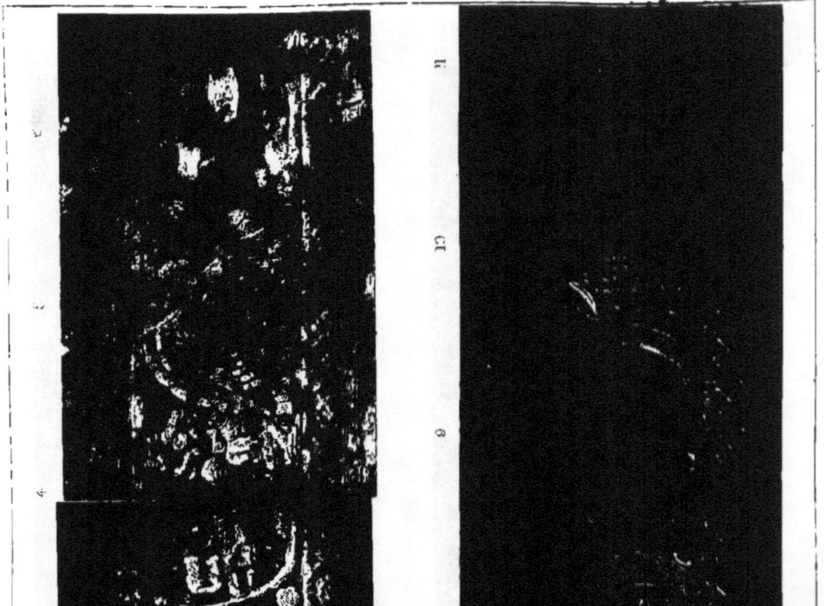

Vincent Brooks, Day & Son

FRONTLETS.

1. 2. 9. 3. 4.

5. 6. 7. 8.

EARRINGS

11. 10. 12.

13. 14.

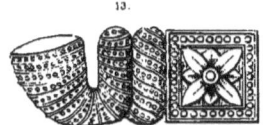

ARMLETS

15. 17. 19.

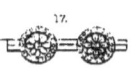

Vincent Brooks, Day & Son.

NECKLACES.

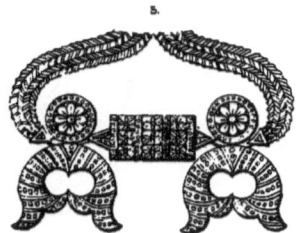

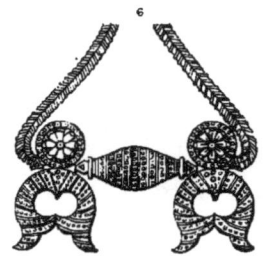

LONG COLLAR.

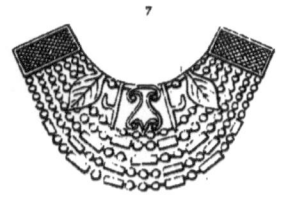

BRACELETS.

1.

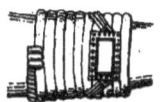

GIRDLES.

2.

SIRIMÁ DEVATÁ.

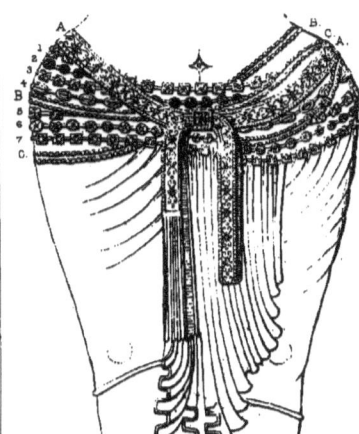

3.

FRAGMENT.

Waist Bells

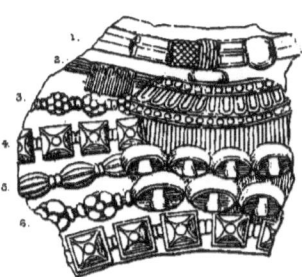

See Plate XLVII.— Nº 5.

ANKLETS.

4.

5.

6.

TATTOO MARKS.

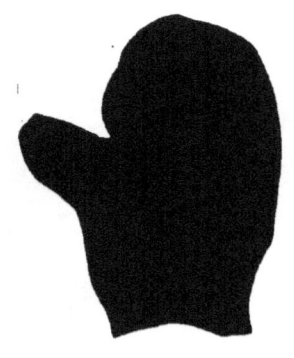

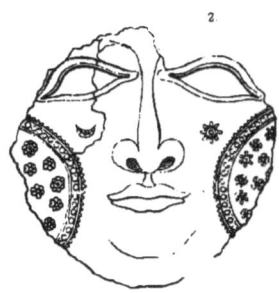

Half Size.

on Figure above

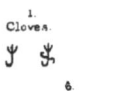

Sixima Devalâ.

Chandâ Yakshini

MODERN MARKS.

1. Cloves	2. Scorpions	3. Sieve	4. Shell	5. Stool

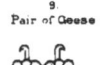

6. Bird	7. Parrot	8. Duck	9. Pair of Geese	10. Peacocks

11. Elephant	12. City of Jhansi	13.	14. City of Urcha	15. Garden

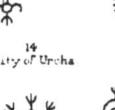

17. Regiment.		18. Sixia's Kitchen		19. Garden

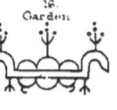

BHARHUT.

PLATE LIII.

2. Gateway Pillar.

3. Gateway Pillar.

GATEWAYS

1 Pillar of E Gateway

+ MATHURA.

COPINGS.

PILLARS of RAILING — S.E. QUADRANT.

A Cunningham del

CORNER PILLARS — S GATE.

PILLARS OF RAILING. — S W QUADRANT.

CORNER PILLARS. — W GATE

PILLARS OF RAILINGS N W QUADRANT

CORNER PILLARS — N GATE

DISPLACED PILLARS.

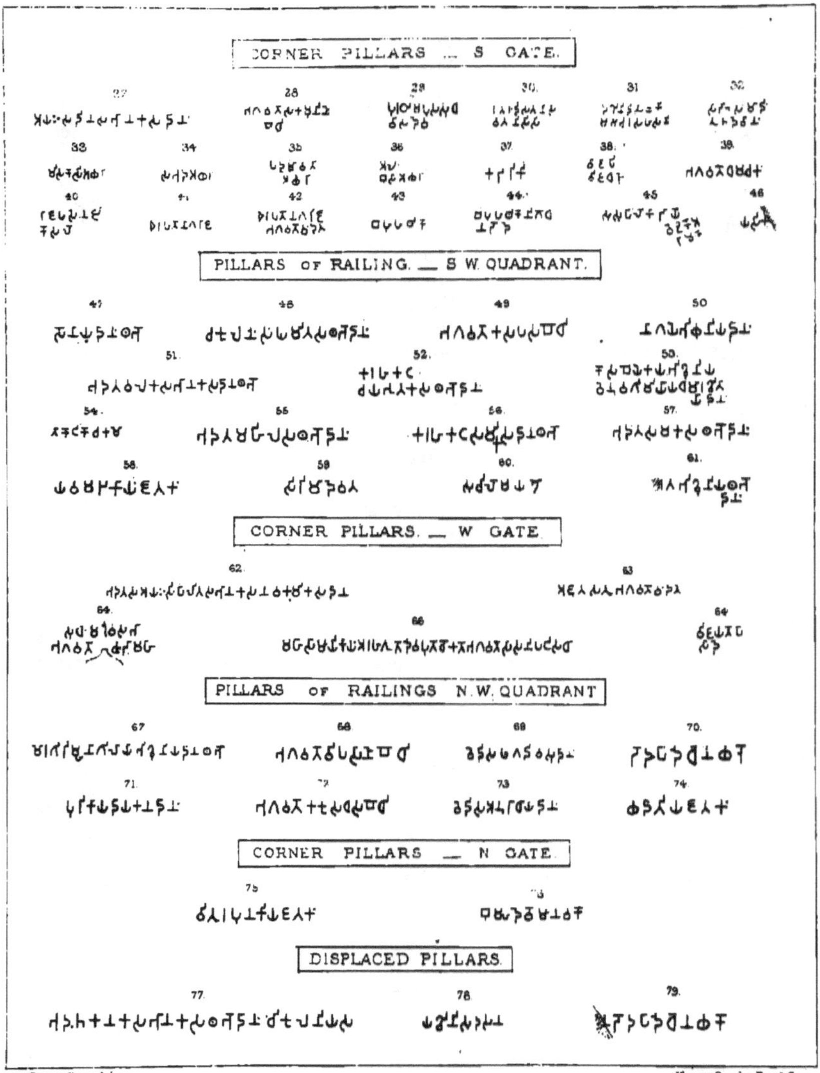

A. Cunningham del.   Vincent Brooks, Day & Son.

PILLARS OF RAILING ___ N. E. QUADRANT.

80.

81.

82.

83.

84.

85.

86.

87.

88.

89.

PILLARS AT BATANMÂRA.

90.

91.

92.

93.

94.

95.

96.

PILLARS AT PATAORA.

97.

98.

99.

100

RAILS.

S.E. Quadrant.

1.

2.

3.

4.

5.

6.

7.

8.

9.

10.

11.
S. Gate.

12.

13.

14.

15.

16.

17.
S.W. Quadrant

18.

19.

20.

21.

Vincent Brooks, Day & Son.

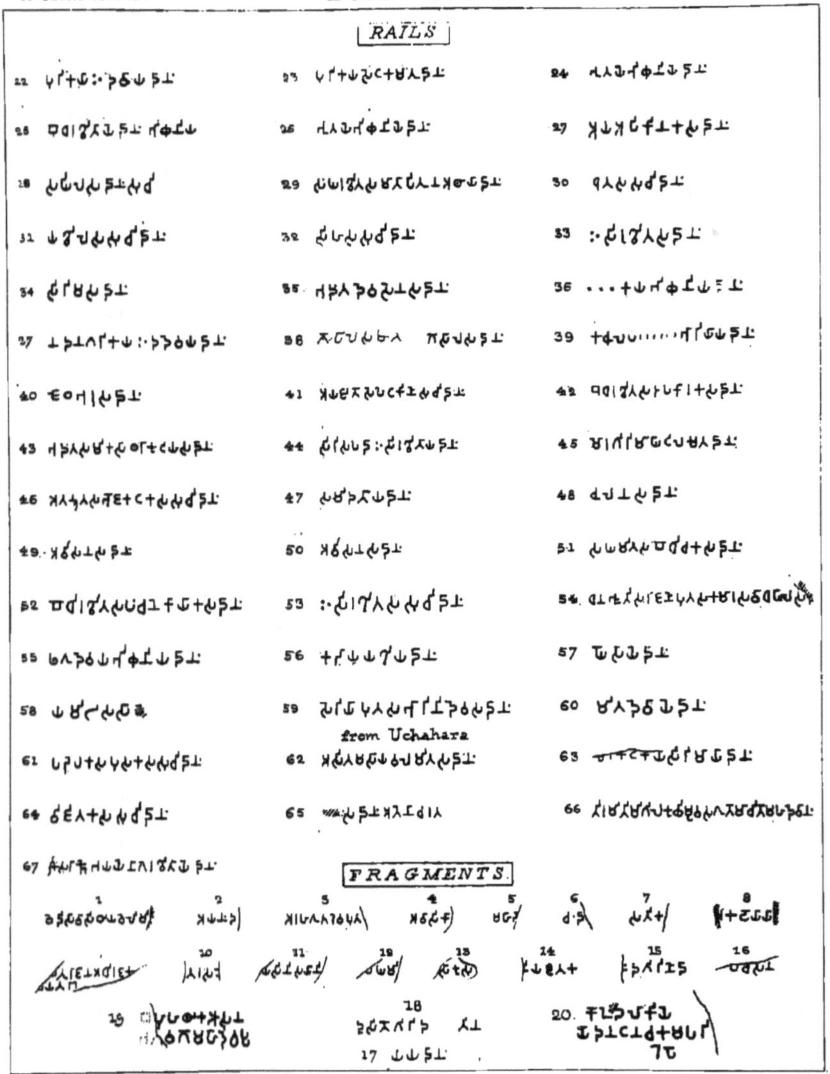

RAILS
22
23
24
25
26
27
28
29
30
31
32
33
34
35
36
37
38
39
40
41
42
43
44
45
46
47
48
49
50
51
52
53
54
55
56
57
58
59
60
from Uchahara
61
62
63
64
65
66
67
FRAGMENTS
1
2
3
4
5
6
7
8
10
11
12
13
14
15
16
19
18
20
17

A Cunningham del.

Vincent Brooks, Day & Son.

THE JETAVANA MONASTERY